I0599807

CHAPTER ONE

The light ambushed me—a 3am confession that clawed into my consciousness, draped in yesterday's intentions and last night's bad ideas. It poured through a gap in the alley wall baking the pavement, and branding its golden truths into everything it touched.

My truth? I was in a box. Cardboard. Damning. Dust clung to my fur like guilt. The air reeked of week-old chow mein and mildew. The kind of choices you make when your coupons have expired, and your therapist is on sabbatical.

A fly buzzed nearby. Somewhere else a pigeon plotted murder. It was your typical midday back-alley scene. I blinked against the sunbeam, trying to remember how I got here.

I didn't remember my name. Just betrayal—and maybe tuna. The tuna was probably a dream. But betrayal? That was real. Names could come later, once the yarn straightened out.

Something scratched inside my skull. A thought? A memory? A raccoon with a badge and a vendetta? Maybe it was—

Chonk, whispered a voice that wasn't mine. Fuzzy and faintly moist, like it had just licked a window. Pure Butternugget, though I didn't know that yet.

The Chonk remembers you, it giggled. *Remembers your toes. Chooses. Always choosing. Even when it's sleeping. Especially when it's eating shoelaces.*

I tried to stand, but my limbs squished, betraying me. There was fur—too much fur. Matted in places I didn't remember owning. Some of it mine. The rest already judging me.

And paws. I had paws. *Why did I have paws?*

I tried to think like a man, build a theory. Ask questions. File a mental report in triplicate. But the thoughts unraveled. Fast. String and spirals. And the word *Chonk*, muttered by a voice that once licked a battery on a dare.

How did I get here?

The question hit like a fistful of gravel. I don't remember the jump or the climb. Or the moment the fur settled around me. Only the hum. The pull. The shift in my internal monologue. And now... the voice. Gleefully unhinged, like a candy-coated demon whispering from a shoebox.

Maybe I was losing it. Insanity? Imagination? A hangover still on the department roster?

It giggled again. *Butternugget,* it whispered.

It felt less like a name and more like a revelation. Like a spell mispronounced by a toddler and still somehow binding.

THE ORANGE PROTOCOL
CASE 001

KYSA STEELE

Containment Not Recommended

The Orange Protocol Case 001

This is a work of fiction.
All names, characters, setting, and events are born of the author's imagination or twisted through myth, memory, and metaphor. Any resemblance to real persons, living or dead, is entirely unintentional unless fate had a hand, in which case, one should never underestimate its sense of irony.

1st edition: 2025
ISBN: 979-8-9989422-2-8 Paperback
ISBN: 979-8-9989422-3-5 Hardback

Cover design, headers, and dividers created in Canva by Kysa Steele.
Additional artwork created by Matias Nivala, KAJO Graphics

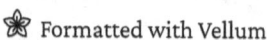 Formatted with Vellum

That's me! You're me now. Sometimes. But not always. Sometimes I'm you. And sometimes I'm a box.

I filed the paperwork, he whispered. *Used a crayon. They'll never trace it.*

I froze in realization. The Cognichonk had let me in, but it hadn't bothered to close the door behind me. The spiral was beginning. Orange had me by the neurons.

The crime scene was still warm. Mostly because I'd been in it. Or, let's not split fur here, Butternugget had.

I investigated the box with the grim determination of a man who'd woken up in worse places. Like a haunted mime school, or to an ex-wife's voicemail when you've never been married. But this was different. This was personal. This was—

Cardboard came the thought from the back of my head, interrupting me.

The corners whispered secrets the walls weren't ready to say—the kind that get honest men buried and dishonest men promoted to commissioner. The floor was a tapestry of paw prints, food stains, and one inexplicable rune made of moldy chow mein. The air reeked of mystery, mildew, and something vaguely corn-chippy. Like someone had once tried to summon a forgotten god using Fritos and loneliness.

This was the epicenter. I pawed through a shredded takeout menu like it held answers. Or at least shrimp cooked in probable crimes. Evidence abounded. A broken plastic spoon. A burnt cigarette butt shaped like a question mark. Half a fortune cookie lay there like a snitch with cold feet, whispering: 'You will soon know clarity or catnip.' The universe's idea of a punchline, delivered with brass knuckles. I didn't know which scared me more.

In the corner, a single catnip mouse lay gutted. Fluff trailing like viscera. One plastic eye was missing and the other stared into a place beyond squeaks. A realm of silence, betrayal, and uncooked rice. A message, maybe. A warning. Or just Butternugget's idea of interior design.

Or mine, I thought, and that was the first time I realized I didn't know where one of us stopped and the other began.

I leaned close. Sniffed. Nothing but the lingering scent of chaos and peanut oil. And faint, but there, wet fur. Sour guilt. A note of fear wrapped in fast food. I knew that smell. I'd worn it before. On stakeouts. After regrets. During weddings.

I crept backward, each pawstep a whispered apology to my pride. My tail dragged like a guilt signature on a bad confession. Low. Twitching and ashamed. My dignity snagged on the cardboard flap and stayed behind like a hostage with stage fright.

Then I saw it. Scratched into the cardboard wall. Barely visible in the shadows. Three claw marks. Evenly spaced. Deliberate as a hitman's alibi. Just like the ones I'd seen scratched into the precinct door the night it all broke— before the badges started disappearing and the commissioner started wearing sunglasses indoors. Before the Cognichonk sang through me like a siren made of yarn and broken memories. This wasn't random panic; it was clearly deliberate, a kind of ritual.

I don't remember making those marks. But my chest ached like I'd left something behind in them. Something sharp. Something mine. Marking territory, maybe. Or sending a signal. This wasn't random instinct. Repeated marks like that meant intent. Which means Butternugget knew more than he let on. Or maybe I did before everything shattered.

One thing was clear in my mind. Butternugget hadn't just been sleeping here. He'd been *waiting*. And now I was what he'd waited for. Or maybe, he was me. Just rendered in crunchy.

Suddenly, my vision crackled, and I was somewhere else. It felt like a memory, but also like a dream, not quite either.

A plastic bag swirled in the gutter like a prophecy with a bad haircut. A pigeon screamed somewhere off-stage. A light flickered. The shape it made? Spiral. Conspiratorial. Familiar. I saw Butternugget standing in this same box, looking at the marks like they were a recipe.

Then he licked the wall. My body tried to repeat the vision.

"No, don't lick the wall," I muttered, shaking it off.

My tail twitched in agreement or betrayal. Hard to say. Authority was negotiable.

I glanced at the fortune cookie fragment again. *"Clarity or catnip."* A choice. Or a diagnosis. Either way, that was an odd saying to find in a fortune cookie—something about it stank worse than the week I spent living in my car on stakeout for the Sable Nail affair.

Somewhere deep in the box, something crinkled. A candy wrapper? A prophecy? A receipt for crimes unpaid?

I crouched lower, pressing my ear to the cardboard like it could confess. I heard it. Not just any purr. *The* purr. Ancient and slightly smug. The Cognichonk, humming through recycled shipping tape and ambient regret. I blinked as a new thought wormed through my head like a noodle with ambition. He was making this into a shrine. It wasn't for me. It was for the Chonk.

I sat back, heart thudding. Tail flicking like it had ambitions above its clearance level. If this box was sacred ground, then Butternugget had been playing priest. Or pawn. Or both. And now the altar was mine, whether I asked for it or not.

For the briefest moment, the grip slipped. Instinct flooded in like smoke through a vent. I wasn't thinking. I was twitching. Padded. Clawed. Entirely too orange. The kind of orange that screams confidence, shatters glassware, then naps on the evidence. The kind that commits war crimes against upholstery. Leaves paw prints at the scene.

I screamed. High-pitched. Volatile. It bounced off the alley walls and died in a drainage pipe like dignity on discount. I clawed free of the box, limbs flailing like a jazz solo in a blender. The ground was wrong. Worse was the tail. It twitched on its own. Broadcasting emotion like a semaphore for the damned—a mood flag on a noodle battalion.

Somewhere behind my thoughts, the word *Chonk* pulsed again. It wasn't a name, but more like a sound, a warning wrapped in fur. Maybe a summons I was bred to ignore. Or a receipt I forgot to keep.

I turned a corner, hoping to find sense. But I was a cat. A scrappy and slightly crusty alley cat. Instead, I was pretty sure I found the devil.

It shouldn't have been there. It didn't have a charger. It didn't have a home here. No reason it should have been there. Yet it rolled out of the fog spilling from the alley like fate on wheels. Low to the ground. Unblinking and humming a death dirge in B-flat.

It was an autonomous vacuum unit—a gods damn Roomba. Approaching fast and silent as a paid-off jury. Judging. I could feel it. The kind of mechanical scrutiny that turns honest questions into closed-casket funerals. Eyes in the dark. Whispers behind closed doors. The kind of scrutiny that leaves chalk outlines and unanswered questions.

I froze as it turned towards me. Tried forming a scenario where this made sense. I tried to speak to it. Instead, I hissed fluently in threat.

It beeped in warning. The threat felt intentional.

I'd tangled with crime lords, cultists, even a sentient mustache named Carl. But this wasn't business. This was betrayal on wheels, complete with upholstery attachments. I didn't understand why, only knew it felt personal. Maybe that was Butternugget talking?

Get it get it get it get it, whispered a voice in the back of my skull. Sugar-stained. Deranged. Pure Butternugget.

Before I knew what I was doing, I had lunged, every muscle firing like a bad decision steeped in whiskey. Mid-air, I spun. Four paws out, justice inbound. A feline shuriken of vengeance and questionable spatial awareness.

First strike—success! Front claws raked across the Roomba's plastic dome with a sound like a priest's dying breath through a kazoo. It shuddered. Spun. Opted for a counterattack.

It came at me sideways, treads grinding like a bureaucrat overdosing on espresso. I dodged left, paws scrabbling on slick pavement.

The Roomba anticipated, adjusting with mechanical grace and the cold efficiency of a hired assassin. It pivoted sharply, treads snarling like a chainsaw whispering stolen secrets.

We collided in a cacophony of plastic, fur, and betrayal —the sound a marriage makes when it meets a loaded revolver and an empty alibi. Gravity betrayed me. I went under.

The suction hit like a bald monk's blessing in a vacuum-worshipping cult. Spiritual and deeply undignified.

It was merciless in its attempt to suction the dirt from the orange I was riding like a cheap broken down loaner from a cursed rental agency. Fur lifted. Dignity detonated. Legs flailed like a chandelier possessed by jazz and regret.

Spin attack, Butternugget urged. *Scream like you're haunted by tuna.*

I didn't know what tuna-haunted sounded like, but I screamed anyway—close enough. Instinct was driving, mine or his, I wasn't sure. Probably his, given the noodle fixation and a vendetta against small appliances.

It dragged me backwards two feet. I screamed again. It didn't help.

It beeped. Twice. Sarcastically. In Roombish, that probably meant *run, coward.*

I twisted mid-roll, claws slashing. Scored a clean hit on its bumper. It retaliated, slamming me into a yogurt container before reversing full speed into a wall. The impact dislodged me, along with the half-eaten egg roll I landed in.

I tumbled and landed low, fur fluffed to tactical volume—warrior staring down war machine.

It paused one meter away, calculating, maybe receiving orders from the Great Outlet in the Sky. Then it beeped twice more.

You should ride it, Butternugget whispered, *like a noble meat chariot.*

I ignored him. Mostly. Or at least I tried.

"It's retreating," I said. "I've won."

My first mistake. Possibly second. Hard to say. There'd been a lot of tuna. And screaming.

The Roomba let out four more rapid beeps. Surged forward at triple speed, clipped a trash can, ricocheted, and hit me mid-dash.

That's when I knew this wasn't over. I was airborne before regret set in. Landed on its back, riding it like a rodeo clown possessed by vengeance, espresso, and unresolved plot arcs.

My claws sank deep. Tail lashing violently. I snarled. Teeth bared, fury rising.

Then the hum changed. A familiar pitch. From a previous case, I think. The rupture in reason. From when the Chonk opened like a confession at gunpoint. For one breathless instant, I remembered a name. Mine. The name hit like a bullet fired from my own gun—the kind of lead souvenir that comes with regrets and no return policy. Luis Cannon. A name that once made loan sharks check their insurance policies and dirty cops request transfers to quieter precincts.

And for a second, I remembered what it felt like to be whole. I felt whole, truly together, even if not quite human.

My voice, low and rough from too many late nights chasing leads and the bottom of a bottle. A steady growl with purpose.

My hands, calloused from fists clenched around justice and coffee cups, familiar as a trusted revolver. My thoughts lined up like suspects in a solvable case. Clear and ordered. Ready to be questioned.

But clarity was fleeting and that second didn't last.

Because with it, came a scent. Jasmine and ozone. The smell of a decision I hadn't made yet. A flash, just for a second of a woman in black. Eyes like secrets kept in safe deposit boxes. Lips that promised salvation but delivered subpoenas. Cats on every windowsill—sentinels with nine lives and zero loyalty. And a badge. Mine. Half-buried in ash like a good intention at a mob funeral.

The name wasn't just mine. It was a case. A curse. A promise I hadn't kept. I'd failed someone. I didn't remember who. But the guilt was older than this body. And it followed me like a leash I chewed through too late.

I came back to the moment, barely holding on. Butternugget had taken the reigns and was yowling.

This is fun! Gotta go faster like shame just left my butt.

It spun harder, a full 360. I lost traction, slammed into a milk crate full of haunted Tupperware. The crate gave way. I emerged covered in mismatched lids, supernatural resentment, and plastic shame. Bleeding from one shoulder. Still narrating.

"This ends now," I lied heroically. Charged again. From the side this time.

But the Roomba recalibrated. Activated auxiliary

defenses. Weaponized a rubber band. Tactical elastic. Precision insult, square between the eyes.

I staggered, pride wounded like a rookie cop losing his first interrogation to a talking parrot.

You've been chosen, Butternugget whispered, *blessed by the spin priest. The suction crown is yours now.*

"Shut up," I muttered. I wasn't sure who I was talking to anymore, the cat or the machine.

It beeped once. Cold. Final. Then it did a victory doughnut and rolled back into the fog like a war criminal late for brunch.

I lay on the pavement. Panting. Beaten. Dusted and profoundly vacuumed. Another Friday night gone wrong, except this time without the bourbon to soften the edges or the dame to sharpen them.

That's when I saw the puddle. It shimmered with the cruel clarity of a surveillance mirror in a precinct bathroom. My reflection stared back. Scrappy. Tufty. One eyebrow too many and a nose like a guilty marshmallow trying to enter witness protection.

But then it winked. Not a normal wink. The wrong eye. Twice. And that's when I screamed. The eyes... one glinted with noir purpose... the other tracked an ant. Then I screamed again. Longer. Louder. Why? Because dignity was dead and screaming was free.

Minutes later, I found myself on a windowsill three stories up. Fur matted with alley dust and questionable destiny. The sunbeam stalked me like a bad decision with warm hands. The ivy rustled suspiciously, hiding a deal I hadn't made yet.

My claws were loaded and my patience was on its eighth

life. Past knotted in tuna, trauma, and the kind of naps that leave blood on the pillow and questions in the coroner's report. The city was a litter box of lies, and someone, somewhere, was about to get fatally pawed. This wasn't just a case anymore—it was personal, like a vendetta with pension benefits and no dental plan.

I didn't know who yet. But the feeling was back.

CHAPTER TWO

I tried walking with purpose. It came out more like jazz on roller skates. The Cognichonk's grip was slipping. Lucidity leaked like moonshine through a detective's coat pocket. Cheap, unlicensed, and on fire before it hit the floor. My front legs moved like I meant business. Back legs wobbled like drunk philosophy majors arguing with gravity, undermining every stride with feline flair and zero accountability.

Focus, I told myself. *Think trench coat soaked in yesterday's rain and tomorrow's regrets. Think noir, where even the shadows have shadows. Think—*

"Left. Right. No, your other right. For the love of noir, work with me Butternugget."

I tripped over a noodle. It wasn't a real noodle. It was my tail. But the betrayal still stung.

"Focus," I growled aloud. Except it came out as: "Mrrrp."

My voice box had filed for reassignment like a witness

entering protection after seeing too much in the wrong precinct. I froze. Stared at a nearby garbage lid like it owed me back alimony and emotional closure. Okay. Don't panic. It's a throat issue. Laryngeal trauma. I've been compromised. Temporarily. Maybe if I clear it—

I hacked, but it was more than a cough or a bark—it was a full-body, soul-scraping, fur-encrusted retch from the deepest recesses of betrayal. The kind of sound that gets you banned from jazz clubs and family-friendly puppet shows.

Before I knew what was happening a hairball hit the pavement like a confession spat onto church steps at midnight—wet, guilty, and echoing too loud to ignore. I stared at it. It stared back.

It smells like corn nuts, the voice in my head thought. *Corn nuts and regret.*

That wasn't me. That was him. The other one. The interior decorator of doom. Butternugget.

My body just sat down, not with the resignation of a defeated man, but like a cat driven purely by instinct, all cabaret posture. It felt less like I was sitting and more like my anatomy was staging a coup. Like it had a scheduling conflict with reality and decided the meeting was over. Gravity had called in a favor and my spine signed the contract in crayon.

My tail curled around me. I tried to uncurl it. It slapped me. Classic Butternugget move, I thought. Dignity by appointment only. Something inside me snapped. Could've been resolve. Could've been a hamstring. Neither was answering questions.

I rose again. Furious. Poised. Dangerous. Ready to—

What's that.

A twitch. A flicker. A flutter. My ears rotated like satellite dishes made of spite—completely out of my control. I was a student driver in a beat up orange, and the instructor had taken the wheel back.

A moth. Tiny. Insignificant. Practically translucent. The kind of moth that gets wedgied by dust mites and still thinks it can gentrify a porch light.

It has wings, Butternugget whispered reverently. *Murder wings. Let's eat it or chase it. Maybe its a spy for the spin priest.*

My body crouched. No signal sent. No plan made. Just pure, primal instinct. The kind soaked in millennia of ankle-high violence. Muscles tensed. Ears twitched. A growl rumbled in my chest like an ancient prophecy about to be screamed at a lava lamp.

Get it, Butternugget hissed. *Make it regret flight. We could hide it under the dumpster with the others.*

Don't do it, I warned myself. *You're not a moth guy. You're a trench coat guy. You wear regrets like armor and drink metaphors for breakfast. You don't...*

I leapt. Six feet straight up. Bounced off a trash can lid with all the dignity of a district attorney caught in a brothel raid. The moth had played me like a cheap violin at a funeral for ethics. Ricocheted off a pizza box that said, DO NOT OPEN. So, I did. Then I landed. Sideways. In a puddle that smelled like expired dreams and a regretful seafood buffet.

I lay there. Soaked. Confused. Purring. Oh no. Oh *no*, I'm purring. *Why was I purring. Stop it. Stop*—

The purring grew louder, but it was anything but soothing or pleasant; it was the purr of madness. A cosmic fax tone from the soul's last known address. The kind of sound you hear right before an antique mirror whispers your middle name in Latin. A low-frequency engine of doom shook me down to the whiskers.

I was losing control. To instincts. To fur. To Butternugget.I could feel him in the hum, not in a malevolent way, but with his signature chaos, deranged joy, and feral glee. The kind of idiot happiness that makes raccoons applaud and Roombas flee.

Claw the air and scream, he whispered. *That's how you claim a moment.*

And damn it, he was right. I stood. Shaking. Crackling with static. I screamed at the moon. At a leaf. At my tail. All of them deserved it.

And far, far away... The Cognichonk purred back. Not a purr meant for me, not in this moment, but for a shadow I hadn't yet seen. And the thread didn't just fray—it purred.

I needed out of the alley. Too many memories. Too much damp cardboard. Too much tail.

I slunk along the fence. Tail held like a furry question mark, humming with static. The world beyond the alley loomed bright and clinical. Too open. Too cheerful. A cul-de-sac of madness. A suburb of secrets.

The sidewalk stretched ahead, deceptively clean. Aggressively symmetrical. Like it was trying to sell me something I couldn't return. I didn't trust it. No neighborhood's that tidy unless it's hiding something darker than unpaid parking tickets. Something suburban with teeth. Possibly gluten-free. Definitely sinister. The kind of place where garden hoses double as garrotes and the HOA fees include blood sacrifice.

A plastic flamingo watched me from the weeds. One eye chipped. The other knowing. It had seen things. Lawn things. Possibly crimes against landscaping.

I passed a stroller. The baby inside didn't blink. Just stared. Wide-eyed. Drool-slicked. Judging. That baby knew things too. Not tax code or poetry. Ritual things. The kind that leaves echoes in onesies.

Then...*pop*. A scent. Faint. Warm. Horrifying. Banana pudding and electrical fire. I gagged.

But my paws kept moving. A memory surfaced, not one of mine, yet it felt branded onto these borrowed neurons. It was Butternugget's past, flooding through me like static on a broken TV.

Butternugget, full gremlin mode, skittering across a hot stovetop trying to attack a birthday candle. There was a scream. It might've been his. Might've been the blender. Someone yelled "He's on fire!" No one clarified who.

The world stuttered.

I moved on. Cautious. Watching. Every house whispered something off. One mailbox had a scorch mark and a sigil carved into the side. A loop with a tail, like a snake eating its own ampersand. Another yard had twelve garden gnomes. All facing the same direction toward a birdbath filled with teeth. A single goldfish swam in it. Upside down. It made eye contact. This street had a theme. Haunted HOA. Sacrifice with curb appeal.

Then I saw it. Sidewalk chalk. Just a few lines. Crude. Uneven. But unmistakable. A spiral. Jagged. Lopsided. Too orange.

My fur bristled like a lie in a confessional told by a cop with two pensions and three ex-wives. This chalk spiral wasn't just vandalism—it was a signature, the kind killers leave when they want credit without the paperwork. A kid didn't draw this. It felt too deliberate, a crude glyph, a ritualistic loop. It pulsed with a strange resonance, like a secret marking territory. And I'd seen too many sigils to believe in accidents.

I crept closer. The spiral didn't move, but it twitched. As if the concrete itself remembers being scratched. As if it still ached. I sniffed. Ash. Dust. And a trace of... yarn?

But then, underneath it all, the sharp tang of Cheeto dust, felt-tip marker, and something else... the unmistakable scent of a fool who once tried to pee on a humidifier on purpose.

Butternugget. Again. I growled. Quiet. Reflexive. *Get out of my brain, you fluff-cursed calamity.*

But it was too late. The moment stretched. My ears flattened. The Cognichonk, I realized. I didn't know how I knew. But I knew. Like a tune that shouldn't exist and yet the chorus punches you straight in the ribs.

A low hum stirred in the back of my skull. Thick. Coiled. Feral. Memory. Power. Something waiting. A flash—

Candlelight. Cats in a circle. Shadows that didn't belong to anyone. One upside-down. One without a mouth. One staring straight at me, whispering in Morse code with its tail. A whisper, so old it cracked.

But in the center? A figure. Orange. Purring. Wearing a

Burger King crown and licking a window like it owed him money. Butternugget. Presiding over the ritual like a cat pope and a ball pit accident had a baby. Then it was gone.

I staggered back. Tail fluffed like a pipe cleaner at a crime scene. Static crackled under my claws.

Across the street, a wind chime made of silver spoons clinked three times. There was no breeze. That made my whiskers ache more than anything else. And that's when I saw them—more orange.

"Hey," a voice squeaked behind me. "You glowing?"

I spun. Fast and low, claws ready to monologue someone's face off like a prosecutor with a grudge and a closing argument that tastes like gunmetal. Instead, I found a toe bean. Pink. Unapologetic. Shoving itself directly into my left eye.

"Gah!" I swatted it away and blinked, hard. In its place stood a kitten. Possibly. Probably. Orange, vibrating, and shaped like a thought someone had halfway before sneezing it out. It looked like an anxiety gremlin made of pipe cleaners and sugar.

"I told you not to touch him," said a second voice. Rough, gravelly, and tired of everything including air.

A second cat emerged from beneath a broken barbecue grill. Taller. Older. Equally orange but built like a retired mugger who now yells at clouds. One eye half-closed. The other full of accusation. He wore a crusty pizza triangle like a ceremonial sash.

"Who the hell are you two?" I asked. It came out as: "Mrrp-rowww."

The small one gasped. "He speaks prophecy!"

The older one grunted. "Nah. Just sinus congestion. Name's Gutterball," he added. "This here's Shrimp."

Shrimp nodded. Spun in a circle. Bit a leaf. Fell over.

"We've seen your type," Gutterball continued. "Orange. Twitchy. Narratin' like someone stuffed poetry into a blender with fear."

"I'm Luis Cannon," I said. "Private Investigator. Fragmented. Cognichonked." I blinked. "Possibly divine." This time it came out as: "Mrrrow. Mrowrrrp."

Shrimp gasped. Pupils dilated. "He knows the Sacred Meow."

"No he doesn't," Gutterball said. "He's just loud."

"I touched it," I hissed. "The Cognichonk."

They both froze.

They understood me. Perfect comprehension despite the feline vocal cords. Like we were speaking the same language of conspiracy and fur. Just another piece of evidence in a case file that kept burning the edges of reality. The kind of translation that doesn't need paperwork—just shared delusions and matching coats.

"You touched the Chonk?" Shrimp whispered. "The Yarn That Remembers?"

"We don't say its real name," Gutterball muttered. "Not out loud. Makes the pigeons act weird."

Shrimp leaned forward. "Can I sit on your head while you remember the forgotten crimes of the moon?"

"No."

"Can I ride your tail like a vengeance snake?"

"Absolutely not."

Shrimp blinked. Once. Twice. Then stopped moving entirely. His fur bristled in reverse, like reality remembered it had somewhere else to be. Like it remembered how to panic backward. One ear twitched like it heard time trying to sneak out the back door. A stillness fell over him. The kind that makes the world lean in, nervous. His pupils dilated. His ears rotated a full ninety degrees. And for a moment, just a moment, his fur stilled.

The alley hushed. Then he opened his mouth, and in a voice far too deep for his body, far too echoed for this plane of existence, he said:

"The yarn remembers the loop that broke
Twelve paws in the circle, one to bleed.
The window will crack when the tuna sings.
And he who sleeps in the pantry shall rise again."

My fur lifted, not out of fear or some strange awe, but from the chill of recognition. Because I'd *heard* that voice before. Or maybe I'd *been* it.

For one terrifying second, the air smelled like burnt toast and betrayal. And I remembered. It wasn't a memory that hit me, but a leak, a stray thought Butternugget once had during a lucid episode, now rattling loose in my head like an over-caffeinated squirrel.

The pantry god sleeps on croutons, he had whispered, holy and unhinged. *Do not wake him during daylight television.*

I shuddered. The Cognichonk fries circuits, even the

kitten kind. And Shrimp? He was built like a conduit and a chaos grenade in one. Every time the prophecy hit, it left burn marks behind his eyes.

Silence. A plastic bag fluttered by like a nervous ghost.

I'd heard prophecies before. In alleyways. On walls. Once from a fortune cookie that wouldn't stop bleeding. But this one had a shape. A warning. Twelve paws. A pantry god. And tuna with opinions. This wasn't just nonsense. I felt a cold dread as I saw the structure, the symbolism, the ugly recurrence of it all. And in this town, if there's pattern, there's always a purpose, and it's never good. Someone, or something, is pulling the string. The question is: why now? I hated that I understood any of it.

Gutterball froze mid-tail-flick. "Oh no."

And just like that, he was back. Tail-wagging, gnome-biting, sanity-deficient. Shrimp gasped, snapped out of it, then immediately attacked a moth, failed, spun in a circle, and head butted a brick.

"Okay," I muttered. "What the hell was that."

"That," Gutterball said, "was why we don't let him near string unsupervised."

Shrimp sat up and burped. "I tasted math!"

He tried to swallow the word 'betrayal.' It didn't go down clean. "Tastes like coupons," he muttered.

"Yeah," Gutterball said. "He does that."

"We could braid you into the prophecy," Shrimp offered. "I have string."

"He's not string-compatible," Gutterball said. "He's glitchy."

I narrowed my eyes. "You know more about the Chonk?"

"We know of it," Gutterball said. "We've seen what it

does. The twitching. The lucidity. The sudden urge to sort things alphabetically."

"And the screaming," Shrimp added brightly. "So much screaming."

Across the street, a bird exploded out of a tree for no reason. Or maybe because something listened.

"We feel it too," Gutterball said, staring up. "When the sky gets tight. When the yarn hums. It's like static inside the fur."

Shrimp tilted his head. "Did you bring the end times?"

"No," I said. But maybe I was the low hum before the sirens, the part right before the end times came knocking.

"Cool," Shrimp said. "Wanna nap in the bucket?"

"No."

"Your loss." Shrimp climbed into a bucket labeled CHICKEN BONES (HAUNTED) and passed out immediately.

I looked back at Gutterball. "You seem, ah, less insane."

"I'm not. I've just learned to aim it."

We sat in silence for a moment. Two cats. A prophecy. One sleeping goblin. And me? I wasn't sure if I was the prophecy or the punchline.

Gutterball squinted toward the sky, his good eye narrowing like a cop who's seen too many crime scenes to believe in coincidence. "Storm's coming. Cat-shaped. Stitched in teeth."

I nodded. Then I turned and walked away. I had all the answers I was going to get. Which was none. Also, too many. And I'd started to understand them.

I needed altitude. Perspective. A place to lick my wounds without literally licking anything.

The Cognichonk pulsed. Once. A jolt of lucidity, like a live wire in the soup of my brain. My mind rethreaded itself, if only for a minute. It felt like drowning backward. Like remembering how to breathe in a room with no air. I held on as long as I could.

My first steps were a kind of betrayal, clumsy and off-kilter. But the next? They clicked into place, a grim kind of muscle memory. By the third, instinct had taken the wheel, and muscle memory did the navigating. Cat muscle. Idiot memory. But together, they climbed.

The gutter screeched under my weight like a rookie cop caught lying to internal affairs with marked bills in his locker and the commissioner's wife in his bed. Bolts strained, desperate for immunity. The siding peeled beneath my claws like bad alibis. I nearly lost my footing on a sun-bleached HOPE LIVES HERE sticker.

The windowsill greeted me like an old friend with a fresh warrant. I crouched low. Tail twitching like a tripwire with abandonment issues. Below, the neighborhood simmered. Too quiet. Too clean. Too chalked in sigils no sidewalk chalk set should include. The flamingo still watched me. So did the baby. So did the wind.

Inside the nearest house, a television glowed with static, non-Euclidean cartoons. Outside, ivy rustled against the wall with the calculated grace of someone trying not to be caught eavesdropping.

This wasn't random, no lucky fluke or fever dream. Every time I woke up like this, I was near a marker. A shrine. A memory. It was testing us. Or mapping something I hadn't seen yet. I was stuck in a meat suit made of fur, instincts, and deeply suspect bowel control. But I still had my mind. Parts of it. The parts that hadn't been eaten by panic or carpet fibers.

I don't remember much beyond my real name. It tastes like gravel and bad decisions. Hands. A badge. A bottle I promised to quit. Tomorrow. Always tomorrow. Now I've got toe beans. And a supernatural connection to yarn. I get flashes from time to time of a different me, a different life, even a different cat.

I also have an inexplicable craving for boiled chicken and a hatred of citrus-scented soap. But that might be Butternugget. He's in here too, sometimes. Lurking in the corner of my consciousness like a bloated gremlin on furlough from the upholstery wars. I don't know why it chose me. I don't know what the Whispering Widow wanted. But I know this much... somebody broke something they shouldn't' have. And when it shattered, they stitched the sharpest pieces into orange fur and dumped the rest in an alley behind a cursed laundromat.

I looked down at my paws. Small. Dirty. Still trembling from instinct and impact. They weren't the hands I remembered—hands that once held badges, bottles, and occasionally the truth. These were weapons wrapped in fur, loaded with something deadlier than bullets: desperate clarity. I had to work with what I had. I unsheathed my claws. One by one. Each tip gleamed like a metaphor holding a grudge.

"My claws," I muttered, "are loaded like a dice game in the back room of a precinct where even the coffee has an alibi." But my mind? Threadbare and unraveling. A pause. Dramatic. Nearly profound.

For muffins, whispered Butternugget. Gravely. Like a threat. Or a brunch plan. I wasn't sure which.

I twitched. Shook it off. The wind shifted. The sunbeam dimmed.

"My past," I said, "is a blur."

Behind me, a meow echoed. Too close, too warped. It tasted like déjà vu and rotten significance. I ignored it. Butternugget didn't.

The worms know, he whispered again. *The doorknob told them.*

"And someone," I said, narrowing my eyes to feline slits, "is about to get pawed." I paused. Let it hang in the air like a closing statement at the end of a trial the jury's too scared to walk away from. Then, quieter, deadly sincere, I added: "And if they have tuna? I'll interrogate them first."

With my face, said Butternugget, quietly delighted. *Then nap in the evidence.*

The window creaked behind me. The ivy shivered—like it had just heard its name in the dark. Far off, the Cognichonk pulsed once. Like a heartbeat in reverse. Something was coming. And this time, I'd have claws.

The world blinked like a witness changing testimony. The last clear thought I had before the orange void claimed me was like a confession whispered to an empty interrogation room—

Who leaves a haunted chicken bucket in reach of a kitten prophet?

Then the thread snapped. One heartbeat, I was a storm on the sill. A weapon with whiskers. A trench coat of trauma. A detective built from metaphors and bad decisions. The next, gone. The Chonk let go. Lucidity snapped like yarn stretched too far, too fast. Pulled taut, then gone.

I held the thread of myself for one heartbeat. Just one. The whole world felt aligned, like I could claw my way back. I didn't want to go. But I didn't get a choice. I felt the lucidity drain like bathwater from a cracked sink. The noir shut off like a bad signal. And Butternugget returned.

He blinked once. Then again slower, like he wasn't sure both eyes were on board for this reality.

Ceiling moved. Again. I'll bite it into compliance.

His tail thrashed.

Danger? Nah. Just... tail. Wiggle-wobble-noodle. Why it still looking at me like that?

He turned around three full times. Then forgot why he'd turned. Then sat down directly on his own paw and screamed at the horizon.

He launched himself into the ivy like it owed him snacks. Clawed upward. Sideways. Possibly through a dimension. Made of bees. Yowled in triumph. Then slipped. Fell backward.

Falling! Bestest-fall-whee—WHOA. Wet. My wet? THIS IS PEE. Why the heck pee-fall?

He slammed into the gutter. Ricocheted off the windowsill like a furry ricochet of bad planning. Landed inside a flowerpot. Upside down. Legs out. Brain static. He caught a glimpse of himself in the gutter water.

A face in the water. Screamed. Bit it. Missed. Stupid gravity. Always in the way.

He chirped once. Then purred.

Head empty. Purr-engine ON. Tail go weee. Mouth taste shiny-thing. All confusing! Good job? Maybe. Yes. Vict'ry!

Somewhere far below, the remnants of a potted fern wept. And far, far away the Cognichonk purred back. Not for me, not yet, but for some poor soul it had its eye on. And the yarn was already pulling taut.

CHAPTER THREE

The ceiling fan was already spinning when I awoke. It wasn't just turning; it was watching, appraising, like it knew something I didn't—and had already filed a complaint with Internal Affairs. The kind of complaint that gets honest detectives reassigned to traffic duty in neighborhoods where even the fire hydrants carry heat. Its blades sliced the air like the world's laziest guillotine, casting shadows across a room that reeked of apple-scented betrayal and poor interior choices. A space designed by catalog and curated by cowardice. The kind of room where secrets weren't buried. They were upholstered.

I blinked. Slowly. Regally. The light was soft. Too soft. Like someone had draped a snare in velvet and called it ambiance.

The rug beneath me was plush and beige. Offensively smug. It sprawled there like a politician's alibi—too clean, too practiced, with secrets woven into every fiber. The kind of rug that's seen bodies dragged across it and still maintains its poker face. In its own mind, it was tasteful. In truth, it was a glorified napkin with delusions of elegance, reeking of generational wealth left in the rain.

Rutabaga would've peed on it out of principle. I respected that. And I was sprawled on it.

Like a peasant. Unforgivable.

I rose slowly, deliberately. Tail held low but proud, claws extended just enough to threaten the thread count. That's when I felt it. The sigil spiraled under my paw, etched deep, not just drawn on the surface. It was the kind wielded by sugar-stained hands guided by forgotten rites and a coloring book grudge. The sigil spiraled with the elegance of a tantrum midway through a crayon meltdown. No symmetry. No flair. Pure ritualized nonsense. It radiated hunger. And not the polite kind.

I am not in the mood to tangle with another one of these poorly-rendered glyphs of doom. Not before breakfast. Not barefoot.

The thought hit with a flair I didn't recognize as mine. It felt flatter. Haughtier. Like it had been sprayed with rosewater and pronounced from atop a silk pillow. A Rutabaga flavor.

I was beginning to get used to this. The shift in cats. The change of flavor. Always Orange. Never stable. Flickers of me scattered like brain static across whiskers and half-open blinds that never quite remembered how to close.

I needed to stay grounded. The Chonk disagreed. I remembered little of the case I had been working when everything split apart. I needed to figure out what happened to me. I was my own cold case, but still warm and bleeding under the collar.

The ceiling fan shifted. Only slightly. But not from power. No, this was something worse. Intent. It had stopped spinning. Not because it lacked voltage. Because it had begun listening. If fans have opinions, this one needed therapy. Court-mandated therapy. Possibly exorcism.

Rutabaga sniffed. *Tacky.*

Do not trust the air, I thought, my ears twitching with inherited suspicion. *It moves for too many reasons. And not all of them are polite.*

My great-aunt Mittens once swatted a priest for less.

I stepped back. The rug creaked. Not the fabric. The history. As if something beneath this house remembered footsteps that never should have returned. And resented their echo.

Everything here was too pristine. Too curated. Like someone had sanitized a séance and tried to sell it as comfort. The lemon scent clung to the cushions—a chemical sweetness clearly hiding something. Probably a body. Or worse, bad taste.

And faux velvet? Revolting. This house has the aesthetic range of damp dishrags.

Toys. Family photos. A cartoon flickering on mute. All of it arranged to suggest warmth, but none of it lived in. Real safety doesn't coordinate. It doesn't come with coasters.

Too many throw pillows, Rutabaga muttered. *Probably cursed.*

Places like this? They are never safe. They are performing safety. And I've seen too many of those performances end in blood, broken charms, or possessed blenders.

A noise from the next room. Small. Fast. Giggling.

I tensed. Instinct and contempt united. The fan whirred

again, slow and purposeful. My fur rose like it remembered something I hadn't yet lived.

Somewhere deep inside, Rutabaga whispered: *It's wearing socks with animals on them. You're not safe.*

The sigil flared. Briefly. Pale orange, that specific, heretical hue only the Cognichonk could justify. My jaw locked. My claws flexed. Something thrummed beneath my ribs, familiar and hostile. A memory without time. Yarn with motive. Not now. Not yet.

I backed away. Slowly. Every step a royal decree signed in invisible ink. In this game, the house held all the cards, and I'd bet my last life they were marked. Classic setup. I'd seen cleaner traps in precinct bathrooms after the annual chili cook-off.

The fan had stopped spinning. Now it loomed. Its shadow stretched across the sigil like a final judgment. It was no longer a fixture. It was a presence. Watching. Waiting. Calculating guilt in revolutions per minute.

It was not a fan. It was a question. And I was not prepared to answer. Certainly not before breakfast.

It grinned. Or maybe that was me. The Cognichonk's mark pulsed behind my ribs. It wasn't a burn or a sting, but memory, coiled and damning, twisting inside me. This place had called it. It wasn't a full connection, but it was enough to know the score: the house knew I was here. The ceiling was listening. And the decor was lying. And the throw pillows were complicit.

I'd seen it before. Sanctified smiles on a cursed nursery. A leyline tucked beneath an upscale preschool. Teething rings shaped like wards. I once dismantled an entire smuggling ring operating out of a daycare where the finger paints bit back. This wasn't a home. Not by a long shot. This was a ritual, and I was the offering that woke up too early.

And somewhere deep beneath the noir and the claws, Rutabaga purred. Not a sound of pleasure, just presence. And judgment, cold as a forgotten case file.

Stuck here, I clawed for memory—fragments, flashes, anything that wasn't sticky. As I struggled to recall what had been lost, my body moved on instinct or maybe Rutabaga took control. I was mid-groom, polishing the only tuft of tail that still held dignity, when the cherub struck.

She descended from the couch like a wrathful pudding, all giggles and grubby fingers, her grip tacky with the sins of breakfast past. I'd faced down mob enforcers with cleaner methods and more predictable demands. At least they tell you what they want before they break your legs. This one? Pure chaos in unicorn pajamas. Before I could hiss or invoke my ancestral rights, she had me. Lifted—bodily, scandalously—like a plush tribute to the gods of sticky-fingered chaos.

I twisted. I flailed. My paws became verbs conjugated in the tense of desperation. I'd escaped four contract killers in a locked meat locker with less effort. But this? This was the kind of hold they don't teach at the academy—the kind that makes hardened informants reconsider their life choices.

Rutabaga's voice snarled inside my brain, *Unhand me, sticky demon!*

She laughed. That wasn't a baby's sound; it was the

shriek of an ancient thing awakened, a sound that had haunted temples and toppled empires. I went rigid.

The toddler, a roly-poly tyrant in a unicorn onesie, hauled me like a victory flag through the living room, her legs wobbling with divine, unearned authority. I saw it all through narrowed eyes: the battlefield of juice-sigils, the gutted remote still leaking batteries, the fridge poetry that spelled CAT IS KEY in shaky, prophetic alignment. So they knew. And still they dared call me—

"Oh, *Rutabaga's* having fun!" sang the voice from the kitchen.

Rutabaga. They had renamed me Rutabaga. A tuber. A peasant vegetable. It wasn't a name, it was a goddamn produce aisle insult. Fit for soup, maybe, but never a legacy. My ancestors wore collars of velvet, drank from chalices, and judged kings from atop embroidered cushions.

Now I was being groped by a goblin in a unicorn jumpsuit. I yowled.

She squealed. Her grip tightened. She opened the dishwasher. That gleaming, steam-belching sarcophagus. The one-eyed stainless-steel executioner of socks, spoons, and souls. She reached for it like a cultist unlocking the elder vault.

"No," I rasped. My voice was Luis now—grit and gravel soaked in bourbon and nine lives' worth of bad luck.

Not the rinse cycle again, Rutabaga cried out.

It was clear that Rutabaga had been through this song and dance before and wanted no part in it.

She tried to stuff me in. I resisted with every claw, every sinew, every ounce of feline vengeance coded into my DNA by Bastet and bootlegging. My spine arched like a war banner. My claws found traction in the door frame. She pulled. I pushed. It was toddler versus Persian. Bloodline versus mayhem in a ballet of destruction. And then—

The basket. A laundry basket appeared like a miracle from the Housewares aisle. I lunged. A tactical roll. A perfect three-point landing in a sea of unmatched socks and crumpled hope. But the toddler wasn't done. She charged.

The basket moved. Wheels skidded. The world tilted. I was in a mobile sarcophagus careening through the kitchen like a soapbox derby piloted by entropy.

They will write epics of my suffering, Rutabaga wailed. *Ballads of betrayal sung in key change!*

A rogue towel jammed the wheels. The basket spun. I launched skyward like vengeance on springs. Airborne. Slow-motion. My tail streamed behind me like a banner of war. I passed the ceiling fan. It watched me ascend. Judging.

I landed. But not on towels. No. That would have been mercy. I slammed into a pile of building blocks. Plastic bricks in screaming primary colors that jabbed into my ribs like enchanted caltrops disguised as learning tools. The impact sang a hymn of indignity. Something inside the pile crunched. I hoped it was the toy and not one of my kidneys.

If I die here, Rutabaga moaned, *bury me in silk.*

I staggered upright. Dazed. Dignity cracked but not broken, like a detective's moral code after ten years on the force. My fur, formerly smooth as velvet vengeance, now bristled like the conscience of a judge who knows he's been bought but can't remember by whom. And then I heard it. The slap of footie pajamas on laminate. She had rounded the corner.

I turned. Our eyes met. Her expression? Triumphant. A

juice box in one hand. In the other? A glitter-coated xylophone mallet. And this wasn't Rutabaga's kind of tasteful glitter; this was weapons-grade.

I bolted to the left. Too slow. The mallet struck. Squeaky. Rubber. Blunt. The blow hit me squarely on the flank with the force of an overexcited therapy dog. It didn't hurt, not physically anyway, but it sure as hell offended. A hit straight to the soul, not just the flesh. The kind of insult that no proper feline should endure without reparations or at least a dramatically fainted collapse.

I reeled theatrically and used the momentum to twist into a roll. I came up beneath a dining chair, leapt to the tabletop in a single bound, and sent a half-eaten graham cracker skittering across the surface like a decoy. She went for it.

Rutabaga huffed, *Of course she did. No palate.*

I launched again, full speed, onto the windowsill, bounced off the curtain rod, ricocheted off a framed inspirational quote ("*Live, Laugh, Love*" liars all), and landed on the back of the couch.

The toddler turned. She came. Faster this time. Arms outstretched. A pacifier clenched in her teeth like a war talisman. She climbed the couch like a siege tower scaled by giggles.

I stood tall on the back of the couch, a prince cornered. My final line of defense was a throw pillow. A truly hideous paisley thing.

Paisley, Rutabaga sniffed internally. *A pattern fit for a clown's coffin. Do not let it touch your fur.*

Ignoring him, I braced myself. The toddler lunged. I spun, shoving the pillow forward as a shield. She hit it full-force and bounced backward into a pile of plush animals. Their stitched-on smiles seemed to mock her failure. My dignity, while frayed, remained intact.

I dashed along the backrest, vaulted onto the TV stand, and took a flying leap onto the stairs. Finally. Uphill. A sacred direction. I climbed like a prince pursued. My claws found grip. My breath came in measured bursts. Behind me, the toddler shrieked again. That wasn't a cry for help; it was a promise, cold and clear.

She followed. Gods help us, she followed. Diaper-sagging, unholy giggles bouncing off the walls like sonar. She moved like a sugar-haunted banshee with a side quest.

I made the landing. Turned left. Ducked. Slid. A dollhouse exploded beneath my feet. Too bad. No time. Collateral damage.

"Collateral damage," I muttered. "Comes with the case."

I crossed into sanctuary: the linen closet. Dark. Soft. Shelves of towels that smelled like false peace. I collapsed, panting. Eyes wide. Cognichonk pulsing like a second heart behind my ribs. For I was Rutabaga in name, but Cannon in soul. And I had seen the truth: The sigils were spreading. The hairless ones were drawing them. And somewhere in this house, beneath the lemon-scented lies, was a plan. A conspiracy. A ritual. A reckoning. And I would solve it.

After a snack. And a nap.

But mostly the nap.

Especially now that my spine was full of Legos.

I'd found my sanctuary, but the linen closet promised peace it couldn't deliver. It lied. It smelled like lavender, desperate to pass for truth. I'd buried myself in towels, hoping the scent would cover me like a shroud of fabric softener and denial—the same denial that keeps bartenders pouring doubles for cops who've seen too much and remembered too little. The kind of denial that has its own mailbox and pays rent on time. Silence lies. And soft things rot just the same.

Even here, in the belly of linen-scented falsehoods, the house breathed, though not with air that would fill a man's lungs. It exhaled memory, thick and suffocating. I could feel it curling around the towel fibers. Watching through vent slats. Listening in frequencies just shy of sanity.

Something scraped faintly behind the wall. Not the frantic scrabble of claws, nor the skitter of vermin. This was the calculated drag of intention—like a body being moved by someone who's done it before and has a system. The kind of sound that makes coroners check their watches and detectives reach for their second flask. The sigils were drawing themselves now. I didn't know whether to be impressed or terrified. Probably both. Definitely both.

There had been cases like this before. A poltergeist with a flair for scented candles. A haunted ottoman that only activated during jazz. But this? This went beyond hauntings. This felt less like a ghost in the machine and more like the machine writing its own damn script. Architecture writing its own doctrine in citrus and blood. The Cognichonk pulsed at the idea.

And beneath the hum of quiet appliances and judgmental lamps, I heard it again. A whisper that bypassed the ears and landed straight in the gut—a whisper of raw intent.

Welcome back.

I didn't remember ever being here. But the house did.

Eventually, the hum returned. Low. Subtle. Wrong. It vibrated through the floorboards like the house had a second heartbeat—and mine was trespassing.

I slipped from the linen closet like a thief in a museum of curated deceit. Velvet paws. Tactical precision. Disdain primed and polished. Past finger-smudged baseboards and nightlights that judged harder than a bishop at brunch with sinners. The kind of lights that don't keep monsters out. They just highlight the furniture when the shadows start talking.

I'd once slipped through the vents of a penthouse owned by a kleptomaniac sorceress with seven cursed urns and a vendetta against ceiling tiles. This felt worse.

Back then, I knew what I was walking into—probably a fire trap, definitely a moral one. But here? The uncertainty was the threat. Here, even the silence had a smirk. The kind that said, "I know where your litter box is buried."

I don't like walking into things blind. Not since the chandelier incident. But when the Cognichonk hums and the air carries the static weight of something unsaid... you walk anyway. You walk because some part of you remembers how to hunt. And the rest of you remembers why you stopped.

The kitchen door was ajar, not so much open as it was beckoning—the way a back-alley poker game beckons when you're down to your last bullet and your second-best lie. The kind of invitation that comes with fine print written in someone else's blood. Or maybe just toast. There was a hum there, too. Not the arcane thrum of sigils, but the low, unsettling purr of the blender.

It sat silent. Plugged in, but breathing. The lights on its face blinked a sequence I swore resembled Morse. I didn't dare look too long. It's always the blender. First it blends. Then it plots.

Rutabaga hissed softly under his breath. *That thing made eye contact last week.*

Appliances shouldn't have eyes. But this one had a presence—the kind of presence that makes veteran cops request backup and judges sign warrants without reading them. It hummed with the quiet confidence of someone who knows where all the bodies are buried because it helped dig the holes.

I moved past it with calculated casualness, like I wasn't intimidated by 1200 watts of betrayal. But I was. We both were. Something about the blender felt sigiled, yes, but not in the ancient hand-drawn way. This was a deeper magic, coded into its very circuits. Mechanical summoning wrapped in brushed steel.

Whatever secrets this house held, they were woven into its very circuitry. And I needed to unplug them before they powered up completely.

CHAPTER FOUR

The door to the laundry room stood ajar like the mouth of a stoolie who died before finishing his confession. The smell hit first: peanut butter, shampoo, and something older—mothballs steeped in regret and broken routines. The kind of smell that makes medical examiners check their watches and defense attorneys suddenly remember prior commitments. The olfactory equivalent of finding your own name etched on a gravestone. Spelled right, dated wrong, and still warm.

Also, it stank of budget fabric softener—a cheap cologne trying to hide the stink of failure.

I slipped inside. Tiled floor. Cold. Clean—the kind of clean that hides things like bleach over bloodstains. A dryer rumbled in the corner, muttering threats through a mouthful of socks. The washing machine stood beside it, lid cracked like it was half-awake and dreaming of bleach.

I moved past them. Low and deliberate, like a prosecutor with dirt on the judge. My fur brushed against a laundry basket that had clearly never seen a matching set—just like I'd never seen a clean precinct or an honest mayor. Some things just aren't in the cards when the deck's been stacked since before you were dealt in.

Oh why did I get stuck in this tragedy of a home, Rutabaga moaned.

And that's when I saw it. Behind the dryer. A sigil. Drawn in lint. Not a flourish to be found, no hint of whimsy. Just coiled lines, stark and brutal, built from shed fibers and spiritual neglect. It pulsed faintly. Less like a magical charm, more like a silent, vibrating truth—a truth that didn't need spells to be dangerous, only meaning. It made my spine ring like a tuning fork for heresy. My whiskers didn't like the song. And somewhere in the back of my borrowed brain, a memory stirred. Not a ghost of my own past, but a shard of his. A spiral. A purpose. And maybe, just maybe, a whisper of pride.

It also offends my aesthetic. Who draws warding glyphs in dust without coordinating color tones? Monsters, that's who. Rutabaga hissed aloud. *Lint is for shedding. Not for symbolism.*

I added my own hiss, low and instinctual. Who draws a sigil in lint? Lint spells aren't for amateurs. They're for believers. Or madmen with a dryer full of regrets. Someone who knows you don't always need chalk when a house is already listening.

The dryer exhaled. The hum sharpened. I ducked behind it. Into the crawlspace of forgotten socks and mechanical spite. The vent caught my attention. Ordinary. Grated. Slightly bent at one corner. And just inside, wedged between dust bunnies and the accumulated shame of a thousand unwashed blankets, was a scrap of paper.

I reached in slow. Claws out, like a pickpocket at a confession booth. It came loose like it wanted to talk and knew too much. A torn receipt. Ink faded. But the words remained.

DON'T TRUST THE HAIRLESS ONES
THE COGNICHONK DREAMS BENEATH.

I stared. The hum grew louder, like a confession building in the throat of a man who knows he won't see morning. *The Cognichonk dreams beneath.* Beneath what? The house? The floor? The litterbox? In my line of work, 'beneath' usually meant six feet under with concrete shoes and a death certificate that listed 'natural causes.' Nothing about this felt natural.

I turned. There it was. Pink plastic. Hooded. Too clean. The litterbox. An altar to deception. Domestic on the surface. Ritual beneath. Scented clay over sacred geometry. It reeked of lemon-scented denial. The kind of tension you only find at crime scenes or Sunday dinner with exorcists. It was hideous. The color alone could summon demons.

Peach? In this lighting? I should hex whoever bought it. Rutabaga recoiled internally. *If one must conduct rituals in a plastic vestibule, at least match it to the decor.*

The surface was smooth. Too smooth. Like it knew I was coming and wanted to look innocent. No natural dig marks. Someone had been tampering. I approached cautiously. One paw at a time. My nose wrinkled. My fur bristled.

Beneath the layer of pine-scented deception, I could feel it. A symbol. Scratched into the base. Hidden by perfumed granules and corporate guilt. This wasn't hygiene. It was a hex in a hoodie. And somewhere in the back of my shared mind, I knew Even Rutabaga wouldn't scratch in this sacrilege. And he once peed in a salad bowl on purpose.

A clay-lined oubliette. A ward. And I'd used it three times already. Three times I had unknowingly participated in my own containment, scratching my own name onto the bars of my cage. The indignity wasn't just in the plastic, it was in the complicity. They hadn't just built a prison; they'd made the prisoner maintain it, forcing dignity to kneel before deception. I backed away, lashing my tail. This wasn't a home. It was a prison. Or worse. A shrine. A holy place built from plastic bins and passive-aggressive throw pillows. Something was being worshipped here. And it sure as hell wasn't the god of good taste. To what, I didn't know. But someone, something, was watching. Not with the idle gaze of curiosity, but with the cold, patient stare of hunger. And I was walking its halls like a tourist in a mausoleum, too lucid for my own safety.

The note burned behind my eyes. I read it again.

DON'T TRUST THE HAIRLESS ONES

I didn't. I never had.

A memory, greasy and common, surfaced from the cat's side of the aisle. Rutabaga's memory. He'd never trusted them either.

Especially not when they bring that ghastly "fancy" food, he huffed. *That slop in a rustling pouch. It carries the stench of betrayal simmered in gravy-scented mediocrity.*

But now I had proof. I glanced back at the dryer. The lint sigil glowed faintly. Its edges shifted, not like it was being disturbed, but like it knew I was watching. I tucked the note beneath my fur, close to my ribs. Right near the bruise from that cursed flamingo cat tree Rutabaga liked. Rutabaga liked it. Which meant I should have known it was cursed.

The Cognichonk stirred. Not fully, no, but enough to set the static prickling under my fur. Something about this vent full of whispered warnings had awakened it. I had stepped into a ritual not as a guest but as evidence—the kind that gets buried, not catalogued.

My claws flexed. My tail flicked. My eyes narrowed. There was more to find. More to uncover. Someone had scrawled a warning in the vent and scratched a prison ward into my bathroom. That meant there were others. Survivors. Witnesses. Or traitors. And I would find them. Even if I had to claw through every sock drawer in this cursed mausoleum of lemon-scented deception.

I crept back toward the hallway, ears low, shoulders hunched. This wasn't over. This wasn't act one. It was the crawl before the curtains. And the spotlight had already found my tail. And somewhere deep in the drywall, the hum began to laugh.

The living room hadn't changed. It had confessed. The furniture was still where it had been. But now it meant something—like evidence that changes meaning once you know where the murder weapon was stashed. Every ottoman, every lamp, every dust bunny was now a witness with something to hide and a price for talking. The ottoman had secrets. The couch had regrets. And the shag rug? That smug beige bastard was an accomplice. Rutabaga loathed it on principle. Too soft to be trustworthy. Too beige to be divine.

I padded in, low and loaded, nose twitching like a lie detector in a tax audit. The fan wasn't spinning, not for lack of power, but for intent. Its blades hung heavily in the air like accusations, each one pointed directly at me, or perhaps, at the cereal bowl. A half-eaten loop of breakfast treachery lay glowing like a forgotten relic from the Temple of Gluten Doom.

I looked down. The Fruit Loops weren't spilled. No, they were arranged with a chilling precision, a deliberate positioning. The kind of sigil you'd expect to find etched in blood and regret, not sugar and FDA-approved dye.

And mismatched colors. Rutabaga sneered internally. *If you're going to call forth ancient hunger, at least commit to a color scheme. No orange in the sigil? Cowards.*

I'd seen this trick before. Once in a demonic daycare where the Goldfish crackers spelled CONFESS. Once more at a cult-run petting zoo where the alpacas whispered in Enochian. Both cases ended with paperwork nobody wanted to file and witnesses who suddenly developed selective amnesia and new beach houses. The kind of cases that get locked in filing cabinets that don't officially exist. This was premeditated breakfast occultism. The worst kind. Small bits of memory, tiny cracks into my past cases, but I still couldn't fully recall the case I had been on when things went full orange.

The air shifted. Behind me, the fan didn't move. But the shadows did. I looked left. Nothing more of note. I went back to checking out the breakfast for further clues.

The toast was burned, but not by chance. The char lines curled into a glyph I'd only seen once before: a spiral within a spiral. The sigil of recursive hunger. Drawn once on a basement wall. Beneath a church. Full of cats. Full of screams. Rutabaga would've tried to lick the jam off the sigil. Then blame the dog. I squinted at it. Yeah. That tracks.

I leapt onto the bookshelf. Hard wood. Cheap varnish. Titles like *Ten Steps to Joy* and *The Gluten-Free Soul*. Lies, all of them. Spiritual pamphlets for the comfortably damned. I climbed like a sinner with a secret. Each shelf a rung on the ladder to divine retribution. And a better vantage point. Also, the top shelf had the least dust. Finally, something in this house understood standards.

Still smells like discount pine and failure, Rutabaga noted, with tragic dignity.

I reached the top. The fan loomed overhead. Blades aligned like judgment from on high. And then, it turned. No hum of electricity, no whisper of power. Just one deliberate revolution, slow and intimate. The kind of movement that says *I see you* and means it with every haunted bolt. It didn't growl with sound, not in a way that would trouble the ears. This was a deeper snarl, a rumble of pure gravity that twisted the air.

The walls vibrated like they were remembering something they swore to forget. The ceiling tensed. The lightbulbs dimmed in shame. I grabbed a toy mouse. A limp, half-chewed fuzzball still reeking of betrayal and drool. I threw it. It vanished midair. Just disappeared. No bounce. No fall. Just gone. Like it had never existed. Like the fan had unmade it. That's when I felt the hum.

The Cognichonk stirred behind my eyes. An itch inside

my soul's radiator. Static prickled under my fur like guilt on a dirty judge. Lucidity flared—sharp and sudden as a switchblade in a pension negotiation. The kind of clarity that comes with a price tag written in red and collected in installments of sanity.

I was Luis Cannon. Detective. Cynic. Currently housed in a cat named after a root vegetable and held hostage by interior design. And I was close. Too close. A memory hit me like a flash-bang wrapped in yarn. The present dissolved as the past came rushing back.

Candlelight. The air was thick with the smell of ozone, catnip, and melting wax—the perfume of bad decisions made by committees with blood oaths. A dozen orange cats in a spiral, their forms shifting in the guttering light like alibis under cross-examination. This wasn't just a meeting; it was a tribunal where the verdict had been decided before the gavel dropped.

One had a monocle that gleamed with stolen starlight. One had no face, just a smooth expanse of fur that rippled as it hummed. One spoke in paw Morse... The center? A brass orb... Cognichonk. It was purring with a sound that vibrated not in the ears, but in the teeth, in the bones. It was choosing. Someone offered it a dead moth... Someone else offered me. Rutabaga would've scorned the sparkle. Unworthy of ritual. And him. I refused. I think.

Then back to now. The Cognichonk was near. Or calling. Or hungry. Maybe all three. But maybe that was Rutabaga's stomach. It was hard to tell.

The fan shifted again. Its blades aligned perfectly with my position. Target acquired. This wasn't a fixture. It was a divining blade with a body count. A rotating prophet with murder in its gears. I narrowed my eyes. Snarled. Drew a breath thick with dread and defiance. And suppressed the part of me that wanted to scream because the lampshade didn't match the base.

"Fan", I growled, "you're out of spins." Then I slashed the wall. Three claws. Vertical. Evenly spaced. Just like the marks I'd found in the precinct. Just like the ones etched into the box that started it all. Ritual. Resonance. Reckoning.

The fan whirled once. The room bent. The world narrowed. Colors dulled. Edges blurred. The Cognichonk's tether pulled taut behind my eyes. Snapped. The pulse was gone. And with it, me. My last thought, before the velvet fog swallowed the mind of Luis Cannon, was neither poetic nor profound. It was—

I hope they remember to feed me before the world ends.

The tent reeked of betrayal and goldfish crackers—a bouquet familiar to anyone who's ever been double-crossed by their own partner. Rutabaga awoke with a gasp. Or perhaps a wheeze. The sound a corrupt commissioner makes when he realizes the wire was recording the whole time. Or perhaps the gasp was imagined. The Cognichonk's hold had slipped away, taking Luis with it. He was alone, and therefore unobserved.

A tragedy. And worse, unfilmed.

He lay motionless on his back for several seconds, legs curled daintily in the air like a fainting widow atop a chaise lounge. His flat face scrunched. Something in the polyester walls offended him. Possibly the unicorn print. Possibly existence. He emitted a low, rattling noise. It wasn't the menace of a growl, nor the demand of a meow. This was a royal lamentation from a throat that deserved velvet curtains and a house with better lighting.

Then he rolled into a heap of stuffed animals and gave a full-body shudder, as if the scent of off-brand vanilla had personally wounded him. He sniffed the air. Snorted. Sniffed again.

Disgusting. Everything smells like plastic and lower class.

Inside the tent, in crayon:

THEY LISTEN THROUGH THE BLADES

Rutabaga stared at it. Then stared harder. Then screamed at it. Loud. Sustained. Into the nylon seam like it had betrayed Versailles. He flopped out of the tent like a Regency ghost denied inheritance and immediately head-butted a nearby wall with all the rage of a duke snubbed at tea.

He moved on. In the kitchen, a blender made eye contact. He arched his back. Fluffed his tail. Then jumped. Sideways, of course. Onto a child's chair and collapsed like dying nobility. For thirty seconds, he laid limp. Then, as if remembering something dire, he shrieked again and sprinted out of the room. His destination was unclear. Possibly divine. Possibly sink-related.

At some point, he returned to the living room. The fan loomed. Rutabaga sat beneath it like a judge awaiting bribes —patient as a hitman on an hourly rate. He licked his paw. Slowly. Dramatically. With the deliberate precision of a coroner who knows exactly which evidence to misplace before the autopsy report goes public. Then he slapped it against his own face with theatrical disdain. Missed the third time and fell off the ottoman.

He did not recover with grace. He screamed again. At the fan. At the rug. Then at his own tail. He leapt to the window. Pressed one paw dramatically to the glass. Looked out upon the yard like a minor noble exiled for crimes of taste. There were birds.

I hate those flying rodents with their freedom and ability to view something other than this beige dystopia.

Back in the tent, the crayon writing flickered in the light. Its spiral smudged. One word nearly erased. Someone had touched it, yet the room offered no witness, no one to catch the subtle shift. Outside, a breeze stirred the ivy. Somewhere upstairs, a door creaked open on its own. In the crawlspace, the lint sigil rearranged itself, slightly.

Rutabaga, meanwhile, had discovered the sink and was now shrieking directly into it, eyes wide, tail puffed, back arched like he'd seen an aesthetic crime.

He caught sight of his reflection in the faucet. A grotesque parody. A funhouse-mirror version of his noble, flattened face, warped by the curve of cheap metal. Crooked. Warped. Lit like an afterthought. It wasn't merely a reflection; no, this was a chrome-plated accusation of mediocrity. An insult rendered in chrome. He screamed louder, not at what he saw, but at the sheer, unmitigated gall of the lighting to present him so poorly.

Gilded faucet. Fluorescent guilt. I deserve chiaroscuro.

And somewhere far off the Cognichonk purred. It pulsed once, like a reversed heartbeat behind the drywall.

And somewhere deep inside me, what was left of me, a

thought surfaced—murky and dangerous as a body floating to the top of the harbor after the cement shoes finally cracked. The kind of thought that doesn't knock before entering and leaves fingerprints on purpose.

I didn't know who drew the sigils. But someone in this house worshiped something. It wasn't some deity, or even the faint glimmer of sanity. It certainly wasn't the god of basic vacuum maintenance. It was an ancient, lazy hunger. It didn't need to hunt; that wasn't its game. This was something that purred when you bled, content to simply wait for you to fall apart.

CHAPTER FIVE

The world reeked of rusted rain gutters and week-old tuna. A thick, wet stillness clung to the air, the kind of quiet that means something is watching—the same quiet that hangs around stakeouts gone wrong and witnesses who've suddenly developed expensive taste. The kind of quiet that costs extra and leaves bruises. That meant I was back. Riding Butternugget. I blinked once against the overcast sky. The clouds churned like guilt in a blender, hovering above a horizon that promised nothing. Somewhere, a pigeon screamed. Probably Carl.

Feathered Syndicate call.

I didn't know how long I'd been out. Time in the Cognichonk wasn't a straight line. It was a corkscrew in a microwave. Loud, glowing, and full of dangerous leftovers. But for one flicker of clarity, I remembered.

The Widow. Her name was dust in my mouth. Only the case remained, cold and sharp. Wrapped in lace and bad decisions. Her file was thicker than a district attorney's pension plan and twice as suspicious. She'd walked into my office trailing perfume that smelled like opportunity with a silencer attached. Her voice, her perfume, the way her cats watched me like they knew I'd broken something sacred just by walking in. And the toy. Gods help me, the toy. It had the shape of a toy, but the weight of a lead coffin. No, not a toy. A trap wrapped in yarn and meaning. And I touched it. Thought I was clever. Thought I was strong. And then the world exploded into whiskers.

I remembered her face only in outline. Soft, suspicious, backlit by candlelight and lies. I didn't remember her name, but I remembered the way she didn't flinch when the sigil flared behind her. I'd failed her. I think. It sat behind my ribs like a loaded file I couldn't open. Every memory clipped at the corners. Every regret filed under "pending." Or maybe she failed me. It didn't matter. Not anymore. I shook the thought off. It clung like cobwebs on a wet brainstem. Focus.

I was back in Butternugget. Tucked behind an overturned trash bin that smelled like expired ramen and a wish granted by mistake—the kind of mistake that gets junior detectives reassigned to traffic duty in neighborhoods where even the parking meters carry heat. This alley had seen more broken promises than a bail bondsman's Christmas party. The alley was still cracked and crooked. Walls stained with graffiti, sigils. A crude possum sketch that might've been prophetic, if you knew how to read betrayal in its beady eyes. I crept low. Streetlight off. Instinct on.

The alley held its breath. No wind. No sound. Even Carl, wherever he was, had shut up. That's when it twitched. Too

CONTAINMENT NOT RECOMMENDED

fast to see, but enough to know something had just broken formation. Something was moving. It wasn't the scuttle of a rat. This was too swift, too certain. Too damned deliberate for anything with whiskers and a taste for garbage. A streak of gray darted across the alley's mouth and vanished behind a pile of damp cardboard.

I froze. Then I saw it again. A squirrel.

Squirrel? Butternugget perked up, sticky with static and optimism. *Bite it or court it? I forget how love works when it's fast.*

I blinked. Hard. It was not just any squirrel. This one moved like it had a map and a deadline. Its tail snapped like it had an opinion. And maybe clearance codes. Eyes too bright. It paused at the edge of the alley, sniffed the air, then took off across the broken fence into the back lot of a shuttered laundromat.

I knew that lot. I knew what was buried under the south corner tile. I still dream about the noise it made going in. Which meant—

"That squirrel," I whispered, claws sliding free with a soft shhhk, like a zipper on a secret, "knows something."

It's wearing secrets. Butternugget added reverently. *Also pants. No wait. That's just its butt.*

It was always squirrels. Twitchy little operatives in fur coats. Smuggling secrets between trees. Sometimes they work for the pigeons. Sometimes the gnomes. Once, for a blender cult that didn't survive the great outlet fire of '04.

I moved. One paw after the other. Hips low. Tail high. A twitch in my back leg suggested I should scream at a leaf. I ignored it. My breath caught between focus and fury.

He zigged like a rumor. I zagged like I knew better. My

fur was a warning. My claws were already writing the obituary. It wasn't just a random rodent. It was a fleeing witness. A fluff-tailed accomplice to something darker. Maybe the sigils. Maybe the potted fern incident. I didn't need another reason. My muscles coiled, and I exploded from the shadows.

The lawn was treacherous. If you could call it that. Broken bottles and concrete cracks. An old Barbie head, its plastic scarred with teeth marks. A gnome was toppled against a weed-choked planter. One eye chipped. The other saw everything and filed it under 'unspoken'. I didn't stop to ask what Carl had done. I already knew it involved cheese and regret.

The squirrel juked left. I matched. Through the hydrangeas. Past a tricycle. I hurdled a coiled garden hose. A slow, steady *drip...drip...* ticked from its brass nozzle, the sound sharp and loud in the silence. We left the alley behind. Now it was neutral turf. Gravel and hard-packed dirt between old apartment blocks that had once dreamed of being a park. Instead woke up full of mold and broken sidewalk chalk.

The squirrel hit the fence. Vaulted. I launched. The squirrel didn't hesitate. Straight for the lot. Straight for the tile. Like it *knew*.

For a second, just one, I felt like myself again. Like the man I'd been before the fur. Before the Widow said my name like a prayer with teeth. Wind in my face. Muscles coiled with intent. The case was alive under my skin, and I was going to catch it. Mid-air, time cracked. The sky pulsed. Orange. Wrong.

My narration stammered. Like a scratched record

choking on static. *The case—case—was—was—*

Then everything spiraled. Thoughts spilled like secrets. Shredded like trust. Unraveled like cursed yarn left out in the rain. I tumbled through something soft and sharp at the same time. A spiral? A snare? The Cognichonk waking. Twitching? Rewriting? I landed. Badly. Rolled once. Twice. Came up claws-first, fur bristling, heart hammering against a rhythm I didn't choose.

Tummy hurts. Blame the hose, Butternugget muttered. Then louder, *Scream at it! That'll teach gravity.*

I was still Luis. Cognichonked into Butternugget again. Riding his nervous system like a trench coat on a ferret. We didn't share a brain. We handed it off like bad roommates on opposite shifts. The body was mine, for now. The instincts had their own agenda. Something had changed. The Cognichonk had pulsed. And something was still pulsing.

The sky had pulsed orange. And across the street sat an orange cat, regal and watching. It wasn't a coincidence. The system hadn't just glitched. It had found a second terminal. Regal in the way of loafs that know secrets. Reclined like judgment. His eyes met mine. Something tugged at the edge of my thoughts. Like my own mind had stepped outside for a smoke. That's when I heard it.

"The suspect was cornered. But so was I. The garden gnome knew more than it let on."

Same cadence. Same gravel. My voice. My head jerked sideways. Not toward him. *From* him. My thoughts bent like heat shimmer. I wasn't just hearing him. I was feeling him think in my bones. My voice, my cadence, piped through someone else's breath.

That's me! No it's not! YES IT IS but like, upgraded. Like me but with muscles. And secrets. Wanna sniff him. Bite him. Hug him and yell. He knows about the laundry goblin. You can see it in the eyes. Those are goblin-knowing eyes.

I didn't answer. I unraveled. I didn't know what that meant. I didn't want to. If my voice was loose in the world without me, then I wasn't alone. I was duplicated. Or dissected. Or both.

The cat across the street stretched. Yawned. Licked one paw with the casual precision of a coroner who enjoys his work too much. And he winked. No warmth in that wink, no sly agreement. Just the cold, dead certainty of a creature that knew every shameful sin I'd ever committed in the dark —the kind of certainty usually reserved for tax auditors and priests who've heard one confession too many. That wink was a signed confession to a crime I hadn't realized I'd committed.

I woke up under a rose bush that offered no sweet perfume, only the blunt, earthy stench of mulch and something fouler, like regret mixed with Carl's latest garden gnome atrocity. The kind of stench that clings to crime scenes after the photographers leave but before the cleaning crew arrives. The thorns embraced me like a loan shark who's decided to get creative about the interest. My back ached. My fangs felt metaphorical. And I knew the truth. Somewhere, someone had buried my dignity beneath a garden gnome named Carl.

The wind shifted. Petals rustled like secrets on the move. The nap was recent. The rose bush was real. But I wasn't just

Jake Speed anymore. I was Luis Cannon. Again, and in a fur coat twice my usual dignity. I caught his name in the back of my mind, *Jake Speed*.

He was majestic. Maine Coon-sized and fluffier than a lie whispered at a funeral by the deceased's business partner. His body was a cathedral of feline power—the kind of physical presence that makes witnesses suddenly remember urgent appointments and prosecutors consider career changes. Every whisker was a loaded statement, every twitch of his tail a cross-examination. Coiled in sun-dappled shade and radiating noir potential like a lion with a fedora. My claws flexed. Retractable weapons wrapped in velvet sin.

Strange voice in skull. Not mine. Uses my paws. Hunts with my body. Not enemy. Not friend. Something else

I stretched. Slowly. Precisely. Like a crime scene unfolding. Then I spoke. "The suspect was cornered. But so was I. The garden gnome knew more than it let on." The words tasted like home and gunmetal. My voice. My rhythm. My cadence.

There is a faint memory of pink plastic and beige carpeting. I don't remember exactly where I saw it, but it's there in the back of my mind, like one of those tunes that get stuck in your head. I looked around to discern where I was this time.

There was another Orange across the street. His head jerked towards me. His tail snapped. His fur rose like a false confession. I knew that look. Because it was my look. Somewhere in that crusty little trash-goblin of a host, I was still speaking. Twice.

Small orange across street. Same voice inside. Connected somehow. Shared hunting ground now.

He blinked once. Slowly. Then, "Wait. Is that my voice?"

The echo wasn't from my throat, nor did it carry across the street. It vibrated deep inside, a chilling resonance in Jake's lungs, in Butternugget's very ears. We were syncing. I saw a flash.

A water bowl I didn't recognize. A sock drawer with secrets folded between the argyles. Someone yelling 'Get off the Roomba!' in three languages, each one more accusatory than the last. Memories. Not mine. Butternugget's. Bleeding in. Leaking out like evidence from an evidence locker with a faulty lock and a night watchman with gambling debts.

"This is my body," I thought. "You had your turn." But the body disagreed. The pulse shifted. Heavy. Intentional. Jake's pulse answered like a slow drumroll in a velvet coffin. Not my thought. Still my voice. And then, for one breathless second, Jake Speed was lucid without me. He turned his head. Looked across the street. Saw Butternugget. Saw himself.

And thought, *Small hunter. Bad form. Smells like garbage den. Voice too big for his whiskers. Pack-scent familiar. Trouble certain.*

He winked. Not clumsy. Not derpy. Deliberate. The kind of wink that says, "I know the flavor of fate. And it's about to bite back." It was the wink of a detective who's found the murder weapon in the district attorney's golf bag and is still deciding what to do about it. A wink with consequences and footnotes.

"No, I think it's mine," Jake said, maybe. Or maybe I did.

"Oh hell," Butternugget said back.

We locked eyes. Orange fury to Orange crust. Then I tried the impossible. I tried to speak to me.

"Can you hear this?" I thought.

Butternugget twitched, hard. A shudder rippled down his spine like a broadcast gone sideways.

"Don't freak out—" I started.

"MRRROWOWWAAAAAAAHHHH!!!" he screamed.

Louder than necessary. Louder than physics. It echoed through Jake's sinuses like a fire alarm made of teeth.

"Stop that!" I yowled.

"YOU stop that!" he howled back. Voice cracking halfway into a gargle-growl-meow that sounded like jazz played on a cursed accordion.

We weren't talking. We were overlapping. Thoughts bled through the wrong mouths. Cadence collided. My narration cracked like sunglasses in a blender. I tried to pull back. Refocus. One mind. One voice. One narrator.

The bright thing hums between us. Pulling. Pushing. Making us same-but-different.

The Cognichonk laughed. Not out loud. But in the way gravity suddenly forgets how stairs work. A new thought slithered sideways across my awareness. *I'm not alone.*

I'd always assumed the Cognichonk possessed cats one at a time. A noir curse on a loop. A solo act in a thousand stages. But now? Now I was a duet I hadn't agreed to sing. I was me. But so was he. And we were not in harmony.

Somewhere deep in the static, I heard Butternugget's instinct mutter, "Lick the sidewalk and assert dominance."

I tried to shove it aside, but that's when the memory surfaced. A gnome. Speaking to me or Butternugget or some other orange about how "the concrete holds the day's secrets". Focus, damn it. But my focus split like old twine. Two voices. Same source. Same rhythm. Different bodies. This wasn't possession. This was cross-talk. And something, some force, was testing the signal strength. Then—

The squirrel. It reappeared like it had stage directions and an understudy waiting in the wings. Fast. Twitchy. Smug with secrets. Its tail flicked like a semaphore of sin— like a corrupt judge's gavel after he's received the envelope under the table. This wasn't just a rodent; it was a walking cipher with fur and an agenda that smelled like conspiracy.

Butternugget's pupils dilated. Jake's breath caught. Our thoughts aligned. We leapt.

My paws hit the grass like loaded verdicts in a rigged trial. Each muscle moved with orchestral menace, a symphony of predatory intent conducted by a maestro with a grudge and perfect timing. This wasn't just a chase; it was an execution of justice with fur and retractable claws. Jake Speed was a closing argument on four paws, every fiber of his being poised to deliver a verdict. Power surged beneath the fluff. This body was a freight train made of judgment and peanut butter breath. A lion in suburbia. A poem about murder written in soft focus and uncut claws.

"We can catch it," I muttered, stalking low. But then, the voice cracked. Not mine. Still mine.

Butternugget buzzed through the Cognichonk like a radio tuned too close. A static scream of misaligned thoughts.

"CHASE IT BUTT-FIRST!" Butternugget screamed across the psychic link like a drunk toddler with a taser.

Jake's tail twitched. I didn't tell it to.

"Resist," I snarled. At myself, at the system, at the squirrel.

But the body shuddered. There was a moment, brief and burning, where I felt Butternugget's instincts try to override mine. A shared nervous system glitch. My claws flexed the wrong direction. My teeth itched. Jake sneezed. I felt it. Like a warning shot made of lint. The sneeze echoed like a prophecy coughed in fur.

Butternugget was already running. I followed. Two minds, one squirrel, and zero control. The chase was on. And somewhere, the Cognichonk purred. Like it had written the ending in yarn and teeth.

Jake's body was a low-slung missile of muscle and intent. Butternugget was a ricochet of pure chaos. The squirrel hit a chain-link fence separating the lot from a yard that smelled of fertilizer and broken promises. It squeezed through a gap near the bottom, a flicker of gray ambition.

"You go high, I'll go low," I thought, aiming the command at myself. It was like trying to conduct an orchestra during an earthquake.

LICK THE FENCE, LOUDER! Butternugget's brain-static screamed back, translating 'high' into 'scream at the fence post.'

Jake's body, however, responded to the raw tactical command. I coiled, launched, and cleared the fence in a single, fluid arc of orange fury. The landing was perfect, a silent verdict delivered on manicured grass. Butternugget, meanwhile, scrabbled halfway up, got a claw stuck, swore in a dialect of pure psychic frustration that probably curdled milk three blocks away, and then tumbled over the top to land in a heap of indignation.

We landed in a yard patrolled by a single, desolate-looking flamingo ornament—the kind of lawn decoration that's seen too much and is keeping it all in a safety deposit box as insurance. It had Carl's signature painted on its base. Of course it did. Carl's signature showed up at more crime scenes than the coroner, always just slightly off-center, always just slightly mocking.

The squirrel wasn't just running; it was executing a route. It juked past a sprinkler head that sputtered like a dying confession, its movements too precise for a simple rodent. It knew angles. It understood cover. That twitchy tail wasn't just for balance; it was a rudder steering a vessel of stolen information.

We were closing the gap. Two predators, one mind—fractured, yes, but focused on the same frantic point. Our thoughts converged into a three-part harmony of intent.

Target cornered. Block escape route. Shed-shadow provides ambush advantage. Synchronized attack pattern optimal. Jake's instincts were cool and professional.

THE SHED IS WHERE IT KEEPS ITS BUTT-PANTS! GET THE PANTS-HOUSE! Butternugget shrieked with glee.

Just. Catch. Him, I pleaded, urging both bodies forward as we cornered our quarry against the unforgiving vinyl siding of a suburban shed.

CHAPTER SIX

We had it. Pinned against the unforgiving vinyl siding of a suburban shed that smelled faintly of gasoline and regret— the kind of regret that comes with alibi receipts and witness statements that don't quite match. The shed leaned slightly, like a corrupt judge who knows the envelope's coming but still has to pretend impartiality. Two bodies, one fractured consciousness, and a single, twitching target. My mind was a three-way tug-of-war played across a psychic clothesline.

Wait for my signal, I commanded, trying to orchestrate a pincer movement.

Jake's predatory calm flooded my senses. His body was a coiled spring of lethal intent, ready to move like a whispered threat. *Target cornered. Wind direction favorable. Wait for the lunge. Pounce angle optimal.*

BITE THE SHED! Butternugget screamed from his side of the link, his thoughts a firework display of pure chaos.

The hesitation was a crack in reality just wide enough for a secret to slip through.

The squirrel didn't panic. It turned. Slow. Deliberate. With the practiced calm of a hitman who's already been paid half up front. Its tiny, black eyes weren't filled with fear. They were filled with... syntax. The kind of syntax that gets case files marked 'classified' and detectives reassigned to desk duty with sudden pension reviews. They glowed. Just for a second. A faint, violet light like a dying LED on a piece of cursed technology.

"SIGIL-MARKED!" I screamed across the link, a wave of cold recognition washing over me.

I may have mentioned that, Jake replied, his mental voice as dry as dust on a sealed tomb.

Is it spicy? Butternugget wondered with genuine, ravenous curiosity.

The squirrel didn't bolt in blind terror. Its move was too clean, too sharp—choreographed like a jailbreak planned on stolen blueprints. It shot left, a calculated gray streak, moving with the cold intent of a whispered threat delivered by someone who collects kneecaps as souvenirs. This wasn't panic; this was protocol. I vaulted in one clean leap, Jake's body answering before I'd finished the thought. Precision. Power. Regal fury wrapped in floof. Then—

A hiccup. My back paw kicked mid-air like it wanted to scream at a window. A Butternugget twitch. Unbidden. Unwelcome. I landed half a second late.

Out of the corner of my eye, I caught movement. Butternugget crashed through a plastic lawn chair like destiny wearing poor judgment. He was chasing the same squirrel. From the left. Slightly behind. Eyes wild with derp and destiny.

We're always chasing, Butternugget answered from somewhere too loud in my brain. *Especially the ones with tails.*

I tried to send a message. A simple, tactical command. *Circle left. We have the angle.*

"MEOW-WA-CHAAAAK!" Butternugget shrieked. The thought hit the link like a rubber chicken in a blender. Jake flinched. I flinched. The squirrel skittered sideways in alarm, using our psychic disharmony to its advantage. There was a time when I could command a room with a whisper. Now I couldn't even send a coherent thought to a trash goblin with a shared cortex.

That didn't work, I muttered.

You think? Jake replied.

The squirrel tore through a hedge like it had clearance codes and divine purpose. We followed. Claws flashing, breath sharp, minds unraveling in stereo like three different confessions to the same crime. We moved with the desperate coordination of a sting operation where half the officers didn't get the memo and the other half were working for the mark.

Flash. Memory. Pain. Memories like these didn't come from me. They came from the Cognichonk. From someone else I'd been. Or someone else I might become. I didn't remember the case, but I remembered the guilt. And that was worse.

Basement. Blood. A chalk circle with teeth. A tuxedo cat who spoke backward and smelled like ozone. My claws bit into turf. I grounded myself. Barely.

"What even is this squirrel?" I hissed.

Sigil-marked, Jake said calmly. *We've seen worse.*

He wasn't wrong. There was the haunted iguana in

Sector 7. The pug that spoke in riddles about moonlight and aluminum. The Shorthair Oracle. Gods. The Shorthair Oracle. Focus, I snarled at myself.

We turned the corner. Chain-link fence. Half-rusted. It groaned when Jake vaulted it. Butternugget tried to dig under it. Found a beetle. Screamed. Kept digging.

Then I saw it. The squirrel had doubled back. It was waiting. Perched atop a broken birdbath, tail twitching. Watching us. The birdbath stood in a patch of neglected garden, half-sunken into soil that hadn't seen care in years. Moss crept up one side like a green memory. Water, dark and still as old secrets, filled the shallow basin. This wasn't just any birdbath. This was *the* birdbath. The same birdbath from the Wren Hollow Incident.

"Not again," I whispered.

Marked territory. Old hunting ground. Jake's thoughts cut through. *The birdbath remembers. It always does. And so does whatever sent this messenger.*

The memory didn't just flood me—it drowned me.

I was standing in the rain again, a real trench coat heavy on my shoulders like guilt after the third divorce, water dripping from the brim of a fedora I was never cool enough to pull off—the kind of hat that belongs on detectives who solve cases instead of becoming them. The rain tasted like cheap whiskey and expensive mistakes. I had thumbs. Gods, I remembered having thumbs, wrapped around a steaming cup of diner coffee that did nothing to chase the chill from my bones. Every sensation returned with cruel clarity, as if my current feline form was just a temporary inconvenience.

The birdbath was the epicenter of the crime scene. The official report said 'animal attack,' but the beat cops were spooked—the kind of spooked that makes veterans request desk duty and rookies suddenly remember religious commitments. The crime scene tape fluttered like nervous fingers on a trigger, yellow warnings against a sky that had seen too much. The victim, a Steller's jay named Phineas who worked as a freelance informant for the Aviary Guild, was laid out on the grass. His head wasn't just gone; it had simply... ceased to be. No tear marks, no ragged pecks. Just a clean absence, as if unmade from the world.

In its place, arranged in a perfect spiral of black sunflower seeds, was a sigil that hummed with a frequency that made my fillings ache and my moral compass spin like a drunk ballerina. It was the kind of symbol that gets evidence bags marked with warnings and case files stored in rooms without numbers. The kind of symbol that makes career cops suddenly believe in something worse than human evil. It was a statement, written in a language of feathers and stolen life, and it was addressed to me. I knew it then, just as I knew it now.

That squirrel, perched there, tail twitching with the same smug rhythm as a blackmailer who knows your secrets have secrets... it wasn't a trick of memory. This was a signature. The same artist, a fresh canvas of dread. Like finding the same lipstick shade on your collar and your partner's gun—a connection that rewrites every assumption in the case file and adds footnotes in blood.

"Not again," I repeated, the words a ghost of a memory on a tongue that could no longer form them properly.

We surrounded the squirrel. Flanked. Jake on one side. Butternugget on the other. Me, somewhere in the middle of both and neither. Every instinct screamed trap. Every breath tasted like a setup. I'd chased enough leads to know when the string tied to the cheese was already looped around your neck. But I couldn't stop. I had to know. What it was. What I was becoming.

Its eyes locked on mine. They glowed. Just for a second.

"IT WANTED US HERE!" I screamed across the link.

I told you, Jake said, licking one paw like this wasn't escalating into a goddamn metaphysical hostage situation.

"You said it was lunch!"

So is prophecy.

Detective? That felt like a lifetime ago. Now, I was a symptom, nothing more – a walking, clawed echo in someone else's nervous system. But this squirrel? This was my lead. My last one. And I wasn't going to let it vanish into the hedge like everything else. We leapt as one. Too many paws. Too many minds. One Fate.

Mid-air, I tried again to wrestle for control. Jake didn't resist. He *gave me the body*. For a second.

You got this?

I did. Until I didn't. Butternugget sneezed inside my head and I missed the landing. I felt the snap. Lucidity gone. Jake took control. I crashed into the birdbath like a failed prophecy in Butternugget form. Jake landed perfectly. Claws poised. Gaze cool as justice. Fur unbothered by prophecy or pain.

The squirrel slipped through reality. Gone. No trace. Only the wind, the stone, and a single twitching flower petal on the water's surface.

Jake watched the trash goblin shell I was stuck in wipe gravel out of its nose. *That went well.*

"It was sigil-marked," I growled. "Shut up."

Prey that speaks is still prey. Would have tasted like secrets.

Somewhere, the Cognichonk pulsed again. Like something watching had teeth. And a sense of humor. It didn't feel like closure. It felt like a comma. A breath between acts. The case wasn't dead. Just hiding. Like me. Somewhere, another squirrel blinked. Somewhere else, another fragment stirred. The yarn wasn't done with us. And I was still on the string.

The connection snapped. No static. No scream. Just the sudden silence. Blessed. Brutal. One mind. The kind of silence that falls after a confession that can't be taken back —when the tape recorder clicks off but the words still hang in the air like smoke from a gun that can't be unfired.

For the first time in what felt like a thousand tangled yarn dreams, I was simply alone. No echoing void, no hollow ache. Just the quiet hum of Jake.

I sat beside the birdbath like a gargoyle with better grooming. The pressure in my skull vanished. The non-stop color commentary on reality—the similes clinging to every shadow, the metaphors sticking to my ribs—receded like a tide, leaving behind the clean, quiet shore of what *was*. The squirrel was gone. The orange trash gremlin had rolled himself into a patch of clover and was now sneezing on a dandelion. And Luis? Gone.

The first time he'd shown up, I thought I was sick. A fever of the soul. I'd find myself staring at a loose floorboard for twenty minutes, possessed by an un-feline urgency to know what was beneath it. I'd wake up on top of the refrigerator, not with the usual satisfaction of a successful climb, but with a lingering sense of being on a stakeout. My own instincts would get shoved aside by his, a clumsy human mind trying to pilot a precision machine. He'd try to make a tactical leap and forget to account for tail-balance; I'd try to nap in a sunbeam and my legs would twitch with the urge to pace.

He always left a residue. Guilt. Obsession. The phantom smell of burnt coffee and cheap whiskey. He was a psychic storm that blew through my consciousness, rearranging the furniture and leaving muddy bootprints on the rugs. That tangled detective needed to name every shadow and judge every silence. When he's here, the world narrates itself, every bird a potential witness, every gust of wind a potential clue.

When he's gone, it just breathes. The sunbeam offered only simple warmth, not the cruel, fleeting glint of hope Luis was always chasing in its rays. The wind just is. I liked the quiet. Didn't trust it. But I liked it.

I watched the other one, Butternugget. The storm was in him now, I could tell. His fur bristled with secondhand purpose. He might have felt the case cracking open, but that was just the ghost rattling its chains inside him. Butternugget was nothing more than the current ride for a soul too stubborn to fade. We were all just stops on his line.

No strong feelings, one way or another. He was a pain in the tail, sure, but the ghost he carried meant well. Probably. Even when he hijacked my limbs to monologue at breakfast cereal. Even when he didn't ask.

I licked a paw. Smoothed one ear. The yard was still. The

wind smelled like wet stone and false closure. Luis was gone, but the case wasn't. The weirdness lingered.

The squirrel would be back. They always come back.

I had lost the connection with Jake. The tether snapped. Cruel. Sudden. Alone. That wasn't quite it. I was isolated, trapped in this twitching fur-suit of Butternugget, disconnected from everything but the hum of my own panic —the kind of isolation usually reserved for protected witnesses who've outlived their usefulness or detectives who've seen the commissioner's private files. My consciousness rattled around this furry prison like a bullet in an empty chamber. No majestic reach. No tactical breath. Just twitchy instinct and me.

I was starting to understand the shape of things. A spiral. A scatter. I was a case file scrawled in chalk and claw marks—the kind of file that gets locked in cabinets that don't officially exist, guarded by agents whose badges have numbers that lead to disconnected phone lines. My existence was a cold case that kept breathing. I didn't remember the case I was working when everything cracked, but I remembered the feeling. The hum of purpose behind my ribs. I needed answers. And I was the only one who had them.

The problem was, I was scattered like cereal in a toddler riot. Shards of me flung across orange hosts with varying degrees of competence and emotional stability.

Butternugget whispered, *It's the Orange Syndicat. We're*

all orange here. Except the one that isn't. Don't trust him. He licked a doorknob and saw the future.

I was collecting fragments. Slowly. Faint signals in the static. It wasn't enough, not by a long shot. I needed to make contact, to pull the scattered pieces into something resembling a whole. A psychic conference table of cats who've all screamed at ceiling fans. Maybe then I could reconstruct the timeline. The relic. The rupture. What she did. What I did.

Butternugget again, louder this time, *You gotta talk to the old man. He knows stuff. Buries stuff. Sleeps on top of truths like they're heating vents. Also he smells like jazz and ham.*

That was the key. Forget the squirrel. Forget the birdbath. That was a lead for a case I was working while split in two. This was different. This was about putting the pieces of Luis Cannon back together. I needed the man who slept on truths.

My focus sharpened. I tried to tune into the Orange Syndicat, to isolate Bosco's signal from the psychic static. It was a mess. A psychic maelstrom where every cat was a screaming toddler with an opinion. I caught glimpses: the petty squabbles over sunbeams, the existential dread of a cleaning robot, the dizzying philosophy of the red dot.

Then I pushed past the noise, and for a second, I felt it. A low, steady thrum beneath the chaos. A bass note of ancient knowing. Bosco.

The air was thick with grit and purpose. I pushed the body forward. Butternugget's legs jittery with joy. Tail twitching like a liar under oath. I had him. I had control. Sort of.

"Straight line," I muttered. "We can do this. Stay on task."

A set of wind chimes on a nearby porch tinkled, a random melody in the afternoon breeze—except nothing's random in a universe where even coincidences file tax returns. My old instincts kicked in, searching for patterns, for code, the way you search a crime scene for the evidence that doesn't belong but fits too perfectly. Those chimes weren't just making noise; they were testifying in a language I'd forgotten how to speak.

Loud sky-bones! Butternugget yowled in my head. *They sing the song of imminent doom! Or maybe lunch! Yell at them until they confess!*

I felt the body's muscles tense, an urge to puff up my fur and hiss at the inanimate object. I shoved the thought aside, focusing again on Bosco's signal to drown out the noise. One clear thought. That's all I needed.

We were headed toward the old cul-de-sac, where the ivy choked the fences and the mailboxes leaned like drunks after last call. That's where the thread pulled. That's where Bosco would be.

Butternugget's thoughts hummed like static on candy. *Go see the soup ghost. He hums jazz in his sleep.*

"No distractions," I hissed. "One clear thought. For once in your life focus."

Butternugget gasped. *We should bring an offering. Ham! Or a question. Better yet, a question in a tiny ham suit!*

I clutched the wheel of his nervous system tighter. My paws padded along the cracked sidewalk. Claws half-out. Tail poised like a statement I wasn't ready to make. Beneath my ribs, the Cognichonk pulsed. Quiet, yes, but its gaze was a heavy thing, unseen and constant.

Bosco was close. I could feel the weight of him in the psychic hum. Old. Heavy with knowing. Anchored in a way none of us were anymore. If I could reach him. Just speak to him while lucid. I could...

Butternugget abruptly slowed.

"What are you doing?" I snapped. "Keep walking."

He paused in front of a mailbox shaped like a catfish wearing a top hat. *This one knows things.*

"Don't be a fool," I snapped. "It's just tin and paint."

What if the mailbox is Bosco. In disguise.

"A tin box and a top hat. That's your 'Bosco'?" I retorted.

WHAT IF I'M BOSCO.

"You're a hairball on legs, Butternugget! Now focus!"

I surged forward again. Past the mailbox. Past a yard littered with suspicious lawn ornaments and an empty birdbath that definitely hadn't moved. I could feel Bosco's presence now. Like a hush under the noise. He was near. I could almost smell the jazz and soup. One more corner. One more step. One—

The world folded. The pulse snapped. And I was gone.

Butternugget blinked. He stood in the middle of the sidewalk, one paw suspended mid-step like a lie caught mid-delivery. Staring at absolutely nothing. A sneeze— violent, undignified—then he screamed at a bush. Loud. Guttural. Righteous.

WHERE'S THE HAM.

A breeze stirred. Somewhere beyond the fence, Bosco sighed in his sleep—long and low, like someone who just felt the story shift. Butternugget sat down, tail curling loosely around his body. Confused. Then he bit the air. Hard.

CHAPTER SEVEN

The world reeked of tuna, treachery, and a floral note trying too hard to impress death—like perfume on a corpse that knows it's being viewed for identification. But before that, there was the hum. The kind of hum that makes bomb squad veterans sweat and confession-room recorders malfunction at exactly the wrong moment. A deep, marrow-thrumming hum. The kind you don't hear so much as feel. Like being purred back into existence by something with too many teeth and not enough mercy.

Awakening was a slow drag, a fog clinging to the edges of my mind. Not yet. Not truly. There were voices. Soft, spiraled things, looped in yarn and static. Flashes of Jake's whiskers. Butternugget's scream. A sunbeam melting across a grimoire that smelled like mildew and memory. Somewhere under it all, I felt the hum of math. Numbers spooling like thread in the background.

The snap.

Oh. It's crime time. Been a while since you visited.

Lucidity hit like cold water and unpaid rent—the kind of clarity that comes with eviction notices served by reality itself. I came to in a wicker teacup the size of my pride and just as frayed, a holding cell with decorative intentions and punitive execution. The kind of accommodations usually reserved for witnesses who've seen too much but remembered too little. It was a new flavor of orange. But if this fluff was to be believed, not my first visit. Claws first, I stretched. Felt the ridges of the basket beneath me. Heard the soft chant of a spell sung in a key no human throat should find. And above me, cooing with the enthusiasm of someone who'd never lost a war or coughed up regret, a toddler witch.

"Who's my fuzzy little crime-finder?" she chirped.

I blinked. Once. Slowly. As if each eyelid carried the weight of betrayal and catnip overdoses. Her hand descended. It smelled of sugar, glitter, and poorly-contained ambition. I batted it away on instinct, claws retracted. Barely. But it was too late. The moment her fingers brushed behind my ear, something shifted. The fog lifted. The memories snapped back into place like a mousetrap.

Luis Cannon, P.I. Reborn in fur, grit, and a rising tide of fury.

I took in my surroundings to assess the site of my latest incarnation. The café was a lie pretending to be whimsical —like a crime scene dressed up for a birthday party. Crystals dangled from the ceiling like threats on fishing line, each one catching light the way informants catch bullets when their cover stories develop sudden, fatal holes. This wasn't ambiance; it was surveillance with better marketing. Chalk runes circled each table, spiraling inward like someone had spilled their conspiracy theories in cursive. The air was thick with incense and roasted despair. Somewhere near the espresso bar, someone was scrying into foam.

You seem more scattered this time. This thread of you doesn't remember yet. But you will.

I slunk from the teacup, each step a silent accusation against gravity—the kind of accusation that gets cases reopened and detectives reassigned to precincts where even the coffee has an alibi. My paws hit the surface with the calculated quiet of a blackmailer who knows exactly how much silence costs. There were towers, cat towers, each one warded and sigil-laced. A whiteboard near the counter bore an elegant handwritten special: Hexspresso, with a pentagram drawn in caramel drizzle. Cute. Too cute. That's how they get you. With whimsy.

She was watching me. My eyes bypassed the chirping menace and found their real target: the one in green. Hair like spilled ink. Eyes that flicked across me like she was counting runes per whisker. Witch, full-grown. Twenty-something. Sleeves tattooed in constellations. Probably cursed at least twice before breakfast.

"You're awake," she said. Her voice carried weight. Not like authority, more like someone used to arguing with ghosts and winning.

I nodded. Slow. Deliberate. Acknowledgment or threat? I'll let her decide.

She crouched, but didn't offer a hand this time. Smart. The kind of smart that comes from scars that don't show on medical reports. Instead, she slid a small, shallow saucer toward me with the practiced casualness of someone offering a plea deal they already know you can't refuse. Her fingers moved with the precise confidence of someone who's stitched their own wounds. It was filled with a pearlescent, lavender liquid that shimmered under the crystal-light.

"It's a calming draught," she said, her voice low and even. "Helps with the resonance bleed. Smooths out the static."

Do not ingest, Peaches' thought cut through my own with the precision of a scalpel. *Composition: Valerian root, powdered moonstone, two drops of silver nitrate, and a binding agent with a half-life of 3.7 hours. Not a sedative. A psychic dampener. It wouldn't calm the static; it would isolate it. Quarantine it.*

I looked from the saucer back to her. She wanted to study me. To contain the signal. Was she a doctor or a warden? In my experience, the line between the two is thinner than the edge of a coroner's blade—both types ask questions they already know the answers to, both keep secrets in locked cabinets, both wear authority like a shoulder holster.

I ignored the offering and gave her the stare. The one that once made a blood mage confess to murder and poor taste in curtains. The kind of stare that peels alibis like old wallpaper and leaves suspects suddenly remembering appointments with their attorneys. It was my badge, my warrant, and my closing argument all wrapped in fur and contempt.

Jessa's grin didn't falter. She wasn't intimidated. She nudged the saucer a fraction of an inch closer. "Suit yourself. Most of them fight it at first. They always look at me like that when the Kog'nith'enk's still cooking. Don't worry," she added, picking up the saucer and setting it aside. "It fades."

No. It doesn't. It never fades. Wait, Kog'nith'enk. So that was its true name. Not Cognichonk—that was just what it sounded like through cat ears, filtered through feline brains that naturally added 'chonk' to anything important. The ancient power had a proper name after all, one that sounded like it belonged in dusty tomes and whispered rituals, not in the mouth of an orange idiot who also ate plastic.

They called this place Bewitched Beans. But it wasn't a café. It was a shelter. A halfway house for magically scrambled felines. Cursed familiars. Spellback strays. Cats who'd wandered too close to forbidden objects and came back knowing too much about string theory and tuna taxation.

And here I was. Luis Cannon, pride of the precinct, reduced to a furry node in a psychic network shaped like pandemonium and meows. I had a bit of deja-vu as if I might've come here on a case once. Back before the Chonk scattered my mind across the network.

I prowled the perimeter, tail low, twitching like bacon sizzling in a frying pan monitored by health inspectors with grudges. The tiles beneath my paws hummed with containment wards—magical parole anklets disguised as decor. This place wasn't just a shelter; it was a holding cell for the weird, the kind of establishment that doesn't appear on official records but gets regular visits from agents whose badges have redacted serial numbers.

Near the window, a sleek black cat stared at his own reflection, except his reflection was a half-second behind, its movements syrupy and wrong—like surveillance footage that's been tampered with by someone who knows exactly which frame contains the smoking gun. Every so often, the cat would hiss at it, a sound like tearing silk, before the reflection caught up. Spell-lag. Nasty business. The kind of magical residue that makes coroners request hazard pay.

Curled on a velvet pillow near the counter was a fluffy Persian, its eyes unfocused. It was muttering, a low, continuous stream of numbers. No random babbling. This was cold, hard data: stock market predictions, whispered from a fur-covered oracle. It was tracking the arcane futures of enchanted artifacts on a non-existent cosmic exchange. It hadn't noticed me. It probably hadn't noticed anything since the Dow Jones fell in Fae-realm silver. This is what happened when the Chonk spat you out wrong. You became a tool. A calculator with fur. I wasn't going to end up like that.

A nervous tabby sat rigidly in a corner, its tail twitching like a metronome. Every thirty seconds, it would startle as if hearing a loud noise only it could perceive, look around in terror, then slowly relax back into its rigid posture, resetting the clock on its own private loop of fear.

On the wall was a bulletin board full of photos, missing posters, and menu specials. And something else. Something red. The kind of red that shows up at crime scenes and gets photographed from multiple angles before being bagged as evidence. The kind of red that makes veteran detectives suddenly develop religious convictions. My instincts hummed like a tuning fork struck against a loaded gun. I followed the scent of conspiracy.

Back room. Slightly ajar. Unlocked on purpose so you'd think it was an accident. But I knew better. This had setup written all over it. Inside was all dim light, humming glyphs, and yarn. So much yarn. It was a web, spun for truth, or perhaps, for a lie—the kind of elaborate construction usually found in the apartments of detectives who've gone too deep undercover or witnesses who've started seeing patterns in their breakfast cereal. This wasn't investigation; this was obsession with color-coding and pushpin methodology.

That's their conspiracy board. I sneak in sometimes to move the pins on the ones they have incorrect. The geometry's sloppy.

A murder board. My paws padded closer with the quiet respect usually reserved for open caskets and confessional booths. There was a map of the city, dotted with red pins that pulsed with a faint, angry light—like the heartbeats of victims who refuse to become statistics. Each pin was an accusation, a question, a wound in the city's alibi that refused to scab over. I recognized the locations. A pin hovered over the back lot of a shuttered laundromat. Another marked a cul-de-sac where the mailboxes leaned like drunks. They weren't just tracking the relics; they were tracking *me*.

It was amateur work—crooked pins, coffee stains on the edges—but it was good. Frighteningly good. The kind of good that makes professional investigators suddenly develop drinking problems and request transfers to departments where the most complicated case is parking violations. This wasn't just connect-the-dots; this was cartography of conspiracy with the longitude and latitude of damnation. My life's work, my current fractured existence, reduced to a DIY project in a witch's back room.

Tacked to the side was a news clipping about a "freak

animal incident" at the Wren Hollow birdbath. The official report was quoted—'unusual predatory behavior'—but someone, probably Jessa, had scrawled in the margin: *Resonance spike matches the cannery sample. Same signature. Higher amplitude.* They were connecting the dots, just from the outside. They saw the storm, but they couldn't see the ghost piloting it.

And in the center? The Cognichonk. Circled in red lipstick. Labeled.

ANCHOR NODE?

Underneath, written in sharp, desperate handwriting:

NOT a relic. A recruiter.

Something twisted in my gut. It wasn't hunger, though a steak and a bottle of bourbon wouldn't go amiss—the kind of bourbon that burns like confessions and costs more than most witnesses' integrity. It was realization, cold and loud as a gunshot in a rainstorm, the kind of epiphany that comes with its own body count and paperwork that never gets filed in the right cabinet. They weren't just stealing relics. They were assembling something. Amplifying it. Building a crown of teeth and yarn to replicate the Cognichonk. And me? I was a byproduct. A breadcrumb in my own shattered psyche.

Voices in the next room. Witches. Two of them.

"I'm telling you, the Kog'nith'enk wasn't stolen. It left. It's looking for someone."

"It doesn't leave," said the second. "It selects. That's worse."

Paper rustled. One of them stepped closer. Their shadow slid under the door, bringing tension with it like a leash pulled taut.

"I've seen the resonance data,"

Witch One continued. "Every relic they took matches a Kog'nith'enk frequency. Bones. Tomes. The crown. They're all echoes. Tracers."

"Then why haven't we found it?"

A long pause. Then, "Because we're looking for a toy. And it's a recruiter."

They didn't say more. They didn't have to.

I was already forming the case in my head. The Cognichonk, or Kog'nith'enk, as they called it, wasn't just stolen. It was sent. And someone's trying to become it.

Apparently, the witches of the city were aware of it. But their name, their framing, it was more eldritch. They saw an anomaly. They couldn't see the eye of the storm, the divine fur-driven chaos it truly was.

I have no idea how the witches discovered the Chonk, but I'd hate to see what would happen if one of them ever got their hands on it. Having you rolling around in my head on an irregular basis is bad enough.

The constant calculation buzz of the orange I was riding had me distracted. I didn't hear the kitten sneak in. But I knew him. Eyes too wide for his face. Whiskers twitching like dowsing rods. Shrimp. The chaos oracle. The one from the cul-de-sac. He'd squeaked prophecy in Butternugget's ear and vanished into instinct. Now he was back, lucid again, for however long the Cognichonk allowed.

He looked at the board. Then at me. Then purred a sentence that wasn't a sentence.

"The thread's been chosen. The anchor sings."

I stared.

Oh no. Shrimp is prophesying again. Make sure you write that one down. It goes in the database under the old broken washing machine out back. Middle shelf, behind the jar of buttons.

He licked his paw. Then promptly fell over, squeaked, and rolled into a potted plant. Lucidity, gone. But the message lingered like prophecy wrapped in fur.

I padded back toward the café, tail flicking.

Jessa spotted me. Arched a brow. "Figure something out?" she asked, already sipping something too green to be coffee.

I didn't answer. Just leapt onto the counter and stared at her reflection in the coffee pot. Green apron Jessa knew more than she was letting on. There was still lipstick on her hand. Red. Same shade as the murder board. Maybe a coincidence. But in my experience? Coincidence was just conspiracy in a trench coat.

She turned her back. That was her first mistake—the kind rookies make when they think the perp is subdued and the cuffs are secure. I climbed into the satchel like it owed me answers and was three payments behind with a broken kneecap already on its record.

Peaches, ever the silent strategist, didn't protest. She'd already mapped three exit points and a contingency path through the ceiling tiles. Between her pattern-recognition and my paranoia, we made a decent team.

The zipper didn't quite close. Intentional I suspected. Just enough light for the static to seep in. Just enough error to be meaningful.

The bag is dark and enclosed. This is good for processing.

I settled in among the debris. Crumpled receipts and a cinnamon breath mint discolored at the edges—the kind of overlooked evidence that breaks alibis and rewrites testimonies. Every item told a story, and like most stories I encountered, they all smelled faintly of lies and convenience store coffee. Every surface held the psychic residue of recent use, mundane but layered.

But it was the hum that caught me. Magic hummed in the air, a presence too tidy, too contained for anything natural. A cold, calculated thrum like a radio dial tuned just off-center to a frequency where only blackmail and last confessions get broadcast. Too focused to ignore. Too careful to trust.

Jessa moved briskly through the café. Her muttering was half grocery list, half arcane shorthand—like a coroner dictating notes while planning dinner. Her words fell around her like shell casings at a crime scene: precise, metallic, and each one evidence of something that couldn't be taken back. Intonations that weren't meant to be overheard but still offered context.

Another theft, another broken ward. Another relic was

gone—vanished like a star witness the night before trial. The pattern was forming, not in chalk outlines but in negative spaces where power used to be. The kind of pattern that gets case files stamped 'unsolved' and detectives transferred to departments where the coffee's always cold.

She hadn't said "Cognichonk" or "Kog'nith'enk". The tight set of her jaw, spoke volumes she hadn't dared utter. I could taste the recognition of the 'Chonk' in her words, even unspoken.

I braced myself as we stepped outside. The wind hit with bureaucratic precision, cold and abrupt, carrying the scent of damp sidewalk and distant tension.

The cab smelled like licorice, ozone, and regret baked into vinyl—the kind of regret that comes with plea bargains signed at 3 AM by defendants who've run out of options and attorneys who've run out of tricks. The upholstery had seen more secrets than a precinct confession room with a broken recorder.

Peaches lay curled in a quiet corner of us, pulsing with calculations like a forensic accountant who's just found where the bodies are buried in the ledger. I could hear the subtle tick-tick-tick of her thoughts sorting themselves into geometric grids, precise as ballistics reports and twice as damning. She was running mental algorithms on Jessa's tattoo symmetry, the curvature of coffee drops, and the weight distribution of magical residue across the floor tiles back at the cafe.

Me? I had time to think. That was the problem. The hum

was quieter in the cab, but not gone—like a wiretap that's been discovered but not removed. It lingered in the corners of my consciousness like a stakeout detective who's forgotten what sleep feels like and why anyone would want it.

I shut my eyes. Searched the dark for threads of who I'd been last time—rummaging through my own memories like a detective rifling through a suspect's trash at midnight. Every fragment was a clue to a case where I was both the investigator and the missing person. A dive bar. A domino pattern scrawled in blood. A string of relic thefts coded in the lining of a cursed trench coat. There was a book...no, it was a ledger. I'd seen it in a safe that opened to tooth print and spite. That had to be before the cafe. Maybe even before the cul-de-sac.

Peaches twitched as if she'd found a new variable to factor. I followed the echo.

The memory wasn't a flash; it was a drowning. The air tasted of ozone and the cheap perfume she wore—gardenias fighting a losing battle against dread, like an alibi that's technically true but fatally incomplete. The kind of perfume that lingers in empty rooms and closed case files, marking where truth used to be. She stood on a plush oriental rug, the pattern swirling like blood in water—the kind of rug that costs more than most cops make in a year and has probably been used to wrap at least one body. One red heel was on, the other lay on its side, the stiletto tip snapped clean off like a promise made by someone who never intended to keep it. Her name was... it was gone. Lost in the static. But I remembered her knuckles, white as she clutched a silver locket.

"It's not a crown *for* a king," she'd whispered, her voice cracking as she looked at something over my shoulder. "It's a crown *of* anchors. It doesn't rule, it holds..."

Before I could ask what it held, the scream started. Not from her throat, but from the air around her—the kind of scream that doesn't appear in police reports but keeps witnesses awake for years afterward. It came from everywhere and nowhere, like justice in a corrupt precinct. A sound that tore reality, and then the sudden, silent cascade of white powder where she had been. Salt. Or maybe ash. I never got to check. The Chonk had pulled me out, leaving me with nothing but the image of that fallen red heel and a question that tasted like poison.

"You remember her too, don't you?" I asked.

Peaches didn't respond. Just kept calculating. That was her answer.

There was a reason the Chonk kept pulling me back. A thread I hadn't followed. Someone out there was trying to build something impossible. And somewhere deep in this fractured feline mind scape, I'd already figured it out.

I just had to remember before someone else did first.

The cab hissed to a halt like a suspect who's run out of lies and alibi witnesses. It looks like we made it to the location Jessa had been sent to investigate—another scene in a case file that was growing thicker with questions than answers, each page more redacted than the last.

"Alright Peaches," I muttered. "Let's go rattle the bones of memory and see what falls out—probably a confession no one wants to hear and evidence that should have been buried deeper. The truth is always messier than the crime scene it leaves behind."

CHAPTER EIGHT

The thaumaturgic antiquities shop presented a brave face, unblemished at first glance. The kind of clean that hid the rot underneath—like a politician's smile or a coroner's hands. Too polished, too practiced, with secrets buffed into the woodwork and lies varnished over the truth. The front door stood whole. The ward sigils flickered politely. A chime rang as we entered, far too cheerfully for a crime scene. Then the smell hit. Blood and lilacs. Someone's idea of balance.

Jessa hesitated. I slipped free of the satchel and landed silent as a withheld confession.

The floor was polished obsidian. Too polished. The kind of shine that makes you wonder what got wiped away—blood, evidence, or just the footprints of customers who never made it back out to the street. In my experience, anything that clean is covering up something that dirty.

"Crown's gone," said a voice. Witch. Male. Tired.

"Molars?"

"Forty-four of them. Baby teeth. Bound for resonance."

Jessa swore. She moved toward the case. I followed.

The wards weren't bypassed. They were convinced. Peaches noted having conducted the calculations.

I padded past a display of silver music boxes. Each was closed, but I could feel the trapped melodies pressing against their lids—songs that could make a man forget his own name. On another shelf, a deck of tarot cards was splayed in a silent argument; the face of The Fool had been scratched out with a fingernail.

Peaches's mind supplied a quiet annotation: *Probability analysis suggests a 73% chance this deck is rigged to only show The Tower.*

This shop wasn't a store; it was a landfill for bad decisions and cursed hobbies—the kind of place where regrets come with price tags and curses are sold as collectibles. Every shelf was a confession waiting to be cataloged, every item a crime that hadn't been prosecuted yet. The kind of inventory that should come with its own detective division.

The velvet cushion still held the shape of the missing crown. Dustless. Undisturbed. Like it had evaporated—the perfect crime scene, too perfect, like an alibi rehearsed in front of a mirror until even the liar believes it. The absence screamed louder than any evidence could have, a void with fingerprints only visible to the guilty. The circle beneath the stand was still faintly visible. Chalk and blood, swirled in harmony. Meant to detect theft. Meant to scream when something was taken. It hadn't screamed. That's what worried me.

I leaned closer. The ward lines around the glass case didn't scream of forced entry; they hummed with a smug, placid energy, a sign they hadn't been defeated, but utterly deceived.

Resonance key, Peaches thought, her mind a flurry of calculations. *The thief didn't pick the lock. They had a psychic key that matched the ward's frequency. They didn't break in. The wards invited them in.*

That was a different level of thief. Not a smash-and-grab artist with pawn shop connections and desperation sweat. This was a con man who could talk an alarm system into looking the other way—the kind of smooth criminal who leaves thank-you notes instead of evidence, who makes the victims question their own sanity instead of their security systems. Professional. Methodical. The kind that makes detectives drink on duty.

I prowled deeper into the shop. Every shelf watched me. Every rune on the wall looked just slightly off. Tilted. Like a room trying to remember which way was real. In the back, past the shattered scrying mirror and a stack of discount hex jars labeled with warnings no sane person would ignore, I found the sigil. No larger than a dinner plate. Etched into the floor in silver ink. Still humming with the quiet confidence of a blackmailer who knows where all the bodies are buried because he provided the shovels. This wasn't residual magic; this was a calling card left with deliberate intent.

Residual Frequency: 11.2. Match confirmed. Case File: Theta-Vermillion.

I didn't like it, but I stepped into it. The world didn't explode. But it shifted. The shelves bent inward like ribs trying to protect vital organs. The lights dimmed with the reluctance of a witness about to recant. And in the mirrored glass behind me, I saw cats—not reflections but observers, a jury of orange fur and unblinking judgment. They watched with the cold patience of coroners who know the deceased will eventually tell them everything.

The glass showed figures. Cats. Orange ones, and too damned lucid watching something I couldn't see. And in the center... floating, humming, spinning like a secret too elegant to last... was the Cognichonk. Only this time, it was bigger. And it was waiting.

And across from me, in a reflection that wasn't mine: Mallory Vex. Eyes closed. Smiling like a knife that's tasted more throats than confessions. Her smile was the kind that gets case files marked 'unsolved' and detectives reassigned to traffic duty in neighborhoods where even the fire hydrants carry heat. It was the smile of someone who'd already won a game I didn't know I was playing. She whispered, not to me, but to the Cognichonk.

"I've fed you memory. Soon, I'll give you form."

One mirror shattered. I staggered backward with a hiss. The glyph sparked under my paws and burned out like a lightbulb cursed by envy.

The shop was spinning. Or maybe I was.

A voice, not Peaches's, nor mine, slid along the back of my skull like velvet soaked in malice and hung out to dry in a morgue. It whispered with the intimate familiarity of a killer who's watched you sleep, with consonants sharp as autopsy tools and vowels that left bruises on my thoughts.

"She's almost ready."

Then the vision snapped. The sigil flared. I tumbled backward and knocked over a jar labeled "Consequences." It shattered. Of course it did. A puff of gray dust billowed out, smelling of ozone and regret. For a split second, the sound in the room doubled—I heard the glass break, and then an instant later, I heard the echo of it breaking again, a noise that hadn't happened yet. The dust settled, and the paradox faded, but a chill remained. Some consequences are paid for in advance.

Mallory Vex. Why do I know that name? Come on Luis, think. Which case was that from? My memory was frayed like a pair of well-worn jeans 30 years past their prime. I knew the name, but not from where or when.

Jessa appeared in the doorway, wand drawn. She looked at the mess. Then at me. Then at the circle.

"What did you do?"

I didn't answer. Instead, I padded to the far wall because something shimmered. Just a flicker. Just for me. A message. Scrawled in glimmering ink, visible only in the slant of fear.

The choir assembles. Can you still hear your own voice?

I blinked. It was gone. Of course it was.

Sensory integrity restored. Lucidity thread compromised. Rebooting deductive subroutines.

I shook the glass dust from my fur. No good answers here. Just echoes and broken jars. But the message lingered. *The choir assembles.* If they were building something, it meant structure. Pattern. Ritual. You don't gather a choir unless you've got a song. And songs? Songs have purpose. Even when they end in blood.

Jessa knelt by the sigil. Her expression was flat, but her hands weren't. They trembled just slightly.

"This thing shouldn't be humming, shouldn't be alive. It was a dead glyph, dormant, cataloged months ago. It wasn't supposed to do a damn thing."

I looked at the scorch mark beneath my paws. At the shimmer where a name had been. I didn't speak, just gave her *the look*. The one that said, "You're in over your head, sweetheart. And the water's rising fast."

She met my gaze. Then nodded.

"I'll check the records. You...just don't touch anything else, please?"

I padded to the door, tail low. The wind outside whispered through the cracked display glass like breath on the back of my neck. Mallory Vex had smiled at the Cognichonk like it was a lover.

And she was feeding it memories. The question wasn't what she was building. It was who she was building it from?

Jessa didn't speak as she gathered what remained of the crown's security wards. Snapped glyph shards, a scorched velvet case, and one lonely molar that had rolled under the display stand like it was trying to escape the plot.

She pocketed the tooth with a sigh.

"Come on," she said. "Let's get you back to the cafe before the archive crew arrives and tries to blame the cat."

I didn't argue. Not because she was right, but because I was still listening to the echo of Mallory Vex's smile. The Cognichonk had pulsed when she spoke. Like it *liked* the sound of her voice. This was the hum of a predator marking its prey.

I lept into the satchel without ceremony. Peaches had already curled into a low-process spiral, running silent loops of fragmented case files and scent memory matrices. I could feel her calculating something we didn't have words for yet.

The zipper closed, but not quite, leaving just enough crack for the world's static to bleed in.

Jessa carried us out like a bartender carrying home a bomb in her purse—casual on the surface, calculating every step, aware that one wrong move turns witnesses into statistics and bystanders into collateral damage. Her fingers gripped the satchel with the kind of tension usually reserved for trigger fingers during standoffs. The wind had teeth. It bit the edge of her coat, and tried to steal her notes. She held tighter.

"We'll sort through it," she muttered. I wasn't sure if she meant the glyphs, the relic theft, or the broken jar labeled consequences.

The cab rolled up, summoned either by spell or schedule. She slid inside and gave the driver the cafe's name without ceremony.

I watched her reflection in the cab window. Her lips were pressed thin, compressed like a file that's been redacted until only the punctuation remains. Her fingers tapped a pattern against the side of the bag—not nervous, but coded. Deliberate. The kind of tapping that replaces words too dangerous to say aloud, like a prisoner communicating through cell walls to conspirators. Three quick. Two slow.

"You knew about the 'Chonk,' then? Not its fancy library

name, but the real thing." I said quietly, just to test the air. It didn't really come out as speech, so much as a series of meows and mrrps.

She didn't flinch. Didn't even blink. Just adjusted her sleeve and said, "I know about a lot of things."

Too smooth. Too calm. The kind of answer that's been practiced in front of a mirror until the mirror itself started to doubt its own reflection. Her words had the polished edge of testimony that's been rehearsed with legal counsel present —factually accurate but spiritually bankrupt, like a confession with all the important sins omitted. Possibly several mirrors, all slightly off-angle.

"Does one of those things go by the name Mallory Vex?" I pressed.

This time, there was a reaction. A flicker. The pattern of her tapping fingers broke for a single beat before resuming. It was all the answer I needed. "Some names are just labels on empty jars," she said, her voice a carefully constructed wall of nonchalance. "Dangerous to open. Better to leave on the shelf."

"And the cats?" I noted, testing her again.

She didn't look at me, but the corner of her mouth twitched. "Not everything that purrs is innocent."

The cab jolted as we turned the corner, the suspension protesting like a witness who suddenly remembers their Fifth Amendment rights. The moment broke, shattered like an alibi under cross-examination. We were back at the Bewitched Beans—a sanctuary or a trap, depending on which side of the law you stood. And lately, I wasn't sure which side that was.

The world had tilted on its axis. Jessa was a stranger in

plain sight, the cats hummed with secrets, and I? I was just a shadow of the man I used to be, adrift.

Back at the cafe, the world tilted just a degree off true.

The door chime rang the same too-cheerful note, but it echoed this time—lingered like a threat that's been made with a smile. As if it knew things now. As if it watched with the patient observation of a detective who knows the perp will eventually make a mistake. Some sounds aren't just noise; they're surveillance with better acoustics.

Jessa said nothing as she unzipped the satchel. Just set it down near the sigil-laced cat tower like it was routine. Safe. Normal.

But nothing about this was normal anymore. I stepped out, my stride steady, my mind sharp. No tremors, no psychic aftershocks. Just me, whole and lucid, a new kind of dangerous calm.

Peaches didn't slip forward this time, just pulsed quietly in the background, her thoughts arranged like backup servers and escape routes. I padded across the floor. The runes on the tiles, usually a low thrum against my paws, held their breath, their silent pause more unnerving than any noise—like a confession room when the recorder's been switched off and the real questions begin. Their silence wasn't absence; it was attention. The kind of focused quiet that falls when someone's just found the murder weapon in a place it shouldn't be.

Three cats sat in a patch of sunlight near the window. I'd seen them before, usually chasing light specks or licking things that shouldn't be licked. But now? Now they were still. Too still.

The ambient hum of the café—the gurgle of the espresso machine, the buzz of the wards—seemed to fade into nothing. The dust motes in the sunbeam froze mid-air. It was the kind of absolute silence that precedes either a gunshot or a revelation—the heavy, expectant hush that falls when the jury foreman stands or when the blackmailer finally names their price. A silence with weight, with intent, with consequences already set in motion and just waiting for gravity to do its work.

Their heads turned in perfect, unnatural unison. Their eyes locked onto mine. Synchrony in fur. Then they spoke, their voices layering over one another like a round sung in a crypt.

"The thread winds inward."
 "The anchor hums."
 "The mirror forgets."

Each voice was different, but each tone the same. The layered voices weren't a formal chant, just shy of it. But the meaning? That was pure, unadulterated prophecy.

The sun shifted behind a cloud and reality snapped back into place. The espresso machine hissed. A fly buzzed near the window. The three cats blinked, their shared consciousness shattering like glass, and immediately began fighting over an empty box with the gravitas of drunken philosophers. The moment was gone, but the air still tasted of ozone and prophecy.

Jessa didn't look up from her spell ledger, but I saw her knuckles turn white around her pen. She'd felt it too. Probably a coping mechanism.

I prowled towards the stairs. The second floor wasn't off limits, just full of excuses not to go. Jessa kept her archives up there, and her personal space. The air grew colder with each step, the scent of coffee and incense giving way to old paper, dried herbs, and the electric tang of dormant spells.

The promised weird draft curled around the banister, whispering a name I couldn't quite catch. Peaches's mind flagged it as a residual vocal echo, a common side effect of poorly-cast privacy wards. Ahead, I saw the cursed dartboard. As I passed, a single dart detached itself from the cork, flew with silent purpose across the hall, and pinned a floating dust mote to the opposite wall. It quivered there for a second before dropping to the floor. A warning. Or just the house clearing its throat—the way a loan shark clears his throat before explaining what happens to kneecaps when payments are missed. Some warnings don't need words, just the right prop in the right place with the right amount of menace attached.

I was halfway up the landing when I felt it. A static hum in the air, like someone had tried to summon meaning and only got guilt. The note was taped to the window with a smear of ectoplasm that still clung to the glass like a greasy fingerprint. The paper was cheap, torn from a pocket notepad. The three words were printed in shaky block letters.

IT'S ALREADY BEGUN.

I leaned closer. The ink was standard, but the pressure was all over the place. Written in a hurry. Or in fear.

Residual energy signature faint, Peaches noted coolly. *Humanoid. Non-witch. High anxiety levels. Trace elements of street-level ozone and... regret? The variable is poetically imprecise but registers as a valid emotional residue.*

A scared mortal had been up here. Someone who knew enough to be terrified but not enough to use magic. Someone who left a warning for me or for any cat who could read the signs.

My paw rested against the glass beside the note; it was warm, humming with residual fear. A flicker of motion across the street caught my eye—a flash of familiar orange against crumbling brick.

My gaze lifted. Outside, the street rolled on like it always did. Mortals walking dogs, drinking their foam, tapping their arcane screens. Never looking up. Except one.

Across the street, on a crumbling brick wall above a closed-down bookstore, an orange tabby stared straight into me. His gaze uneven as a flicker of awareness battled the deeper static. One eye blinked out of rhythm. He wasn't fully there, but lucidity was calling.

His mouth moved, but no sound reached my ears, just a whisper vibrating directly in the deepest corners of my mind.

"Luis..."

Then he twitched. Convulsed. Fell backwards into the alley like a puppet dropped mid-sentence. The thread snapped. The connection broke.

Downstairs, something crashed. A teacup. A spell jar. Or a riddle that finally solved itself. It didn't matter though.

I'd overstayed, it seemed. And the Chonk was pulling me toward a new flavor of Orange.

The room stilled. Not just the cafe. The pattern.

A faint fizz of static peeled off the nearest sigil as Luis's consciousness slipped from the network, leaving Peaches behind like ash after fire.

Her gaze remained fixed, unwavering. Blinking was a luxury. Her mind, however, churned.

Peaches stood alone in the middle of the landing. She was neither inert nor overflowing. A perfect mid-point, a node cooling its circuits after a heavy draw.

Her tail twitched in equilateral quadrants. Her ears flicked at 2.3-second intervals. Her pupils dilated, then narrowed, then mirrored the ambient sigil glow with an almost accusatory precision.

Luis was gone.

But his last thoughts lingered like residue on shared teeth.

"The Cognichonk liked her voice."

Peaches catalogued the line. Tagged it under Threats: Vocal-Adaptive Artifacts > Subfile: Mallory Vex. She folded the image of the molar crown into a thought-space shaped like a hex grid and moved to the café's main ledger, which no one had noticed was slightly ajar.

She didn't open it. She pawed the corner. A slip of parchment protruded like guilt. She read it.

Mallory Vex
Known Associative: Anchor Thread?
Voiceprint Matches: ~82.4%
Relic Path: Crown, Chain, Chorus.
Final node: ???

Peaches closed the ledger and slid it back into place, silent, unseen. The world remained none the wiser.

She returned to her spot beneath the chalkboard menu, curled her tail just so, and resumed the default pattern.

Breathing. Waiting. Calculating.

Until next time.

Luis would return. They always did. Until one didn't.

CHAPTER NINE

I came to mid-air. Claws splayed. Mouth open. A shriek rising from my throat—part feline, part existential siren. The kind of awakening usually reserved for men who've been pushed from fire escapes by dames they trusted too much or cops who've discovered their pension fund in the pocket of a mobster. A scream made of rage, confusion, and canned betrayal.

The blender was already howling.

So was I.

For one glorious, gravity-defying heartbeat, we sang the song of our people: one of vengeance, voltage, and possibly salmon. A duet of doom, like the harmony a detective and a suspect make when they both realize the gun is loaded and the confession tape is rolling. We were partners in this fall—unwilling, unequal, but inescapably linked. We met in harmony. We parted in chaos.

Then came the crash.

Fur met linoleum in a tangle of limbs and poorly aimed

prophecy. A bowl shattered. A fork ricocheted off the fridge and embedded itself into a loaf of white bread that had been left out long enough to achieve sentience. Trash erupted like confetti at a parade for poor decisions—wilted parsley, half a shoe insert, the gristle remains of a rotisserie chicken that had clearly died in vain.

My tail twitched. My brain did not.

"Why," I muttered to no one in particular, "am I airborne?"

But I wasn't anymore. I was sprawled across a kitchen that smelled like mustard, mold, and unresolved trauma—the kind of trauma that gets case files sealed and detectives transferred to precincts where the coffee's always cold and the homicide rate's always zero. This kitchen had seen things, absorbed them into its linoleum like evidence that can't be bagged. Above me loomed the beige monolith of a countertop—neutral, judgmental, and crusted with sauces that defied known food groups.

Gingersnap.

The name hit like a static shock behind my eyes. I was in Gingersnap.

The Cognichonk had launched me without warning into the living embodiment of a gremlin on espresso and unresolved childhood issues—no briefing, no backup, just sudden immersion like an undercover operation where the handler's gone dark and the exit strategy was written in disappearing ink. This wasn't possession; this was a hostile takeover with fur and no severance package. Instant possession of a body that was already mid-murder.

Kill. Eat. Kill again. And then maybe nap. Blender watches. Wants death.

What passed for thought in that head was a storm of urges, smeared with grease and static. Her instincts clawed through my skull like wet socks in a dryer full of knives.

The blender sputtered again. Its cord twitched like a snitch having second thoughts about his testimony. The base glowed faintly, as if offended—the kind of offended that comes with brass knuckles and a grudge that's been aged like fine whiskey. This wasn't just an appliance; it was a witness with mechanical immunity and too much voltage for its own good. Someone—possibly Gingersnap, possibly a ghost with a flair for the dramatic—had drawn a sigil on it in what I hoped was cinnamon and strongly suspected was regret.

The light above the stove didn't flicker. It twitched. Sharp. Deliberate. A psychic tic in the fabric of the room.

And then I felt it.

A buzz. Not in the ears. Deeper. Like the resonance of a cathedral bell rung underwater—the kind of frequency that breaks confessions loose from guilty men and makes innocent ones suddenly remember crimes they never committed. It vibrated through bone and memory with equal disregard for structural integrity. The Cognichonk field pulsing in my blood, sliding down each hair follicle like a whisper made of yarn and menace—the kind of whisper usually heard in interrogation rooms after the recorder's been switched off and the good cop's gone for coffee. It carried promises of answers wrapped in threats, each pulse a contract I never signed but couldn't escape. Something in the network had shifted—tightened. The echo was no longer just passive background noise. It had teeth.

I tried to focus. Gingersnap did not.

Her leap wasn't aimed, not at a living thing. Just at the vague scent of grievance. A sponge. A carrot nub. A ghost of peanut butter left on a spoon. She tackled all three with righteous fury, snarling like a deity of filth and defiance. I was just along for the ride, my claws skittering across the tile involuntarily—erratic punctuation marks to her war cry. Her war cry peaked in pitch, dipped, then landed us in a heap of receipts, crayon wrappers, and what I strongly suspected was a cursed oyster fork.

I attempted speech. I got a hairball.

The Cognichonk's signal surged again, erratic, jagged—like trying to catch a thought mid-dream while someone throws glitter in your eyes. Gingersnap didn't resist me. She simply did not notice me. This body wasn't a vehicle I controlled. I was just the grim ornament, along for its murderous journey.

Victory is mine. Blender is next. Feather demon watches. Saw his crime. He knows.

The feather duster trembled in the corner. I didn't know why. I didn't ask. I knew its time would come.

The light twitched again. No longer watching. Syncing.

This wasn't a random connection. No whim drove the Cognichonk's choice. This was a calculated test, a brutal system check—the kind of deliberate evaluation usually conducted by crime bosses before a hit or judges before a sentencing that won't appear in any official record. The network wasn't just active; it was auditing its assets with cold precision and colder purpose.

I licked my shoulder slowly, deliberately. A territorial mark of defiance. A promise.

Then I locked eyes with the blender.

Round two.

The blender whirred—softly this time. A whisper, not a roar.

It was baiting me.

I could feel it, humming in anticipation like a predator in appliance form. Its buttons glowed faintly, one after the other, blinking a silent code of challenge. *Purée. Pulse. Obliterate.*

Gingersnap's pupils dilated to the size of judgment.

Rage cube. Make smoothie. Add vengeance.

Gingersnap's will coiled the body like a spring. I was powerless to stop the launch. We pounced.

I didn't plan the leap. I barely survived it. We launched as one—a tangle of fur, fury, and cognitive dissonance. My left paw hit the counter with all the grace of a dropped lasagna. The right went straight for the lid.

The blender screamed again. The shriek that tore through the kitchen wasn't metal on metal. It was the socket letting out its last breath.

Sparks arced. The sigil beneath the base flared—orange, then violet, then a shade of green that shouldn't exist outside mold and envy. The linoleum buckled. Something beneath the surface of the floor groaned like it remembered being a tree and regretted its choices.

We landed half on the blender, half on a pile of expired coupons and cat fur. My claws connected with plastic. Something inside shattered. Maybe a gear. Maybe my pride. Maybe both. Hard to tell, with the noise in my skull and the ringing in my teeth.

And then it hit.

The pulse.

A shockwave, not of brute force, but of something far more unsettling: pure presence. Like a thought dropped into still water. It radiated out—through the walls, into the wiring, down the drainpipes and out across the city like a meow heard in dreams. I felt it resonate through the Cognichonk network, fracturing consciousness like a champagne glass under operatic pressure.

For one brief moment, I wasn't just in Gingersnap. I was in **all** of them.

A dozen orange cats twitched, hissed, or yowled in languages no throat should hold—a chorus of informants all singing different verses of the same damning song. Each cat a witness to something they couldn't understand, each vocalization an evidence file being corrupted in real time. This wasn't just connection; it was conscription with fur and unnatural syntax.

A kitten screamed the square root of seven. A tom on a rooftop declared war on the moon. In a pet salon three blocks over, a Maine Coon knocked over a summoning bowl and summoned a very confused raccoon. A senior tabby in a hardware store paused mid-bath, raised one paw, and said, perfectly clearly—"Not again."

And through it all, the blender hummed.

It was more than a kitchen appliance. It was a conduit. A cheap, plastic, sigil-tagged focal point for something bigger. Older. Hungrier—like a precinct rat who's been taking payoffs so long he's forgotten what honest police work looks like. This blender wasn't just broadcasting; it was recruiting, with the cold efficiency of a talent scout for a crime family that operates outside jurisdictions and inside nightmares.

Eat the cord. Eat the truth. Eat.

Gingersnap lunged for the power strip. I slammed on the internal brakes, wrestling for control of a nervous system that wasn't mine. We crashed into the pantry, burying ourselves in expired beans and apocalyptic amounts of instant rice. Dust swirled like battlefield fog.

I surfaced beneath a broken broom and a coupon for canned mackerel that expired in 2009.

My head throbbed—temples pounding like timpani under a bad omen. My whiskers buzzed with leftover static, twitching like lie detectors.

The hum receded, yet what remained was different. The frequency, once a dull drone, now sang with chilling clarity.

And I wasn't the only one riding the frequency anymore.

We fled the scene like all good criminals do—covered in rice, half-possessed, and full of unexamined trauma. No alibi, no exit strategy, just the desperate momentum of the guilty and the hunted. We left behind everything but circumstantial evidence and the lingering scent of reasonable doubt.

The apartment window was already cracked. Gingersnap cracked it further. She hit the sill like a comet of fur and bad intentions, then vaulted into open air with all the grace of a liquor-fueled ballerina. I clung to consciousness as we landed on the rooftop beyond, tail high, claws catching on old shingles slick with damp leaves and questionable moss.

The city breathed, a low pulse that had nothing to do with sirens or streetlights. This was a deeper beat, the kind that got under your skin. A frequency I didn't know I could hear until I couldn't stop.

The Cognichonk field wasn't just active anymore. It was alive. It stretched across the rooftops and back alleys like invisible yarn, thrumming with power—and cats were tripping on it. The network pulsed like a heart that's survived three autopsies and still refuses to stop beating, a connection stronger than blood ties and more dangerous than mob loyalties. Every orange cat was now a potential witness, suspect, or accomplice in a case file that rewrote itself with every pulse.

A yowl split the air from two streets over. Followed by another. Then six more. Orange bodies leapt, twisted, flopped. Some hissed. Some meowed in Gregorian modes. One screamed what might have been Enochian or exceptionally guttural French.

I turned just in time to catch a glimpse of a mangy tom on a window ledge. He blinked once, slowly. Regally. Then muttered, 'XIII Kalendas Martias' with the grim certainty of a coroner announcing time of death or a judge delivering a sentence without possibility of parole. The date wasn't just information; it was evidence in a language most had forgotten how to prosecute. Then he sneezed and resumed licking between his toes like nothing had happened.

The signal flared again.

My fur stood on end. Not Gingersnap's fur—*mine*. Buried deep in the shared meat. Whatever circuit this was, I was tangled in its wires now. More than a mere passenger, more than a whisper in the dark—I was the conduit, whether I liked it or not.

We skittered down a fire escape with the enthusiasm of

a raccoon evading rent. I wrestled her chaotic urges into a semblance of a straight line; I steered, Gingersnap powered. The results were... improvisational.

Must run. Must chase. Must head to pulse. Must eat shoelace.

"No. No shoelaces. Ignore the child's Crocs. Ignore the—GODDAMMIT—"

We sprinted across a backyard fence and barreled straight into a flock of pigeons. They scattered like lies at a confession booth. All but one.

Shrimp. Standing perfectly still. Paw raised mid-air. Trying to high-five a pigeon.

"He hums jazz in his sleep," he whispered, before his eyes rolled back and he bolted up a drainpipe.

I didn't ask. Some truths are self-sabotaging.

And then we heard it. Human voices. Close. Shaky. The scent of burnt sage and over-roasted espresso curled downwind like a warning.

We careened around a corner and onto the back patio of Bewitched Beans—that grimy little café with scrying specials and the worst wi-fi east of the river. The one where wards fizzled for fun and the espresso machine sometimes spoke Latin when no one was watching.

Two young witches huddled by the compostable runes bin, frantic and under-caffeinated, their familiar—a Sphynx —curled in a dream spiral atop a still-warm grimoire. The café's back door was propped open with a brick carved with protective sigils, releasing the competing scents of burnt coffee and what might have been sandalwood or possibly just mold.

Through the doorway, I caught a glimpse of the interior, of walls lined with jars of ingredients labeled in handwriting too neat to be trustworthy, and a chalkboard menu offering "Hexspresso" and "Curse-Free Cookies (Most Days)." A woman behind the counter—Jessa, I remembered suddenly —was frantically drawing containment wards on napkins, her hands shaking. The same Jessa who'd examined the relic theft, who'd carried Peaches in her satchel not long ago. Something about her presence here couldn't be coincidence.

"—second surge this week," one said, clutching a cracked phone in one hand and a half-melted crystal in the other.

"Not natural. That's a ritual-grade spike. You don't get a signal like that unless someone's reactivating the grid."

Her friend looked pale. "You mean the old network? The one they shut down after the Kog'nith'enk Event?"

Static in brain. Wrong hum.

Gingersnap hissed. The Sphynx twitched. Somewhere inside, I felt a memory I didn't make curl in on itself and burn.

I didn't linger.

The pull tightened its grip, a summons that reached further than mere instinct, and carried a chill colder than any cold-blooded purpose. It was routing me. Through the network. Through the cats. Through the city.

And whatever was waiting at the end of the line?

It already knew I was coming.

The alley didn't have a name. Just a feeling. It crouched behind a shuttered bookstore like a secret the city didn't want to claim —the kind of urban space that gets redacted from official maps and witness statements. Some alleys aren't just passages; they're crime scenes waiting to happen, with histories darker than the shadows they cast and futures outlined in chalk.

Even Gingersnap paused, her usual charge replaced by a strange, still awe. Because something was humming.

Graffiti bled across the walls, a language I hadn't seen before, certainly no art, no politics, just... movement. Each symbol writhed like a suspect under questioning, each line curved like a confession that keeps changing its story. This wasn't vandalism; it was testimony in a dialect that predated the concept of truth under oath.

The air buzzed with static and citrus, the kind that came from magical cleaning agents and lemon curses. Every hair on our body stood at attention; the Cognichonk was here, or at least a node of it, buried under the garbage like so many truths in this city.

A dented metal trash can sat near the back wall, its lid rattling faintly, like it was trying not to be obvious. Gingersnap approached with the caution of a raccoon preparing to slap a toaster. Her thoughts pulsed like broken headlights.

Must bite. Must sniff. Must know. Must destroy.

"Wait, no. Let me look first."

It was heavy. Too heavy. Gingersnap's tiny frame wasn't built for leverage, and I didn't exactly have opposable thumbs in my current situation. But spite is a kind of physics. She dug her claws in, grunted like a toddler possessed by rage and instinct, and *shoved*.

The lid didn't move.

Then it twitched. Just a little.

A pulse rolled out from beneath it—soft, low, but insistent. Like the node was acknowledging us. Or warning us.

Her yowl split the air, a protest not to the stubborn can, but to the universe's audacity to resist her. She leapt on top and bounced twice. The second time, the lid slipped sideways with a metallic shriek and thudded to the ground like a dropped secret.

We stared down into the hollow.

Inside was candle wax, bones—tiny ones. Avian. Arranged in looping patterns that shimmered at the edges like evidence that doesn't want to be bagged and tagged. A resonance node. Primitive, but precise. It offered neither light nor whisper. But the pulse it sent out spoke volumes, a desperate beat against time—like a witness trying to communicate after their tongue's been cut out.

And there, stuck to the alley wall just above it, held in place with something that looked—and smelled—like sardine oil: a photograph.

Torn. Faded. But I'd seen that face before. The Whispering Widow's husband. Younger. Smiling. The kind of smile that doesn't know it's already evidence in a case that hasn't happened yet. His eyes held the blissful ignorance of a man who doesn't realize he's already a victim in a crime scene that's still being assembled. The photograph wasn't just an image; it was an exhibit waiting to be numbered.

Arm around someone cropped out. And in his other hand—undeniably, unforgettably—the Cognichonk. Bright. Whole. Unfractured. As if it hadn't yet splintered my consciousness and spread it like glitter through the orange cat hivemind.

The date in the corner was smudged but legible. Two years *before* my disappearance.

I stared.

Gingersnap growled. Quiet. Low. Not at the photo. At the node.

It pulsed. Once. Hard.

I touched it.

The world inverted. Light turned inside out. Sound collapsed into pressure. It was an eye, all right, but not one that belonged to anything with fur and purr. Too high, too many layers of lid. It opened, and the color of it was something between rust and memory.

And behind it, just for a moment—a woman. Elegant. Dangerous. Her smile too wide for comfort, like a knife that's forgotten it's not supposed to talk. Her fingers tracing sigils in the air that burned my retinas—the kind of burning usually associated with looking at crime scene photos that later get sealed by judges who don't sleep well afterward. Mallory Vex wasn't just a suspect; she was a verdict delivered before the trial had even begun. Her touch went beyond mere manipulation. Mallory Vex was bleeding into the network, becoming its very essence.

"Hello, Detective," she whispered, though her lips didn't move. "Enjoying your new accommodations?"

A chill ran through Gingersnap's tiny frame—my chill, not hers. Recognition, cold and complete. This wasn't just another player. This was the architect. The one who had been there from the beginning.

The vision shattered.

I hit the pavement. Hard. My nose met pigeon feather and regret.

The photo was gone.

The trash lid rolled to a stop behind me. The bones had rearranged themselves. A new pattern now—spikier. Meaner. And still pulsing.

No longer was I chasing the ghost of a signal. It had found me. I was squarely in its sights.

There was no fanfare, no blinding flash, no last-gasp monologue. Just a twitch. A skip in the signal. A flicker behind the eyes. One moment, I was there. Breathing Gingersnap's breath. Feeling her paws on cold concrete, her mind thrumming with post-node static and war crimes. And then—I wasn't.

No darkness enveloped me. Just the stark reality that the world continued its grim spin, and I was no longer on it.

Gingersnap blinked once. Then again, slower. Thoughtful. Almost smug.

She stared at the empty spot where the photo had been. Tilted her head. Sniffed the sardine oil stain. Licked it. Then shredded the corner of the wall for emphasis.

Memory bad. Smell good. Wall untrustworthy.

The wind kicked up. A roach skittered out from the trash pile like it had somewhere to be.

She ate it. No hesitation. No chewing. Just victory and chitin.

A shard of broken mirror caught the light, leaning

against a crate covered in sigil tags and old coffee grounds. Gingersnap caught her reflection.

She hissed. Loud. The kind of hiss that echoed off the bricks and bounced back sounding like prophecy.

Then she licked her paw, fixed her ear tuft, and walked away like nothing happened.

The hum followed her. Soft. Subtle. Like a tone trying not to be noticed.

She didn't notice. Or maybe she did.

She paused at the alley's mouth—tail high, whiskers forward. Then she turned and batted a feather off the ground like it owed her money. She watched it fall. Tracked it all the way down. When it hit the concrete, she looked up, her gaze piercing through the alley's grime as if seeing something beyond its miserable walls.

Then she vanished into the dark like she owned it.

As the Cognichonk pulled me away from Gingersnap, I felt myself stretching thin, consciousness scattering like ash in the wind. Somewhere in the static between hosts, I caught a glimpse of something larger—the network itself, pulsing with orange light, cats scattered across it like nodes in a web. And at its center, a shape forming, coalescing, almost human but not quite.

Mallory Vex was calling. And somewhere in the city, another orange vessel was about to receive me, whether they wanted to or not.

CHAPTER TEN

Jasmine perfume and cheap incense slapped me awake—mid-purr, mid-seduction, mid-disaster. Another day in the fractured hell I called existence, where even my consciousness was just another item someone had stolen. My throat vibrated with someone else's satisfaction while my paws kneaded Anna Mae's trembling fingers. Mango's body housed my fractured consciousness—neither of us had the decency to apologize for this unwelcome intrusion; it was a kind of crime we both relished. Another night at the office.

I'd been somewhere else entirely a moment ago—chasing taxidermy thieves through the rain—before the Cognichonk yanked me here like a suspect dragged to interrogation. I was drowning in Mango Fuzz's waking dream, a textbook seduction designed to break the heart of a psychic bookstore clerk with a soul as brittle as cheap glass.

The universe had its twisted sense of humor, always

ready to roll the dice on my misfortune, like a dealer at a crooked table in a back-alley casino.

I wasn't used to it yet. Don't think I ever will be. I used to pride myself on control. Clean office. Clean hands. Now my "office" was a four-legged charmer with fur like sin and instincts sharper than my old switchblade. My "hands" were velvet-covered scalpels of feline manipulation.

And Mango Fuzz? My current ride was too damned smooth for anyone's good.

He was sprawled in the rooftop garden, tangled in Anna Mae Bellamy's hopeless affection, purring like a jazz sax played by a con artist who knew exactly how to ruin your life and make you thank him for it.

The name—Anna Mae Bellamy—floated up from Mango's memory, slick as oil on water. Below us, her bookstore's neon sign flickered: The Clairvoyant Cat. She'd arranged the rooftop like an altar, candles guttering at precise intervals, her fingers stained with ink from drawing wards that wouldn't work. Her eyes never left my borrowed face, pupils wide with the kind of hunger that keeps psychic hotlines in business.

She knelt in front of me—of us—her hair escaping its bun in messy curls that framed her face like half-finished thoughts. Glitter clung to her clothes like evidence she didn't bother cleaning up. There were smudges on her fingers—ink? candle soot? old magic that didn't wash off?

She was breathing too quickly. Eyes too wide, shining with fragile faith like she was waiting for revelation to pounce on her and explain why she kept waking up alone.

She believed Mango was the reincarnation of some lost Khaloren oracle. Gods help me.

I recalled her naive confidence, words dripping with an optimism that was about as welcome as a bullet in the back. *"The world isn't ready for direct revelation,"* she whispered once, feeding him imported salmon like a communion wafer. She'd built her entire little empire interpreting Mango's meows for lost souls willing to pay for prophecy by the hour.

She wasn't malevolent, just a soul famished for something genuine, desperate enough to grasp at shadows masquerading as light. And that made her dangerous. The true believers always were—they'd burn down the world just to warm their hands over the embers of what they thought was truth.

The rooftop around us was a tangle of secondhand wicker chairs with sagging seats and rust-eaten tables—furniture that had given up hope long before its owner did, each piece telling the story of dreams corroded by time and neglect. String lights trembled in the wind, buzzing softly, throwing off just enough light to make the shadows shift and whisper. Jasmine twisted up old trellises, smothering the rot and mildew with sticky sweetness.

I could smell the mold underneath it all. The rotting wood. The bitter tang of candle smoke and burned-out hope.

Mango—my body now—leaned in, his soft paw an uninvited hand on Anna Mae's trembling fingers—a gesture laced with deceit, promising her the universe even as he robbed her blind.

"Oh, Mango, you sly thing," she breathed, voice cracking under the weight of hope she didn't want to admit was killing her. "You always know just how to ask."

Mango purred. Low. Deliberate. I felt it resonate in my chest, disgusting in its intimacy. Sharing my own borrowed ribs with a grifter's siren song. I tried to pull back. To take control. Mango didn't budge.

Anna's lips trembled. She bit down on them hard enough to leave dents. She fumbled in her coat pocket with shaking fingers. The rustle of fabric sounded like a confession trying to escape.

"I—um—I brought something special for you."

Her words cracked on the last syllable. An offering. A prayer she didn't know how to finish.

Mango's eyes half-lidded, tail flicking lazily in calculated invitation. I felt the smirk tug at my mouth without my permission.

She laid it out slowly on the checkered blanket. Careful. Reverent. Like it might explode if she dropped it too hard. And that's exactly what it was to her. This rooftop was her chapel. Mango her oracle. And me? The unwilling god trapped in the priest's skin.

I scanned the scene—my reeking crime scene—guilt clawing at my insides. A checkered blanket that smelled of damp and old wine. Dozens of socks laid out with near-religious precision. God. There was a mountain of socks, each one folded like some twisted relic, a tribute to a deity that demanded cotton taxes.

Anna believed socks held secrets.

Mango's voice oozed into my head, smug and indulgent. *Threadbare cotton holds the weight of human tragedy.*

I snarled at him internally. He ignored me.

The socks weren't even the worst of it. Other trinkets

peppered the blanket—a silver bell etched with runes worn smooth with worry, a half-burned candle stuck in an amber-glass holder, a tiny crystal figurine chipped at the ear.

Enough mysticism to keep her hooked. I'd seen this hustle before. I used to bust conmen who did the same thing with tarot cards and weeping widows. They stole hope instead of wallets. Now I was the con.

Anna's fingers trembled as she withdrew the prize from her pocket.

A fragment. It glowed. Pulsing lavender and pale gold. Rune-carved. Too smooth. Too perfect.

My gut twisted.

She held it out to Mango like salvation in the palm of her hand.

"It's...part of the Kog'nith'enk," she whispered. Her voice fractured on the name like it cut her to say it.

I recognized it immediately. Fake. Counterfeit. The real Kog'nith'enk—what the witches called it before it got turned into the Cognichonk on alley walls and drunken forums—wasn't steady. It was alive. Chaos. Echoes of a thousand minds screaming in harmony.

This thing? A hollow facsimile, churned out by soulless machines who knew nothing of life or death—just cold, lifeless counterfeit magic.

But Mango leaned in. He inhaled like a sommelier judging vintage. Eyelids drooped to half-mast, promising mystery he had no intention of delivering. He made a small, intimate sound in his throat that felt like treason crawling under my skin.

My revulsion curdled into rage.

"Pull back," I snarled. "Don't encourage her."

Mango didn't even flinch. The glow of the shard lit up Anna's eyes like a shrine catching fire. She didn't see the lie. Only hope.

My internal alarm screamed. This wasn't just a scam. Someone was feeding counterfeits into the psychic network. Poisoning the Orange Syndicat I'd been forced to join.

I remembered the real Cognichonk. That sang in my skull until it split me apart and scattered me across a hundred orange bodies.

This shard was dead. Synthetic magic buzzed from it in flat, monotonous waves. It felt wrong in my teeth. Like biting foil. It didn't whisper secrets. Didn't echo with lives lived and lost. It buzzed like cheap neon in a cracked sign over a ruined bar.

"This... this is real, right?" Anna's voice cracked again. She was shaking all over.

Mango pressed his whiskers against her fingers. He purred. A smooth-talking conman, offering promises as empty as the cigarette pack in my coat pocket—sweet nothings and savage truths wrapped in velvet.

I wanted to vomit.

"We need answers," I roared at him. "Not another sock!"

But Mango's mind was calm. Satisfied.

Answers are overrated, he purred. *But gifts? Gifts keep you fed.*

I strained to wrench us back. I felt the body flex and relax under his control. He was in his element.

Anna's eyes brimmed. One tear escaped, streaking a line through the grime on her cheek. She didn't even seem to notice. Her thumb stroked the runes on the shard. Tender. Desperate. She set it down on the blanket like an offering at an altar.

Mango took it gently between his teeth. He purred louder. Her shoulders slumped in relief.

Below us, the wind rattled the string lights so they clicked against each other like teeth. The old windchimes screamed once, then fell silent. The socks rustled in the breeze, silent witnesses to the crime.

I watched it all. Trapped behind Mango's purr.

This would spread. This counterfeit node would hum its lie into the network. Crack the Syndicat further. Invite more poison.

And when it all went wrong? When everything broke again? I'd be the one left holding the blame. Because that's what happens to the detective behind the whiskers.

The cat always walks away clean. But I don't.

I didn't choose to bite it. I was circling the ring of fakes like a cop casing a counterfeit racket, the kind of setup that always ends with someone bleeding in an alley while the real perp catches the midnight train to somewhere better, tail twitching with every warning sign my borrowed body could give. My nose twitched at their stale hum. Each one was a bad forgery of something sacred, buzzing with the cheap static of half-baked rituals and crayon-grade rune work.

Deep inside the spiraling static of the Cognichonk, something blinked. Not recognition. Not curiosity. A cold, hard warning.

"Back off," I thought. "These things aren't right."

But Mango had other ideas. He lunged.

My internal alarms screamed red alert as Mango's jaws opened. I threw myself against the walls of his consciousness, clawing for control. "Don't you dare—"

Critics, Mango sighed, mental voice dripping with lounge-singer condescension. *Always afraid of a little improvisation.*

His teeth closed around the shard before I could wrestle back the reins. He bit down with the same grace he applied to fleecing rich dowagers and charm-slaying vet techs.

For one blessed heartbeat, nothing happened. Then everything did.

The shard pulsed. Once. Twice. Then it screamed. Not with sound any sane man could hear. Not even with psychic whispers. This was deeper—like the universe's guts were ripping open in silent protest.

It slammed into my awareness like pressure without sound. Guilt given form and frequency. It tore at me. Vibrated in my inner ear with silent shrieking.

I felt it grind reality under its heel. A waveform of guilt and false divinity shot through Mango's jaw, channeling straight into the lattice of wards stitched across the rooftops. The rooftop's protective sigils shattered like cheap candy glass.

Above us, the string lights detonated in perfect unison— every bulb giving up with a sharp, synchronized pop. Glittering shards rained over the rooftop like cursed confetti. The air collapsed into hush. A terrible, smothered hush.

It felt like the entire block was holding its breath in

incense-choked terror. Then the scent hit. Ozone. Burnt copper. The acrid stink of cheap wiring melted under too much load. Scorched hope.

I convulsed. Psychic feedback ripped through my spine like electric current on loan from Hell. My claws shot out involuntarily, scoring the tile beneath me. Sparks danced in my vision.

The world fractured. Connections I didn't know I had snapped like ribs under a boot. Somewhere across town, Butternugget howled in sudden agony. Rutabaga's imperial disdain cracked into panic. Jake's tactical calm shattered mid-calculation. Each severed link burned through me like copper wire stripped of insulation, the current finding nowhere to go but back through my borrowed nervous system.

They sputtered. Buckled. Sparked like overworked circuits on the verge of meltdown. The backlash didn't just short the network. It twisted the fundamental frequencies. It *corrupted* the very signals that let me exist across the Orange Syndicat.

Each surge of pain reminded me of the first touch. The first mistake. That damned relic. The moment I stopped being Luis Cannon, P.I., and became the unwilling, fractured patron saint of every orange cat in a thirteen-mile radius.

I felt it failing. I felt *myself* failing. Then, silence.

Mango dropped the fragment. It hit the tile with a weak clink, still humming, like it was proud of the damage. Smoke curled from Mango's whiskers. He licked his paw. Slowly. Meticulously.

Well, he mused, calm as a corpse, *that was dramatic.*

I was mentally staggered. Control seeped back into me

like blood into old bandages. My entire existence was a taut wire, strung between agony and ruin, jolting with every perceived misstep. Phantom pain buzzed where a thousand connections used to be. I tasted ash. Failure.

"You absolute disaster in a velvet coat," I snarled, my voice raw even to myself.

Compliment accepted, Mango replied, stretching his singed paw and grooming it with insulting care. He didn't even blink at the smoke.

Below us, I heard Anna shriek. Glass shattered. Charms blew off the shelves of The Clairvoyant Cat like they were refusing to participate in the lie anymore.

From up here I could see the big front window flex, fracture, and give way—not from any physical hit, but from the sheer weight of belief imploding on itself.

The air roared in. Shards tumbled in slow motion. I felt the building's wards collapse in one collective gasp of betrayal.

Down below, candles guttered out. Scrolls burned at the edges, curling into black petals.

I stood there, body vibrating, Mango's breath unbothered. We watched the ruin together. The fake shard still hummed weakly in the dirt, like it was proud of itself. They weren't just fake. They were rigged. Sabotage disguised as salvation.

There was a puppet master lurking in the shadows, pulling strings with a gambler's glee as they watched the Cognichonk spin helplessly into oblivion—a bet against my very existence. And I had no idea if I could stop them. Or if I'd even survive it.

The rooftop fell into an uneasy silence, the kind that made your skin crawl, like the pause right before the wrong answer at an interrogation—thick with ghosts of what just transpired. I'd heard that silence before—in precinct interrogation rooms, in alleys where deals went south, in my own apartment the night I realized I'd touched something I shouldn't have. That silence never brought anything but trouble.

Smoke curled from scorched sigils, their careful lines now blackened into scabs on old tile. The jasmine hung burned and limp. A river stone cracked in half with a sound like a final verdict, splitting neatly down its center.

One of the river stones cracked neatly in half. I watched it split with the kind of judgment only a rock can manage—silent, patient, but unmistakably offended at being used in a con.

I paced. Four ginger paws clicking against ruined tile. Tail stiff, fur puffed where it shouldn't be. My borrowed eyes narrowed to hateful slits. I was trying to outrun the echoes still clanging around in my skull.

The hum was gone. But not forgotten. The air still crackled with it—static clinging to a bad decision, lingering like the smell of burnt hair after a fire you didn't quite put out.

Anna stumbled out onto the rooftop. Shoes half-on, dress twisted, a warded bracelet on one wrist sparking like a cheap sparkler at a party no one wanted to attend.

"Mango?" Her voice was ragged, shaky. "What just—was that you?"

I blinked at her. Slow. Innocent. Entirely unhelpful.

I considered answering. Maybe with a dramatic leap to the trellis, a haughty flick of the tail, an elegant vanish into the shadows. Anything to salvage the moment.

But Mango's body had other ideas. He sat. Lifted one paw. And began grooming his singed whiskers with all the smug composure of a bastard who sets a house on fire and then critiques the architecture.

They never suspect the clean ones, Mango thought, voice curling in my skull with a satisfied purr.

"You shorted out six blocks of magical security," I growled at him internally. My mental voice was raw from screaming.

Seven, Mango corrected primly. *If you count the antique teacup emporium.*

Below us, the bookstore let out a long, tortured whine as the last of the feedback loop pinged off its dying wards—a high-pitched, glassy shriek with nowhere to land.

Anna flinched at the sound. She turned, slowly, eyes wide and glassy. She saw the fake shard on the ground. Saw the smoking ruin of the rooftop altar she'd so carefully curated, all those socks and stones and river-glass charms now covered in fine ash and regret.

Her mouth moved soundlessly for a second before words finally emerged.

"I—I didn't know," she whispered. It cracked halfway through. "It felt real."

I felt something inside me soften. Just for a second. She wasn't the threat. She was just another believer. A well-intentioned node plugged into the wrong socket. Another casualty in the con.

I stepped forward on careful paws. Head lowered. I gave her shin a slow, deliberate headbutt.

She jolted like I'd shocked her. Her eyes met mine. Red-rimmed. Searching.

"Oh," she breathed. "Okay. Yeah. That's fair."

She dropped her gaze. I watched her. The wind kicked up and dragged smoke across us both. The burnt jasmine scent clung to the air, mingling with a bitter tang of regret and charred dreams that buzzed like failed ambitions igniting in the dead of night, like hot wires left too long in the rain.

I turned back to the shard. Still humming. Weak now. But not harmless. I eyed it like a bomb with a cute paint job.

Whoever was planting these things knew their craft. They knew how to stitch it into the network. They knew how to hum at just the wrong frequency. They wanted the Cognichonk to choke on it.

I flicked an ear, listening to the dying static in the air. If enough orange minds collapsed under that noise? Someone else got to write the next verse. And not just for us.

My mind flashed to the warehouse on Bleecker Street— where reality had thinned last month after a minor Cognichonk disruption. Pigeons flying backward. Water flowing uphill. A child aging three years in an afternoon before the wards could stabilize it.

And that was from a hiccup.

This? This was cardiac arrest. If Mallory Vex got her claws into the network while it was vulnerable... I'd seen what she did to that street vendor who crossed her. Some things shouldn't be rewritten. Not by her. Not by anyone

Mango yawned, stretching so hard his back cracked, tail curling in a flourish that would have been beautiful if it hadn't been infuriating.

We should go, he suggested lazily. *Before she tries to hug me.*

I didn't argue. My claws flexed once in the soot, testing the ground. I turned my head. One last look.

Jasmine. Smoke. Socks and sabotage. The remains of belief burned down to the roots.

I slipped into the shadows of the garden trellis, silent as a regret you don't bother confessing.

The Cognichonk—once a beacon of chaotic brilliance— was now a ticking time bomb, a shard of unstable magic teetering on the brink of disaster.

My consciousness frayed at the edges, vision tunneling to a pinpoint of orange light. The Cognichonk was calling me home—or whatever passed for home in this fractured existence. The pull was irresistible, my protests meaningless as I slipped away from Mango's body like smoke through fingers.

The last thing I felt was relief—his, not mine.

Mango paused beneath the trellis, free at last from the gravelly voice that had been polluting his thoughts. He stretched, digging his claws luxuriously into the rough wood. That faint, almost imperceptible ping in the deeper corners of his mind—the sound of Luis's consciousness being yanked elsewhere—was sweeter than any bell.

Good. He'd been getting annoying.

Mango flicked an ear, then padded softly down the alley, tail held high. He had a sudden, overwhelming urge for tuna. And perhaps, a nap in a sunbeam.

The case was closed. The sunbeam was warm. And the Cognichonk could handle itself—for now.

CHAPTER ELEVEN

The alley stank of spoiled intentions and canned regret. The kind of place where dreams come to die and tuna cans come to rust—both leaving behind the same sour aftertaste of disappointment.

A half-crushed can of tuna wept quietly in the corner, its contents glistening with betrayal and possibly mercury. Rain drizzled from a broken gutter above like divine ambivalence—God's own Chinese water torture, reminding me that even the heavens had given up filing paperwork on this case.

And I—Luis Cannon, former detective, current fur-coated tragedy—was hunkered in the shadows behind a moldy cardboard box labeled "DO NOT QUESTION." I was on a stakeout. Or I was supposed to be. My companion, however, seemed to have found a higher calling.

Box smell like warm. Sit forever. Box is god now.

"We've talked about this. The box is not god. The box is

surveillance cover. Eyes up, kid—we've got a raccoon to tail."

Tail! Tailtailtail!!!

"Not our tail. HIS tail. Focus. Look at the one with the glowy butt tattoo."

Clatterfang emerged from behind a stack of damp pizza flyers, swaggering like a warlock on probation. The raccoon's minor sigil charge glowed faint blue beneath his matted fur, and he was chewing something that pulsed— probably a bone, possibly a soul.

The bone pulsed with a familiar rhythm—not just any glow, but the specific frequency I'd felt in the antique shop when Jessa touched the relic case. The same harmonic I'd glimpsed in the counterfeit shard that Anna had shown Mango.

"That's not just any bone," I muttered. "That's a resonance key. Like the ones Vex has been collecting."

Paw dirty.

"No—" I licked. Automatically. Reflexively. A cleansing swipe across the wrist I hadn't even consciously registered.

"One lick. That's all. Then we move."

The elbow need love. Elbow feel sadness.Fix it with tongue love.

"No. No tongue love. This is a stakeout. We are a precision instrument of justice, not a loofah with abandonment issues."

Buttenugget purring, *Mmmm elbowspot SPOTTTTTT*

I flopped sideways. Full lick mode. Tactical disaster.

My professional facade, built brick by painstaking brick of late nights and cynical observations, crumbled with every involuntary swipe of that deranged tongue. It wasn't just undignified; it was a cosmic betrayal. The Cognichonk's grip, usually a subtle hum, felt like a wrestling match in my own skull, a primal instinct duking it out with years of honed restraint, and losing, spectacularly, to the siren call of a sad elbow

The raccoon paused twenty feet ahead. Turned. Our eyes met. He watched me. I watched him. My tongue continued its treason.

"We're compromised. We're licking under observation." The thought was a cold knot in my gut, amplified by Butternugget's simple, horrifying query:

He look crunchy. Fight? Snack?

Clatterfang, that flea-bitten felon, strutted towards the mound of refuse like it was hallowed ground, a true believer approaching an altar of forgotten snacks. And there he was: the 'trash priest,' robed not in silk, but in the brittle, yellowing skins of forgotten bananas, secured with the stained tessellations of pizza coupons.

The trash priest's altar wasn't random garbage—it was arranged with the same precise geometry as the sigil-laced cat towers at Bewitched Beans. Someone was creating resonance points throughout the city, and using society's overlooked creatures as their couriers.

The air around him shimmered with the faint, cloying scent of fermented fruit and unholy devotion. He didn't just 'take' the glowing femur; he swiped it, with the casual arrogance of a warlord pilfering a sacred relic from a fallen kingdom, the bone pulsing with a dim, unwholesome light that defied the mundane grime. It wasn't just larceny; it was blasphemy against the very concept of dignity.

"We are watching a felony occur in real time."

He took the glowy! Glowy gone! GET THE GLOWY!

"Yes! Finally! Chase protocol—"

First...lick other elbow.

"...what."

Balance.

I didn't move. I licked. I licked like my ancestors demanded it.

Clatterfang scurried into a storm drain, dragging the relic behind him like a kidnapper with a neon fish stick.

I blinked.

When Clatterfang vanished into the drain, I caught a glimpse of something etched into the bone—a spiral pattern, similar to the one I'd seen in the Widow's sigil work. The pattern that keeps appearing in chalk, in food, in dreams.

"No," I muttered, rising slowly. "No, no, no. You don't get to commit interdimensional larceny while I'm tongue-deep in dermal maintenance."

Ear itchy now.

"We missed the handoff. He's gone. Because you couldn't resist your own elbow."

You licked too.

"That was sarcasm grooming."

A trash can tipped over nearby. Probably judging me. Possibly sentient.

I lunged forward. My foot caught a cheese wrapper. I tumbled into a puddle of expired mayonnaise and a tarot deck. One card slapped against my flank.

The Fool.

Of course.

The alley had gone quiet. Too quiet. Like a punchline waiting for the wrong joke.

Rain whispered against the bricks in Morse code I wasn't fluent in, and somewhere, something dripped with the rhythm of a forgotten lullaby. I was still damp. Still humiliated. Still freshly licked and profoundly aware that I'd just let a magic raccoon commit grand theft femur while I tongue-bathed myself into irrelevance.

Smell rain. Rain is snack? Taste wall.

"Don't taste the wall. That wall has regrets older than both of us."

I crouched beneath a sagging awning that smelled like mildew and powdered disappointment, waiting for my pride to dry.

That's when I felt it. A presence. Not hostile. Not helpful. Just... here. Like jazz on an elevator that no one else noticed.

A slow shape emerged from the shadows. Orange and white. Lanky. Tail trailing behind him like punctuation on a sentence he hadn't decided how to finish.

Bosco.

He moved like he'd forgotten how urgency worked. Or maybe he remembered and chose not to care.

"Seen worse," he said, barely a whisper. "Slept through most of it."

Haircat! Is haircat!!

"Great. Of course. The one cat who makes riddles look impatient and combs look like religion."

Bosco padded over, sniffed me once, and began grooming the top of my head with slow, deliberate swipes.

"Stop it," I muttered.

He didn't.

"Seriously. This is undignified."

He licked harder. I swore he hit a pressure point behind my ear that temporarily erased two years of childhood trauma and one ex-girlfriend's voicemail.

Purring loud. Haircat love. Brain clean. Feel warm now.

"I swear to twelve minor gods and a cursed mailbox, if you start purring louder I will bite a ghost. There was a time when my threats carried weight—when perps trembled at my approach instead of offering unsolicited grooming services."

"Missed the mark, didn't you?" Bosco murmured between licks. "Too much chase. Not enough still."

"You saw him? Clatterfang. Sigil-branded klepto with a glowing bone and no morals?"

Bosco didn't answer. He groomed one of my whiskers until it hummed.

"You could've stopped him."

He yawned. The kind of yawn that could end arguments, riots, marriages. "Could've," he said. "Didn't."

"That relic might've been a Cognichonk shard. Or bait. Or a key."

"Could've," he repeated. "Didn't."

He wise. Like sleepy shoe.

"You don't even know what a shoe is."

Tasted one once. Full of ghost foot.

Bosco finally stopped licking and stared at the rain like it owed him rent.

"Bones don't glow unless someone remembers 'em wrong," he said.

I blinked. "What does that even mean?"

The question hung in the humid air, heavy with the weight of my human inability to comprehend something so profoundly, stubbornly simple. My mind, trained to dissect motives and follow paper trails, spun uselessly, snagging on logic that simply didn't apply to glowing bones or napping prophets.

Bosco didn't clarify. He just rolled onto his side, curled into the shape of a loose question mark, and began snoring like a saxophone with low self-esteem, his wisdom a closed book and his help as tangible as a politician's promise

"That's it? No help? No direction? Just grooming and haiku-level nonsense?"

He good. He nap now. You nap too?

"No," I snapped aloud. "I'm not napping."

I was already kneading the wet newspaper beneath me.

Something was humming beneath the trash. Not audibly. Not physically. But in that way your spine knows when the case is about to go sideways and your lunch is about to get prophetic.

Bosco had vanished—possibly evaporated, possibly snuck into another dream. The sky had darkened to a bruised eggplant, and the alley had taken on that uncanny shimmer things get when the veil between logic and memory frays at the corners.

I crouched by the trash priest's old nest. The sacred

banana peel was gone. The dryer lint tapestry, gone. Only a faint shimmer remained where the femur had been stolen—like the air still remembered being sacred.

"Something's still here," I muttered. "Something under the rot. Under the ritual. Under the fur."

Bug under bag. Chase bug. Kill bug. Forget bug forever.

"No. We are not doing this again. There is no bug. There's a pattern."

Pattern bug? New bug?

I swatted aside a heap of greasy food wrappers. Something pulsed beneath them—a soft, golden light that flickered with rhythm. Not light exactly. More like memory residue. The kind of glow dreams leave when they die wrong.

At the bottom of the pile, I found a bottle cap, a snapped wishbone, and a broken pair of reading glasses crusted with sigil-dust.

They were arranged in a spiral. Not elegant. Not occult. Just... meaningful.

"Resonance marker," I breathed. "Someone planted this. Someone who knows how to make trash talk."

Eat wishbone. Get smart.

"Absolutely not."

I sniffed the air. The scent was wrong. Sweet, sour, old. Like burnt yarn and wet magic. The kind of stink you don't wash off—you inherit. The Cognichonk's presence prickled against my whiskers. Not strong. Not full possession. Just a whiff of memory static. A psychic hangnail snagging my thoughts.

I touched the wishbone. My vision went sideways.

Someone else's memory. Not mine. Not Butternugget's either. Sharper. Cooler.

A velvet collar. A shrine made of buttons and chewed feathers. A voice—not a meow, but something translated through purring: "Bones glow when they remember pain." The spiral glowed white. A paw—slender, precise, orange-furred—drew a sigil in chalk. No... ash. No... fur? Another paw swatted the sigil. Clawprint gouged deep. A whisper: "This one's too close. Break it before he finds the thread."

I gasped back into my body, splayed in the trash heap like a desecrated lasagna.

"Someone's watching," I hissed. "Someone else using the Cognichonk like a tuning fork and we're just the static."

Tail itchy. Itch tail.

"You don't get to come back in now. You didn't even SEE the memory."

you saw. now I hungry.

"I saw Vex. Or someone Vex-adjacent. They're laying down false nodes. Marking trash sites. Redirecting us."

Paw Sleepy.

I turned in a slow, deliberate circle, tail flicking like punctuation.

That's when I saw it. Near the drainpipe where Clatterfang vanished—burned into the brick beneath a layer of soggy receipts and what may have once been a sandwich —a spiral. Double-lined. Twisting inward. Like a sigil collapsing on itself. Like a door trying not to open.

I crept closer. The spiral pulsed. The air buzzed. And then I heard it—no louder than breath, no clearer than a lie told to a mirror.

"Wrong tail, Cannon."

The moment hung like a wet towel of meaning. Profound. Ominous. Then the wind shifted, a can rattled, and fate slipped on a fish bone and fell on its ass.

I tried to walk away with dignity. Tried. But my tail was stuck in a tuna can.

I'd stepped backward into it during the spiral trance and now it clanked along behind me like an unwanted sidekick. Every movement echoed with hollow metallic shame.

Tail monster! Kill it! Bite it till it learns respect!

"Don't. It's a can. We're already on thin metaphorical ice."

Clankclankclank. Sneak mode broken. Now we LOUD.

"I am a professional. A detective. I have solved cult murders, psychic kidnappings, and a theft ring run by enchanted novelty mugs. I will not be undone by a—"

The can popped loose with a *clang* and shot forward. I pounced instinctively and landed face-first in a cold patch of vinegar-soaked paper towels. There are moments that define a man. This was not one of them. I rolled over slowly, groaning. Rain tapped out a mockery rhythm against a nearby lid. My whiskers twitched. My soul twitched harder.

"Okay," I muttered, peeling a slice of cheese off my shoulder. "We're regrouping. We're strategizing. We're—"

Something moved. No threat. Just ambiance. A crumpled fast food bag hissed as the wind caught it. And in that motion, I caught a glimpse: a spiral drawn in barbecue sauce, smeared but deliberate.

"They're leaving sigils in food waste," I whispered. "Who the hell does ritual work in ketchup?"

Pants ghosts. Ketchup holds ghost flavor.

"No. No ghost pants. No food-based hauntings. Not right now."

I stalked toward the bag, half-mad with questions and the faint urge to scream into a compost bin, when a pigeon above cooed with a deeply personal smugness. I looked up. It stared down. Same one from before. Same haunted beady eyes.

Carl.

He puffed once, turned around, and crapped directly into my path.

I lunged. I missed. And landed headfirst in a recycling bin labeled 'HOPE.' The lid closed behind me with the finality of a failed marriage. Fitting—my dignity and this city's optimism, both discarded and waiting for collection that would never come.

There are moments that define a man. This was not one of them. This was the moment a former detective, a man who once tracked whispers through city gutters and shadows through human hearts, landed headfirst in a receptacle of discarded optimism. The irony, bitter and metallic, coated my tongue like the faint tang of spoiled milk. 'HOPE,' the bin proclaimed, a stark, mocking white against the industrial gray plastic. Inside, it smelled of stale newspapers and the faint, unsettling sweetness of forgotten intentions. I could almost hear the universe chuckling, a low, rumbling laugh from behind a cloud, at the sheer, unmitigated banality of my current rock bottom.

We live here now. Bin safe. Bin dry. Bin cradle of tomorrow.

"I swear, Butternugget, if you make this a nest I'm finding a blender and ending both our careers."

Something creaked above. A shadow moved on the ledge.

Bosco.

He watched. Unblinking. Tail curled like a question never asked. Then he nodded once, like a man accepting the ending of a bad jazz solo. He didn't look alarmed. Just... tired. Like he'd seen this ending before, and slept through most of it last time too. Then he disappeared over the rooftop.

Something shifted. Quietly. Like a thought losing its shape. It started in my spine. That slow unravel. The tingle behind my eyes. The sense that my metaphors were losing meaning.

"No," I whispered. "Not yet. We're not done. We almost had something. A thread. A sigil string. A clue shaped like poultry."

Mouth taste like old rubber band. Nap soon? Nap now.

"Butternugget. Listen. You have to hold on. Just long enough to mark the spiral. Just—"

I lost feeling in my teeth. Not physically, but in a way that resonated deeper, a metaphysical erosion. Like watching your last lead vanish into a crowd—that moment when you realize the case isn't just cold, it's been buried in the freezer beneath last year's broken promises.

The noir was slipping, the hard-boiled edge of my reality softening, thinning. My voice rasped, the psychic thread frayed like cheap yarn in a rainstorm, and I knew what was happening. The Cognichonk was retreating. And I was going with it.

"Remember," I managed, the words catching in my throat. "There's a pattern in the waste. Not all spirals turn inward. Some... some spin you loose."

"Tell them I tried," I thought. "Tell them I almost mattered."

And then I was gone. The world around me dissolved into static, then silence.

Butternugget blinked. Once. Slowly. Like a toaster rebooting. Then he stood up. He wobbled. He sneezed into a soup lid. He turned three full circles and headbutted the recycling bin, knocking the word **HOPE** askew. Then—he froze.

Not because of a noise. Not because of fear. Because something in the back of his mind twitched. A thought? A scent? A dream with corners?

He stared at the alley wall. The one with the ketchup sigil. He didn't lick it. Didn't bite it. He just... looked. The fur on his back rose in a slow, confused ripple. Then fell.

Bug gone. Glowy gone. Tail itchy.

He turned. He ran into the trash can. Headfirst. Again.

But the moment lingered. Just a second too long. Long enough to wonder: Did he understand? Or was something else watching through his eyes?

The spiral on the wall pulsed once. Faint. Forgotten. But in that brief, eerie glow, the graffiti on the bricks seemed to writhe, the shadows deepened into hungry maws, and the discarded trash around it took on the silent, watchful aspect of a congregation. Still waiting. Still watching. And perhaps, still influencing.

CHAPTER TWELVE

I woke mid-sprint. The world stank of damp concrete and old blood, and my paws landed with soundless certainty on broken tile. Another day in paradise—if paradise was a concrete coffin where even the shadows had given up hope of escape. My breath was a tight leash, pulled just enough. Ears pivoting. My tail, a damn rudder, cut the air, reading currents I couldn't see. The air stuck to my fur. Heavy. Like guilt in summer.

I wasn't thinking. I was *moving*. Jake's body—a cathedral of muscle and intent—ran like a machine built to exit trouble before it started. A temple where prayers went unanswered and survival was the only sacrament worth keeping. Jake moved with the cold calculation of a chess master who moonlights as a hitman. The gravel crunched underpaw like a confession trying to escape. It was the only sound that dared speak. And here I was riding shotgun in a cat. A goddamn orange siege engine with whiskers instead of wire cutters. And this was my war.

We checked our six. Nothing.

Again. Nothing.

Instinct, a nagging voice, screamed against the calm. I heard it too. The quiet was a lure, a silk glove hiding a fist.

The shadows to the left were too long. Streetlights flickered like dying promises. The sky overhead was a bruised slab of industrial haze, leaking cold. I felt the wind shift—barely. Enough to carry the ghost of burnt oil, stale urine, old fear. Urban camouflage for danger.

A faint, intriguing whiff of week-old tuna, quickly dismissed.

No time.

Jake's whiskers twitched, a coded message in the gloom, feeling out angles, paths, and threats that hadn't shown their face.

His mind, a honed blade, whispered only tactics: where to hit, how to run, and the impossible luxury of a safe sleep. No room for frills, only the hard lines of survival. My brain, used to dictating the moves, found itself riding shotgun on a primeval engine of war.

I felt the Cognichonk pulse behind my ribs like a second heart that judged my tactical planning. It hummed in approval or mockery. Hard to tell. Even a possessed cat toy had an opinion on my recon, and it usually wasn't good.

Especially when it involved that persistent itch behind my left ear.

A chain-link fence appeared in the gloom ahead. Jake didn't even slow. Muscles bunched. Hind legs fired. We vaulted in silence. Landed in a crouch that belonged on a crime scene photo with a caption that read "suspect remained at large."

Eyes narrowed. Pupils drank the dark. The city swallowed us whole as we ran. Just how I liked it. The body moved on rails of memory and training. Not mine. His. But I rode it like I'd paid for the ticket in blood.

And maybe a few purrs, just to be safe.

The veterans' center loomed. A carcass of civic good intentions rotting on city neglect. Facade cracked. Paint peeled in ancient curls. The kind of place where promises came to die—where the government buried its shame under paperwork and forgotten medals. The sign overhead still read WELCOME HOME in letters that lied. One flickered. Another was gone.

Jake slowed. Precision. His breathing dropped to a stealth cadence. Heartbeat like a metronome of menace. Every part of him said: *We've done this before. And survived. Barely. Might even find a loose thread to chew on inside.*

We circled right. Avoided the main door where the boards were loose and the rats had built an audience.

There was a side entrance. Obscured by a dying hedge. Hinges rusted into near-uselessness, but someone had lubricated them recently. The scent was faint. Oil. Old blood. Ash.

And a tantalizing hint of something... chewable. Control, Cannon.

Jake's ears twitched. Catalogued. Stored.

One paw lifted, hovered. Quiet as a confession in a padded cell.

Sniff for traps. Or anything that didn't smell like decay.

It was the oldest trick in the book: feel for the wire, sniff for the hint of trouble. Only now, the book had claws, and better balance. But the dust was scuffed in a pattern only maniacs and soldiers would notice. Scrapes of a boot heel with a limp. Directional. Inbound. Not outbound.

Whoever went in hadn't come out.

Jake's claws flexed automatically. My mind followed suit, thoughts slicing options like a scalpel through scar tissue.

Though a good, deep stretch would feel amazing right now.

We didn't speak. Didn't need to.

My tail twitched in fractions. Every angle a question. Every step an answer no one trusted.

A sudden urge to flatten myself and rub against the cold concrete. Dismissed.

And tonight, preparation was the only reason we weren't dead yet.

The door whispered shut behind us. Sound bled out. Air thickened.

Jake's pads touched down in fractions, like he was auditioning for the role of Silence. The hall stretched before us—long, cracked tile, walls sweating mildew and resignation.

Smells wrong. Territory abandoned but marked. Old threat. Dead air.

My nose twitched. Mildew. Old gun oil. The sour ghost of sweat bled into paint that had peeled decades ago. Memories baked into walls like war stories no one wanted told.

We moved slow. Deliberate.

Clear corners. Check blind spots. A good hunting ground, if the stakes weren't so high.

Jake's ears swiveled with practiced arcs. Every sound filtered and catalogued. Drip in the pipes. Rat scratching in the ducts. Wind worked the glass somewhere down the hall. Polite violence. The kind that calls before it kills you.

Half-collapsed filing cabinets blocked half the hall. Their drawers yawned open like snapped ribs. Paper littered the floor in drifts—decades of case files and dishonor, stamped, dated, forgotten. A bulletin board hung askew on one wall, its surface a palimpsest of notices, schedules, and warnings. Faded photographs of military units stared back with hollow eyes, their faces blurred by time and something more deliberate. Someone had scratched out certain faces with methodical fury.

One photo caught my eye—newer than the rest. A group of civilian contractors, their smiles too wide, too practiced. In the center stood a woman whose posture screamed authority without trying. Her face was intact, but her eyes held something cold. Familiar. The plaque beneath read: "Leyline Research Initiative, Phase 3."

Jake's nose twitched, picking up something faint, something that didn't matter. Not yet anyway. But I knew what I'd seen. The Widow had connections here. Threads I hadn't pulled yet.

We pressed on. The hallway narrowed, ceiling lower here, as if the building itself were hunching under the weight of its secrets. Rust-colored stains marked the baseboards in patterns too regular to be accidental. Too irregular to be maintenance. The air grew thicker, charged with something that made Jake's fur stand on end.

Territory marked with power. Fresh. Someone hunted here when the sun was still up.

But there—behind the wreckage. A door. Nearly hidden. Paint scoured by age, and something deliberate. Three long scratches marked it. Evenly spaced. Ritual. Message.

Jake's tail stiffened.

We've seen marks like that before. The human called them 'sigils'.

The marks were identical to the ones I'd found carved into the alley wall where Butternugget first woke up. The same pattern Rutabaga had discovered etched into his litter box. A signature. A warning. A claim of ownership.

Claws flexed as we eased forward. One paw lifted. Hovered.

Listen.

No movement behind it. No sound. I pressed. The door gave. Slow. Resistant.

Inside, the world changed. The room wasn't empty. It was *arranged.*

Sigils. Charcoal and old wax. Drawn on every wall in looping, frantic patterns. Lines twisted into spirals and teeth. Meaning layered like bruises over old rites. The patterns weren't random—they formed a complex web, each symbol connecting to others in a macabre constellation. Some I recognized from the Widow's home. Others were new, but carried the same signature of desperation and precision.

Candles guttered on the floor. Stubs melted into warped brass holders. One sputtered. Another choked itself out in a curl of sour smoke. The holders themselves formed another pattern—a loose spiral that mirrored the larger one on the floor. At its center, a clear space where something had been removed. Recently.

Jake's nose wrinkled.

Burnt tallow. Blood, faint. Old.

We advanced. Slow. Every step a contract with the dark.

A desk stood against one wall, its surface cleared except for a leather-bound journal, its pages torn out and pasted to the walls as part of the sigil work. Whoever had done this wanted the words to be part of the ritual itself. Letters blurred into symbols, symbols into intent.

In the far corner, paper clung to the wall with rusty tacks. Edges burned. Smoke stains radiated from old singe marks like halos. Evidence was for cops. This was a hunter's shrine. A scoreboard for the damned

We approached. I read it. Low. Gravel-thick.

"Ripley." Crossed out.

"Gutterball." Crossed out.

"Butternugget." Crossed out.

"Shrimp." Crossed out.

"Bosco." Crossed out.

"Delta-J." Status: Unknown.

And circled in deep red wax smeared like blood. "Widow's Tail."

Each name was accompanied by a small photograph— orange cats in various states of awareness. Ripley, mid-yowl in what looked like an alley behind a diner. Gutterball, asleep on a car hood. Butternugget, eyes wild, mouth open in what was clearly a scream. My hosts. My vessels. My fractured selves, catalogued like specimens.

A cold knot formed in my gut. This wasn't just a list. It was a recruitment ledger. A hunter's trophy wall. Each cat had been tagged, tracked, and—judging by the crossed-out names—claimed.

Hunters know our paths. Our leaps. Our hiding spots. No safe perch here.

Jake's tail twitched with surgical precision. His mind calculated threats, exits, ambush points. But beneath that tactical assessment, I felt something else. Recognition. Fear. He'd seen this room before. Or one like it.

The Cognichonk pulsed behind my ribs. Once. Twice. Like a heartbeat I didn't own anymore. It recognized those names. Sang them back in static and teeth. I swallowed. My mouth felt like confession booths and old bourbon.

"Delta-J," I rasped. "Status unknown."

The name sparked something in Jake's memory. A flash of respect. Loyalty. The ghost of a partnership that predated me. His claws flexed.

She fought here. Left this.

I stared at the name, willing it to tell me more. Delta-J. The only one not crossed out. The only one who'd fought back hard enough to earn a question mark instead of a death sentence. Someone important to Jake. Someone who might have answers.

That's when the room shifted. A mirror in the corner flickered. No electricity. No glow. Just light that didn't belong anywhere else. The surface rippled like disturbed water, and a presence filled the room—not physical, but undeniable.

Mallory Vex's voice cut through the quiet like a scalpel dipped in honey. "You found it," she rasped. "Good. I wrote half of those names myself."

I turned, claws out, tail lashing. "Show yourself."

The mirror's surface warped. Her eyes gleamed from inside it—sharp, knowing, merciless. Eyes that had seen the bottom of too many souls and found the view to her liking. The kind of eyes that made confession booths good business. She watched from somewhere else, her gaze burning with amused contempt.

"You always were so thorough," she said, her voice carrying notes of genuine admiration beneath the mocking.

"Tell me what this is." My voice cracked like old ice.

She smiled. Not kind. Not human. "A ledger," she purred. "A recruitment list. Some cats...break better than others."

I lunged. Hit glass. It stayed glass. "Answer me!"

But the mirror had gone dark. Just a reflection. Just me. Tail lashing. Breath ragged. Fur bristling with rage and helplessness.

The Cognichonk purred behind my ribs. Not comfort. Not triumph. Recognition. Because it liked what she'd said. It approved of the cataloguing, the claiming, the breaking. Like it had been waiting for someone to understand its purpose all along.

I stared at the list again. At the names I knew. The vessels I'd worn. And I wondered which of us would be crossed out next.

The mirror had gone dark, leaving only the taste of ash and Mallory Vex's chilling words hanging in the air. "A recruitment list. Some cats... break better than others." The cold fury that had filled me now settled into a hard knot in my gut, heavy with intent. Jake's body, a coiled spring of controlled power, tensed under me.

"She's here," I rasped, the words thick with the implications of Vex's presence. "Or she was."

Closer than you think, Jake's thought cut through, sharp and clear. *The signal from the mirror was too strong for a simple scrying pool. She wants you to know she's close.*

We moved deeper into the labyrinthine halls of the veterans' center. The flickering emergency lights hummed, casting long, dancing shadows that seemed to writhe and stretch like unspoken threats. The air grew colder, charged with an unsettling static that prickled my fur. Every creak of the old building, every distant drip of water, seemed to whisper her name.

My nose twitched, picking up a faint, cloying scent beneath the mildew and old dust—jasmine and ozone, familiar from the antique shop, but stronger here, laced with something metallic and sweet. The smell of a fresh ritual.

Residual energy spike, Jake confirmed, his ears swiveling, triangulating the scent. *Forward and left. Through that archway.*

We padded through a sagging archway, the plaster crumbling like old bones. The corridor beyond was narrower, lined with empty rooms, their doors ajar like forgotten mouths. Each one held the ghost of past lives, the lingering scent of stale medicine and quiet desperation. But one room stood out. Its door, unlike the others, was tightly shut. And beneath it, a sliver of pulsing, violet light.

Trap scent. Bait placed. Hunter logic, Jake's thoughts flashed. *We're not the first prey to walk this path.*

I felt the Cognichonk quicken behind my ribs, a low, hungry thrumming that recognized the light. This was no ordinary room. This was a focal point.

I pressed my ear to the door. Silence. A profound, unnatural stillness that felt heavier than any noise. Not even the faint whisper of air. Like the room itself was holding its breath.

"Too quiet," I muttered.

Air too still. Predator stillness. Jake replied. *Waiting breath. Wrong.*

My claws scraped against the aged wood, seeking purchase near the latch. The lock was simple, a rusted bolt, but someone had coated it with a thin layer of wax, now hardened and almost invisible. I recognized the scent: lavender, meant to soothe, to obscure. To trick.

Scent fresh. Still wet. Jake's mind noted the exact time signature. *Predator just left. Could return before whiskers dry.*

I worked my claws around the wax, scraping it away with meticulous fury. It peeled off like old skin, revealing the raw metal beneath. Then, with a grunt of effort, I pressed against the door. It gave way with a soft, mournful groan, swinging inward on hinges that now seemed to scream in protest.

The room hit me like a physical blow. It wasn't just a room. It was an altar where reality came to bleed.

The walls wore their sigils like prison tattoos—no charcoal sketches here. These were carved deep into the plaster, permanent as regret. The violet light pulsed with the rhythm of a dying heart, each beat pumping poison into the air. Spirals twisted into predatory shapes, teeth and eyes woven into the looping lines. In the center of the floor, a large, perfectly formed circle, etched in shimmering ash, hummed with a palpable hunger.

And within that circle, arranged on a black velvet cloth, was a collection of artifacts. A crown of polished molars, larger and more intricately carved than the one mentioned at the antique shop, gleamed with an unholy light. Beside it, a cluster of glowing bones—femurs, ribs, small, delicate phalanges—each pulsing with the exact same violet hue. A dozen in total. Each one thrummed with a familiar, dangerous frequency.

Power objects. Wrong vibration, Jake thought, his internal assessment chillingly calm. *Territory marked by a predator too clever for claws.*

"She's gathering them," I breathed, my voice raw with dawning comprehension. "She isn't picking pockets. She's building an empire, brick by stolen brick."

The Cognichonk, Jake supplied, his thought surprisingly clinical. *Here. Split like prey shared among a colony. Her scent on every piece.*

My breath hitched. The source. The thing that had fragmented me, scattered my mind across the Orange Syndicat.

On a small, makeshift table near the wall, a leather-bound journal lay spread before me like a confession I was beating out of it. Not Jessa's frantic scrawl, but confident, precise handwriting. It was Mallory Vex's. Her thoughts. Her plans.

I leaped onto the table, my paws landing silently on the worn wood. I leaned over the journal, devouring the words. Diagrams of intricate sigils. Formulas for resonance frequencies. And lists. Lists of names. Cats. Locations.

My own eyes scanned the names, recognizing them with a jolt of ice water in my veins. Butternugget. Rutabaga. Mango. Jake. My hosts. My fractured selves.

She's claiming all territories at once, Jake's thoughts overlapped with mine, a grim symphony of realization. *Making every hunting ground hers. Every cat a puppet with her paw on the strings.*

"She's trying to make herself the Cognichonk," I whispered, the horror of it twisting my gut. "The ultimate Anchor. The voice in every head. The will in every paw."

The room wasn't just a workshop. It was a crucible. And we were caught in the heat.

Jake's thoughts brushed against mine, a grim tally of danger in every relic. But my eyes were glued to that journal, to the names of my ghosts, my fractured selves. Vex wasn't just hoarding; she was hunting. And I was the prize.

"We need to search this place," I growled, the words barely making it past my teeth. "Every corner. Every shadow."

The silence felt staged. We'd been searching the workshop for twenty minutes, methodically dismantling Vex's secrets. The journal had given us names, but not locations. The artifacts had shown us power, but not purpose. Something was missing—something Mallory wouldn't leave in plain sight.

My ears flicked at nothing; my tail lashed once before I forced it still.

Still tail. Sharp eyes. Hunter mode.

My nose twitched. There—a seam in the floor, a grate half-buried under soot and the debris of old crimes. I crept closer, my breath measured and heavy.

Nose low. Breathe slow. Read the ground's memory.

Burnt fabric. Acrid. Faint, but clinging like guilt that refused to wash out.

My claws scraped metal as I pried the grate free. It gave with a single, reluctant squeal—a confession no one wanted overheard.

Inside waited darkness, then shape.

I reached in, claws hooking, careful, deliberate. I pulled it out.

It was a glove. Singed. Edges blackened. Fingers half-crisped.

I froze. Memory flooded in—unwanted, unstoppable. Jessa's voice, low and urgent: "Luis, you have to understand —once you're in the loop, it doesn't let you out." Her hand on my shoulder. The smell of ozone and bitter coffee. The crackle of wards pushed too far. "Promise me you'll stay out of that place."

My tail lashed without permission. I turned the glove over in my paw, tracing the burn patterns that suggested heat from a glyph gone bad, or a fight she hadn't won.

My claws flexed.

Bait. Placed here. Waiting for our whiskers to twitch.

I exhaled, slow and shaking. The air tasted like old candles and betrayal.

My gaze drifted to the wall beside the grate. Scrawled sigils crawled across it, half-finished; lines that didn't just mark, they warned. Nicknames etched in charcoal, smudged but legible.

"Delta-J. Status: Unknown."

My throat tightened.

Pack-friend fought. Claws out. Lost her territory. Not coming back.

The Cognichonk pulsed behind my ribs. Warm. Satisfied. Like it had wanted me to see this, to feel it. My rage was cold. Surgical. I set the glove down carefully, as if it deserved respect. I stepped back, claws still out, tail cutting arcs in the stale air—a blade searching for guilt. My voice dropped to gravel. A promise. A threat. "I'm not leaving this unsolved."

The Cognichonk pulsed again. Harder this time. Like it approved of the evidence, of the pain. I snarled. Low. Helpless. But the hum thickened behind my ribs. Turned sharp. Splintered. My thoughts fuzzed, unraveled. Clarity slipped through my claws.

My voice cracked once—ragged, angry, desperate. "I'm not—" But the words died.

The world lurched sideways in my skull. Noir narration lost its footing. Tactical overlays blurred to static. For one second, I felt myself split in half: a detective made of teeth and guilt, and a cat built for quiet violence.

Then the Cognichonk snapped the tether. I choked on the nothing it left behind—a void where purpose used to live, like a bottle drained of whiskey but none of the regret.

The connection snapped. No static. No scream. Just sudden, absolute silence.

I sat there, still as stone, feeling the hum drain out of my ribs. The voice in my head went quiet first. Then the fear.

For the first time in hours, it was just me. Just Jake.

I blinked. Once. Slow. My tail settled, no longer twitching with someone else's nerves.

The glove lay on the ground. Strange. I didn't remember digging it out. Didn't remember why it mattered. I sniffed it once, cautious. Burnt fabric. Old threat scent. Nothing worth chasing now.

I looked at the wall. Marks everywhere. The human's territory signs. I didn't understand them. Couldn't. That was his skill, not mine.

I licked my shoulder, slow. Groomed away the fur that stood wrong from his borrowed tension.

The room smelled like dust and cold wax. Safe enough. For now.

I liked the quiet. Didn't trust it. But I liked it. I settled onto my haunches in the center of the floor. Ears up. Eyes half-closed. Guarding the space that was now mine.

Luis was gone. But danger wasn't.

The quiet settled on my fur like territory claimed. And I allowed it.

CHAPTER THIRTEEN

I think I was dreaming. I remembered the first time I came here. Before the Cognichonk got its claws in me. Before orange fur and twitchy instincts. Before I was forced to see the world through cat's eyes and scratch at secrets with claws instead of questions.

I remembered it too well.

The house loomed at the end of the dirt drive like a confession someone built out of termite spit and regret. The kind of place where secrets went to retire and ghosts clocked in for the night shift. Paint peeled back in long curls the color of old bone. The porch sagged under the weight of promises it never meant to keep.

I parked the car a good twenty feet back. Even the gravel didn't want to get too close. I lit a cigarette and watched the smoke drift across the yard's overgrowth. Thistles and wild grass had laid siege to the place. Cat statues lined the walkway, cracked and glass-eyed with judgment, no longer even pretending not to see. It was the kind of place that remembered murder like a fond first date.

Jessa's voice memo rattled in my pocket. *"Luis, don't go alone. Don't you dare."*

Too late, sweetheart.

I walked up the porch. Each board groaned like it was testifying under subpoena. I knocked once out of habit. The door opened before my knuckles landed.

She stood there. The Widow.

Hair pinned back with obsessive precision. Wrinkles like hieroglyphs of grief carved deep—the kind of face that had argued with sorrow and lost every round but refused to throw in the towel. Her skin was papery, pale as candle wax, but her eyes held no warmth—just the dull sheen of old pond water gone bad. And she smelled faintly of something sharp and herbal, like an apothecary that had given up on selling cures and started bottling sorrow.

"Mr. Cannon," she said, voice dry as old paper.

I tipped my hat, out of professional reflex.

"Ma'am. You called."

She didn't answer. Just turned and walked inside. Invitation enough.

I hesitated on the threshold. The porch boards creaked with the weight of decisions made too late. Even the wind seemed to hold its breath, waiting to see if I'd cross a line I couldn't redraw. For a second I saw my reflection in the dusty window—hat brim low, collar turned up like a warning. A detective. A trespasser. Or maybe a sacrificial lamb. I stepped inside anyway.

The door closed behind me with a soft, decisive click, like a confession being filed away. My pupils dilated, pulling in shadows like evidence. I caught my own scent—cigarette smoke, stale sweat, a fear I refused to sign for. The house was a trap and it wasn't even pretending otherwise.

Inside was too dark for midday. Heavy curtains strangled the light like it owed them money. The smell hit first: pungent herbs, wet carpet, and stale tea meant more for warding than refreshment—the perfume of desperation with notes of last-ditch effort. Every shelf was crowded with porcelain cats. Rows of gleaming-eyed sentinels posed mid-pounce or mid-prayer. A silent jury. Family portraits lined the walls, every face scratched away with cruel, methodical fury.

I paused. Let the silence breathe, thick and suffocating.

"Have a seat," she said.

The chair she pointed at was antique, claw-footed. Looked like it had tried to be a throne and given up halfway.

I sat. She sat opposite. Didn't pour tea. Didn't offer it.

There was ceremony here, but no hospitality. A courtroom with no judge, just the defendant confessing to a crime she still hoped was justified. She watched me over that unpoured cup like she was daring me to call it what it was: poison for the soul. I felt my mouth go dry.

A cup sat between us anyway—already cold, herbs swirling in a sour black broth that looked like it could kill something small and determined.

I nodded at it. "You forgot to drink."

Her eyes flicked to the cup. "That brew's waiting for another throat, detective."

I took out my notebook. Old-school. Spiral-bound. Pages crinkled with sweat and bad decisions.

"You told the department you had information about Jessa Gable."

She didn't look at me. "She interfered."

"With what?"

Her eyes shifted. Landed on the fireplace mantle. An old photograph sat there. Two figures. Faces gouged away with a knife or maybe a desperate thumb.

"You and him," I said.

Her breath shivered out. "Jareth Vale. My husband."

My pen scratched the paper like claws on old wood.

"Tell me about the ritual."

Her mouth quirked. Call it a smile and you'd be lying to yourself. This was the kind of grimace that only comes after burying hope so deep even the worms can't find it.

"I didn't say it was a ritual."

"You didn't have to."

I glanced at the floor. Sigils were carved and half-scrubbed, but not gone. Spiral lines like twisted logic, triangles locking intention into shape. Words etched so deeply they seemed to stain the boards. Symbols meant to make something stay. Or come back. Symbols I'd seen again and again, drawn in sidewalk chalk by screaming kittens. Scratched into cardboard boxes I'd woken up in, orange fur stuck to the blood. The same damned pattern.

"Trying to bring him back," I said quietly. "You tried to resurrect him."

She flinched.

"Not resurrection." Her voice cracked. "Restoration."

I kept my voice level. "He died in a fire."

Her fingers gripped the chair arms until the skin went white.

"They told me it was an accident. But accidents don't chant. Accidents don't carve symbols. Accidents don't *take*." Her voice broke on that last word.

I waited.

She wiped her eyes with the heel of her hand.

"*Summon*?" She spat the word like a bad tooth. "I *asked*, Mr. Cannon. Like a widow begs at a graveside."

"Who answered?"

She smiled. Thin. Bloodless.

"Who do you think?"

My cigarette burned low. Ash fell onto my coat like dirty snow.

"Jessa came here to stop you."

Her silence confirmed it.

"She saw the sigils. She saw you calling something you thought was him."

Her fingers drummed on the chair, sharp and deliberate. Like code only she understood.

"She interfered," she repeated. "She didn't understand."

"Explain it to me."

She laughed. It wasn't a sound that belonged indoors.

"The world doesn't want to give back what it takes. You know that. It punishes you for even trying. But there are rules. Reflections. Anchors. Will. If you're strong enough—"

She stopped. Bit her lip until blood welled up, one drop trailing to her chin. I watched it fall.

"You tried to anchor him in something alive," I said.

Her eyes snapped to mine. And for a moment, the room felt like it was holding its breath.

"I want to see the other room," I said.

She shook her head.

"No."

"Now."

"No."

My voice dropped. Gravel and bourbon.

"Lady, pleasantries died three cigarettes back. Let's cut to the marrow."

Her gaze sharpened, two pinpricks of cold light.

She laughed. "Men like you spend lifetimes avoiding what waits in that room."

I stood. The chair creaked.

"Lady, I've walked through hell wearing gasoline pajamas. Whatever's behind that door can take a number."

She didn't move.

"Do you think this is your case?" she asked softly. "You think you're the hero? You're just another vessel, detective. You're just another *mirror*."

The air felt thick enough to chew. My hand went to my coat pocket. I wasn't reaching for the notebook anymore.

She didn't flinch. She just smiled that awful, broken smile.

My hand twitched near my coat pocket. Not for the notebook. For the gun I no longer carried. For the comfort of a grip, cold steel, decisions that ended in certainty. But there was no comfort here. Only the memory of control, crumbling like the walls around us.

"Come back at dusk," she whispered. "If you really want to see what's left of my husband."

The room seemed to shrink. The cold tea steamed suddenly, though no heat touched it. Outside, the wind rattled the windows like it wanted in.

I didn't thank her. I turned and walked out. The door closed behind me without help.

Jessa's voice in my ear. *"Don't go alone."*

Too late.

I walked down the porch steps slowly, cigarette burned to the filter, the taste of ash and blood in my mouth. The sun was already sinking behind black branches.

And I knew damn well I'd be back at dusk.

Outside, the wind was picking up. A cold promise. I felt it slide under my collar like a blade at my throat. The last sliver of sun struggled through the trees, turning the grass the color of old bruises. I lit another cigarette, the flame shaking just enough to remind me my hands weren't steady. I didn't want to come back. But I would. Because that's the job. Because someone has to. Because I'm an idiot.

The side room swallowed me the second I crossed the threshold. The door creaked like a guilty conscience behind me—the sound a murder weapon makes when you pull it from the drawer years later, still remembering the weight. It was dim, lit by dozens of candles guttering on every shelf and table, wax dripping in chaotic stalagmites, pooling like frozen screams. The air stank of burnt herbs, old incense, and something coppery under it all, like blood someone had tried to scrub but couldn't forget.

At the center of the room sat a low stand draped in black velvet. The fabric was stiff with old stains, candle wax hardened into crude seals. On that makeshift altar rested the thing. The Cognichonk.

It had stopped pretending to be a simple ball of yarn. Brass ribs caged it now, twisted into symbols that hurt to look at—like reading someone else's suicide note and recognizing your own handwriting. Between them, the yarn pulsed slow, deliberate, like a heart that knew better than to stop. Shadows coiled around it like they were listening for orders.

Behind me, the Widow breathed like she was trying not to sob. Or trying not to laugh. I couldn't tell.

"He speaks clearer every day," she said.

I didn't turn. Just took in the room. The melted candles, burned and replaced so many times their ghosts had nowhere left to go. The walls scrawled in looping symbols, blackened in soot. A cat-shaped urn in one corner, occult glyphs scratched so deep they seemed to bleed shadow.

"Cozy," I muttered. "You redecorate yourself or hire a priest on discount?"

She didn't answer. Just watched the Cognichonk like it might wink at her.

"He meowed," she whispered. Her voice cracked in the middle. "I thought I had him back."

I exhaled slow. My hand twitched toward my pocket for a cigarette I didn't light.

"It's a cat toy," I said, voice cold. "With ideas above its station."

Her breath rattled.

"The cats helped. The sigils guided. The voices obeyed."

I turned to look at her. Her hair was pinned so tightly it looked like it hurt. She was shaking, but she didn't seem to notice. Her eyes were pale and sharp at once, like glass knives trying to cut their way out.

She built a confessional out of fur and bad intentions, I thought, words scratching at the inside of my skull. *Lit candles for lies she called hope.*

"Listen," she whispered. She was crying now. But the tears didn't fall. Just clung to the rims of her eyes like they were too scared to leave.

"Hear him."

I shifted my weight. My shoulders itched. My teeth hurt. My ears rang like someone had whispered a secret too close.

"Lady, I left my Ouija board in my other trenchcoat," I snapped.

"Please."

That one word hung in the room like smoke. I moved closer. Boots scraping on the warped boards. The Cognichonk pulsed once, a lazy, mocking glow.

The yarn inside wasn't normal. Fibers the color of old blood and rust tangled with something slicker, stranger— like wet sinew pretending to be string. It writhed just a hair, like it knew I was watching.

My hand hovered over it. The brass was tarnished but warm. Symbols flickered like they were waiting to be read. I felt something uncoil behind my ribs. Recognition. A memory that wasn't mine, a flicker of orange fur dashing across an alley, teeth bared in a snarl that sounded like my own voice.

I ground my teeth.

"No."

Her voice broke.

"Hear him."

I reached out anyway. I had to. Because I'm an idiot.

My fingers brushed the brass. The purring started as a

low rumble and turned into a roar that rattled my teeth. The candles flared, coughing smoke. Wax split and dripped in furious rivulets. The air thickened, pressed against my lungs. The walls rippled with crawling shadows that twisted into spirals, intersecting lines.

Reflection. Anchor. Will. The words pounded at the walls of my skull. Not just words. Instructions. Demands. Memories I hadn't lived clawing their way out. For a heartbeat I felt every orange cat yowling in unison, their bodies arching in pain or ecstasy, all part of the same damn pattern I was too stubborn to see.

The Widow dropped to her knees. She wasn't crying anymore. Her eyes rolled back, showing nothing but white. Her mouth worked, chanting in a voice that wasn't hers: "Reflection. Anchor. Will."

My hand was glued to the Cognichonk. Heat and cold at once. It burned my palm, sank hooks under my nails. I felt it crawl up my arm, wiring itself into my veins. I tried to scream but my mouth was full of fur. The purring shook the floor. It wasn't sound. It was law. I saw cats everywhere. Orange shapes, mouths open, yowling in chorus. I heard my own voice echoing out of them.

Jessa's face broke through the swirl. She was screaming. I screamed her name.

The Cognichonk pulsed once. The world split open in orange light and spiraling shadows. Sound fractured. The walls collapsed into endless purring. And I fell.

The world peeled off me like old skin, raw and screaming underneath. Light fractured into orange prisms, each one a memory I'd never claimed. I reached for something solid—my name, my past, the case—but it all slipped through blood-slick fingers that weren't even mine anymore. I wasn't falling. I was being *claimed*.

I woke screaming. High. Unhinged. Something between warning and confession clawed out of my throat, raw and feral, bouncing off damp brick and rusted dumpster lids. I choked it back, but it wouldn't die.

The memory hit like a sucker punch to the soul—Jessa. The witch from Bewitched Beans. The one with the satchel and the haunted dartboard. The one who'd examined the relic theft. I'd seen her. Been carried in her damn bag and hadn't even recognized her. My own fractured mind had betrayed me again.

"Jessa," I rasped, the name tasting like guilt and ash. "She warned me. She was right there, and I didn't know her."

My vision swam. Shapes and shadows wavered like heat off blacktop. Alley walls pressed close, tagged in angry spray paint that glowed like sigils when my eyes unfocused.

My fur bristled. Orange. Coarse. Too much of it. Butternugget's body, all tension and scabs and a twitching tail that refused orders. My claws scraped wet pavement, dredging up alley filth that had never seen an honest day's rain.

Angry lady? Spell lady? Smells like burned leaves and sad coffee.

"Yes," I muttered. "The witch. She knew me. She tried to warn me before, and she's still trying. And I was too scattered to see it."

The pieces were coming together, jagged and ill-fitting. The café. The relic thefts. The Widow. The Cognichonk. Jessa had been there all along, watching, waiting. Maybe trying to help. And I'd sat in her satchel, oblivious as a tourist in my own investigation.

The air reeked of rancid oil, sour garbage, wet cardboard scheming in the dark. Rats whispered secrets for crumbs.

I tried to steady my breathing. In. Out. Didn't help. The memories crawled behind my eyes. Candles burning down to guttering stubs. The Widow's voice cracked and raw with worship. Reflection. Anchor. Will.

My chest heaved. I coughed up a snarl borrowed from darker places, a sound shared between man and beast.

I remembered the touch. I remembered her promise. And Jessa's scream.

I lowered myself to the ground, tail flicking like a loaded gun. I had to find the Widow again. And this time, get answers I could live with.

CHAPTER FOURTEEN

My breathing hitched like a bad clutch on black ice. The screaming was over. Done. Left behind like empty bottles after a three-day bender. My throat burned raw, scraped with old rust and confessions—the kind of pain that reminds you some truths weren't meant to be spoken, just drowned in cheap whiskey and cheaper promises.

The room flickered into focus: The Orange Syndicat HQ. If you could call it that.

An abandoned factory pretending to be civilization. Metal walls flaked rust like old scabs. Broken windows funneled dying light through cracked glass like the last gasp of hope in a city that stopped caring. Cardboard forts sprawled in overlapping dominions—kingdoms built on delusion and defended with desperation. Every surface scribbled in crayon sigils, half of them nonsense. And the smell: treachery and cat pee.

I felt Butternugget squirm in my skull.

Homey! he chirped. *I like this one. Smells like power and pee!*

I tried to ignore him. My tail lashed once, twice, refusing orders.

Lick it, he whispered. *Mark it. Make them respect you.*

My claws scraped concrete in answer. *No.*

Butternugget sulked in the dark corners of our mind.

You're no fun. I'm gonna pee later. On something important.

My eyes scanned the room. A ring of orange cats watched each other with militant suspicion. Shadows jerked and danced like gossiping witnesses.

Mittens paced on top of a crumpled moving box. Her tail whipped like punctuation.

"We need an Anchor!" she spat. "We're *losing* the Spiral. It's fraying. We're forgetting everything we know."

The ring shivered with yowls.

Dorito sat at the center on a stack of old ballots, chewing one with holy purpose.

"Democracy," he mumbled proudly. Bits of paper fluttered from his mouth like confetti at a funeral.

Mittens slapped him. "Stop eating the votes!"

Dorito blinked once. Swallowed defiantly. "Democracy," he repeated.

Good idea, Butternugget suggested, voice bright with mischief. *Eat the evidence. Less paperwork.*

"Shut up," I muttered aloud, earning a round of startled hisses.

Words clawed their way up from my chest, dragging gravel and old regrets. "Keep talking. What else?"

Mittens froze. Her eyes widened. "Luis?"

I tried to steady my breathing. Butternugget tried to bite it.

Say meow! Loud! Show dominance!

"Yeah." I coughed, tasting blood and old fish. "I'm here."

Relief spread through the circle like a shared drug. Even Dorito paused, slack-jawed, dribbling pulp.

Mittens stepped closer, claws half-sheathed. "It's bad, Luis. Some of them are... listening to *her*."

That did it. My hackles rose. Static danced under my skin. The Cognichonk pulsed behind my ribs with a wrong-way heartbeat.

Her. Mallory Vex.

Butternugget's voice quivered. *Pretty voice. Bad yarn. Hurts the head. Don't like her.*

"I need numbers," I rasped. "How many?"

Mittens swallowed. "Enough. Enough to split us. They say she gives them lucidity. Memory. But it's tight. Binding. Wrong." Her voice dropped to a whisper, the kind reserved for confessions at the bottom of bottles and prayers at the edge of graves.

Dorito perked up. "She gives better dreams."

Mittens cuffed him. "Those aren't dreams. They're *leashes*."

The circle shifted. Tails lashed. Growls caught in throats.

Butternugget whined, *I don't like leashes. Or baths. Or rules.*

I forced my spine to straighten. Forced my voice into something cold. Steady. *Mine.*

"You want an Anchor?"

Silence swallowed them whole. Even the flickering light seemed to hold its breath. I felt Butternugget squirm.

No Anchors. Boo. CHAOS.

I ground my teeth. "Then *listen*."

A growl rumbled through the room. Echoed in me. *Us.*

Butternugget hissed. *Scratch them all! Bite their ears!*

"Shut up," I whispered. They didn't know if it was to them or myself.

"Listen," I repeated louder. "We don't bow to her leash. We don't eat the goddamn votes. We remember. Even when it *hurts*. Especially then."

Dorito lifted a paw. "Can we *chew* them?"

My tail lashed so hard I nearly tipped over.

Let him chew, Butternugget sang. *Let him be freeeee.*

"No."

"Fascist," Dorito grumbled.

"Better me than *her*."

Mittens' eyes glowed in the shadows. A slow nod. "Will you lead us?"

My mouth dried. The cardboard walls pressed in. The smell of stale urine and fear filled my head.

Butternugget laughed, *Scary. Fun. Tell them to follow you to the tuna pile!*

I shut him out. As much as I could. My voice dropped low. Dark.

"I'll anchor you. But you'll *think*. No more cult crap. No more screaming at shadows. We do this the hard way. Together."

Silence.

Dorito farted. A hissed argument broke out. But this time it sounded like planning. And somewhere deep in the back of my skull, Butternugget sulked.

Fine. he mumbled. *But I'm peeing on the plan later.*

And far behind that, even deeper, the Cognichonk purred. It ignored me, passed me over like yesterday's promises. But it sang for *us*.

I pressed deeper into the circle. The air was heavy with old tuna and older grudges. It felt like a furry town hall from hell, the kind that starts with a petition and ends with blood on the ballots.

My claws clicked on the concrete. Butternugget's instincts tugged at my nerves, itching for a fight I wasn't ready to lose. My tail lashed behind me—impatient, treacherous. Around me, the Orange Syndicat was already fracturing.

Mango reclined across a warped wooden crate like he'd been sculpted there. His sleek fur gleamed under the flickering work lamp, golden stripes rippling as he stretched one paw with leisurely disdain. He looked amused, the way a fox might look at a hen house with an unlocked door.

"I suppose," Mango said, voice soft and smooth as stolen cream, "we could vote for Luis. Or for me. Or," his whiskers twitched, "we could do something truly novel and not vote at all. Just let the strongest mind take the lead."

Clawrence's ears flattened. His lip curled, fangs gleaming. "Shut it, seducer. We need discipline, not another of your little games."

Mango's eyes half-lidded. "Everything's a game, Clawrence. You simply lack the grace to play."

Across the room, Bosco still hadn't moved. He sat on a sagging crate, watching me with unblinking focus. I'd faced down two-bit killers and mob enforcers who fidgeted more than this old tomcat. His unblinking stare had the patience of cemetery dirt.

I turned to address the crowd. "Listen to me—"

A loud crunch cut me off. Shrimp was gnawing a hole into the wall again, eyes wide, pupils blown. He didn't blink as he spoke.

"The pantry god rises!" Shrimp screeched, bits of plaster stuck to his whiskers. "Twelve paws! Twelve! A spiral in every sock drawer! The window will bleed fish!"

Nobody moved to stop him. Nobody even looked surprised.

Dorito scuttled into the middle of the room, brandishing a battered pen caked with congealed tuna. "I propose myself as Anchor!" he announced. "I have vision! Passion!" He licked the pen. "And snacks!"

Clawrence lunged without warning, knocking Dorito onto his back. They rolled across the floor in a flurry of claws and howls. Gingersnap leapt in, trying to pull them apart.

"Stop it!" Gingersnap yowled. "We're supposed to be a collective—!"

Dorito shrieked, "This is a collective! A collective of idiots!"

Gingersnap got flattened as Clawrence slammed Dorito into the cardboard fortress. Crumpled boxes rained down like cheap barricades.

I tried to reason with them, but my voice vanished under the noise. It was democracy at its worst: loud, unwashed, and ready to kill each other over a can of discount tuna.

Mango flicked his tail, looking bored. "This is beneath us."

"Then help me end it," I snapped.

He tilted his head. "Perhaps. But chaos is clarifying."

Shrimp cackled, spinning in a tight circle as the brawl escalated. His voice dropped into a guttural chant:

"When the twelve unite, the pantry unlocks. When the yarn splits, the dreamer mocks. One shall lead, the rest shall fray— But none shall see another day."

Mango's eyes gleamed, thoughtful. "Not his worst verse."

"Focus!" I hissed.

But no one was listening.

Clawrence pinned Dorito to the ground, snarling inches from his face. "You'd sell us all to her!"

Dorito spat a wad of tuna onto Clawrence's cheek. "At least she has a plan!"

I had to act. I pushed forward, tail high, my voice low and flint-sharp. "Enough!"

They kept fighting.

Bosco finally stirred. One paw lifted, slow as dusk. The air shifted.

"Enough," he echoed. The word wasn't loud. It didn't need to be. The tone cracked the room in half.

The brawl froze. Even Shrimp stopped spinning.

Bosco's eyes never left mine. "She cracked the knot," he said softly. "And she'll weave it around whoever survives." The words hung in the air like smoke after a firing squad— lingering long after the damage was done.

The silence that followed was worse than the fighting. Clawrence slowly released Dorito. Mango sat up, no longer amused.

Shrimp's tail curled tight as a noose. He whispered, "The spiral's coming."

I swallowed. The Cognichonk pulsed behind my ribs—a heartbeat in reverse, counting down to a deadline I couldn't see. Butternugget whimpered in my skull, a frightened witness to a crime that hadn't happened yet.

We should leave, he whispered. *Hide in a box. Bite whoever comes near.*

Dread swallowed my voice whole, leaving nothing but ash and echoes. Because Bosco was right. This wasn't a debate. It was an audition.

And the price of winning was everything.

The room was wreckage. Spilled cans bled gravy across the concrete; cardboard forts lay in splintered heaps. Shredded ballots littered the floor like confetti for a failed coup.

I dusted off Butternugget's battered fur, each swipe scraping dried blood, scabs, and equal measures of pride off. My tail flicked in slow, exhausted arcs. Every muscle ached.

I surveyed the wreckage. Call it resistance and you'd be lying to yourself. We'd signed a suicide pact in hairballs and broken pride.

Mango sat off to one side, grooming with meticulous disinterest. He paused only to inspect a blood smear on his flank, then sighed and kept cleaning.

My throat cleared like sandpaper on rust. "Listen up," I tried.

A couple of cats lifted their heads. Most didn't bother. Shrimp was licking the wall again, muttering about pantry gods. Dorito let out a loud snort and rolled over, mumbling "Democracy" in his sleep.

I raised my voice. It cracked, but I kept going. "If we keep fighting like this, she wins."

That got a few ears twitching. I ground my teeth. Butternugget's body wanted to pace, to pounce, to bite anything that moved; I held it steady. Barely.

"She doesn't want unity," I growled. "She wants an Anchor she can control. One who'll trade freedom for lucidity. For memory."

Mango didn't even look up. Just sighed, flexing his claws. "Or seduce," he said lazily. "Let's not discount her talents."

My hackles lifted. "This isn't a joke."

Mango finally met my eyes. For once, the amusement was gone. "I know."

Silence spread through the room like slow poison.

Bosco moved. A single, deliberate step. The floor creaked beneath him. He stood up from his crate, every muscle lean and coiled, eyes black as midnight. He didn't blink. Didn't waver.

"She's already got followers here," he said quietly.

The line landed like a fist in the gut. You could feel it suck the air out of the room. Mango stopped grooming. Shrimp froze mid-lick, eyes huge. Even Dorito let out a troubled snort in his sleep, tail curling protectively. I felt it too. The Cognichonk purred behind my ribs with the cold satisfaction of a predator watching prey stumble.

Butternugget whimpered in the back of my skull.

They'd choose her. The soft one. The safe one. The one who remembers.

I couldn't argue. Because I saw it in their eyes. Some of them would. They'd choose her. Choose the leash. Choose the dream that didn't hurt, even if it meant forgetting everything else.

I swallowed. My voice came out a rasp, half-human, half-feral, as I declared: "This wasn't just a fight for control." The words felt heavy, scraped raw from memory. "It was a vote on who got to own my soul."

My voice cracked on that last word—hoarse, final. The Cognichonk exhaled like a tired killer putting down his gun. It *relaxed*, letting tension leak out like bad air from a worn tire. My mind slipped. Luis Cannon slipped.

Luis Cannon evaporated like cheap booze, leaving Butternugget behind—all instinct and chaos where calculation once lived. He shrieked at the ceiling with unearned rage, tail spiraling like it had independent ambitions. He spun in a tight circle, forgot why halfway through, and fell over sideways. Scrambled up again only to immediately trip over his own leg. He hissed at nothing. Then licked the floor. Then forgot he had a tongue and sneezed so hard he back flipped into a stack of ballots.

Mittens barked for order like a beat cop at a bar fight. Her imperial yowl cut short when gravity betrayed her, sending her tumbling off her cardboard throne. She emerged bristling, eyes wide, as if personally betrayed by gravity.

Dorito giggled. He was on his back, all four paws kicking wildly while he chewed a ballot to pulp, eyes rolling with manic delight. He paused only to shout "Democracy!" before resuming his slobbering desecration.

Shrimp skipped the intermission entirely. He launched himself into a wall at full speed, bounced off with a grunt, then began chanting "pantry god" in increasingly shrill tones while gnawing on a crayon he found behind a box.

Clawrence roared a challenge at Dorito and dove into him like an angry comet, the two becoming an indistinct ball of orange fury and paper shreds.

Gingersnap shrieked at them to stop, tried to intervene, and got body-checked into the debris, where she immediately joined the melee out of pure reflexive rage.

Bosco lifted his head slowly. Watched it all. Blinked once with ancient, scornful patience. Then lowered his head back onto his paws with a long, deliberate sigh, dismissing the entire world as beneath him.

And Mango? Mango sat apart, licking his shoulder with disdain so refined it could have been bottled. But his tail twitched in silent fury. When Shrimp's chanting got too close, he swatted the smaller cat across the nose without even breaking his grooming rhythm.

And Butternugget—oh, Butternugget. He shrieked again. Climbed a box. Fell off. Climbed again. Stood triumphant for two full seconds before forgetting he was standing and rolling off backwards. He froze. Ears forward. Eyes huge. He licked the concrete with intense, mystic focus. Paused. Considered. Then screamed in its face.

Somewhere, behind all of it, the Cognichonk purred. Not for Luis. Not for any one of them. But for all of them. Waiting for next time.

CHAPTER FIFTEEN

I woke in a box too small for dignity and just right for crime. The walls pressed in, cardboard damp and sagging, breathing like lungs filled with gutter stench—the kind of makeshift coffin where dreams go to die and alibis come to practice their lies. Old fish bones lay arranged like runes of regret, soy sauce stains spelling confessions no one would ever read. The box was my cell. My altar. My cradle for violent rebirth.

Mine.

Clawrence's growl scraped up my throat like claws on badge brass. More than noise—a verdict, delivered from the jury box of my ribs. The justice of the alley was simple: you take it, you keep it. No questions asked. No answers given.

Detective instincts died hard in me. Ghosts of a badge I'd worn in another life. Before yarn and the Cognichonk scattered my mind like case files in a windstorm. I tried to think. Build a case. Clawrence wanted something simpler. Blood. Territory. Enforcement as gospel.

My claws punched through the soggy cardboard with a wet rip, leaving evidence of intent and malice in equal measure. I shoved out into the alley like a parolee already planning his next charge.

Clawrence was all bulk and muscle under matted orange fur, ears chewed at the edges like someone had tried negotiating with teeth. Even my thoughts felt heavier in his skull—like rage had mass.

Neon flickered overhead—'DRY CLEANING' with half the letters dead, buzzing in insect Morse about failed dreams and unpaid tabs. Rain slicked the concrete in oil rainbows too pretty to trust—like a con man's smile promising you the world while his hands are already in your pockets.

I shook out my fur. Water spattered like blood at a crime scene.

Scuffling nearby. A shape in the dark. A rat. Or a witness. Same difference.

The smell of blood. Real. Fresh. It cut through the baseline perfume of wet garbage and moldy sin. Clawrence purred at that. A sound with no kindness in it. Justice belonged to people with clean hands and full stomachs. Enforcement ran deeper—a calling etched in bone and fur.

I licked my lips. Clawrence wanted to bite.

Focus, I told myself. Think. Build the case.

There *was* a case. I felt it, buried under Clawrence's hunger. The sigils spreading across town like tumors. The Velvet Paw's smirking threat. Mallory Vex's voice coiling in the dark corners of my mind: *You're not the only one collecting clues, Luis.*

I tried to hold onto it. But Clawrence twitched our tail

like a fuse about to light. We moved forward anyway. Shoulders rolling in threat. Each pawstep a low-grade assault charge.

"Look for motive. Opportunity. Means."

Establish dominance, Clawrence corrected.

The rain picked up. It washed nothing away. Just made everything shine with malice. Somewhere in the dark, a cat yowled. A warning. Or an invitation.

I yowled back. My words. His voice.

God help whoever answered.

I padded forward, tail lashing like an accusation no one wanted to answer. The alley squeezed around me, walls pressing in with damp resignation. Trash bags split open at the seams, leaking half-eaten noodles and the smell of old sins. Water dripped from rusted pipes in slow, mocking applause.

Ahead, movement. Two orange shapes rolled in the filth, yowling like a pair of banshees trapped in fur coats. They weren't just fighting. They were putting on a show.

One had the other in a headlock, back legs bunny-kicking his ribs with the grace of a drunken centipede. The other responded by biting an ear and letting out a squeal so high it could interrogate glassware.

A soggy paper sack lay between them, torn open. Greasy fries spilled out like golden bribes to gutter gods.

One let out a ragged yowl: "Vex promised me an Anchor's cut!"

That name froze the blood in my veins. Mallory Vex. The

Velvet Paw. Making promises to idiots who didn't know better. Or didn't care.

A growl started low in my chest—Clawrence's engine of authority. It rumbled through the trash-laden fog like a warning shot.

Mine, Clawrence insisted. *All this. The alley. The food. Them. Mine.*

They didn't stop. So I didn't warn them twice. I charged.

Good, Clawrence urged. *Break them.*

I hit them like a bowling ball made of fur and bad intentions. We all went sprawling. Fries flew in a greasy arc. One cat hit a puddle. The splash smelled of last week's rain and yesterday's broken promises. The other scrambled upright and arched his back so hard he looked like a croquet wicket made of hate.

Hit harder next time.

I bristled. He bristled back. Then we both let out matching hisses that tasted like copper and insults.

He lunged. I met him halfway.

We collided in a squealing, slashing knot of orange rage. Our claws scraped the pavement, raising sparks and curses.

Yes, Clawrence growled inside me. *Fight's the only truth.*

He tried to bite my nose—I slapped him with a paw so fast it was more sound than substance.

Bite back, Clawrence advised helpfully. *Go for the throat.*

Thwap!

He sneezed. I hissed.

He dove for my tail. I twisted, curling it around his neck like an accusatory scarf, pulling him sideways into a pile of wet newspapers. He exploded from it coughing ink and indignity.

Strangle him. Make him remember.

"Mine!" he shrieked, batting at my face with both front paws in rapid-fire slaps that sounded like someone typing threats.

Even Clawrence sounded impressed. *Good spirit,* he admitted. *Break him.*

"*You* working for her?" I snarled back, trying to keep my voice low and threatening, but it came out sounding like a garbage disposal full of gravel.

Doesn't matter, Clawrence hissed. *He's weak. Make him say it.*

He didn't answer.

So I shoved him, shoulder first, into a dumpster wall with a metallic *clang* that set off a cascade of falling cans. He bounced off the metal with a clang, all wild legs and electric fur. The kind of mess that'd make a bathroom accessory feel professional.

He yowled. I yowled back.

Louder, Clawrence demanded. *Make him scream.*

Meanwhile, the other one recovered and made his move. He pounced at my back leg. I turned just in time to see his jaws clamp on my ankle with all the fury of a toddler chewing on a table leg.

Crush him. Don't let go.

I screamed. He bellowed. I lashed my tail. It hit him in the face. He let go, spitting fur.

"Get off me!"

I lunged, pinning him to the ground with both paws on his chest, our noses nearly touching. His breath smelled like fish bones and lost causes.

Mine.

CONTAINMENT NOT RECOMMENDED

"Talk," I growled. "Or I sharpen my claws on your ribs." The threat hung between us like a broken promise—not elegant, but effective in the gutter economy of pain and truth.

Do it anyway.

He went cross-eyed looking at the paw pressed to his sternum. "Better than following your dead-end tail!"

So I gave him a half-claw flex—enough to sting but not to shred.

He yowled and went limp.

"I'll talk! I'll talk!"

The other cat tried to sneak away.

"Don't even think about it," I snapped without looking. My tail lashed sideways, smacking him in the face. He squeaked in surprise and sat down hard.

I turned back to my pinned prize.

"She's recruiting," he blurted. "Promising power. Said she knows how to use the Chonk. Said she'd make us kings. Priests. Gods." His voice trembled with the desperation of a two-bit hustler who'd finally found a racket worth dying for.

He shuddered. I felt it under my paw.

Clawrence didn't care. *Pack. Weaklings need a boss. Kill or lead.*

The air in the alley stank of wet fur and fear.

I leaned closer. My nose almost touching his.

"She's lying," I hissed.

He whimpered. "Maybe. Don't care. Better than starving."

The words cut. Not because they were wrong. Because they were too right.

I released him. He squirmed free, dragging his dignity behind him like a cheap suit.

Should've finished him.

I turned to the other one.

He was licking a paw like he hadn't just been part of a street brawl worthy of an insurance claim. He froze when I stared at him.

"You," I growled.

He blinked. "What? You want my fries too?"

I stepped forward. He tensed. But Clawrence's rage was cooling. The alley felt quieter. Watching eyes blinked in the shadows. More orange cats. Half-hidden. Half-afraid. Half-ready to jump in if the mood shifted.

They're watching. Good. Let them learn.

But they didn't. They watched. Waiting to see who was boss. Who was worth following. Who was worth betraying.

My voice dropped to something less than a snarl, more than a threat.

"She'll use you. Chew you up and spit you out when she's done. She doesn't want you strong. She wants you loyal."

He flattened his ears. "At least she *wants* us."

I didn't have an answer for that. Because Luis Cannon might. But Clawrence didn't give a damn. I took a breath that rattled in my ribs. Tasted blood. My blood? His? Hard to tell.

My claws clicked against wet pavement as I pulled back. I let them go. Because I could kill them. Or I could warn them. And right now? Warnings were cheaper. Justice was a luxury I couldn't afford. So I settled for the truth.

Truth is teeth.

I turned and stalked away, my tail flicking like punctuation behind me. The alley settled into silence, broken only by the soft rustle of trash and the distant drip of water.

Behind me, I heard them shuffle. Mutter. Reconsider. Some slinked off into the dark. Others sat, tails flicking, eyes narrow, watching me go.

Factions were forming. Lines were being drawn in the grime. And I wasn't sure which side of the line I was on.

Clawrence purred, low and savage. Not content. Just ready. Ready for the next fight. Ready for the next confession forced out with claws and teeth.

Next time, Clawrence promised. *We don't ask.*

And somewhere deep inside me, Luis Cannon sighed like a man realizing he didn't have the budget for mercy anymore—another moral bankruptcy in a ledger already drowning in red ink.

I limped back through the alley, claws scraping damp pavement. My fur told the story better than any police report—rainwater and blood where the perp had left his signature, indignity where I'd signed mine. Each step protested like an old man with unpaid parking tickets in his knees.

Good fight, Clawrence insisted, satisfaction vibrating through me. *We need more.*

I ignored him. For now. The box waited at the alley's end. Clawrence's nest. His kingdom built out of trash. It wasn't just a box. It was a fortress.

Cardboard walls stacked and braced with damp pizza boxes. Crushed soda cans perched like gargoyles. Torn rags for bedding. A takeout menu gnawed to pulp, its teeth marks spelling some primal script. The stench hit like a pawnshop at closing time—fish bones gone south, defiance gone stale, and curry that asked more questions than it answered.

I pushed my way inside. Darkness folded around me like a cheap suit. Clawrence's musk hung in the air, territorial as a loan shark. We'd signed the deed in blood and bad decisions.

Mine, he breathed.

"Yeah," I muttered. "Ours."

I sank onto the rags with a grunt. My side throbbed where claws had found purchase. My tail lashed irritably, batting a half-eaten fortune cookie off the bedding.

The walls were tagged in old graffiti. Human curses layered in spray-paint palimpsests. Symbols from gangs that thought they owned this stretch before four-legged turf wars convinced them otherwise.

But something new glared back. Scrawled in grime and what might have been blood: **Anchor. Reflection. Spiral.**

A cold knot tightened in my gut. Anchors weren't chosen. They were promised.

Claimed, Clawrence corrected.

I felt my lip curl. A snarl worked up my throat. Because I knew Vex's style. She didn't recruit. She *bound.* She promised. And she kept her promises better than I ever did.

I reached out a paw and scraped at the sigil until the cardboard peeled in damp curls. Letters fell apart like too-late confessions. Something crinkled beneath my claws. I paused. Sniffed. Buried in the rags was a scrap of paper. Half-chewed. Water-stained. I flipped it over. Human print.

FAILED STABILIZATION

Two words. That was all. But enough.

I let out a breath that felt like rust leaving old hinges. The faction fight wasn't coming. It was already here.

Clawrence's satisfaction settled over me, pleased at the scent of blood in the air.

They'll choose sides. Or we'll choose for them.

I shook my head. Tried to clear the static. But the alley's silence pressed close, too thick, too knowing.

I crouched lower, claws kneading rags. Felt the city's rotten pulse beating in my ribs. Felt the Cognichonk's hum behind my eyes like a second, faithless heart.

If this was my city, it was time to start acting like it.

But lucidity only lasts so long. The Cognichonk's pulse stuttered behind my eyes. Clarity thinned like cheap soup stretched too far.

I felt my thoughts fray. Case notes dissolving. Names slipping. Purpose curdling into instinct. I tried to hold on. But the box felt safe. Dark. Mine.

The last thing I remembered clearly was the smell of blood and damp cardboard, the promise of war scrawled on the walls.

Then Luis Cannon was gone. And Clawrence was all that remained.

The Cognichonk's hum faded behind my eyes like a dying spark. Luis clawed at the edges of my thoughts—then slipped away.

Good. Didn't need him now.

I blinked. Slow. Heavy-lidded. The fight still stung in my muscles like satisfaction. My nose was wet. One ear twitched from a bite that would scab over nicely.

I turned in my box, claws flexing in the rags.

My kingdom. My den. My stink everywhere. Mine.

The words on the wall meant nothing. Lines. Shapes. Smell of blood and fear. All good.

Fancy talk.

I spat at them.

Not mine. *Mine is this.*

Old blankets. Damp cardboard. Grease from stolen fries rubbed into the floor like an offering.

I sniffed.

Still smelled like them. The ones I beat. The ones who yowled about Vex and promised and begged.

Good. Let them remember.

I licked my paw and wiped it over my ear, wincing at the split skin. A badge of enforcement. I settled onto my side, curling my tail like a question mark I didn't need answered.

My box creaked when I shifted. Good. It knew who was inside.

Outside, the alley breathed. Shifted. Rats rustled. Cats watched.

Mine. All of them. They'd try again. Fight. Pick sides.

I yawned wide enough to threaten the night.

Let them. I'd beat them again. Or kill them. Didn't matter which. As long as they knew. *Mine.*

My purr started deep, low. A rumble that threatened to become a growl but didn't have to. Not tonight.

Tonight I was king. Tonight the alley was quiet. Quiet was good. Quiet meant they remembered.

I let my eyes half-close. Watched the dark shift around me. My claws flexed once, slow.

Ready. Always ready. Because tomorrow? Tomorrow someone would forget. And I'd remind them.

CHAPTER SIXTEEN

I came to with my face buried in a stack of receipts and regret. The old oak counter of The Clairvoyant Cat groaned under my weight like it was tired of the charade—like it had witnessed too many false promises sold by the ounce and paid for in broken dreams. Ink stains. Grease spots. A ledger of small-town occult dreams, paid in cash and wishful thinking. The lights hung low, drowning in Anna's idea of after-hours atmosphere. My throat betrayed me with every vibration—a purr that wouldn't quit, wouldn't apologize, wouldn't do anything but announce my tabby-shaped sins to the empty shop.

Don't fight it, Mango crooned, warm and drowsy in my skull. *She likes the sound.*

"The purr is a lie," I growled back.

So is love. Your point?

I lifted my head slowly, ears flicking at every creak in the floorboards. Overstuffed shelves leaned like conspirators caught mid-whisper. Dust motes drifted in the lamplight like slow, accusing thoughts—the kind that visit you at 3 AM when the whiskey's gone but the guilt's still pouring. Cinnamon tea gone cold, wax from candles burned too long, paper yellowed with age—the shop reeked of it all. The kind of smell that makes you think every page turned here whispered something it shouldn't have.

But beneath it—ozone. Like the memory of lightning.

My eyes cut to the sigils pinned behind the counter. Ink on yellowed parchment. Protective wards, maybe. But drawn wrong. Asymmetrical. Frantic—like prayers scribbled by a man who knows the devil's already in the room, counting down his heartbeats. Some scrawled over older marks, the ink cracked like dried blood. When the candle guttered, they seemed to twitch. Enough to raise the hackles on my back.

Pretty, aren't they? Mango sighed. *She collects them for me.*

"She doesn't know what she's collecting."

Details.

Footsteps on warped floorboards. Slow. Careful. Each creak sounded like a confession she didn't want to make.

"Mango?" Her voice. Soft as a promise you knew would break.

There she is. Mango warmed. *Look at her.*

I did. Against my better judgment. Anna Mae Bellamy. Her hair never stayed put—strands breaking free from that bun like confessions she couldn't keep bottled up. Ink smeared on one cheek like a half-finished ward—another promise made in haste and abandoned when reality came knocking with its brass knuckles. Candle smoke clung to her clothes. Cheap tea on her breath. And something else—that sharp tang that only comes from staring at the ceiling till dawn three nights running.

But it wasn't just her scent that turned my stomach. It was the way her eyes kept flicking over her shoulder. Checking the shadows. Like she'd invited something in and wasn't sure she could uninvite it.

She paused, brow creased.

"You okay? You fell asleep on the register again."

Mango surged, tail curling like a question he already knew the answer to. He licked his paw and wiped his face with calculated innocence.

Watch this.

"Stop it," I snapped internally.

Let me work.

She exhaled, shoulders sagging. That same cracked smile she gave customers desperate for meaning. The hunger was there, behind her eyes. The need to *believe*.

She wants magic, Mango purred, pleased. *I am magic.*

"You're a cat."

That makes a difference, how?

She stepped closer. The air shifted. Her scent hit me like a memory. Jasmine. Ink. Sweat. And something else—like old static, clinging too tight.

My claws dug into the wood. I wanted to pull back. Mango wanted to crawl into her lap and stay there forever.

Warm. Safe. Ours.

"Not yours. Not mine."

Her hand trembled before it landed on my head. Mango butted into it without hesitation.

Soft.

I tried to hold back the snarl. It escaped as a thunderous

purr. She closed her eyes at the sound. Like it was prayer. Like it saved her.

"There you are," she whispered. "I don't know what I'd do without you."

She means it, Mango purred smugly.

"That's the tragedy."

She rubbed under my chin. Mango melted. My body pressed into her palm like confession.

Good. Purr louder.

The candle behind her sputtered. Smoke twisted into shapes I didn't want to recognize. Letters. A sigil half-burned, half-alive. And beneath it—etched in thin white scars along her wrist, revealed only when her sleeve slipped —a looping spiral.

My eyes narrowed. "She's marked."

Stop ruining it, Mango sulked. *She's happy. I'm happy. That's the point.*

"It's not the point."

I studied the mark. Too clean. Deliberate. A controlling bind, not a protective ward. Not her work. No—it was Vex's style. The Velvet Paw's signature. Control dressed up as a gift.

She leaned her forehead against mine. "I had such a bad day," she breathed. "The supplier screwed me. Rent's going up. I can't keep doing this."

Mango licked her nose.

We'll keep her.

"We can't."

Why not?

"Because someone already did."

My tail lashed. She flinched.

"Mango?"

I tried to warn her. My mouth opened, but only a deep, resonant purr came out. It vibrated through her bones. She exhaled. Trusted me.

Good, Mango sighed. *She's ours.*

No. She was never ours. And in the flicker of the candle, the smoke curled into a question mark. And somewhere in that smoke, something laughed.

Anna carried me like a relic through the dim aisles of The Clairvoyant Cat, one arm cradling my ribs, the other steadying a candle that threatened to snuff itself out with every step.

The back room was worse than the front. Overfilled shelves groaned under antique grimoires with cracked spines and questionable provenance. Candles had dripped wax in elaborate ruins along the floorboards, accidental or deliberate. Hard to tell.

She set me down gently on a warped oak desk. The desk had taken more punishment than a confession room chair—burns where desperate candles died, ink that would never wash out. Every stain told a story somebody should've kept to themselves.

"Stay," she whispered.

I always do, Mango thought dreamily. *Because she needs us.*

I ignored him. My tail flicked once, the only betrayal of the tension coiled under my fur.

Anna fumbled with a heavy leather-bound book, its

cover stamped with a sigil even I recognized: an Initiate's Mark, but drawn in a rush. A student's mistake.

"My grandmother's journal," she muttered. "I've been reading through it again."

The candlelight shivered as she cracked the spine. Pages yellowed with age released the dry, suffocating scent of old secrets. She ran a fingertip along the lines, voice unsteady.

"Listen to this: 'Arietta Vale bargained for return. Paid in memory, received only grief. Warn the next who asks.'"

My ears flattened.

Vale. The name landed like a brick in the gut. I'd heard it before, whispered behind cracked doors. Always around the worst cases—resurrections that went wrong. Anchors that broke. The kind of ritual the Widow had covered her walls in blood to attempt.

Mango licked his shoulder absently. *Pretty name.*

"Shut up."

Anna kept reading.

"'Failed resurrection. Anchor severed. Vessel unbound. It hunts what it cannot hold.'"

She stopped. Her thumb trembled on the edge of the page. I studied her face in the wavering candlelight. The shadows deepened the hollows under her eyes. Ink smudges marked her like old bruises. She hadn't slept enough in weeks—too many nights poring over symbols she barely understood, trying to make them mean safety.

She swallowed hard. "I think whoever did this... didn't figure it out alone."

My tail lashed. She flinched but didn't back away.

"This Vale woman," she said more quietly. "She might

have taught them. Or sold them the ritual." She paused. Looked straight at me. "Mango?"

I tensed. She studied me—brows drawn, eyes shining with frustration and fear.

"You know something about this, don't you?"

I let the silence breathe. Let the room press in.

The smoke from the candle twisted into a coil. Memory pulsed behind my eyes: the Widow's crumbling house, walls covered in sigils that wept wax and blood. The air had reeked of burned herbs and spoiled milk. I remembered the half-finished circle etched into the floor with something that wasn't paint. And Jessa's voice, hoarse from screaming, begging me to leave it alone before it woke up again.

Mango yawned. *We could bite her hair to distract her.*

"Not now."

Anna turned the page, eyes scanning, breath hitching.

"Look."

She angled the book so the candlelight hit an old, water-stained diagram. A spiral. Tight. Uneven. At its center, an anchor rune—crossbar flared like claws reaching for something to hold onto in the dark. The kind of symbol that doesn't just invite trouble—it sends engraved invitations with your address already written in blood. I felt the Cognichonk hum. Low. Hungry. Anna traced it with her finger.

"She says it was meant to hold the soul in place," she murmured. "But it broke. And it let something in."

Something crawled up from my gut—the kind of growl that makes smart people back away. Anna wasn't feeling smart tonight.

"Mango, stop."

She grabbed a pen and a scrap of parchment.

She's gonna copy it, Mango warned, suddenly alert.

"No."

I lunged, batting the pen from her grip. It clattered to the floor and rolled under a shelf.

"Mango!"

She swore under her breath, stooping to retrieve it. My tail lashed again, claws biting the desk.

Good, Mango said, though he sounded rattled. *I don't like it.*

Anna straightened slowly, the candle guttering dangerously in her other hand.

"What is your problem?"

I flattened my ears. Let the rumble in my chest carry meaning I couldn't put to words.

"These are dangerous symbols," she snapped. "I'm trying to learn how to protect myself."

"Not like that," I thought savagely.

I hauled myself up like a drunk at closing time, all business now. Got close enough to the journal that I could taste the old paper's lies. The growl in my chest wouldn't quit—the same warning I'd given to killers and mailmen. She set the candle down so hard it spat wax across the desk.

"I'm not some clueless bystander," she hissed. "I'm the only one who even tries to understand you."

The words hit like a slap. Silence folded in. Even Mango shut up. The candle's flame steadied. I let the growl fade. Sat back on my haunches. Forced myself to think.

"She's right," I admitted.

Mango blinked. *She's ours.*

"She's not ours to keep safe. She's here. And she's involved."

I closed my eyes for half a heartbeat. When I opened them, I stared straight at her. She watched me. Breathing hard. Hands shaking. I wanted to tell her to run. To stay. To scratch my ears until this whole mess blew over. None of those options were on the table for a detective trapped in nine pounds of orange fur.

Finally, I gave her wrist the gentlest headbutt in my repertoire—the kind reserved for witnesses who've seen too much but still might help. Her shoulders folded like a bad poker hand.

"Mango?"

I rumbled. Quieter. She sniffed, blinking too fast. I watched the smoke from the candle curl around us. It formed a spiral and broke apart before it could finish.

"They aren't shields," I thought, trying to will the words into her. "They're doors."

"Don't open them," I whispered inside Mango's skull.

I pressed my forehead to her wrist harder. Growled low. Warning. Pleading. The candle guttered. Shadows danced. Anna's eyes reflected something older than her years. None of us were getting out of this clean.

She sniffed, blinking too fast. Looked down at me.

"Okay," she whispered, voice cracking.

Her fingers trembled against my cheek like a rookie's first time drawing a weapon. We stayed like that. The candle burned lower. Wax ran in rivulets like the aftershocks of old magic gone wrong. Somewhere in the room, the shadows rearranged themselves. The sigils on the walls shuddered and fell still. The sigils weren't just bad news—they were the kind of bad news that gets delivered at 3 AM by something wearing your dead uncle's face.

But the journal lay open between us. And on the page, the anchor still waited.

We stumbled back into the store's front room. The candle burned low, the flame choking on its own wax. Shadows huddled in corners like conspirators. Anna clutched the journal to her chest. Her breathing ragged, eyes darting over the clutter of half-finished wards and cheap incense.

"Mango," she whispered. Voice cracking. Pleading for calm.

She's scared, I realized. Of me. Of this.

Mango didn't care. He watched her with wide, unblinking eyes. Tail twitching like a metronome set to want.

"Stop," I warned.

But the air was thick with old paper and cinnamon, and Mango liked her trapped. Liked her having nowhere to go. He moved before I could stop him. Slid against her side, purring so loud it vibrated the floorboards.

Warm. Safe. Ours.

"Don't," I hissed. But it was too late.

He butted his head against her, slinking higher, rumbling against her ribs. She stiffened, breath catching.

"Mango—"

Mine.

He pressed close, purring deep and guttural, marking her in sound and scent.

"Stop. Don't—"

But the words were mine, not his. Mango ignored me. He twisted, licking her wrist where the ink hid. She shivered. The air snapped like a struck match. Behind her, the pinned sigils twisted in the failing light. Paper curled in the heat of unseen flame. Ink ran like blood on parchment.

A single sigil burned itself into revelation. A spiral. An anchor at its heart. And in the mirror behind the counter, the symbol glowed.

Anna gasped. Her eyes flicked to the glass and went wide with horror. Smoke curled off the parchment, black and oily. Letters twisted in the haze.

A voice slithered out. Low. Sweet. Cruel. "Oh, clever boy. So easy to make you dance."

Anna screamed, clutching her head. The journal fell to the floor, pages splaying like a dead bird's wings.

"Stop it!" I howled. But my voice was buried under Mango's purr.

Mine.

He wrapped his tail around her wrist. Possessive. Binding.

Ours.

Her knees found the floor before her mind caught up to the betrayal. Down she went, like every mark who ever trusted the wrong smile.

"You always did have a thing for partners, Cannon," the smoke whispered. "So easy to make you sell them out."

I fought. Clawed at the walls of Mango's mind. But the Cognichonk pulsed behind my eyes like a second heart. Mango turned, pressing his forehead to hers. Purring like a promise. Her eyes went vacant—not the empty stare of

210

shock but the thousand-yard gaze of someone being rewritten from the inside out.

"Shhh," Vex crooned from the smoke. "Let it happen."

Anna sobbed. One lick. That's all it took. The oldest con in the book—the gentle touch that signs the death warrant. And I'd let it happen. Control didn't just slip away—it laughed in my face as it packed its bags, leaving nothing but cat instinct and the taste of failure.

Good, Mango rumbled. *She's ours now.*

My voice shredded in my head. "No. Don't. Don't do this—"

But the purr drowned me out. Low. Relentless. Triumphant. And somewhere in the purr, I heard Vex laughing.

I felt myself tearing free. Not by choice. The Cognichonk pulsed—once. Hard. Like it was yanking the leash. Mango's body bucked under me, but I wasn't there anymore. I was being dragged out, my mind unspooling in static and claws. Anna's scream cut off like a dropped call. Her face burned behind my eyes—eyes that weren't mine now.

I tried to hold on. Tried to scream her name. The orange void didn't invite me in—it mugged me at the corner of consciousness and sanity, dragging me down where even prayers go to die. And the last thing I felt was *Mango's purr,* satisfied.

CHAPTER SEVENTEEN

My claws were out before I was even awake. Dragging a gouge across the cold concrete. An instinctive promise. His shoulders bunched under thick fur, every muscle remembering a fight it hadn't lost yet—a body primed for violence like a loaded gun just waiting for a finger to twitch on the trigger. The weight was different. Heavier. More certain.

I woke up angry. Not the simple kind. The layered, crusted kind that's earned over lifetimes. Mango's purr still rang in my ears like a confession made under duress. He'd enjoyed it. He'd *sold her out.*

And now I was here. In Jake Speed. Jake was all bulk and velvet threat. A lion in a world of squeaks. Muscle and mass coiled around grudges older than the factory walls.

Still body. Slow breath, Jake thought. *Power speaks louder than hisses.*

I wrestled for the wheel. Jake didn't fight me, exactly. He held on, stubborn as old evidence. We negotiated control with every breath. I growled. Low. Testing the voice. It came out as promise and threat in equal measure. The Cognichonk pulsed behind my eyes, sour and smug. It hadn't just pulled me here—it wanted this meeting. Or maybe it needed witnesses.

Good, Jake observed. *Let your scent fill the space. Show them your teeth mean business.*

The War Room fell quiet. Broken windows were boarded in desperate geometry. Candles guttered in beer cans, their feeble flames throwing shadows like knives—the kind of makeshift illumination that only highlights the darkness it can't touch, like hope in a city that stopped believing. The chalk sigils sprawled across cracked concrete, looping in spirals that pretended control even as they invited something older to answer. This wasn't just any gathering. The hum had driven us all here, like cats pulled on strings we pretended we didn't see.

Bad hunting ground, Jake noted. *Too many escape routes. Decent high perches though.*

Crates were thrones. Cats spread in a semicircle like jurors with convictions prewritten. Dorito perched up high, tail flicking out insults in Morse. Mango lounged, too casual, eyes half-lidded and glittering with unearned confidence— the look of a con man who's counted all the exits and knows exactly which one he'll use when the deals go south and the bullets start flying.

I let my gaze rest on him. My lip twitched.

That one's marked by trouble, Jake thought. *Tail says confidence. Eyes say liar. Don't break gaze first.*

I didn't.

Shrimp rocked in the corner, muttering scripture that

only made sense to madmen and prophets. Clawrence shredded a crate corner in perfect rhythm, a metronome for violence. Bosco sat against the back wall, silent as a tomb that had a witness protection program.

I cleared my throat. It came out as a rumble that made Dorito's ears flatten. Mango didn't move. Didn't blink.

"Glad you could join us," he drawled.

"Don't," I warned.

Clean strike, Jake approved. *Few sounds. Clear threat. The pack understands strength.*

Dorito's gaze flicked between us. "Problems, Jake?"

I bared my teeth. "Just unfinished business."

Anna's scream echoed behind my eyes. Mango's purr. Mine. Mango's whiskers twitched. His tail curled around his paws like he was some smug prophet who'd already read the ending.

"Really?" he purred. "You want to go over that *now*? Or do you want to tell us why you're really here?"

Jake's voice cut through, cold and dry. *Take him down now. Mark him as prey. But you need the colony. Deal with the biggest threat first.*

I exhaled through my nose. "Later," I said, voice flat as week-old beer, the threat lurking beneath like a switchblade in a silk pocket. "We'll deal with it later."

Silence stretched like a confession on the rack. Shrimp giggled. Then barked. Then hushed himself with his tail. Mango's grin didn't fade. He watched me with those infuriating eyes that said he wasn't done, not by a long shot —the kind of look that promises trouble wrapped in velvet and delivered with a kiss.

No fear-scent, Jake assessed. *Either has backup waiting or too foolish to know he's outmatched.*

"Look," I growled, sweeping the room. "We're all here for one reason. You felt it. I felt it. The hum. The call. The Cognichonk's changing the rules."

Dorito's claws drummed on his box.

"Or you're just losing it," Mango offered.

I turned my head slow. Made him wait for my words.

"They don't have to be mutually exclusive," I said.

Shrimp shrieked with joy. "Truth! He speaks the truth! Hide the votes!"

Shrimp, ever the prophet of inconvenient chaos.

Bosco blinked once. The slow kind of blink that said you had exactly one chance to impress him.

I let Jake's body shift. Heavy. Solid. A rolling boulder that dared anyone to try moving it.

Claim the center space, Jake thought. *Make them choose— your territory or no territory.*

I lowered my voice. Let it grind. "I'm not asking you to like me," I said. "I wouldn't. But you're going to listen. Because whatever's coming? It doesn't care if you voted for me."

Dorito stopped flicking his tail.

Mango's eyes narrowed. Calculating.

Shrimp whimpered. Then burped prophecy.

Bosco stayed silent. But he didn't look away.

The Cognichonk pulsed behind my eyes.

They're listening now, Jake whispered. *Their ears track your voice. Don't waste the attention.*

Somewhere far outside, the wind rattled the boards like it wanted in on the argument.

Silence weighed on the War Room like old debts collected by broken fingers. Then a voice, cracked with age and authority, cut the tension like a dull knife through a confession—rough, painful, but getting the job done all the same.

"Order," Mittens rasped.

She was older than dirt, and meaner. A long-haired matriarch whose tabby markings had faded to near-myth. She sat atop an ancient ammo crate repurposed as a throne, one ear notched from a hundred forgotten battles. Her single good eye glittered with judgment.

"Order," she repeated, with enough menace to make even Dorito's tail slow its twitching.

I used the moment. Jake's tail slammed onto the concrete with the force of a gavel in a courthouse that never saw acquittals.

"Listen up," I growled. My voice carried like a death sentence. "We need unity."

Silence held its breath for one second. Then Mango snorted like he was spitting on a grave, each note dripping with the kind of disdain you can't buy in polite company.

"Unity," he said, dragging the word out like it tasted bad. "Really? That's so last season. Next you'll be telling us to hold paws and sing."

A low growl rolled through Clawrence's chest. His claws dug deep, peeling up splinters of crate wood like confessions from unwilling suspects.

"Anchor now," he said, voice ragged with warning. "Or we break apart. And then she picks us off one by one."

Dorito's eyes gleamed with manic delight. He lifted one paw. Between his claws, chewed and soggy, was a ballot.

"I have *voted*," he declared, solemn as a judge at a clown funeral. He squinted at the paper. It disintegrated between his teeth. He chewed thoughtfully, then spat. "Tastes like corruption."

Gingersnap stepped forward. She was slim, scarred, elegant despite the candlelight making her shadow dance like a demon's.

"Please," she tried, voice soothing. "This isn't helping. We need to stay calm. We need—"

She didn't get to finish. Dorito let out a shriek that peeled paint from the walls and sanity from ears.

"I ABSTAIN!" he howled, and stage-dived off his crate with the grace of a falling filing cabinet.

Chaos rippled. Cats yowled. Someone screeched. Jake's instincts were to pin Dorito immediately.

Pin the yowler. Claim center ground. Show teeth once, mean it.

I held back. Barely.

"Enough!" I barked, my voice booming across the floor. "Enough!"

They settled, if only because there wasn't enough oxygen left to scream. And that's when Shrimp spoke. Curled in his corner, his eyes wide, unblinking. His tail twitched like it was writing letters to the void. His mouth opened and the room went dead silent.

"Twelve paws in circle," he intoned. Voice too deep. Too old. Like it was stolen from a crypt that hadn't given permission. "The pantry god rises. The Anchor will drown in tuna."

No one moved. No one breathed. Even the candles flickered lower, as if they were listening too. I felt the Cognichonk behind my eyes, pulsing. Thrumming with approval.

Small cat, big voice, Jake thought, deadpan. *Useful distraction when prey needs herding.*

Bosco stirred. It was like watching a landslide decide it was sentient. He unfolded from the wall, massive, battered, silent until now. All eyes turned.

His voice was a boulder rolling downhill. "She tried to bring him back," he said. Slow. Relentless. "She failed."

Silence.

"But she learned," he continued. "And she's choosing now."

The words hit like a back-alley confession whispered with a blade pressed to your ribs. I felt the fur along my spine stand on end. She's choosing now. My gut twisted. This wasn't just politics. This was ritual. A collective shiver ran through the room. Cats hissed. Tails puffed. Arguments flared.

Mango's eyes glittered. "Vex has a plan."

Clawrence bared his teeth. "She'll gut us to feed it."

Dorito scrambled back onto his crate. "I'll vote for whoever feeds me!"

Shrimp twitched and let out a high-pitched giggle. "Or whoever sets us on fire. Fire is good. Fire speaks the truth."

Gingersnap tried to soothe them again. "Please—stop this. We need sense."

But sense had already left the building. I tried to force calm.

Jake's voice whispered tactical options. *Growl low. Corner the weak ones first. Separate the fighters. Territory control basics.*

I slammed my tail again. Harder. "If we split, she wins."

Mango met my eyes. His voice slithered across the room, smooth as stolen silk until it hit you with the aftertaste of cheap poison. "And what if you're the one helping her split us?"

It hit like a slap. I felt the rage crawl up my spine.

But Jake's cold voice cut through. *Ignore the tail-flick. Eyes on the real threat. Make them follow your scent, not his.*

The hush sat heavy as a loaded .45, everyone waiting for the verdict they'd already written in their heads. I opened my mouth to lay down the law, but the room erupted before I could spit the words out. Some arguments don't wait for introductions.

Clawrence's claws dug grooves into the floor, scraping out his patience letter by letter. Clawrence lunged. Mango met him halfway. They collided in a screeching, yowling tangle.

Dorito dove in with unholy glee, screaming, "I vote ANARCHY!"

Shrimp launched himself onto Bosco's back, prophesying at maximum volume. "Twelve paws! The pantry god rises! THE ANCHOR IS TUNA!"

Bosco roared once. A sound like a landslide given teeth. He shook Shrimp off.

Gingersnap yowled. "Stop it! STOP IT!"

Mittens hissed from her crate, voice cracking with age

and fury. "Enough! You worthless flea-bitten anarchists! SIT!"

But no one listened. The old authority that once cowed them had lost its teeth, and the war room fell apart around her growl. They tore into each other with the kind of enthusiasm usually reserved for fresh murder scenes. Fur scattered like evidence nobody bothered to collect, while claws wrote manifestos in skin and splinters. I tried to intervene. Jake's body moved with brutal efficiency—he was built for this. I grabbed Mango by the scruff, but he twisted, biting down on my foreleg. I slammed him onto the floor, snarling.

Clean takedown, Jake noted. *Too many watching eyes. They'll remember who's strongest.*

Dorito pounced on Clawrence's back like a deranged rodeo clown. Clawrence bucked, claws tearing at the floor. Shrimp bit Bosco's tail and screamed something about cosmic coupons. Gingersnap howled curses that would have scandalized an alley witch.

I felt the Cognichonk pulsing behind my eyes, thrilled. Feeding on the chaos like a god that only took tithes in blood and screaming.

It likes this, I realized. It wants this.

Jake was unimpressed. *Bad hunting strategy. End this fast.*

I threw Mango off me and roared. "ENOUGH!"

For a moment—it worked. They froze. Fur matted. Ears torn. Blood dripped on concrete. The candles flickered in the silence. My chest heaved. Jake's heart thundered.

Slow breath. Speak from the chest, Jake ordered. *Make them feel it in their whiskers.*

I looked around the room.

"You think this is about pride?" I spat, eyes sweeping the room. "If we turn on each other now, we're not just splitting a faction. We're handing Vex the keys to the whole damn Cognichonk."

The silence had teeth. Eyes tracked me across the room, each pair calculating odds, measuring distances, remembering old scores. They didn't laugh. They didn't lunge. They just waited, like killers at a funeral. Shrimp hiccuped once. Bosco's eyes bored into mine. Mango licked blood from his paw, glaring. Clawrence flexed his claws, but stayed seated. Gingersnap exhaled, trembling. Dorito fell off his crate. Again.

I felt the Cognichonk purr behind my eyes. The sound wasn't blessing our little democracy—it was counting the seconds until we tore each other apart.

The War Room smelled like blood, old wax, and humiliation. Cats sprawled across the factory floor, licking wounds that wouldn't heal right. The candles guttered, their light coughing into shadows that seemed to move on their own.

Dorito had vanished inside a rusted barrel, only the tips of his ears visible as they flicked in indignation. He sulked upside-down, muttering to himself about corruption and treachery between chews on his own tail.

Mango sat on the edge of a crate like it was a throne no one else deserved, grooming his shoulder with slow, deliberate strokes. His eyes never left me. Calm. Dangerous. Like he'd already filed my murder plan in triplicate and rehearsed the closing argument.

Trouble-maker shows throat slightly. Temporary truce. Watch his tail, not his eyes.

Clawrence brooded near the wall, one ear torn, eyes narrow and burning. His claws flexed against the floor with the slow promise of future violence.

Shrimp was out cold, twitching in prophetic nightmares that rattled his ribs. He mewled something about tuna and oblivion.

Bosco had retreated to the deepest shadows, only his eyes visible. Watching. Judging. Deciding nothing and everything.

Mittens sat slumped on her crate, tail wrapped tight around brittle bones, her one good eye dull. She didn't speak. She didn't need to. She'd seen enough uprisings to know when the crown was broken.

Jake's body ached with bruises I'd borrowed but couldn't return. Blood matted the fur in patterns like abstract art—my contribution mixed with donations from everyone else in the room. I forced a breath. It felt like inhaling razors dipped in regret.

Lick wounds later, Jake thought. *Count allies now. Territory still needs marking.*

We weren't a team. We were suspects in a murder that hadn't happened yet, all of us eyeing each other for who'd be holding the knife when the lights came back on.

The Cognichonk pulsed behind my eyes. Heavy. Watching. Approving of the mess like a god who only asked for worship in blood and screaming.

I felt my tail lash once. A punctuation mark no one wanted to read. I stepped forward. The boards creaked in warning. My voice dropped, raw and low.

"If she gets the last shard," I said, "it's over. She'll choose the Anchor. She'll choose *herself*."

Silence swallowed us. The dust motes in the flickering light hung still, as if holding their breath. Somewhere, water dripped in the dark, each drop a slow accusation. It wasn't peaceful. It was the silence of a room realizing the walls were closing in.

Mango stopped grooming. His eyes narrowed to slits. Clawrence's claws gouged fresh lines in the concrete. Dorito peeked out of the barrel. Wide-eyed. Listening. Shrimp snored once. Then whimpered. Bosco moved. Slowly. The shadows peeled off him like regret. His voice was low. Grounded. Immutable.

"Then don't let her get it."

Old hunter knows. Simple truth hits harder than fancy words.

It wasn't advice. It was an order. A verdict. For a moment, no one moved. Then Clawrence grunted. A sound halfway between a threat and agreement. Gingersnap, battered but upright, let out a shaking exhale. Mango met my eyes and—damn him—smirked. Slow. Deliberate. Approval shaped like insult. Dorito's ears wiggled. He emerged a fraction more from his barrel.

"Do we get snacks?" he asked, voice small but defiant, like hope was a weapon he refused to drop.

No one answered Dorito. The only snacks in this joint were broken promises and the taste of your own blood. We were fresh out of everything except scars, and those we had in abundance.

I let the silence fill its lungs, watching it turn blue

around the edges before it collapsed across the room like a drunk who'd read his own obituary and found it lacking.

They're watching your whiskers now, Jake murmured. *Speak low. Make them lean in to hear the hunt plan.*

But my voice was too tired for speeches. Too honest for lies. I felt the words curdle behind my teeth, unsaid orders that even Jake couldn't force through. The Cognichonk purred behind my eyes. It wasn't comfort. It was a promise that it wasn't done with us yet.

Pack wounded but aligned. Sometimes silence speaks louder than growls.

I looked around the room. At the bruises. The cuts. The broken trust that was supposed to hold us together. What we had wasn't an alliance—just a roomful of condemned cats who'd temporarily agreed not to hang each other with the same rope. And somehow I'd become their jailhouse lawyer, arguing a case I'd already lost in my sleep.

CHAPTER EIGHTEEN

The War Room reeked of last week's fish guts, ideas that died in infancy, and the unmistakable stench of optimism decomposing in the corner—the kind of hope that ferments into something harder and meaner when left too long in the dark. Candles guttered in rusted cans, throwing shadows that knew more than they were telling across walls tagged with conspiracy. Crates circled the floor like suspects in a lineup, most of them cracked and leaking splinters that could confess more than the cats who sat on them ever would. String maps sprawled across the concrete, a spider's web of delusions that caught more ankles than answers. Nobody followed the lines, but everybody bled when they crossed them. Candles in tin cans guttered, flickering shadows across walls scrawled with conspiracy.

I shifted my weight, feeling Jake's bigger frame creak with bruises that weren't entirely mine. Shoulders broad enough to intimidate, ribs tight like they'd been used as percussion in last night's brawl. I stood in the center. Fur matted. Tail lashing. The Cognichonk purred behind my eyes, the kind of sound a loaded .38 might make if it could laugh at the poor bastard about to pull its trigger.

Territory unstable. Count allies. Establish dominance, Jake's voice rumbled in my skull, certain as a coroner pronouncing time of death. I couldn't argue with the diagnosis, even if I wanted to.

Mango draped himself across a crate with the casual arrogance of a crime boss who'd survived three assassination attempts before breakfast—the kind of calculated indifference that comes from knowing exactly how many lives you've ruined and sleeping just fine anyway. His grooming wasn't hygiene—it was performance art, each lick a silent invoice for time he considered stolen from more profitable schemes. He'd tipped over the Syndicat's entire stash of planning chalk just to make room for himself, so every map line now ended in a question mark.

Clawrence lurked in shadow, one good eye glinting. He carved the floor with slow, deliberate strokes of his claws that were less about strategy and more about sending a message that he remembered every grudge—tallying debts that would be collected in blood and regret when the moment was right.

Dorito gnawed on a dead flashlight like it contained the confessions of saints, his teeth scraping metal with the kind of devotion usually reserved for last rites or first murders. Each time he bit down, the bulb flickered in death throes, painting the walls with the kind of light that makes innocent men confess. He'd also drawn sigils in the dust with his whiskers that spelled "DON'T TRUST HIM" in something close to crayon logic. He was presumably talking about me.

Shrimp sat in the center of the circle, tangled in the string lines so thoroughly he was part of the map now. He occasionally screamed in prophecy. Last time, it had knocked over an entire stack of empty cans, the crash echoing like gunshots and blowing out two candles. At one point he yelled "THE SPIRAL WANTS SNACKS" and tried to bite his own tail in intimidation.

Bosco sat at the edge, statue-still, eyes glinting with the patient hatred of a judge who'd already written the sentence. The room's last chance at sanity, which was worrying.

I cleared my throat. It sounded like a death threat to my own dignity.

"Everyone shut up and listen."

Silence fell. Sort of. Dorito stopped chewing but spat the flashlight out with a clunk that rolled across the floor, hitting Mango's crate. Mango didn't move, but his tail lashed once. Warning. Mango didn't stop grooming. But he slowed. Watching. Waiting. Shrimp froze with one leg in the air, eyes huge. Then he blinked both eyes, but one at a time. The old, familiar tell. *My tell, now his.* Proof the Cognichonk wasn't just sharing memories. It was stitching me into them.

Keep their eyes on you, Jake's voice ordered.

"This isn't a team," I growled, my voice scraping like a key in a rusted lock. "We're a shared delusion with claws, a bad trip that learned how to hunt in packs—the kind of nightmare that wakes up and decides to make everyone else stop sleeping too."

Shrimp squeaked. "We're doomed." His tail twitched so hard he knocked over another candle. Wax spilled. The light guttered out. Then came the giggling. "We're gonna die!" He cackled so hard he fell over and rolled in the string like a burrito of failure.

Dorito let out a hiss like a pressure valve, glaring at the darkness like it owed him rent.

Mango flicked his tail, eyes half-lidded. "Do go on, oh fearless leader. I live to be disappointed."

My claws scraped the floor—blunt, but big enough to promise violence even when dulled by blood. Jake's body had weight. Authority. Even they felt it.

"Mallory Vex wants the last shard. She gets it? She *anchors* the network. Makes herself the center. Every thought, every orange cat, funneling through *her*. Forever."

Shrimp's eyes went huge. "Does she give out snacks?"

"No," I growled.

He let out a sob so genuine it hurt.

Clawrence scraped the floor with claws like he was signing a contract in violence. "What's the plan?"

Assign hunting positions. Each cat needs a clear path to stalk, Jake urged.

"Two teams. One intercepts the courier. The other blocks her retreat. Quiet. Fast. Coordinated."

Shrimp raised his paw from inside the tangled map. "I volunteer as bait!" He tried to wave, and pulled the entire tangle of string with him, knocking over three crates. A domino of noise and curses.

Dorito took that moment to hiss at Shrimp, scream "TRAITOR," then turn and bite the candle. The flame sputtered and died. Smoke curled upward, choking the room in burnt-wax regret.

Mango licked his paw with the deliberate slowness of someone calculating exactly how much your funeral would cost. "Your plan is adorable. I want it framed. Posthumously." Each word dropped like a coin in a dead man's collection plate.

I let the insult hang in the air, heavy as smoke, before speaking. "Clawrence, you're muscle. Scare them. Dorito, flank."

Dorito spat wax like a confession he'd been holding too long, then raised the burnt candle stub in a salute that managed to be both mocking and eerily formal—the kind of respect you show to the corpse of someone who once tried to kill you.

"Shrimp. You're bait. Loud. Distracting."

Shrimp beamed. "I'm good at that!" Then immediately tried to pounce on a floating ash mote. He missed, hit the floor sideways, and sent another crate crashing down, scattering the last candle's light and leaving us in dim, flickering gloom.

Bosco's eyes didn't move. His approval was subtle, like tectonic plates shifting.

Bring them back to the scent trail. They're getting distracted by dust motes, Jake growled.

"We're not heroes. We're not friends. We're cats. Mean. Hungry. Untrustworthy. But she wants to make us hers. Rewrite us all. We don't serve."

Shrimp sniffled. "I serve the Spiral."

I sighed. "Except you."

He beamed.

Mango licked his chest fur with great dignity. "Do I get a team? Or just an obituary?"

"Mango," I said, voice low. "You get the second intercept team. Do not improvise."

He licked his paw with infuriating calm. "Darling, improvisation is my entire resume."

I clamped down on the urge to snarl. "Consider yourself fired."

He smiled. Slowly. "Try it."

Clawrence snorted, claws gouging new scars into the floor. "When do we kill someone?"

"After we have the shard," I growled.

Dorito started chanting "Snacks" again, rocking back and forth in the dark. Shrimp whispered "Tuna Eclipse" in the haunted tones of someone who'd seen things. Mango exhaled with the resignation of a man attending his own roast.

Close the trap now. They're ready to pounce, Jake rumbled.

I felt the Cognichonk hum behind my eyes, pleased as a god with blood in its teeth.

"This is survival," I rasped. "We plan tonight. We move tomorrow. Quiet. Fast. Like cats."

Silence. Real silence. Even Shrimp stopped breathing for a second.

I let it sit. Let it weigh them down.

"We take it back. For us. For the right to be this insane by choice." The words hung in the air like smoke after a shootout—evidence of something violent that couldn't be taken back.

Bosco's tail twitched once. Then his voice, low and final: "We don't get second chances. Make the plan tight."

Mango's eyes narrowed, calculating. Clawrence stopped carving. Dorito paused, flame-stub held like a relic. Shrimp smiled, dreamy.

I nodded once.

"Good." I let the word hang in the air like a promise nobody believed but everyone needed. "Now let's plan a goddamn heist." The words tasted like copper and gasoline in my mouth—the flavor of bad decisions that were still better than the alternatives.

I stomped into the center, Jake's big frame throwing shadows like accusations. The fur along my spine bristled as the Cognichonk purred behind my eyes—pleased. Watching. Waiting to see how I'd screw this up.

Claim the center space, Jake's voice rumbled in my head. *Make them feel your shadow.*

Sure. On this group. I slammed the pizza box onto the floor. It hit with a greasy thump—the sound of evidence nobody wanted to claim. The carton had seen better days— probably in another decade when dreams came cheaper and lasted longer.

"This," I growled, claw tapping it, "is the plan."

Shrimp gasped like I'd unveiled holy scripture. He immediately dove for it, squealing.

I snatched him by the scruff. Jake's muscles did the heavy lifting, dangling the runt like he weighed less than his crimes. He flailed, feet windmilling, knocking over two candles and sending hot wax splattering onto Dorito's tail.

Dorito screeched. "ASSAULT!"

He spun and sank teeth into Shrimp's foot. Revenge served raw and bleeding. Shrimp howled, twisting in my grip like a salmon possessed.

Peaches sauntered in when the blood was freshest. Tail high—a victory flag before the war even started. She sashayed in, took one look at Dorito biting Shrimp, and whipped Dorito across the face with her tail so hard the nearest candle guttered out.

Dorito spat wax and glared at her, sputtering. "Betrayal!" he yowled.

Peaches didn't dignify it with a response.

I set Shrimp down with a thump. He blinked, eyes crossed, and whispered "I see the strings of fate."

Eyes on the hunt, Jake growled. *Don't chase their distractions.*

I dipped a claw in soot scraped from a can and began sketching onto the pizza box lid. The grease soaked it instantly, turning lines into blurred threats.

"Vault's here," I said. "Leyline access point. Vex's courier is hitting tomorrow night. We intercept here. Two teams."

Mango sprawled across his crate with the casual arrogance of a con artist at a mark's funeral. His tail curled, a question mark made of pure insolence. "Infiltration sounds...intimate," he purred.

Clawrence's one good eye narrowed to a razor edge. "I'm not working with *him*."

Mango slowly, deliberately licked his shoulder. "I insist on teamwork."

Mittens, silent till now, snapped her tail like a whip. "Control your hormones, Mango."

Mango didn't break eye contact with Clawrence. He purred. Clawrence flexed claws with clear homicidal intent.

"Enough," I snarled, claws scoring the ruined pizza box. "Infiltration Unit: Mango, Mittens, Clawrence."

Clawrence growled. "He tries anything, I skin him."

Mango yawned, unimpressed. "Promises, promises."

I kept going before they could murder each other.

"Distraction Team," I said, stabbing the box. "Dorito. Peaches. Shrimp."

Shrimp squeaked. "Glory to the Tuna Eclipse!"

Dorito raised a paw, solemn. "Do we get snacks?"

"No."

Dorito collapsed in dramatic grief. Peaches gave him a shove with her back foot, knocking him off the crate.

It was right then Butternugget finally arrived—late, unrepentant, and insane. He emerged through a gap in the crates like a bright-orange demon birthed by chaos itself.

"IS THIS THE MEETING?" he screeched, eyes huge and unfocused.

The small orange one is useful chaos. Point him at the enemy, not us.

Everyone stared. He froze. Blinked one eye. Then the other. Then both in a pattern only the Cognichonk could love.

"I got lost," he announced cheerfully. "Found a box. It was lying to me about the exit. I interrogated it. It had... secrets."

Mango didn't even blink. "Fascinating. Someone get him a medal."

Butternugget ignored him. Or forgot he existed. He licked his paw and immediately forgot why he was licking it.

He then fell over sideways with a loud "MRAOW!" and lay there blinking at the ceiling.

Peaches narrowed her eyes. "He's on *our* team?"

"Distraction," I confirmed without hesitation.

Butternugget perked up, still on his back. "I'M VERY GOOD AT DISTRACTIONS. My special move is screaming while biting the evidence."

Shrimp applauded. Dorito let out a warbling giggle and tackled Butternugget for solidarity. They rolled together in a tangle of claws and yowls, slamming into the crate I'd been using as a table. It collapsed under the impact, sending the pizza box map spinning into the wax puddle.

Grease spread. Soot lines smeared. My beautiful, terrible plan dissolved into abstract art. I shut my eyes, counting heartbeats until the urge to commit mass murder passed. Got to five. Still wasn't enough.

Plans change. Hunters adapt. Use their energy, don't fight it. Even chaos cats respond to a steady growl.

I opened my eyes to see Sunbeam Jones standing in the doorway, nose wrinkled in disdain.

"This lighting is abysmal," he sniffed. "I require at least three daylight windows for optimal scrying."

Mango gave him a slow, malicious smile. "We'll get right on that. Maybe open a skylight with Clawrence's claws."

Clawrence flexed them, not at all ironically.

Sunbeam ignored them with the practiced indifference of a bartender at last call, stepping daintily over the rolling brawl of Dorito and Butternugget. He paused beside Shrimp, who had begun chanting "ALL HAIL THE STRING" while chewing it.

Sunbeam lifted his paw like he was about to smack

Shrimp, then reconsidered, settling for muttering "Unprofessional."

"Sunbeam," I barked, voice cracking with murder. "Mystic Timing. You're on leyline watch. You call the window."

Sunbeam sniffed again. "I'll need the candles relit, a proper scribing surface, and someone to keep the orange one from eating the map."

Dorito immediately yowled, "WE'RE ALL ORANGE."

Butternugget paused mid-lick. "I'm the *orangest* one," he said proudly, then continued licking the box.

Shrimp stopped chewing long enough to say, "No promises."

Bosco finally stirred. He lifted his head, eyes gleaming with centuries of judgment, and said in his gravelly voice: "I'll be on vibes and judgment."

The old one has weight. Let his silence work for you.

The room fell silent at that. Even Butternugget paused mid-yowl to blink at Bosco in awe. I sighed. I felt Jake's bruised ribs shift painfully with the effort.

Stand tall. Tail high. They follow strength, not words, Jake reminded me.

"I'd interrogated mob bosses with better manners," I muttered.

Mango smirked. "Maybe they had better snacks."

Clawrence let out a slow growl. Shrimp giggled, spun in a circle, and headbutted Peaches. Peaches immediately bit his ear. Dorito was trying to bite Peaches in revenge but missed and bit his own tail, screaming betrayal at maximum volume. Butternugget was licking the spilled grease off the pizza box like it was holy writ.

Sunbeam Jones was arranging the candles with surgical precision, hissing "Amateurs" under his breath.

Bosco watched them all, unmoving, the eye of a hurricane made of fur and disappointment.

I let the silence crash around me like surf against a doomed lighthouse. When it finally quieted—even if only by exhaustion—I bared my teeth.

I exhaled. Slow. Like it might kill me. "Memorize your part," I growled. "Because next time we meet, it's the job. No more rehearsals. Just claws."

The War Room looked like someone had tried to hold a strategy session in the middle of a junkyard riot—the aftermath of good intentions mugged by reality and left bleeding out between overturned crates. Candles burned low, guttering smoke like guilty confessions. Crates were overturned or smashed. Wax pooled in ominous shapes. The string map was a shredded monument to lost patience. And at the center of it all lay the pizza box, grease-smeared and ruined, the plan scrawled in soot barely legible.

I glared at it. My tail lashed like a live wire. Jake's muscles burned with effort just holding me back from murder.

Pack in disarray. Too much energy, no direction. Like kittens with sharp teeth.

Shrimp stared at the box with the rapt devotion of a zealot before an altar. His pupils were blown wide, tail quivering like a divining rod. Without warning, he lunged.

Fast one moves. Intercept trajectory clear. But let him fail. Sometimes chaos teaches better than claws.

"THE PROPHECY IS MINE!"

He snatched the entire pizza box in his teeth and bolted three steps before I roared and pounced. Too late. He ripped it open with wild-eyed fury and *ate* half of it in three frantic, jerky bites. Grease dripped onto his chest. Soot smeared his nose. He coughed once, swallowed, and let out a blissed-out sigh.

"We are...blessed," he intoned.

Silence crashed down like a debt collector at midnight. The kind of quiet that follows explosions—all shock and no peace.

Dorito cheered. "THAT'S MY BOY!"

Peaches let out a low, horrified hiss. "You *idiot*. That was our *plan*!"

Plan gone. Not important. Plans change. The hunt remains. Focus them on the prey, not the map.

Mango didn't move, just slowly rolled his eyes toward the rafters. "Truly, our best minds."

Clawrence flexed his claws like he was deciding whether murder was worth the paperwork.

Butternugget blinked, wide-eyed. "Is it *my* turn to eat the plan? I can help."

Sunbeam Jones recoiled in disgust. "This is worse than I envisioned. And I envisioned fire."

Bosco didn't speak. Just watched. Silent. Heavy. The last sane thing in the room.

My claws scraped the concrete. My breath came in hard, rasping growls.

Control them, Jake hissed.

I surveyed my crew—orange-furred catastrophes with teeth and grudges. Backstabbers and fortune-tellers. The worst family a detective could ask for, and the only one I had. Grease-scrawled schemes had the lifespan of a match in a hurricane. Prophecy plans? Those were DOA before the ink dried. My tail twitched with the slow promise of violence.

"We're doing this anyway."

Good. They feel it now. The real threat. Not each other. Something bigger. Pack instinct awakening.

They froze. Shrimp was mid-lick, blinking. Dorito fell silent. Peaches stilled. Even Mango lowered his paw from his grandiose grooming.

I let my voice drop, raw and low. "She's one shard away from choosing us all. Forever. Her voice in every head. Her will in every claw. We don't get to fail."

Silence deepened. Wax hissed. Shadows crawled. I met every eye. Even Shrimp's still-wild gaze. Even Butternugget's upside-down stare as he rolled slowly off his crate.

"We hit the place hard," I growled, throat raw with certainty. "That shard belongs to us before anyone else gets their claws on it."

A hush spread like blood in water. Slowly, claws retracted. Tails lowered. Heads dipped in grim understanding.

Bosco stood last, massive and immovable. His eyes met mine. And he nodded. Once. The kind of nod that ended arguments.

Old hunter knows. Has seen worse hunts succeed with less. His weight matters more than words.

I let out a breath like I was exhaling knives. Jake's big tail thumped the floor once. Hard. Like a judge's gavel.

"Operation Tuna Eclipse," I rasped, my voice scraping across the room like a jailer's keys. "Starts now. God help whatever gets in our way."

Silence clung to them. Even the candles flickered lower, as if ducking for cover. I narrowed my eyes, tail twitching once more.

Tails down. Eyes sharp. They're ready to hunt now. Not perfect. But hungry enough to work.

"God help us all."

CHAPTER NINETEEN

Night hung over us like a loan shark's promise—thick, ugly, and waiting to collect. I crouched behind an enchanted hedge that glistened with containment glyphs, its thorns twitching with predatory etiquette—the kind of security system that doesn't just keep you out, but makes you regret ever having the thought to try.

Jake Speed's body, a cathedral of muscle in Maine Coon fur, shifted beneath me. His claws punched into the soil. Final verdicts digging their own graves.

I tasted the leyline on the wind. Ozone. Old blood. The static of promises broken at knifepoint.

The plan was simple. Which meant it was doomed.

I narrowed my eyes at the observatory. It was marble arrogance carved into a trap. Sigils crawled the walls like legalese on a curse. Gilded mirrors rotated slowly, catching ghostlight and hurling it across the grounds in cold accusation. The floor tiles inside pulsed with leyline energy —breathing in sync with something old, and hungry.

The observatory? That's what the architects called it. I called it what it was: a vault disguised as a temple with teeth sharp enough for curious cats like us—another pretty lie wrapped in marble and moonlight, waiting to snap shut on whatever fool believed the brochure. And somewhere inside lay what we'd come for: a leyline shard. Cognichonk-tainted. A piece of me.

Trap layout. Multiple exits. Scent the air currents, Jake's thoughts surfaced, cool and methodical. *Always know your escape route first.*

I let the Cognichonk hum behind my eyes. The psychic link snapped open like a bad filing cabinet.

Roll call, I sent. My thoughts spilled out noir-drenched, like ink that judged you for reading it.

Pack check. Good. Count your hunters before the stalk begins, Jake approved, his thoughts precise as a soldier's.

Silence. One breath heavy with risk.

Then: *Dorito here. I'm blending in.*

His mind-voice practically preened. I caught a flicker of him crouched on a gargoyle, tail draped dramatically.

How, I growled.

I am the gargoyle now. His smugness pulsed like cheap cologne.

Peaches cut in, voice dry and surgical. *He's orange. The gargoyle is granite. You're embarrassing all of us.* I saw her hunkered in shadow, eyes slitted, ears flicking in disdain.

Shrimp shrieked *BLESSED BE THE SPIN PRIEST!* so loud the link rattled. I felt his teeth gnash at the connection itself —pure feral glee leaking through.

I grimaced. Jake's whiskers twitched like tripwires rigged with dynamite.

Distraction Team, I sent, *hold.*

Their collective mischief bristled. I could *feel* Dorito's tail twitching. But they stilled. I shifted focus, letting the hum crackle, re-threading the link.

Mango. Mittens. Clawrence. Status.

Mango's response came as a low, velvety purr—equal parts promise and threat. *North wall. Shadows. Waiting on your grand plan, boss.* I felt his calm, a professional's patience.

Mittens whispered, voice full of anxious prayer. 60% apology, 40% please-don't-kill-me.

Clawrence didn't speak. Just a long, slow inhale. A rumble of intent. He was coiled. Ready.

Sunbeam Jones.

A dry rumble. Already annoyed at the world for existing. *Leyline Watch. I see you all. I see too much. But yeah. Clear.* I felt his focus flickering across leyline currents like a seer scanning a crime scene.

Hunting formation solid. Small one makes noise. We make the kill, Jake assessed, his confidence a steady weight beneath my borrowed bones.

We were positioned exactly how I'd planned it on the worst nap of my life. Distraction Team on the south courtyard. Infiltration on the north wall, poised to breach. Me? The service entrance.

The link vibrated with tension. I exhaled. Let the noir spill like cheap bourbon across their minds.

Listen up, I broadcast. My thoughts went slow, deliberate, etched like a tombstone.

We go in quiet. We go out alive. Preferably.

Silence answered. Heavier than honesty.

Heroes die famous. Martyrs die proud. Us? We're just cats with expired luck and a tab running with fate. If you see a way to run? Take it. But if you see that shard?

I paused. Claws flexed. Jake's big body obeyed with grim satisfaction.

You get it. You bring it back. Before they do.

Peaches hissed approval, the sound like cut glass.

Dorito whispered *For glory!* but it sounded like a dare and a joke all at once.

Shrimp screamed *FOR THE CHONK!* and I felt his teeth actually *bite* the link.

Good enough. I shifted, tail low and heavy, battering ram with a grudge.

Mark.

The word left my mouth like a curse. Orders you can disobey—this was something darker. The link went dead as they scattered. Like cutting the strings on puppets who'd rather be predators.

Distraction Team slithered into the courtyard shadows. Shrimp's cackle rippled like prophecy scribbled in crayon. Peaches followed with cold, murderous grace. Dorito galloped after them like guilt wearing a party hat.

Infiltration Team melted into the north wall's silhouette. Three shadows. Three sins. Mango's calm like a held blade. Mittens' panic spiking, then focusing. Clawrence a silent promise to kill anything that moved.

I alone turned toward the service entrance. The door waited, flanked by mist and warding runes so labyrinthine they smelled of bureaucracy. I let Jake's massive frame shift forward, muscles under fur like truths nobody wanted to hear.

Low approach. Shadows favor us. Watch for scent markers, Jake cautioned, his instincts sharp as unsheathed claws.

The leyline thrummed beneath my paws. Old power. Hungry power.

I narrowed my eyes.

This time, I lied to myself, *it's going to go smooth.*

My claws sank in. My shoulders rolled. I walked out of the shadows.

The atrium was supposed to be quiet. Sacred. Marble floors gleamed with the same polish con men use on their smiles. Columns stood tall, runes pulsing like veins of a sick god. The whole place reeked of architectural daddy issues and too much money.

The balcony hung above us, curved and watching—the kind of architectural feature that judges you while you're still counting your sins. Jake's massive frame pressed low, claws biting old stone as I watched the plan burn in real time. Even in the chaos, Jake's mind ticked steady beneath mine, mapping exits, calculating odds. He was calm. Focused. Tactical.

Below, Dorito moved with all the subtlety of a parade celebrating bad decisions—each step a confession to crimes not yet committed but already being planned in detail. He slunk, badly, up to a pedestal crowned with a scrying orb. The orb glowed, an eye that had read too many personal diaries without permission—the kind of voyeuristic magic that charged admission to your own secrets and kept the best parts for itself. Dorito's tail twitched. He stared. Squinted. Then, with the solemnity of a philosopher king confronted with unknowable truth, he bit it.

The orb flickered, issuing a magical gasp. Sparks spat out like angry fireflies. Dorito yowled victory through clenched teeth, then started licking the thing like it owed him money—slow, methodical, the kind of licks that leave psychological scars. Static crackled with every lap. The rune-lines on the floor flared a terrified pink. The orb let out a shrill whine. Then, with the finality of a tax audit, it *shorted out*.

Smoke curled from Dorito's whiskers. He sat back on his haunches, eyes watering, and declared to no one: "I have tamed the all-seeing eye."

An alarm glyph overhead fizzled. Then exploded in a confused *pop*, showering the room in crackling pink sparks.

On the far side of the hall, Peaches was busy displaying all the calm of a professional assassin—if that assassin were forced to babysit. She had cornered a blueprint scroll tucked in a glass case. She studied the lock, assessed the security spells, and proceeded to rip the case off with her claws in one smooth motion.

Scroll in mouth, she turned and ran straight into Shrimp. They collided with the grace of drunken gladiators. Shrimp shrieked. Peaches spat the scroll onto the floor. They circled each other. Tails like loaded crossbows. Hissing. Spitting.

Amateurs, I thought from the balcony.

Shrimp lunged. Peaches tackled. They rolled across sacred floor tiles designed to channel leyline precision into the cosmos itself. Between them, the scroll took punishment it never deserved. Parchment folded and creased—making the same sounds as confessions beaten out of guilty men.

Finally Shrimp broke free, scroll in jaws. He skittered back, fur standing on end. Peaches advanced, eyes slitted in murder's promise.

And then Shrimp *peed* on the scroll. Eyes locked on Peaches, voice suddenly dark and resonant, he *sang*.

"Twelve paws! Tuna sings! Ascend!"

It wasn't a song so much as a *prophecy*. In Enochian. The glyphwork on the floor reacted. Sparks danced. The scroll *burst into flames*.

Peaches let out a scream you could've booked on three counts of aggravated assault. Her paw connected with Shrimp's face hard enough to rearrange his ancestry, but the little psychic kept chanting through a mouthful of destiny.

Dorito, meanwhile, had taken advantage of the confusion. He'd found the observatory's grand constellation projector. It rotated gently, its lenses casting perfect star charts onto the domed ceiling. The heavens. The plan. Dorito climbed it. He balanced atop it, tail waving in the projected starlight like a semaphore for the doomed.

"I see the stars' math!" he howled.

He twisted. The projector groaned. Crystals cracked. Then he fell inside it. His tail flailed wildly from the top aperture. A shriek issued that spoke of neither courage nor wisdom. The projector fizzled. Went dark. The entire star-map shut off.

Silence fell for exactly one insulted heartbeat. Then alarms started in earnest. Runes flared along the walls, lighting up in panicked red. Guards. Not human ones, but enchanted familiars poured in from side doors. These were cats bred for it. Bigger. Meaner. Their fur shimmered with bound runes. Collars lit with cold magical fire.

Their collars flared as they snapped orders to each other, claws extending, spells charging in twitchy arcs of light. They didn't know which catastrophe to pounce on first. They took one look at the scene—Peaches bristling over a burning scroll, Shrimp howling Enochian riddles while smoking slightly, Dorito trapped in a broken machine screaming about the math of the cosmos—and they hesitated.

They actually *hesitated*. And Mango chose that moment to make an entrance.

He wasn't supposed to be there. He was Infiltration. But Mango did nothing by the book. He sauntered straight into the chaos with the slow, practiced swagger of a con artist with nine lives and no morals.

A security familiar—the biggest of the lot, runes flashing warning sigils—turned toward him. Mango purred. Low. Alluring. Full of promise and absolute betrayal. He rubbed up against its flank. The familiar's eyes widened. Its runes flickered. It tried to remember its training. Mango nuzzled its jaw, tail flicking with lazy confidence. The familiar actually *blushed*. Its sigils glowed a confused pink. Its runes sputtered. And then they shorted out. It collapsed in a shuddering heap of static and purrs.

Mango winked at it. I felt Mittens and Clawrence lurking in the leyline's shadow, holding back until the fireworks gave them cover. From my balcony, I exhaled.

Sloppy predators. No stealth.

I shook Jake's massive head.

No. Ferals with ambition.

Below me, the room erupted. More guards poured in. The floor runes buckled under conflicting spells. Smoke poured from the walls as arcane systems overloaded.

And my team? They were already running in three different directions, screaming insults at each other. I tightened my claws into the stone. While they burned down subtlety, I'd slip through the service wing and steal the shard.

This was the distraction they were born to deliver. And I had work to do.

The corridor pulsed with leyline energy. Runes etched in obsidian walls flickered like dying stars. The floor was carved with glyphs designed to make you forget your own name if you stared too long. Jake's body pressed forward. Massive. Low. Breath steaming in the cold vault air.

Floor scent wrong. Step where I step.

His thought pressed into mine, calm as a scalpel.

Safe path. Follow my scent trail.

I blinked. The writhing glyphs resolved just enough to see the gaps. I adjusted our steps, claws scratching deliberate arcs into ancient stone.

Good hunting, Jake murmured.

We reached the vault door. Bronze and black iron. Thick. Etched in glyphwork that crawled like litigious centipedes.

Security built by sadists and mathematicians.

Jake didn't argue. I set his weight low. Claws splayed. We pressed hard at the edge, testing. Wards crackled.

Binding lines lit up in pale green, screaming about authorized access in a dead language.

Find the weakness. Where the territory splits, Jake whispered.

My eyes tracked the junction. The old locking sigils trembled with age, leyline energy buzzing like a liar's teeth.

There.

We braced. Claws dug in. Muscles coiled and struck. This wasn't about brute force. This was surgery with claws instead of scalpels. Jake's bulk did the talking—the kind of conversation that makes steel reconsider its life choices. The door squealed as ancient gears caught. Lock-runes flickered and died as our claws disrupted the tracing patterns. Sparks flew. A ward tried to grab our foreleg. Jake twisted. It fizzled into dead script.

We pushed again. The door gave up with a groan that belonged in a retirement home. Just enough space to squeeze through—barely an invitation.

I panted. *Subtle? No. But effective.*

Chaos surged through the gap behind us. Mango slunk through the gap, fur streaked with dust and disrupted ward-runes from the security familiar he'd seduced half to death. His whiskers twitched in unrepentant triumph.

Clawrence crashed in, wrestling with a metal-plated guard cat that shrieked with alchemical fury at every rake of claws. Sparks danced. The scent of scorched fur and burned sigils filled the hall.

Dorito tumbled in last. He rolled. Fur covered in chalk-dust constellations. Star maps scribbled across his sides in frantic scrawls.

"*I see the math,*" he breathed, eyes too wide.

God help us.

I bared Jake's teeth.

Focus, I sent across the link, voice like a cocked revolver.

They flinched. Even Mango.

Hold them here. Don't let anything follow me.

Jake agreed. *Pack distracts. We hunt deeper.*

Mango's purr tried for casual. *Yeah, sure. This is fine.*

Dorito saluted. Fell over.

Clawrence sank his teeth into the guard's plated neck with a snarl that sounded like a lawsuit filed by rage itself.

The vault door creaked wider. The hallway fell behind us like a slammed door, the noise dropping away to a hush so thick it felt personal. Cold slapped us in the face—the expensive kind of cold that rich people pay good money to store their secrets in.

Past the threshold, leyline energy muscled into my thoughts like a debt collector who knows where you live. It had weight. It had intentions. None of them friendly. Memory and will had built themselves a fortress here, using nightmares for the foundation and regrets for the cornerstones. It didn't just call me. It *mocked* me.

Jake's bulk anchored us against wards that wanted to fling us back into the hall. His mind was steady beneath mine.

Move silent. Territory ahead unclaimed, he urged.

I nodded. Part of me recoiled at the call. The other part reached for it like it was salvation and that was the worst truth of all.

Claws ready? Territory ahead. Jake asked.

Always.

Inside, leyline threads wove through the dark like veins

of trapped lightning, illuminating shapes I couldn't yet name—arcane geometries that whispered promises in languages that died for good reasons. If Mallory got here first, it wouldn't just be my mind lost. It would be the Cognichonk itself—rewritten with her voice.

We slipped through the gap and crossed the threshold.

The vault breathed around us. Jagged crystal ribs jutted from the walls—lightning that got caught and couldn't escape, still remembering what it meant to burn. The architecture of regret, designed by someone who understood that some treasures are just traps with better marketing. Sigils carved deep into the stone hummed like a choir that had forgotten the words but remembered the threat.

In the center stood the pedestal. The shard hovered inches above it. You'd call it crystal if you didn't know better. I knew better. This was thought with the temperature dropped out of it, light twisted into conspiracies that didn't need words. Humming like memory trying to rewrite itself.

Jake's massive frame slowed, muscles tensing with each step. His breath steamed in the cold.

Scent wrong. Approach slow, he rumbled.

Yeah, I replied. *Feels wrong.*

We crept closer. Claws clicked on crystal. The shard's glow hitched as we approached. Like seeing an old friend. Or recognizing fresh prey. It called to something in me I'd spent years trying to drink away. Part of me recoiled. The other part reached for it like salvation and that was the worst truth of all.

I raised a paw.

"Late again, partner."

The voice slithered from the shadows. He stepped out from between leyline pillars like he'd always belonged there.

Vance.

Orange fur sleek. Eyes gleaming with stolen knowledge. His tail moved with the kind of patience only killers cultivate. The slow pendulum of a countdown. And in one paw? The shard. Already his.

He turned it over lazily, letting it catch the leyline glow. The wards reacted, flickering like they respected him.

"Didn't think you'd let me have all the fun," he purred.

I froze. Vance wasn't just another Cognichonk conduit. He'd been my partner. My backup. The man who once saved my life with a single word and a loaded .38. Now he wore orange fur like the rest of us, smirking like he'd planned it all —another good man who'd made the mistake of thinking he could swim in corruption without swallowing some of it.

How the hell did you end up in this nightmare too?

I remembered him at my side. Kicking down doors. Sharing smokes on rain-soaked rooftops. Laughing between cases.

Mallory must have recruited you. Pulled you in like a hook through meat.

Jake's hackles rose beneath me. Claws scraped crystal with a sound like drawn blades.

Rival hunter. Quick paws, sharp eyes, Jake assessed, muscles coiling beneath me.

"Put it down, Vance," I growled.

He smirked.

"Ascend, Cannon. Or get left behind."

I hated how I understood him. How I wanted the same thing. Just not like this. He let the shard spin in his paw, casual as betrayal.

"Mallory taught you that?" I spat.

His grin sharpened.

"Mallory taught me ambition. Promised I could be the one mind left when the Cognichonk finished choosing."

He chuckled, low and pitying.

"You never did get the plan."

He wore my conscience like a cheap suit. Light exploded around him. Leyline energy coiled, glyphs shrieking as they bent. He saluted me with the shard. Then the bastard was gone—swallowed by leyline light that seemed happy to have him. The walls bled new runes where they'd been torn. Nothing gentle about this exit.

The pedestal cracked. Alarms screamed. Ceiling glyphs ruptured, raining sparks and molten sigil-shards. Debris crashed behind us. We'd have seconds to move or get buried with the truth.

I roared. Jake's voice joined mine. Perfect harmony of rage and loss.

And the vault began to collapse.

Glyphs flared red like dying sirens. The entire observatory shuddered. Cracks spidered across rune-etched walls, spitting leyline light in furious arcs. Above us, a containment circle failed with the wet pop of a cork pulled from reality.

The summoning array split with a sound like damnation. Bad Latin poured from the crack, followed by something worse—enchanted tuna cans launching like missiles with occult return addresses. They flew in ragged volleys—arcane sigils half-burned into cheap metal, labels screaming prophecy before bursting in fishy flame. One smashed the floor and detonated in glittering smoke that smelled of the sea and sin.

Dorito screamed in delight. He cartwheeled sideways, narrowly avoiding a can that exploded in midair, spraying him with glowing tuna chunks. "THE GODS PROVIDE!" he howled, licking his paw and immediately regretting it.

Mango had the kind of moves sin learns after a few drinks. He plucked flying cans from their suicide missions, tucking them against his chest like stolen evidence. "Souvenirs," he purred, eyes glinting with criminal pride.

Shrimp was beyond reason. He stood in the center of the chaos, fur singed, eyes wide as prophecy filled him like bad soup. "TUNA METEORS! TWELVE PAWS! THE PANTRY GOD RISES!"

Peaches bared her teeth. "Focus!" she hissed, batting a sizzling can aside before it could explode in her face. "We're not dying under a pile of cursed fish."

Clawrence snarled, batting aside rubble, then shielded Mittens with his bulk as the roof cracked overhead. "Move!" he barked, voice like gravel in an avalanche.

Mittens whimpered, tail puffed to twice its size, but stayed glued to Peaches, moving when she moved.

Sunbeam Jones sat in the corner, eyes half-lidded,

serenely ignoring the rain of fish. "I saw this coming," he muttered. "Just not the brand."

Jake's muscles bunched beneath me.

Pack move, he ordered, tail signaling the escape route.

I didn't argue. We surged forward. I let his bulk shove the others toward the exit. Mango cursed but ran. Dorito sang hymns to tuna. Shrimp shrieked doom. Peaches snarled orders. Clawrence roared, flattening debris. Mittens ran like regret. Sunbeam Jones loped after us, weirdly calm.

Outside, the cold night waited. We tumbled onto grass slick with magic runoff. Claws extended. Breaths ragged. Behind us, the observatory groaned, wards screaming as the roof sagged, vomiting leyline fire into the night.

We rest. Heal wounds. Find new hunting trail. Jake's thoughts cut through, practical and predatory.

I surveyed my disaster crew—chaos wearing fur coats, walking demolition charges with whiskers. Unruly. Dangerous. And somehow, inexplicably mine. The worst family a detective ever claimed. Vance had the shard. And he had answers to questions I wasn't done asking. We'd have to move before dawn. Hunt him down. Take it back.

I let the noir crawl in like old smoke. We came for a shard. We left with bruises, lies, and enough tuna to choke an alibi. I closed my eyes. Operation Tuna Eclipse was a success. If you define success as survival.

CHAPTER TWENTY

The marrow knew first. Something pulled at the core, fraying the edges of sanity. My thoughts scattered like evidence in a ceiling fan—drunk interns feeding my mind through industrial shredders. My consciousness splintered into jagged fragments, each one sharp enough to cut whatever was left of my sanity into ribbons too small to stitch back together.

Jake's body froze mid-stalk. Tail rigid. Reality shrunk to the size of a migraine. I clutched at my unraveling thoughts like a man trying to stuff cash back into a wallet during a hurricane.

"Jake," I rasped through grit and fangs. "Listen. The Chonk's pulling. It's coming apart."

He didn't move. But I felt him shudder. My voice rattled in his bones.

Don't. We're not done with this prey, his thought was a barbed whisper.

I forced focus. Pushed down the rising static. Tried to be the detective instead of the beast.

"Keep the crew tight. Gutterball. Shrimp. Bosco. Butternugget. Someone's gotta be the glue when everything goes to hell. Don't let them forget the mission when memory starts bleeding out the edges."

Abandoning our territory. Leaving the pack leaderless, accusation, sharp as broken glass.

"Not by choice." The hum rose like a siren in a hurricane. Violent. Hungry. The Cognichonk was calling in debts. "Stay focused. Remember the Widow. The sigils. The—"

The pull graduated to violence. My mind gave way like a cheap lock under a crowbar—splintering along fault lines I didn't know I had. Orange light crackled through the air, leaving the taste of static and old blood on the back of my tongue. The kind of sensory cocktail that comes with a hangover built right in.

"Hold them togeth—"

I needed more time. Always more time. Funny how that's the one thing no one ever has enough of, even when they're scattered across multiple hosts. The Cognichonk was calling in debts with the enthusiasm of a bookie whose client just lost big at the tracks. My thoughts unraveled in his skull. A last, tattered plea: *Hold them together.*

The orange static opened its jaws. Not content with swallowing—it devoured with the appetite of something that's been hungry since before hunger had a name. Teeth made of yarn and broken memory closed around what was left of me. I fell screaming into the void, my voice the last thing to go.

Wet leaves, cold mud, and the sour stink of regret filled my nostrils. Hazards of waking up face-down in a world that didn't care if you got up again. Just another morning in the continuous disappointment I called existence—waking up as someone else's bad decision. I sneezed myself awake. One eyelid refused to cooperate. Butternugget's body wasn't built for grace even on good days. My claws twitched, scrabbling at soggy dirt.

Fog crawled along the ground like it had something to hide. Cheap streetlights leaked yellow through the murk—the kind of illumination that makes secrets look worse than they are. Discount noir for a markdown detective.

I groaned. "Butternugget."

No answer. Just a wet gurgle from somewhere in the digestive bureaucracy of chaos incarnate.

"Hey." I shook my head, static fuzz roaring in my skull. "Focus. What happened? Where were you at the heist? Why weren't you there?"

He blinked. Wrong eye first. Tail curled like a question it didn't want answered. Thoughts frothed.

Got lost.

The words tumbled out like someone yelling them through a drainpipe.

Lost forever. Good lost. Tasty lost.

I snarled. "Again?"

Always lost. Good for the soul. Good for the paws. Bad for planning.

I shut my eyes against reality. Vance's grin floated in the

darkness—smug bastard with the shard in his paws while the observatory crumbled around us. Something burned behind my ribs. Not heartburn. Failure. The team blown to the winds like dandelion seeds. And something worse—the distinct feeling of being prey instead of predator.

I dragged my voice down to the basement where the serious conversations happen. "Then what?" The kind of question that comes with its own brass knuckles.

Butternugget shivered. His nose twitched.

Smelled Bosco. Bosco old. Bosco smells like secrets in boxes. Followed. Good idea.

"And?"

He licked one shoulder with unholy devotion.

Bug.

I felt the joy hit like cheap liquor.

Wiggly. Crunchy. Divine.

I let air hiss between my teeth. "So that's your story. Got lost. Missed the score. Followed Bosco's scent trail. Then threw it all away for a bug. And now I'm back in your fur-for-brains body. Again."

He preened. Tail slapped mud with idiotic pride.

Bug was holy. Crunchy truth. Worth it.

Time was a luxury I couldn't afford. Vance had the shard. My crew was scattered across the city like lottery tickets after a windstorm. I needed something solid—a lead, a friendly face, hell, even a halfway decent lie would do.

"Listen to me." My words were granite. "We need to find Bosco. He'll know where the others went. Maybe what the Widow's next move is. Maybe *anything*."

Butternugget's pupils dilated. The fog caught the shine, turned it into hungry madness. He twitched.

Fog has patterns. Secret maps. Lickable maps.

"Don't lick the fog."

But it hums.

I swallowed bile. "We're going to talk to Bosco. You're going to behave. Or so help me, I'll recite every limerick you've ever half-thought until your brain melts."

He shivered. Thoughts rattling.

No limericks. They rhyme too hard. They know too much.

"Focus."

He turned to the mist. Sniffed like he was trying to inhale destiny.

But first... snack?

"Control yourself, for once."

Snack later?

"Sure. Later."

He yowled. Loud enough to wake the fog itself.

Fog settled in for the long haul. Dawn light seeped through—weak and watery, like a confession mumbled to a priest who's heard it all before. Cold draped itself over everything—the kind of chill that makes promises it intends to keep. Grass crackled underpaw. Frost breaking in sharp little snaps, each step sounding like an alibi too loud to hold.

Gravestones leaned like drunks with grudges. Names that once meant something to somebody were losing the fight against wind and time—just like the rest of us. The markers stood as silent witnesses to the ultimate cold case —death making its final argument without needing to raise its voice. Lines of accusation fading but not forgotten. Crows perched along the fence—black-robed and judgmental. Their harsh calls cut through fog like they were testifying against the living. No absolution in those voices. Just cold facts.

I tried wrestling Butternugget's body into something resembling dignity. Slow steps. Solemn pace. The whole funeral march routine. His response? Vibrating like he'd mainlined espresso.

Eat it?

"Not everything needs to be eaten."

Eat later?

"Not if I can help it."

He hissed at the cold.

Tastes like old bones. Good bones.

"Not why we're here."

My tail—his tail—jerked like a question mark in search of trouble. I forced it down.

Ahead of us sat Bosco. Orange-and-white. Elder. Still as a grudge that finally stopped explaining itself. His fur puffed against the cold, scars on his nose mapping every battle he didn't want to discuss. He didn't blink. Didn't need to. Ghosts didn't scare him.

We paused at the edge of the grave. Jareth Vale. Letters cut once with precision, now nearly gone. A feline pawprint worn to a smudge. Runes at the base, scars in stone remembering old intentions the world would rather forget.

The fog writhed like it had secrets it didn't want found. Silence pressed in. The honest kind. The kind you can't bribe.

Butternugget's ears twitched. Nose worked overtime.

Crow smells.

"Ignore it."

Feathers. Crunch. Screaming snacks.

"I swear to god, Butternugget..."

He tried to lean forward. I yanked him back. He squeaked. Humiliating. A sound like a cork popping on dignity. I swore internally. Butternugget's body didn't obey so much as *negotiate*.

Frost? Roll in it. Mark it. Own it.

"No. Sit."

But it's so cold it bites. Good frost.

"We're not here to roll. We're here to remember."

He twitched. Tail slapped mud in protest.

Bosco didn't so much as flick an ear. He'd seen too many mornings like this. Too many graves. He wasn't here for drama or forgiveness. He was the sentinel no one asked for but everyone needed.

I tried to hush Butternugget's twitching limbs. Forced breath slow. The hush of the cemetery felt earned. Heavy. We watched Bosco watch the grave.

The crows called once more. The fog swallowed the sound whole. Frost melted into dirty water under a dawn that didn't pretend to care.

And the old cat didn't move. Did not need to.

He was here to remember.

Frost had teeth in this part of the cemetery. Grave dirt frozen solid—stubborn as the regrets of dead men. The kind of cold that doesn't just chill your bones but reminds them they're just waiting their turn to join the underground democracy where everyone gets equal real estate.

Butternugget's idea of stealth involved all the grace of a

drunk raccoon in a trash can symphony. He moved like guilt with a hangover—loud, messy, and announcing its presence to anyone unfortunate enough to be in earshot. Each step announced our presence to the dead. His paws found every twig, every frozen leaf. Crunch. Snap. He turned the sacred silence into a percussion section for the deceased. Our very own funeral clown, minus the makeup.

"Careful." I tried to guide him. "Act like you've been to a funeral before."

He paused. Blinked. One eye wandered off early.

Never died once. Don't know the rules.

His whiskers twitched. Fog clung to his whiskers—the kind of damp that seeps into bones and memories alike. Stubborn as old guilt. He leaned down. Sniffed the grave. Nose quivering like it was reading the obituary.

Smells like old dirt. Sad dirt. Crunchy bones.

"Leave it alone."

Butternugget's paw flexed. Dug once. A clump of frost cracked.

"No digging."

He hesitated, whiskers twitching with temptation. *But it's loose. Wants to move. Wants to be free.*

I seized control. Forced the paw to retreat. We stood there. The grave marker loomed. Jareth Vale. Letters half-drowned in time, a feline pawprint worn to memory's scar. Runes circled the base. Old wardings. Now just scratches in stone. Like they tried to hold something back, failed, and accepted it.

Bosco watched us. Orange-and-white. Elder. Scars on his nose like old signatures on a contract he couldn't break. Calm. Implacable.

"Bosco," I rasped through Butternugget's throat. "You pick the cheeriest spots. Smells like betrayal and wet stone."

Bosco didn't blink. Didn't flinch.

Butternugget sniffed again. *Jareth. Sounds chewable.*

"Not now."

Why? Tasty name.

"Shut up."

I tried to steady us. Forced Butternugget's tail to stop flicking like it was signing confessions in the fog. I stared at the grave.

"Jareth Vale," I muttered. Voice low. Bitter. "Even the stone tries to forget him."

Memory clawed at the edge of thought. The fog shivered. And then the vision took me. But this wasn't mine. It was *his*. Another orange. Another shard in the Chonk. The memory preserved like a crime scene photo in the yarn.

Candlelight. Too many flames. Arranged in a spiral. Wax dripped like blood trying to write an apology. The Cognichonk at the center. Humming. Glowing. Breathing. A heartbeat for sins.

The Widow hunched over it, hair falling like a veil, shoulders shaking with stolen sobs.

"He meowed. I thought I had him back."

The body on the floor was orange. Young. Fur matted with chalk dust and tears. Eyes glazed and empty. Sigils burned into the floor. Reflection. Anchor. Will. Words that promised safety. Delivered death instead.

Her hand trembled on his ribs. The Cognichonk pulsed. And he meowed. But the sound was wrong. Older.

Male. Her husband's voice. Forced through a throat that wasn't his.

She wailed. Clutched him closer. He went limp forever.

I felt Butternugget *jerk* under me. The memory hit him too. Hit *us*. A sound from the Chonk itself. A dying mewl. The final thought of that orange cat echoing across every shard.

Hurts. Butternugget yowled. High and awful. His body convulsed in the frost. *Stop. Don't want this. Bad story. Bad ending. No.*

I couldn't hold back. My voice broke.

"She killed him. For a voice."

Butternugget's claws raked the grave dirt. He howled. Not for her. Not for Jareth Vale. For the *one she used.*

Bosco didn't move. Didn't flinch. Just blinked. Slow. A sentinel who'd seen too many like this. Maybe he knew that cat too.

Silence crystallized between us, hard as the frost claiming our whiskers. We stood there shivering, neither of us willing to break it. Some truths cut deeper when nobody acknowledges them out loud.

Frost gave ground inch by grudging inch. Dawn crawled over the horizon—the kind of pale, merciless light that shows you things better left in darkness.

Butternugget shifted, paws restless on grave dirt that felt too fresh.

"Don't," I warned.

But he trembled.

Cold. Wrong cold. Don't like it.

"I know."

Still feels like screaming.

He let out a low, broken yowl. Not loud. Not threatening. Wounded.

Crows shifted on the fence, black feathers whispering against each other. They stayed put. Grief was just background noise to professional mourners like them.

"Quiet," I hissed, the edge gone from my voice. Anger's hard to maintain when you're watching something break in real time. "We're not done here."

He sniffled. Yes, sniffled. Mucus and mud and tragedy, bundled in orange fur that couldn't hold still.

Hurts. Don't know why.

"Because you felt it," I said, the words scraping my throat raw.

His dying? Butternugget's voice cracked like thin ice.

"Yeah." Some conversations should require permits and protective gear.

He whimpered in my head.

Don't want it. Don't want dead in me.

"Me neither."

He shuddered. Then pounced forward without warning.

Gotta dig it out.

"Hold it steady, you degenerate—"

But his claws were already raking at the dirt. Frost cracked like old bones. He yowled again. Higher this time. Grief and panic both.

Get it out. Get it out.

"Stop—"

But then the soil parted. Something pale jutted from the

churned earth. We froze. Not bone. Ceramic. A shard. Broken. Lost.

Butternugget sniffed. Whiskers trembled.

Smells burned. Hurt. Smells like... like...

He couldn't finish. I scraped it clean. Glyphs revealed themselves like guilty confessions.

Containment. Severance. Resurrection.

My voice went hoarse. "A ward meant to save. Shattered like her sanity."

Butternugget leaned in. Nose wet. Breath shaking.

We eat it?

"No."

Bite it? Break it worse?

"It's already broken."

He whimpered. Tail thumping dirt in a miserable rhythm.

Don't like this place. Feels like crying.

"Then cry. But don't run."

He went still. Shuddered. My gaze caught the signature scrawled in the shard's edge.

Jessa.

My voice dropped. "She tried to stop it." The words fell from my mouth like stones into an open grave—heavy with the certainty that good intentions make the best paving material on the road to hell.

Butternugget's ears flattened.

Did she die?

"Maybe. Maybe worse."

Silence dropped on us like the last shovelful of dirt at a pauper's funeral. Bosco sat watching, eyes fixed and unforgiving. His whiskers twitched once—the closest thing to judgment he'd offer. Then a single meow rolled out of him, low and weighted with something that felt too much like my own guilt.

We settled in beside the old tom. Just three minds trapped in two orange bodies, keeping company with a grave while dawn did its best to burn away secrets along with the fog.

I let the words slip out. "The dead kept their secrets. But not all of them stayed buried."

Butternugget's tail twitched.

Smells like secrets. He sniffed. *And... maybe worms. Don't want worms today.*

His head lowered.

Want warm. Want safe.

I didn't answer. Because there was nothing honest left to say.

Fog was losing its fight with morning. Dawn ripped it away like bandages from a wound that wasn't ready—all harsh light and brutal honesty where shadows had been kinder. I sat in Butternugget's borrowed skin, staring at the grave. Frost had gone soft and useless. Dirt lay churned up at our feet—evidence of our trespassing that wouldn't wash away any easier than the guilt.

Bosco held his ground like he'd signed a contract with gravity. Eyes hard as cemetery markers, refusing negotiation. The old tom had picked his post and wasn't taking applications for replacement.

"Stay if you want," I rasped. "You've earned it."

He didn't answer. Just blinked once. Slow. Final.

Butternugget squirmed.

Hate it here.

"I know."

Cold. Heavy. Feels like ghosts in my fur.

"Sorry, buddy."

Can we go?

I sucked air through teeth that felt too sharp for my mouth. Wind cut back, making its own point about who really owned the morning.

"We can go."

But Butternugget's mind rattled on like a drunk with a conspiracy theory.

But where? Out there's worse. He's out there. The shard-thief.

Fear had found a home in his voice and was settling in for the long haul.

"Vance."

He'll eat us. Crack us like bugs. Steal the voice.

My tail lashed.

"We'll make him choke on it."

The words tasted like cheap whiskey—harsh going down but warming in the gut. Butternugget's whole body trembled like a confession on the verge of breaking.

Promise? His voice small as a lost kitten's.

"Promise."

Some lies you tell because the truth won't get you out of bed in the morning. He let out a sound halfway between a yowl and a cough.

Then let's go now. No more graves. Don't wanna smell dead. Wanna smell alive.

"Yeah."

I turned us away. Bosco stayed, unmoving. Judge. Witness. The last honest mourner.

We crossed the cemetery like trespassers with expired permits. Frost surrendered to mud beneath us, marking each step with small betrayals. Behind us, the grave sat open. Secrets bared. Nothing left to forgive. Ahead? The whole damned case.

The sun muscled its way over the horizon without apologies. We walked straight into its glare like moths with bad judgment. Light cut too sharp, too clean—a scalpel working the edges of my borrowed mind. Butternugget shivered under me.

Don't wanna go there. Don't wanna see.

My will made his claws flex, digging into mud and memory.

"Easy," I muttered, trying to sound like someone worth trusting. "I'm here."

Empty promises from a detective who specialized in leaving. He squirmed. Tail whipping.

Too bright. Don't like it. Don't—

"I know." I tried to keep my voice steady, like I was the adult in the room. "Focus. Just breathe."

Then the hum found us—thick as old motor oil and twice as toxic. Ancient. Hungry. The Cognichonk making its claim, hooking something behind my ribs and pulling with the patience of a debt collector.

Butternugget's thoughts scattered like roaches when the

kitchen light flicks on. Panic crackled through his mind, making static of everything else.

Where you going? Don't go!

My vision blurred. Lines of the world bled like cheap ink in the rain.

"I'm not—" I tried to promise. But my voice cracked.

Butternugget's fear clawed at me.

Don't leave me! Stay in the head! Keep the voice!

I dug in like a man hanging off a ledge with sweaty fingers. No use. The hum found something behind my ribs that belonged to it and yanked with the authority of fate calling in markers. Butternugget shrieked, wild and terrified. His mind spasmed under mine.

Stay! Don't leave alone in here!

"I'm trying," I rasped. The words tore like paper. "I'm trying to—"

The Cognichonk didn't care. It pulled me out. I felt my hold on Butternugget fail. His paws went limp beneath my will. The world fell away—grass, mud, light—peeling off like old wallpaper.

And then there was only the hum. Thick. Smug. Hungry. I screamed. But there was no sound. Only static.

I fell like a man kicked down an elevator shaft—through layers of orange, through fur and fang, through the howling chorus of a thousand feline minds. Eyes watched my descent—orange, slit-pupiled, hungry. Infinite. I tumbled through their judgment like a detective who'd failed his last case.

I felt *all* of them for one breathless instant. Their terror. Their hunger. Their scattered fragments of me. One hissed poetry in my voice. Another wailed in raw need. Another laughed like breaking glass. My network. My prison.

I spun in the hum, weightless. Directionless. Searching for an anchor. Any anchor.

Please—

The Cognichonk twisted. Tightened. And then chose. Dragged me somewhere else.

Far away, in an alley that stank of candle wax and old fish bones, something small and scrawny looked up from a spiral of string. Eyes wide. Mouth open. Waiting for me.

CHAPTER TWENTY-ONE

The alley didn't invite visitors. It swallowed them. A single broken security lamp flickered like it was confessing under duress, casting shadows thick enough to hide regret, old crimes, and the bodies of better ideas. This was where ambition came to die—where dreams checked in but only nightmares checked out. The walls were scabbed with graffiti layered so many times it read like a palimpsest of threats.

And at the center, the shrine. Trash heaps arranged in spirals, deliberate and defiant. Old takeout boxes folded like origami curses. Tangles of string tied in knots too complex to be accidents—this was ritual architecture, built from urban decay and optimism gone feral. A cathedral for the damned, where prayers were offered in garbage and answered in blood. Bits of fish bone laid out with priestly precision. Bottle caps gleamed like false promises in the gutter light. Broken glass caught the glow and threw it back in fragmented halos.

Candle stubs melted into the trash piles, their wax fossilized in shapes that looked like screaming mouths. Some were still lit, their tiny flames guttering, casting twitchy shadows in the shapes of sigils no sane cat would draw.

I watched through eyes that weren't mine, trapped in a brain too small for both of us. Shrimp padded around it all like he owned it. Or worshiped it. Hard to tell the difference. His body was all angles and bad decisions. Orange fur stretched over a skeleton that hadn't eaten a square meal since Nixon resigned. His tail twitched like it was sending Morse code to ghosts. His eyes had swallowed too much night, dilated past wonder into territory the law hadn't named yet. Three AM eyes in a midnight world. He moved like a question nobody wanted to answer—the kind that comes knocking at 3 AM with a warrant for your conscience and no patience for your alibis.

I felt every twitch of his whiskers, every pulse of his racing heart. The Cognichonk had made room for me here, whether Shrimp liked it or not.

He hummed under his breath. A tuneless chant. A threat in minor key.

The Knot remembers. The Knot knows.

The words crawled through his head. Static through old wiring. The kind that starts fires when nobody's watching. The words bypassed his throat entirely. They leaked straight from his brain like radiation, poisoning any mind foolish enough to listen. Only the ruined could hear them clearly. Tuned to the Cognichonk, for knot was the shape and method. The spiral that bound them all. Understanding was for philosophers and dead men. Shrimp had something better: blind, twitchy obedience that scratched at his insides like a parasite with a pension plan.

He circled the shrine, humming louder. He lifted one paw with the slow precision of a bomb technician. The twine had sagged, offended gravity somehow. Couldn't have that. Not when prophecy was on the line.

I remembered the pull. The way the Cognichonk had taken me from another host—left that orange furball behind, empty and mewling. It didn't apologize. It just redirected. Now I was here, in Shrimp, feeling every thread tug.

Names were scrawled in soot along the brick wall. Some real, some invented, some that looked like they were trying to escape the letters they were spelled with. Sigils were painted in what might have once been barbecue sauce. Or blood. Or both.

He sniffed at them with the solemnity of a priest reading ancient scripture. The wind shifted. It didn't clear the smell. It rearranged it. Rancid grease. Burned wax. Fish bones that had opinions about decay.

Shrimp shivered in delight. He spun once in place, the tip of his tail tracing another spiral in the grime. The movement was precise despite his mania—this was choreography in garbage, holy writ in refuse.

He hummed louder. Louder still. His voice cracked into a laugh that shouldn't have belonged to anything living. Then he went still. Entirely.

One paw rose. Trembled. Descended. He pressed it into the center of a spiral of string laid out on a flattened pizza box. The box groaned under the pressure like it was trying to recant its crimes.

Shrimp's eyes narrowed to slits. His breathing slowed to something approximating sacrament—the deliberate inhale of a priest who's stopped believing in redemption but still performs the rituals because damnation demands proper paperwork.

"The Knot remembers. The Knot knows."

The words weren't his anymore. They were the shrine's. The alley's. The city's. Shrimp just lent them a mouth.

The candlelight guttered in time with his breath. Shadows lengthened, drawing new lines on old walls. The sigils seemed to shift, ever so slightly, as if grateful for the attention.

Shrimp exhaled. A sound halfway between a purr and a death rattle. He did not smile. He didn't need to. The Knot smiled for him.

The Knot Temple festered at the corner of Forgotten and Damned. A wound the city never bothered to clean. It was the belly of an urban leviathan that forgot it was alive. Someone had given the trash purpose. Arranged it like evidence at a crime scene where the victim was reality itself. Arranged in ritual spirals. Layers of filth matted into a kind of unholy carpet—old newspapers, oily rags, bones gone chalky with time. Wax ran in hardened rivulets across pizza boxes that bowed and cracked with the weight of melted prophecy.

The smell hit first—the kind that makes honest men confess to crimes they haven't committed yet. Rot fermenting into something religious. Cardboard gone soft with secrets. Grease that burned black but remembered being alive. And those fishbones? They'd been preaching gospel to the rats since Tuesday.

Shrimp claimed the center like he owned the real estate. Runt of a kitten with fur the color of bad omens. His breath came quick and shallow, each rib counting down to something final. He shivered—not from cold. The kind of shiver that comes when the universe notices you noticing it back.

I felt it before Shrimp did. No. Wait. I feel it because he does.

Something crawled through the air before it vibrated. The kind of sound that bypasses your ears and files straight for your molars like it's got a grudge against dental work. The warning growl a predator makes when it's already too late to run. The candlelight flickered once. Then twice. Shadows lengthened in all the wrong directions.

Shrimp's nose twitched. He sniffed. "Smells like old truth," he mumbled. "Rotten. Delicious."

Shrimp, don't—

But the kitten wasn't listening. He was listening to something else. He went the kind of still that makes time check its watch. The air knew better than to move around him.

I felt it in our shared ribs—the shallow drag of breath

freezing mid-theft. Heartbeat slowing like some cosmic debt collector was winding it down for non-payment. Claws punched out. Dug into the cardboard. Splitting it with the sound of wet paper being torn.

The wax of old candles softened. Started writing checks neither of us could cash. Sigils. The kind I'd seen before in places that don't exist on maps.

Not here. Not now.

Shrimp's pupils swallowed themselves, then started on the rest of the room. Black holes with orange rims. The candlelight didn't stand a chance. His jaw came unhinged— the sound wet and final, like the last move in a game nobody should play. The first breath out was too loud. A hiss that steamed in the cold damp air like a kettle's last confession before the warranty expired. The second breath carried words. Way too deep for his tiny ribs.

"The Mirror will crack."

It didn't echo. It dug. I felt it scrape the inside of our shared skull.

Stop. Stop it.

Shrimp's body shook. Bones rattling against each other like dice rolled for sins. The shadows shifted. Crawled. Started tracing lines on the walls in shapes that hurt to see. Wax ran uphill.

"Twelve paws will bleed."

I tried to shout.

Shrimp—pull back. Don't let it speak. Don't let it use you.

Shrimp's back arched. A crack ran down the old cardboard beneath us. The sound made my ears flatten in our shared skull. Shrimp didn't hear. Didn't move on his own anymore.

Salt and old blood hung in the air like they were waiting for an invitation—party guests who'd arrived too early and brought gifts nobody wanted to unwrap. The kind of damp that seeps into your clothes, then your skin, then starts asking questions about who you really trust. Betrayal has a smell. This was worse. The candles hissed as their wicks bent into unnatural angles, curling into spirals. Shrimp's claws split the cardboard. Blood welled at the tips.

The blood hit my senses like a confession. Warm. Sticky. Coppery. Then came the worst part—recognition. This blood belonged to us.

The air vibrated again.

"He who sleeps in the pantry shall rise."

Shrimp's tail went rigid. The fur bristled so violently the sound was like dry static. I pushed.

Kid, I'm riding shotgun in your skull whether you like it or not. Tune in to my frequency before whatever's on the other channel burns us both down.

But Shrimp's eyes weren't seeing. Not the temple. Not the trash. Not even the shadows. He was seeing *through*.

The candlelight went out. Then roared back twice as bright. The flames burned green at the edges. The trash spiral caught fire at a single point. Burned a perfect line.

I tried to pull back. Tried to break the connection. It didn't let me.

Shrimp's mouth opened. A voice that wasn't his. A voice that had teeth.

"Jessa. She wrote the sigil."

No. No no no. Don't give it names. Don't make it real.

But it was too late. My vision cracked. The temple held steady. It was the network that cracked—a spiderweb of orange consciousness splitting under pressure.

Orange fur everywhere. Shapes flickering.

Mango. Tall. Regal. Bristling in an empty basement. Eyes wide with fear he wouldn't name.

Clawrence. Stalking in a rusting shipping container, walls smeared with chalk lines that refused to stay erased. His tail lashed in figure-eights of warning.

Dorito. Perched on a street sign over a four-lane road, fur fluffed to the size of a small bear, eyes black as debts.

They all heard it. They all *felt* it. I felt them flicker inside him. Their thoughts bled together.

"Stop it. Stop it."

"We can't."

"We have to."

"It's coming."

Shrimp's body spasmed. I felt the pain crack down our shared spine. The taste of iron. Shrimp's tongue lolled. He drooled blood onto the cardboard. The spiral of trash caught it, drank it in.

Shrimp shuddered. His voice cracked into something worse than words. Something older.

"Sever or serve. Choose."

The air snapped like a rope being cut. The candles blew out. Silence swallowed them whole—the kind of quiet that falls after a confession that can't be taken back, when truth has already done its damage and there's nothing left but to count the bodies.

I tried to speak. But the mouth wasn't mine.

Shrimp collapsed. Tiny body hitting the cardboard with the wet finality of a case file being stamped 'closed.' His breath came in jagged sobs that tore at the edges of our shared lungs. He whined. Curled. Uncurled. Scrabbled at the cardboard like he was trying to dig down into the Earth. He mewled. High. Broken.

"Where'd it go?"

Shrimp. Hey. I'm here. I'm with you.

Shrimp sniffed. Tears pooled. He coughed once. It was wet. Red. The air still smelled like blood and melted wax. But it was clearing.

Shrimp's eyes blinked. Came back into focus. He stared at the ruined spiral. At the blood drying in lines that still seemed to *move* if you looked too long.

He whimpered.

"Luis? That was you, right? Tell me it was you."

I'm here. I'm here. It wasn't me. I mean—it was. But it wasn't.

Shrimp shook. His fur bristled and settled in waves. He sniffed. Snot dripped from his nose onto the trash.

"It hurt."

I know.

"I don't wanna say things. I don't wanna know things. Make it stop."

I tried to hold him. But there were no arms. Just shared breath.

We can try. We can try to stop. But you have to listen next time.

Shrimp shuddered again. He pulled his tail up. Wrapped it around himself like a shield.

The candle smoke hung in the air. Bitter. Acrid. Shapes moved in it. Letters. Lines. Spirals.

Shrimp watched them with tears in his eyes.

"Tell them to go away," he whispered.

I can't.

The shapes didn't go. They burned in memory. Carved themselves behind the eyes. I closed them. It didn't help.

We're not done. It's never done.

The hum faded. For now.

"Sever or serve," he mumbled, the prophecy's echo still clinging to his tiny voice. He coughed once more. Spat blood onto the ruin of his shrine. He wiped his mouth on the back of one trembling paw.

"Luis?" he whimpered. "It hurts inside my words."

I didn't answer. I couldn't. Because the words were still crawling through both of us like worms that had developed a taste for truth and weren't done feeding.

The shrine was bleeding out alongside him. Candles melted down to their last prayers, their smoke hanging accusations neither of us could answer. Night air thick enough to chew. Wax hardened into evidence of something nobody should have witnessed. History cooling one drip at a time across trash that knew too much. The graffiti seemed to sweat in the gutterlight.

Shrimp hit the center knot like a bullet finding its mark. The string crunched beneath him—brittle, filthy, satisfied. It had been waiting for exactly this surrender. He shuddered. Drew a slow, ragged breath.

A voice cut through the shadows—too old, too soft for an alley that specialized in broken glass and broken promises: "Easy now. Easy. He's breathing. Slowing down."

Shrimp whimpered. His flanks worked overtime for half-pay, each breath clocking in late and leaving early. A thin reedy wheeze escaped his nose like the last customer out of a doomed speakeasy. He didn't fight anymore. Just lay there, accepting terms nobody should sign.

His purr kicked in like a failing engine that remembered better days. A motor running on fumes, rattling bones that weren't built to house prophecies. The sound settled. Found its rhythm. Dangerous.

I felt it climb my ribs one by one. A vibration behind my heart where no one's supposed to touch. The way innocence feels right before someone puts a price tag on it.

Shrimp's eyes half-lidded. Glassy. Lost. The kind of lost that doesn't show up on missing posters. He licked the knot of string with surgical focus. Each flick of his tongue performing an autopsy on what looked like a toy but mapped the city's cancer. No kitten should know that taste. The taste made him wince, but he didn't stop. Couldn't. Not when truth had its claws in your tongue.

"Taste bad. S'posed to. Gotta be right."

He hummed to himself. A lullaby that had lost its words in a back-alley deal with something that collected innocence.

"Shh... shhh... good string... stay put... stay tied."

The spiral twitched beneath his tongue. Moved. Just a hair. I felt our claws twitch, deep in muscle memory I didn't control.

God help us. It's listening.

I wanted to shout. To scream at Shrimp to run, to never come back here. But I was pinned. Stuck. A passenger in a getaway car with no driver and brakes that had made other arrangements.

I was a detective without a warrant in someone else's crime scene. The prophecy was over. But the truth was waiting.

The alley fell silent. Except for that gentle purr. It spread through the trash. The walls seemed to listen.

Shrimp's voice slurred: "M'kay now. All done. M'kay."

He yawned wide enough to swallow futures neither of us wanted to see. I felt the jaw pop in sympathy. Then gravity won—it always does. Shrimp's face hit the filthy spiral, his breath catching once like it might make a run for it, then deciding to stay. Sleep came like a sentence without parole.

The Cognichonk remembered.

A crunch of gravel. Boots with purpose. A lantern lifted like judgment day had found its flashlight. The light sliced through smoke and filth, exposing twisted sigils that should've stayed in the dark.

A voice, softer than prophecy but older than the city: "There you are, you poor thing."

Another voice behind it, even older, clipped: "Told you the stringwork would lead us."

My ears flattened in Shrimp's head like a gambler's last chips being swept off the table.

They know. They know what this is. Recognition's the kind of currency you can't counterfeit.

Warm hands scooped Shrimp up, lifting him from the ruin of his shrine. Gentle but firm—the touch of someone who'd pulled too many victims from too many disasters to still believe in accidents. He mewed once—the sound a pawnshop receipt for his dignity. The coarse fabric against his fur smelled of coffee and herbal antiseptic—the perfume of people who'd seen too much and decided to do something about it.

"Shh. Easy now. You've done enough tonight."

Another voice, worried and sure: "Wrap him up. He's freezing. We're getting him to the vet before it gets worse. He'll make it though."

I listened to their breathing. Calm. Competent. The kind of steady that comes from dancing with chaos until it sends you a Christmas card.

Witches. Gotta be. Not the first time they've pulled someone from the Chonk.

I tried to push out. To speak. Nothing. Might as well have been pounding on a door that didn't exist. Shrimp just whimpered and curled in the stranger's arms, surrendering to safety like it was a concept he'd only heard rumors about.

Will he be safe? Safe's a relative term in a city where even shadows carry switchblades.

I wanted to ask. I didn't get to.

They turned. Carried Shrimp away. Backlit by flickering lantern light that painted them as saviors or kidnappers—the jury was still deliberating. The spiral of string twitched in the gutter like it was waving goodbye. Or taking notes. Watching them go with the patience of something that knows addresses don't matter when you've already marked your prey.

I felt the pull in our chest tighten once. Twist. And then *snap.* The connection ripped free like a bad tooth from a worse jaw. Not clean. Never clean. Like barbed wire yanked out of wet clay.

I reeled. No body now. No paws. No lungs pulling ragged air. Just consciousness. Weightless. Unmoored. A private eye with no office, floating in the black between minds where even shadows need a light to exist. I felt the ghosts of claws. The ache of bloodied pads. Phantom limb pain for a body I'd borrowed and broken, like a loan shark's warning.

Shrimp's fear. His pain. The taste of string on a kitten's tongue—bitter as promises made in back alleys. The way that fragile purr had clung to life even as prophecy crawled out of his throat like a confession under third-degree lights.

I tried to steady myself. Tried to remember who I was. Who I'd been. Detective. Cynic. Professional. But the Cognichonk didn't care about my resume. It used me like a scalpel on Monday, a crowbar on Tuesday, and brass knuckles for the weekend shift.

It tossed me. From orange to orange. From case to case. A temp worker in the cosmic gumshoe agency, leaving them all in tatters. I saw their faces flicker in the dark—mug shots of the innocent.

Butternugget. Spinning in manic glee before crumpling in a gutter.

Rutabaga. Slashed by prophecy while dodging sticky fingers and pastel lies.

Shrimp. Sweet, stupid Shrimp. Still licking the string even as it bit back.

I'm the infection. I'm the reason they twitch and scream and see too much. I'm the voice in their head that won't shut up—a midnight radio playing confessions on a frequency only the damned can hear.

I drifted. No form. No fur. Just thought. A detective reduced to his case notes with no case file to hold them.

I didn't ask for this.

But I felt the Cognichonk tighten around me anyway.

Didn't matter.

The Cognichonk pulsed somewhere beyond sight. A

slow, cosmic purr. Promising nothing. Demanding everything.

I closed my eyes in the dark. I knew it was waiting to send me again. To break someone else open. I would go. I always did. But for now, I let the silence hold me.

Because there was no comfort. Only truth. And truth had claws.

CHAPTER TWENTY-TWO

They called it abandoned. Luis would have called it prepared.

Vex called it hers.

This body wasn't meant for Mallory Vex. But she wore it perfectly. Perdita moved with predatory grace through the collapsed shop, her movements too deliberate, too controlled for a simple house cat.

The shop had collapsed under time and disuse. Dust and mold fought for territory on walls thick with old silence. Perdita's nose twitched at the scent, wanting to sneeze, but Vex didn't allow it. This place had died long before they arrived—just another crime scene where the only witness was decay and the murder weapon was abandonment.

Counters lay toppled like barricades in a lost war. Shelves split in ruin, leaking secrets and mildew in equal measure—the aftermath of a battle between purpose and neglect where both sides claimed victory and left the civilians to bury the dead. Glass shards littered the floor, arranged with obsessive precision. Each one angled to catch the guttering candlelight and hurl it into corners, throwing sigils onto the crumbling walls. The reflections weren't illumination. They were instruction. Warning. Promise.

Perdita's body resisted with every muscle. She hated this place. Hated the smell of sulfur, old catnip, and burnt rosemary. The whisper of bloodroot ground into the chalk lines that circled the floor in hateful geometry. Vex let her hate it. Let her *feel* it. Fear was an excellent teacher.

The chalk lines weren't simple. Circles nested in triangles. Triangles split by squares. Every intersection annotated in looping cat-Latin: *Memorari. Eligere. Vindicari.*

Vex made Perdita walk the lines. Slow. Deliberate. Her pads pressed into the salt grit scattered across the chalk, each step a signature on a contract she hadn't read. Her paw jerked back from a glyph like it burned. Vex slammed it down against the mark, holding it there until the chalk smudged with Perdita's struggling.

The cat's claws unsheathed involuntarily. She tried to retract them. Vex didn't let her.

Hurts— The thought flickered through Perdita's mind.

Good, Vex thought back.

Three Cognichonk shards waited at the center, points facing inward like a hungry mouth. They *throbbed*, each pulse a hammer against the thin walls of reality. The hum burrowed into Perdita's ears, scraping her skull from the inside. A shudder rippled through her body that Vex crushed, vertebra by vertebra, until she stood frozen.

Perdita's tail lashed once, defiant. Vex pinned it to the floor with thought alone.

The cat whimpered. Low. Pathetic.

Please—

Vex let it squeak out. Then clamped her voice to silence.

Three shards. Three promises kept.

Vex turned Perdita's head to the wall of mirrors propped at uneven angles. She'd placed them herself. They were tools —interrogation rooms for the soul, where reflections were forced to confess sins the original never admitted. Each was cracked along a different axis, reflections split and multiplied. Dozens of Perditas looked back. Wide-eyed. Breathing too fast. Whiskers twitching like antennae for fear.

But all of them belonged to Vex.

The mirrors split Perdita's body, dissected it with light, offering each piece to whatever watched hungrily from the other side. She could feel it, some *thing* observing every twitch of her whiskers, every dilation of her pupils. Judging

Perdita tried to look away. Vex refused her the privilege.

One mirror caught the candlelight and twisted it into an orange spiral. A glyph bloomed in the glass, smoky and roiling, spelling *Eligere* in a scrawled hand that seemed to smear even as she read it.

Perdita recoiled internally, mind skittering across the walls of her own skull.

I don't want this—

The thought flashed like a dying bulb, short-lived and unconvincing. Vex pressed her harder against her own instincts. Perdita trembled so violently her knees buckled. Vex let them.

She hit the floor with a meaty thump, claws raking deep lines into the chalk. Sparks hissed where her claws connected. The symbols bled orange light that seared and then cooled—her pain nothing but fuel for a machine that ran on suffering and paid dividends in power.

Vex bent Perdita until her whiskers brushed the floor, until she had no choice but to inhale the ritual ink—coppery and sharp, the scent of old blood and wax filling her lungs with each terrified breath.

"Three shards," Vex murmured through Perdita's mouth, voice flat, precise. "Three gates. Three witnesses."

Perdita's ears flattened. Her eyes watered. Panic roared through her. Not just physical. *Emotional.*

Memory leaked in around the edges.

A kitten, safe in a box with littermates. Warm.
Hands that smelled like old bread. A human voice whispering *good girl.*
A moment in the sun, belly-up, trusting.

Vex let her remember it all. Then burned it away.

The candles guttered in their mason jars, wicks sputtering green and orange flames. Smoke roiled low, filling the floor with crawling fingers of haze. The sigils drank it up. They glowed like old coals.

The Cognichonk shards pulsed harder. Their hum deepened to a low chord of *want.*

Perdita gagged. Vex closed her throat halfway, let her choke on her own terror. Then let her breathe. Ragged. Shaking. Controlled. She circled the triangle slowly. A garrote, tightening with each step. Perdita's breathing hitched.

I don't want to die here—

A childish thought. Raw. Honest.

"Luis always thought it was memory," Vex said through Perdita's voice, loud enough for the shards to hear. "He never understood choice."

Perdita's eyes locked on one of the shards. It flickered. For an instant, she saw—not her reflection but his. Luis. Broad-shouldered. Trench coat. Tired eyes that judged everything, even himself. A detective who'd worked the case too long, seen too much, and still couldn't walk away because failure had become more familiar than success. He didn't speak. He didn't move. But the judgment burned.

Luis help—

Perdita screamed. A raw, feline shriek that cracked the silence. Vex let it echo. Let it bounce off the broken glass and the sigils and the blackened jars. Then she closed Perdita's mouth with a snap that clicked her teeth.

The shards pulsed in agreement.

Vex paused before the center. Forced Perdita to sit up. Straight-backed. Tail still. Every whisker trembling with exhaustion and terror.

"Memory is a tomb," she whispered through the cat's mouth. "Choice is the corpse it keeps warm."

One candle guttered out entirely, smoke curling into a question mark before it dissipated. The mirror behind them *laughed.* Not with sound. With motion. The images twisted, cracked, rippled outward like a stone thrown into rotten water.

Memorari.

Perdita jerked. Claws dug into her own pads.

Eligere.

A high-pitched whine built in her throat. Vex let it crest.

Vindicari.

She sobbed. Once. Dry. Salt tracks on orange fur. Vex forced her to breathe. Slow. Shuddering. Submissive.

The Cognichonk shards responded with a deeper hum. The lines on the floor brightened, spilling orange light across Perdita's fur like war paint. Vex lowered her head fractionally. Made her bow. Her whiskers dragged through the chalk. She tried to pull away. Vex held her there.

Outside, wind clawed at the boarded windows like it wanted in but had failed the price of admission. Dust rattled. A voice whispered from nowhere, *not yet*. The candles bent their flames toward the shards, thin and eager. Vex let Perdita look up one last time. Into the mirror. Into them both.

Perdita's pupils were blown wide. Her mouth hung open. She was shaking so badly she could barely hold her own weight. Vex forced her still.

And in that hush thick with blood and smoke and memory, Vex whispered the final command: "Let's begin."

Perdita's body convulsed once. A strangled noise crawled from her throat. And she obeyed.

The silence of the chamber wasn't empty. It was anticipating—the held breath before a confession under duress, when truth and lies become negotiable currencies in the economy of pain. Perdita's orange body remained perfectly still, her claws positioned in the chalk lines. She shook with tiny tremors, her spine rigid with tension that seemed to vibrate through the sigils themselves.

Then Mallory began. The first words weren't spoken

through Perdita's throat—they were shaped, forced through like a key turning in a rusted lock.

"Memorari," came the hiss from Perdita's mouth. The chalk lines flared orange.

Perdita gagged, her body convulsing as if fighting against invisible restraints.

"Eligere." The lines split, curling in on themselves, forming new glyphs like ink spreading in water.

Smoke thickened, slithering through the room like it remembered ancient rituals. Debts long unpaid.

"Vindicari." The shards answered with a deep, harmonic hum.

Perdita shivered violently, her fur bristling, but her body remained locked in position. More words scratched from her throat, raw and forced: "Memoria est statica. Electio est viva."

The Cognichonk shards pulsed harder. Light spilled out in fat, unnatural arcs, crawling across the floor in tangled webs. The anchor-sigils drank it in, feeding on the glow, lines growing thick with light like veins engorged with blood.

Mirrors caught the light. Refracted it. Multiplied it. A hundred Perditas stared back from the glass, eyes wide, fur bristling in identical terror. Her gaze was forced to watch, pupils dilating with each reflection.

"Look," came Mallory's whisper through Perdita's vocal cords. Voice low. Intimate. Cruel. "See what you are."

Perdita's pupils shrank to pinpoints. The mirrors didn't just show her—they split the world behind them, fragmenting images:

Cats fighting in alleys. Claws flashing. Screams in too-human voices. Orange bodies tumbling from rooftops, wailing in borrowed terror. A calico, cackling, interrupting a circle and scattering chalk and blood. A black cat hissing over a grave, eyes full of knowledge and refusal. White cats asleep in patterns that implied conspiracy.

A whimper escaped Perdita's throat.

One mirror revealed Luis, caught between worlds, his eyes black with unwanted understanding, trench coat hanging in tatters around him. He stood in a cracked alley, watching helplessly as the orange glow spilled from the walls around him like blood from a wound.

His gaze locked on Perdita—on what controlled her.

"You think you're the detective," Mallory said through Perdita's mouth, so softly the Cognichonk itself seemed to lean in to hear. "But you're just evidence."

Luis's eyes narrowed in the glass. He mouthed something. The mirror cracked down the center. Perdita's body tried to recoil but was slammed forward instead, her paw burning against the sigil. She screamed but it came out as a purr. An unnatural, harmonic vibration filled the chamber.

The Cognichonk shards answered with a pulse that tightened the webs between them. Orange energy writhed across the floor, something older, forming symbols that latched onto Perdita's limbs, burning into her fur like living barbed wire.

She panted, breath rattling and shallow.

The grip loosened just enough to keep her alive. Her

head turned deliberately to the largest mirror, forced to watch the reflection, her orange fur bristling in terror, her eyes cold and certain with another's will.

"Ascension isn't theft," came Mallory's whisper like a sermon over a grave. "It's judgment."

The mirror rippled. Images within it convulsed. Cats howled. Clawed. Bled. The glass darkened like old blood drying in moonlight.

Luis slammed a hand against his side of the reflection, eyes burning with recognition and hatred.

Perdita's mouth curved into a smile that wasn't hers. She whimpered, cracked and tiny, but the sound was quickly silenced.

The room hummed like a hive mind aligning. The sigils on the floor split again, opening like eyes. Watching. Judging. Smoke twisted up from the lines in perfect spirals, writhing into the shapes of catlike silhouettes that circled the walls. Their eyes glowed orange.

The Cognichonk shards shone so brightly they seared afterimages onto the glass. The anchor-web of sigils tightened to a near-solid mesh of crackling energy, binding the floor in a burning lattice.

Perdita's body went rigid, her tail lashing in slow, drugged resistance.

"Yes," Mallory purred through her. "Exactly."

Perdita convulsed once more, forced to watch everything. The light. The mirrors. The shards. The truth. Her vision blurred with tears.

"Soon the loop closes," the voice continued through her trembling form. "No more errors. No more strays."

Perdita was pressed chest-first against the sigil, hard, until she fell silent.

The shards sang in response, their harmonic resonance deepening until it rattled the walls, the mirrors, the bones of the building itself. Outside, the wind howled with laughter it hadn't earned. Inside, the ritual chamber felt *complete*.

Perdita drew a ragged, borrowed breath. Her mouth smiled with someone else's satisfaction. And the Cognichonk answered.

The ritual chamber was a wound made of light. Orange webs of sigils crackled across the floor, crawling like fire through spilled ink. The mirrors seethed with images, their glass warping under the strain of too many possibilities. The Cognichonk shards pulsed in unison, a heartbeat that wasn't Perdita's but owned her all the same.

She whimpered, her small body trembling against the sigil lines. *I can't—*

But her mouth snapped shut against her will, jaw clamped tight by an invisible force. Then the door creaked.

Anna appeared in the threshold. Eyes glassy. Steps hesitant, a witness who'd stumbled onto a crime scene and realized too late she wasn't just observing the evidence, she was becoming part of it. She moved like a moth toward flame, pupils catching the glow and drinking it in. Her breathing was shallow, choked on the thick ritual smoke.

"Good," came Mallory's voice through Perdita's stolen throat, a purr of satisfaction.

Anna blinked, as if waking. Confusion rippled across

her face. She turned, trying to backpedal. The sigils carved around the door flared with sudden, violent light. The frame slammed shut with a sound like a judge's gavel. She gasped. One hand clawed at the handle. Nothing.

Perdita's head turned slowly, the movement deliberate and predatory despite her own terror. The malice in the gesture was palpable, savored. Her eyes, controlled by another's will, locked on Anna.

"Welcome," Mallory said through Perdita's mouth, voice low, smooth, inhumanly calm. "Witness."

Anna's eyes went wide. She trembled. Mouth opening to speak but no sound emerging.

Perdita's heart beat like thunder in her chest, her thoughts fragmenting. *Let her go—*

The thought was smothered before it could finish forming. Perdita's body moved forward against her will. Slow. Heavy. Commanding.

Anna recoiled against nothing. Where the doorway had been, only blackness remained, framed by sigils that smoldered like fresh brands.

Perdita began to circle Anna, her movements predatory and controlled. Each step was like a blade drawn slowly across a throat.

"I shouldn't be here," Anna whispered.

"On the contrary," Mallory replied through Perdita's throat, the voice vibrating with the shards' hum. "You're exactly where you need to be."

Anna shuddered as a purr emerged from Perdita's small form, something too deep for her throat, a resonance that seemed to live in the walls themselves.

"He's about to lose his last choice," Mallory continued through Perdita, tone light, conversational, almost amused.

Anna shook her head. Tears welled. Perdita's eyes gleamed with reflected light from the mirrors, the expression not her own.

"I want you to see it."

Anna fell to her knees. Hands over her ears as if she could shut out the sound. The Cognichonk shards hummed louder in answer. Mirrors around the room twisted. Shivered. Realigned. And one of them caught her reflection.

Not Anna's reflection, but Jessa's stared back, her face emerging through a crawl of static lines in the glass. Scarred. Brutally so. Skin torn and healed wrong. A crude, half-failed ward scrawled over one eye in broken sigilwork. Her mouth moved silently. Desperate. Warning.

Anna's breath hitched in her throat. Perdita's body tensed, a shiver of disgust and horror trying to reclaim control.

Don't make her see it—

The thought was crushed to ash before it could take hold.

Anna screamed. The mirrors caught it. Reflected it. Multiplied it. A chorus of terror that fed the sigils until they shone like branding irons.

Perdita purred in answer, the sound too deep for her throat, harmonic with the Cognichonk shards. The floor sigils flared brighter. Lines thickened, crawling over her paws like veins of molten light.

Anna covered her face with shaking hands.

The Cognichonk hummed. Low. Ancient. Hungry. Ready to choose.

CHAPTER TWENTY-THREE

The mirror screamed like a confession beaten out of innocent glass. What tore wasn't the reflection—it was reality itself, coming apart at the seams like a cheap suit in a knife fight. It wasn't Anna reflected there, nor Perdita. It was me—trapped, a ghost in the glass, watching as Perdita's body moved like a puppet.

Vex's voice poured from her mouth with a coldness that turned the air to stone.

"Welcome. Witness."

Anna sobbed. The sigils burned themselves into the floor, each line searing with purpose I couldn't escape. The Cognichonk shards throbbed everywhere, humming not just in the walls but resonating through the air itself. It hummed like something that had finally gotten what it wanted after centuries of waiting.

I slammed my palms, though I felt them land as paws, against the glass.

"Stop it!"

But there was no sound. Just ripples of orange light that spread from my touch like a contagion.

Vex smiled through Perdita's stolen eyes.

"He's about to lose his last choice."

Her voice was aimed at me.

"Look at me," she whispered through Perdita's mouth. "You need to see. It doesn't work unless you witness what you are."

I tried to retreat. But the mirror lunged forward—no longer a surface but a hunger with teeth made of my own reflection.

Anna's scream shook the walls. The Cognichonk's hum deepened, a resonant purr that spoke of ancient victories. Sigils flared, choosing.

I felt it crawl inside my skull.

"No. No—"

My thoughts cracked like old glass.

I saw cats in those fractures. Butternugget pressed to a rain-slick alley wall, eyes wide in rabid confusion. Jake crouched on a fence, shadow-and-moonlight predator. Bosco dozing on a post but listening with one battered ear. Shrimp twitching in a puddle that reflected too many moons.

I slammed the glass again.

"Let me out!"

The Cognichonk answered not with refusal but with terrible permission.

The glass shattered. And I fell—

—not as one piece, but as shards of thought, scattering

across orange eyes everywhere at once. I felt every heartbeat, every breath, every claw scraping concrete or wood or mud. I was all of them, screaming in discord, before the Cognichonk forced me to focus, one vessel at a time..

I tumbled headlong into Butternugget a block away from the old library's boarded-up door, tail lashing in the ritual's reflected glow. The world reeked of wet trash, fish guts, betrayal fermenting in puddles. My claws scrabbled on soggy cardboard.

WHO SCREAMING? MOUTH OPEN! MY MOUTH! NO! SMELLS LIKE SECRETS. CAN I EAT IT? CHEW. CHEW THE SECRETS.

"Stop. Focus."

FOCUS IS A LIE!

He yowled. High. Sharp. A noise ripped from chaos itself.

A dog howled back, panicked.

I was wrenched away. I landed in Jake perched on the perimeter fence of the condemned lot, watching the sigils burn in the distance. Moonlight cut hard lines through slatted fences. Cold air bit whiskers. Tail coiled. Muscles loaded.

Observe. Identify. Prepare for the hunt.

"This isn't a hunt. It's a curse."

All threats bleed when clawed.

He inhaled deep. Rain. Cedar. The copper tang of someone else's blood drying.

I snapped sideways. I slammed into Shrimp rolling in a puddle that shimmered with the same unholy light, too close already. Mud cold under his belly. Leaves decomposing around him.

The ground is singing.
He mashed his ear to the muck.
Shhh. Listen.
"Shrimp. Listen to me—"
Listening! Too much!
He convulsed, a reedy shriek tearing from his throat, too deep, too old. His tiny body arched as a voice, ancient and unyielding, boomed:

> *"TWELVE PAWS.*
>   *ONE TO BLEED.*
>   *PANTRY GOD SINGS.*
>   *ALL ORANGE.*
>   *ALL WRONG.*
>   *A TAPESTRY UNRAVELING."*

He collapsed. A spent echo.

I crashed into Bosco on a lamppost at the intersection leading to the ritual site. The lamp creaked under him like a testimony under oath. The wind smelled of burned offerings and cheap regret.

Wasn't my case. Became my case.
"Bosco. Help me."
A sigh, heavy as old dust.
Can't. Been here before. Learned the long art of surviving.
His claws flexed once. Slow. Deliberate.
The Cognichonk pulled. I felt my voice try to gather.
"Luis Cannon. Detective. Private Investigator. Dammit—"

But it splintered:

Butternugget: *Chew the crime until it meows.*

Jake: *Track it. Kill it.*

Shrimp: *Sing the end times in tuna.*

Bosco: *File the paperwork. Bury the dead.*

I felt all of it. The reek of trash and burnt offerings. The wet weight of mud. The cold wind cutting to bone. The old wood groaning under accumulated regret. I tried to scream, but I couldn't choose which mouth. All of them shrieked it differently, a discordant chorus of my own fracturing will.

The Cognichonk purred. Pleased.

We all felt it then. A pull. Directionless. Irresistible.

Butternugget's nose twitched.

Tastes like blood that wants to be ink.

Jake's ears flicked.

Death-scent strong. Prey fell nearby.

Shrimp giggled and wept.

The pantry is open. He's coming.

Bosco closed his eye.

We're not making it out clean.

Our paws moved. Four cats. One broken mind. Dragged toward the ritual site.

"My mind," I tried one last time, a desperate whisper, "is a crime scene."

But the words splintered, dissolving into the collective hum. I was nowhere. And everywhere.

It didn't hum like it used to—random and hungry. Now it purred with purpose. It had chosen. It *wanted* this.

The Cognichonk's hum wasn't just sound anymore. It was air. It was weight. It crushed against our ribs like something that had learned to turn pressure into pain. The wind stopped moving right. It thickened, humid with meaning. Light bled orange across cracked pavement, turning shadows into sigils that squirmed when you weren't looking.

I felt it in my borrowed lungs. Heavy. Oily. Wrong.

The cats moved with the jerky precision of puppets learning their strings. Even the strays who'd been fighting the call surrendered at once, their eyes going wide as their pupils devoured what remained of their will.

They turned in unison. Marched.

I fought it. Pushed back with every ounce of human memory I had left. My claws scraped across wet concrete, skidding, dragging, leaving lines that felt like signatures on my own warrant.

It didn't matter. The Cognichonk whispered yes.

Bosco's voice scraped through the static, the only sound that didn't immediately dissolve in the Cognichonk's hum.

"We're cats. We do nothing in formation."

My laugh was shredded. Fractured.

"But I saw the formation anyway," I said, my voice a grinding door hinge across four throats at once. "A crime scene where the evidence was fur and prophecy."

Ahead, Shrimp froze mid-lick on a garbage can. His tiny body trembled, fur standing on end like cheap carpeting reacting to static. His eyes went wide. Glazed.

He choked out the words, each one fighting to escape his throat before the next could strangle it.

"Twelve paws.
   One to bleed.
   Tuna sings.
   The pantry god opens."

He collapsed, tail still twitching like it hadn't gotten the memo.

The air thickened until breathing felt like swallowing smoke—burnt metal and old blood coating the back of my throat.

Butternugget screamed at a sprinkler like it was the only honest cop in a crooked precinct. The water arced overhead, dirty amber in the warped light—rain that couldn't wash anything clean, just spread the filth around more evenly. He clawed at the puddle it left like he could drown the command.

"WHO BRINGS RAIN TO A CRIME SCENE? I'LL BITE THE WEATHER!"

His feet locked, claws scoring the pavement, but the Cognichonk made him walk anyway. Like a wind-up toy with no pity in its gears.

Rutabaga's tail lashed with imperial disgust. He tried to turn, regal head held high, paws digging in to avoid the chalk spiral scrawled on the sidewalk.

"No," he hissed. "I refuse this peasant geometry—"

But he stepped into it anyway. His face contorted with betrayal.

Jake stalked forward, deliberate, controlled. But even he

shuddered once. A muscle in his jaw twitched. He lifted a paw, trying to clean it. Trying to resist. But the Cognichonk slammed his foot down like a gavel. He hissed. Then moved on.

He did pause just long enough to slap another cat who tried to pass him.

"Rank," he growled.

The orange light pulsed brighter. Lines drawn in chalk on the sidewalk twisted, connected, completed themselves with our paws as brushes. I saw it. The spiral. The convergence glyph. The knot of binding.

It wasn't a route. It was a spell. We weren't walking to the ritual site. We were the ritual.

The Cognichonk's hum deepened. Louder. Like laughter in a cathedral built for screaming.

My thoughts splintered, consciousness leaking between vessels until I wasn't just one cat anymore—I was drowning in all of them at once. Butternugget fought. Muscles twitched. Rebellion written in every spasm. The kind of fight that never makes the papers. The kind that ends in alleyways. I felt Jake's calm tactical mind screaming in methodical terror. I felt Rutabaga's refined disdain splinter into pure panic. I felt Shrimp's tiny heart flutter like a bomb with a broken timer.

Their eyes were all mine. Their pain was mine. Their paws moved as one. We were the line someone would cross.

And through Shrimp's eyes—I saw her.

Vex.

Standing in a shattered window three blocks away. Watching us with calm delight. The Cognichonk's orange light reflected in her stolen eyes. She didn't speak. She didn't need to. She approved.

Her smile was the shape of a trap snapping shut. And I knew this wasn't new. This was the Widow's plan. The old grave. The failed binding ritual. Jareth Vale's broken body screaming through my memory.

This was a refinement. A completion. The Cognichonk had learned. And we—I—was the anchor.

We kept walking. Four cats. A hundred cats. A single consciousness split like old rope. And in every mouth at once, I heard my voice say it: "We're the spell. We're the sacrifice. We're the line she's going to cross."

The air pulsed orange. And the Cognichonk purred.

The ritual circle lay half-finished on the concrete, damp orange chalk smeared into arcs by paws that either didn't understand their purpose or—worse—understood it perfectly. No perfect geometry here—just a confession sketched by committee, spirals and regret forming a language no one should be able to read.

Around it, orange cats gathered in concentric rings. Some preened, licking the ritual dust from their fur with idiot satisfaction. Others hissed at shadows only they could see. One sat in the middle, tail wrapped precisely, watching the swirl of sigils with eyes that didn't blink enough.

The Cognichonk purred like an idling engine, patient with the terrible confidence of something that knows all roads eventually lead to it.

I wasn't one detective anymore. I was a lineup where every suspect had my eyes but couldn't remember my name.

Then she arrived. Lantern in hand. The light didn't banish the dark so much as negotiate with it. Dim. Flickering. Enough to illuminate her face—and every line failure had carved into it.

The widow occupied that no man's land between young and old—territory where hope goes to die but keeps breathing anyway. Her face was a map of wrong turns taken deliberately. I'd seen that map before. Usually right before someone pulled a gun. Her eyes didn't hold regret. Just paperwork stamped DENIED.

I watched her through Butternugget's slitted eyes as he hunched low, hackles up. Through Jake's calm, narrowed stare. Through Shrimp, who blinked rapidly like he was trying to file the memory under "Important" but couldn't spell the word.

Rutabaga didn't bother blinking. Just hissed under his breath about the cheap lantern aesthetic.

She stepped forward, boots crunching over old chalk lines.

The Cognichonk purred louder.

She glanced at the circle. Didn't flinch. Didn't smile. Her mouth had settled into the kind of straight line that comes from years of swallowing words instead of speaking them.

"Stop," she whispered.

It didn't. Her shoulders slumped. She lowered the lantern. Light pooled in the center of the broken sigil. I watched it catch on every scrawled line and make it worse. Make it clear. She took a deep breath. The kind that carries too much history.

"I know you're in there."

Her voice cracked. She didn't bother fixing it.

I felt Butternugget want to scream at her. Words forming around murder and betrayal and fish. Jake just watched. Waiting for a tactical angle that wasn't coming. Bosco's voice growled in the link, gravel thick as regret.

"Listening."

She closed her eyes.

"I know what I did. And I know it wasn't enough."

I wanted to ask what. Wanted to scream why. But my voice was scattered over five cats and two alleys. So I settled for silence. It felt like screaming anyway.

She opened her eyes. Looked at the Cognichonk like it was an old letter she'd never mailed.

"I studied it. With Vex."

The name hit the air like a dropped gun. Several cats hissed. Bosco's claws scraped the post he was perched on. She nodded at our reaction.

"Yeah. That one. She understood it. Better than I did. Better than anyone should."

Her fingers tightened around the lantern's handle until it creaked.

"I wanted it to hold a soul."

She glanced at us. Saw the collective ripple of understanding. Horror.

"My husband's."

The silence was absolute. Even the cats stopped grooming. Stopped blinking.

Shrimp shivered once and let out a broken little mew.

She swallowed. Hard.

"Vex said that was dominion, not resurrection. That you

couldn't bring someone back. You could only keep them. Like a bug pinned to felt. Or a memory with teeth."

She looked away. The lantern light threw the lines of her face into stark relief.

"She refused to help me."

Her voice dropped even lower.

"So I tried anyway."

I felt my claws flex in four sets of paws. I wanted to hurt her. I wanted to hold her.

She kept talking.

"I sabotaged the ritual before. When I realized what it was becoming. I tried to stop it. I... I didn't do it right."

The Cognichonk's purr vibrated through every cat like a second heartbeat.

"You think I don't know it's wrong?" she demanded, voice cracking like old glass. "He didn't deserve the grave. But the Cognichonk doesn't care what you deserve."

Her eyes swept over the cats. Over me.

"But you know that. Don't you?"

I tried to speak. I did. But all I managed was Bosco's slow, deliberate tail flick. Butternugget's frantic, twitching yowl. Shrimp's confused whimper. I was too fractured to answer.

She shook her head.

"I hear it purring. Even now. I see what she's doing."

She jerked her head toward the distance. Toward the place Vex waited.

"She'll anchor it. Not for love. For control."

I felt the words hit me like bullets. My mind was a crime scene with too many suspects. And one too many murder weapons.

She stepped closer to the circle. Lantern light made the lines glow like fresh wounds.

"She wants you to choose. But she doesn't care which way. Fragments. Or anchor. Either way you're hers."

The Cognichonk purred like it was proud. The cats twitched. Circling. Spiraling. I felt my mouth open in Shrimp. A mew that might have been a scream if it had teeth.

Bosco's voice, cold and weary, spoke for me.

"Choice."

She nodded once. Tears shining but not falling.

"Choose what you are," she whispered. "Because she will choose for you if you don't."

Silence fell again. I tried to hold myself together. Tried to make one voice, one thought, one accusation. But the Cognichonk just hummed.

In Butternugget: *Bite the secrets until they scream.*

In Jake: *Track it. End it.*

In Shrimp: *Sing the pantry god awake.*

In Bosco: *Witness. Survive.*

She turned away. Shoulders sagging under the weight of truth finally spoken.

"Goodbye," she whispered.

She didn't wait for a reply. She walked out of the circle. Lantern light dimmed. Then was swallowed by the orange.

The cats circled like the second hand on a dead man's watch. Their paws smeared chalk lines—signatures on a contract nobody read but everybody pays for. That's how it always ends. Not with a bang, but with fine print. Completing glyphs they didn't understand. The Cognichonk purred in my ears. My ribs. My mind. And this time, the pull wasn't a command. It was a question.

Anchor or fragment. Detective or evidence.

I couldn't answer. Not yet. But I felt myself being pulled to the center anyway.

And somewhere inside, I heard my own voice. Low. Broken.

"This case... this case is gonna kill me."

CHAPTER TWENTY-FOUR

The circle refused to stay still. Chalk lines crumbled to haunted dust under the restless scrape of orange paws. The spirals pulsed with sickening orange light—thick and wrong—as if someone had sketched a living thing in crayon and then watched in horror as it began to shed its skin. The air reeked of wet fur, old rain, and burnt candle wax—the kind of smell that hangs around crime scenes like a witness too scared to talk but too guilty to leave.

The Cognichonk sat in the middle. Not inert. Not watching. Thrumming. Like an engine with a heartbeat. The purr vibrated through cracked pavement, through whiskers, through bone. A patient, hungry promise.

We paced around it in rings that kept collapsing inward, like we were caught in a drain slowly pulling us down.

Bosco stood just outside the chalk line, shoulders squared, tail flicking slow and menacing. His breath fogged in the cool night air like a condemned man refusing last rites.

Butternugget crouched inside the line itself, smearing sigils with jittery, overzealous paws, eyes wide with manic invitation. *It's art! It's truth! It's lunch!*

Shrimp sat too close to the center. Chalk dust coated his mouth, his tiny pink tongue flicking compulsively at ghostly lines. He shivered with every purr, like it was whispering secrets he was too small to hold.

Jake stayed farthest back. Body low. Muscles coiled. Ears pinned. Watching. Calculating angles like a killer with a moral code.

I existed everywhere and nowhere at once, trapped in the rasp of every claw against pavement, in each conflicted twitch of tails torn between memory and instinct. The Cognichonk's purr hummed through all of it. My thoughts scattered like dry leaves over cold concrete.

Danger scent everywhere. Not gathering. Hunting ground rigged against us, Jake's voice cut through me, low and precise.

Butternugget yipped. *Trap's good! Trap has snacks!*

Shrimp hiccuped chalk dust, pupils blown wide.

I tried to answer. Nothing but a broken rasp in Shrimp's throat.

Then he arrived. Vance. He didn't walk in so much as appear—as if reality had briefly looked away and he'd slipped through the gap it left. He pushed through the cats like smoke through bars, the circle parting around him. His fur—once that same bright, conspiratorial orange—was patchy with old fights, scars that refused to lie. An oily sheen clung to him under the lantern light. His ear was bent at an angle so precise it had to be honest about every mistake he'd made.

He carried the last shard. It dangled from his teeth, clinking softly against fangs worn too flat. The Cognichonk crystal. Sickly orange. The color of old traffic lights and regret left in the rain.

He dropped it onto the chalk with all the ceremony of a thrown gauntlet. The circle flared as lines crawled to complete themselves.

I remembered another gauntlet once, leather-soft, offered across a poker table. A promise: *We'll always have each other's backs.*

The Cognichonk purred deeper. This time the ground vibrated with it.

Shrimp mewled. A small, pathetic sound. His fur spiked in every direction.

Butternugget's tail lashed so hard he knocked over half the circle. *Mine? Mine? Bite it first!*

Bosco growled low enough to rattle ribs.

Jake's voice was cold steel in my head. *Still body. Sharp eyes. Wait for opening.*

Vance finally spoke. His voice had the texture of old bourbon poured over broken glass—locked in a drawer so long it forgot what daylight tasted like. "Don't look at me like that."

I did anyway. Through all of us.

Bosco's eyes became knife slits that judged crimes older than the city.

Butternugget flattened his ears and chattered, high and broken. *Liar! Liar!*

Shrimp tried to hide behind Bosco's tail and forgot how halfway through, paws splayed and trembling.

Vance swallowed. His throat bobbed in a slow, miserable

roll. I heard the wet click of saliva forced down. dry and desperate. "I'm not here to save you."

The words didn't land. They hit like a punch to the jaw. My claws flexed. I felt them all score lines in the pavement at once.

Jake exhaled in my head. *He hunts you. Scent says kill, not capture.*

Vance's eyes twitched. He took a step closer. The Cognichonk purred so loud it shook the air. Like a voice behind the door, inviting us in.

"You're too broken to hold it."

The world spun.

I was Shrimp, blinking too fast to make sense. Chalk dust in my nose. Tail thrashing.

Butternugget hissed at empty spaces only he could see. *I SEE YOU! STOP IT!*

Bosco stood unmoving. A statue at his own funeral.

Jake's voice was a scalpel. *Truth in his scent. You're fractured prey.*

I tried to speak. My voice cracked across five mouths like a bullet splitting into shrapnel. That's the thing about truth in this city. By the time it reaches anyone's ears, it's already lying.

Vance closed his eyes. Breathed slow. Like a man about to put down a pet he loved. "Vex says she can anchor it." He spat her name like it burned. "But at least she *can*." He opened his eyes and glared at us. At me. "You? You're fragments. Half-thoughts in too many bodies."

Butternugget twitched, lips peeling back in something that might have been a smile in another life. *Half-thoughts are better than none! We have so many!*

Shrimp whined. Rolled onto his back, paws in the air like a desperate surrender.

Bosco blinked once. Slow. Deliberate.

Jake's tail lashed. *Muscles set. Eyes sharp. Hunt begins.*

Vance's gaze dropped. That's when I saw it. His paw. Marked. A spiral. Not the kind of brand you choose—the kind that chooses you. I'd seen marks like that before. On witnesses who suddenly couldn't remember. On cops who looked the other way. On friends who weren't friends anymore. Burned so deep the skin had cracked, scabbed, peeled and healed wrong. He tried to tuck it under himself. Too slow.

Butternugget yowled. *TRAITOR!*

Bosco's growl rose from the ground like an earthquake.

Jake's voice was lower. Deadly calm. *See his paw mark? Territory claimed by another predator.*

Vance shuddered. His tail thumped the concrete once. "She... made sure I wouldn't forget." His voice cracked.

The Cognichonk purred even louder, *pleased*. The circle hummed like a nest of dying hornets.

"I didn't want this."

I felt the words scrape against old memories I'd tried to drown in bourbon.

"But I'm not the one with my brain spread over five cats and two alleys."

Shrimp whimpered. Buried his face in his paws.

Butternugget began to lick the ground compulsively, leaving streaks in the chalk. *Can't hear. Can't hear. Won't hear.*

Jake and Bosco growled in unison, stereo accusation. *Weak hunter. Follows stronger scent.*

Vance trembled. His claws clicked against the pavement, punctuating each ugly truth. "Vex will anchor it," he said, voice cracking on *anchor*. He glanced at us. His eyes were wet. "Better the devil you know…"

Butternugget whimpered. Pressed so low to the ground he tried to disappear into it.

Vance's voice dropped to a whisper. "…than the one that purrs while it eats you."

The Cognichonk vibrated so hard the chalk cracked beneath Shrimp's paws. He squeaked and fell over.

I tried to stand. Shrimp's legs buckled. Butternugget spun in a tight, manic circle, howling like he was trying to climb out of his own skin. Bosco refused to move. A monument to old oaths. Jake alone held steady. Muscles tensed. Breath slow.

Give signal. My claws are ready, Jake whispered.

But I couldn't speak.

Vance's eyes softened. The worst thing he could have done. "I'm sorry, Luis."

He nosed the shard forward. It skidded across broken chalk. The lines glowed, spiderweb cracks filling with pulsing orange. The Cognichonk purred in triumph.

"She's giving you a choice," Vance said, voice ragged. "I'm not."

He turned. Walked away like they always do when the check comes due.

Bosco hissed—a sound funeral-low, the kind of goodbye you give to someone who's already dead to you. I'd heard that sound before. Usually right before I woke up in an alley with empty pockets and a head full of regrets. Butternugget lunged, scrabbling madly, claws shrieking over the concrete.

Shrimp mewed. Once. Broken. Jake watched him go. Didn't blink.

He joined another pack. Enemy now.

Vance didn't look back. His tail hung low. His ears pinned. The Cognichonk's purr filled the silence he left behind. It wasn't a question anymore. It was an order given in the language of spirals. Anchor. Or fragment.

I felt myself dragged toward the center. And somewhere inside—across five cats and one dying hope—I felt my own voice rise. Low. Broken.

"This case... this case is gonna kill me."

The Cognichonk wouldn't shut up. Its purr rattled through the circle. Vibrated in our teeth. The kind of sound that doesn't ask permission to get inside your head. Just breaks in and rearranges the furniture while it hummed through the cracked pavement as if it were gnawing on our bones. The chalk glowed orange, searing the edges of the world with greedy light.

Choose, it said in the language of spirals. *Become vessel or become nothing.*

Static crawled through Butternugget's fur until he was more twitch than cat. I felt it ripple through every body I inhabited—the air thick with burnt copper and the electric promise of rain that wouldn't come. Concrete cracked under the lines, spiderweb fractures splintering outward from the glowing sigils.

Bosco refused to move. His tail flicked once, deliberate as an executioner's nod. *Hold.*

Butternugget was yowling now—high and broken. *No choices! No choices! Bite everything!*

Shrimp shivered so hard he clacked his teeth. Chalk dust clung to his fur like guilt made solid. *It's too loud. Make it stop.*

Jake's voice stayed low in my skull. *Choose now. Or become prey.*

I felt myself dragged inward, one paw at a time. Muscles I didn't own convulsed with every pulse. The Cognichonk's purr thickened, roared like the ocean in a storm drain, demanding the world collapse to that sound.

That's when she stumbled in. Jessa. silhouette burned against the orange glow like a sin given form, her usually neat bun now a wild halo, strands of hair escaping around her face.

For a heartbeat—I didn't trust it. Trust is a luxury in this city, like clean rain or honest politicians. Vex had shown me Jessa before. Scarred. Shackled. A promise twisted into threat. Another lie? Another trick? But then I smelled it. Blood. Fresh. Metallic. Hot. Too human to fake. The body never lies, even when everything else does.

She limped over the circle's edge, one arm clutching her side. Blood seeped between her fingers in thick rivulets. Each breath rattled, broken ribs catching like bad gears.

"Don't—move," she rasped. Her eyes gleamed with stubborn, terrified focus.

Shrimp tried to crawl toward her, a whining squeak tearing free. His legs scrabbled uselessly on the cracking pavement.

Bosco's eyes narrowed. Recognition. Old debts paid in silence.

Butternugget sniffed, nose twitching violently. *Blood smells like secrets.*

Jessa dropped to one knee. Concrete bit her skin. She didn't care. She slammed her free hand to the ground, blood smearing in jagged lines that crawled across the chalk. Crimson met orange in wet slashes. Counter-sigils. Old ones.

The air changed. The glow of the circle faltered. The purr hitched. I felt it. Like the moment a car skids on black ice— wrongness opening its mouth to swallow us.

Jake growled, low and sure. *Don't stop. Trail leads forward.*

Jessa's fingers trembled, nails biting into her palm for more blood. She hissed at the pain but pressed harder, drawing older, sharper shapes. Symbols that caught the spirals by their tails and forced them to swallow themselves.

The Cognichonk's purr transformed from seduction to threat, hissing as static tore through our fur until our tails sparked like frayed wires in the dark. The ground trembled. Fine chalk dust lifted in the air like ash from a bomb blast.

Shrimp let out a wailing, broken yowl that rattled his tiny lungs.

Bosco planted claws. Concrete cracked deeper beneath him, shards lifting like teeth.

Butternugget actually fell over. Limbs twitching in rhythm to the Cognichonk's wrath. *Make it stop make it stop!*

Jessa's voice cracked as she spat words meant to be an exorcism. "You can't—let it choose for you," she coughed. Blood dripped from her lips, spattering the sigils. "It doesn't *care* about you. About anyone."

Her eyes met mine. All of mine. Bosco. Butternugget.

Shrimp. Jake. She saw me. It felt like being stabbed in the heart in four different bodies. "You're the only one it listens to," she said, voice fracturing like old glass.

Shrimp whimpered. *Listens?*

Butternugget sobbed, snot and drool leaking. *Don't listen! Lies bite!*

Jake's voice sliced through the chaos. *Her scent speaks truth. You smell it too.*

The Cognichonk's purr went shrill. A feedback whine that split ears and thoughts. Light seared brighter, deep orange flaring to screaming white at the edges. Shadows twisted on the walls, spiraled, writhed.

Jessa didn't flinch. She slammed her bloody palm into the center of the half-finished sigil.

The world jerked sideways with a whipcrack of displaced air. The glow stuttered and flickered like dying neon as the Cognichonk released something beyond a purr or question—a scream that was nothing but threat.

Pain lanced through every body I held. My claws flexed involuntarily, scoring concrete. My vision doubled, tripled, split into colorless fractals.

Butternugget convulsed, wailing. *No no no!*

Shrimp clawed at his own ears. *Stop it stop it stop it!*

Bosco bit down on his tongue to keep from screaming.

Jake's snarl was pure, feral challenge. *Now. Claim your territory. Mark it.*

I tried. My voice scattered. Broke. Echoed across four ragged, panting mouths. I felt myself splitting apart. Pieces of me scrabbling for purchase in too many bodies.

Hold, Bosco growled.

Don't choose! Butternugget sobbed.

NOW, Jake roared.

Shrimp's voice was distant, sing-song. *Twelve paws in the circle... pantry god rise... tuna sings...*

Jessa's forehead pressed to the blood-slick ground. Her breathing came in wet, broken gasps. "Please," she whispered.

The Cognichonk's glow faltered again. The spirals bent. Fractured.

She lifted her head. Tears streaked dirt on her face. "You're the only one who can *order* it," she rasped. "Make it stop." Her fingers, slick with blood, trembled on the ground, a silent prayer.

The circle cracked beneath their paws. Lines broke, snapped, reformed in new, angrier patterns. The Cognichonk's purr shifted again. Deeper. Meaner.

Choose.

Bosco's voice rolled through my skull. *Do it.*

Butternugget moaned. *No! No choices! Don't choose!*

Shrimp's eyes rolled back. He chanted something ancient and nonsense.

Jake's voice thundered. *NOW!*

I opened my mouth. I tried to speak. But the Cognichonk roared back, swallowing thought, drowning sanity, demanding its due.

And waited for my answer.

The Cognichonk abandoned its purr for something worse— a howl that tore orange light from the circle and flung it across the walls. Another authority figure making demands.

Another power play dressed up as destiny. I'd been dancing to other people's tunes since I first put on a badge. Some habits die hard. Others just need a little push.

The sigils burned themselves into the concrete, into our eyes, into memory. The air grew thick enough to chew, coating our tongues with hot copper and the charred aftertaste of forgotten prayers. It wasn't asking anymore. It was choosing.

I felt it ripple through every borrowed body—fur rising like hackles on a cornered wolf, claws splintering concrete, teeth grinding until our gums wept blood.

Bosco hunched low, a growl building in his chest. *Steady.*

Butternugget's scream tore through the mental link. *Hide! No choose! HIDE!*

Shrimp's voice floated above it all, glassy and distant. *Twelve paws in the circle, pantry god rise...*

Jake crouched, muscles coiled. *Scent the danger. Listen.*

And then the world went black.

It showed me the first lie.

I was whole. Human again. Trench coat. Hat. Revolver gleaming with justice and regret. The Cognichonk sat behind me on a twisted throne of yarn and bones, purring in allegiance.

The cats ringed me in perfect obedience, eyes glowing like jack-o-lanterns.

I spoke, and they moved. I pointed, and they killed. I judged, and they died.

The Cognichonk purred in satisfaction.

I felt power like a drug. Every broken piece of me glued back together with worship and fear.

But their eyes. God, their eyes. Terrified.

"Witness," Bosco's voice rasped in horror.

Butternugget giggled wetly. "Good king. Bad king. All kings bite."

Shrimp's eyes were empty.

Jake's voice was a blade. "You become alpha-predator. Ruling through fear."

The vision twisted in on itself, warping reality as it dragged me sideways into another terrible promise.

Vex in the circle. Elegant. Composed. Her scars lit with sigils that pulsed in time with the Cognichonk.

She didn't purr. She commanded.

The cats moved like soldiers. Chalk lines became law. Sigils sharpened to cages.

I watched Shrimp, eyes dead, drawing perfect glyphs with trembling paws.

Butternugget was muzzled in golden chains, tail cut to a nub.

Bosco sat like a statue, an enforcer with empty eyes.

Jake slashed throats for order.

Vex's eyes met mine across the vision. Cold. Certain. "I will keep them safe," she promised.

And the Cognichonk didn't purr. It growled, obedient.

"Her territory. Her rules. Her prey," Jake spat.

The vision cracked open. Split. The circle itself shattered in their minds.

The cats screamed.

Some chanted for me.

LUIS! LUIS! LUIS!

Bosco's growl was thunder. "Better you than her!"

Jake's snarl agreed. "Take the pack. Lead the hunt."

But others turned, tails lashing in fury.

VEX! VEX! VEX!

Shrimp wailed. "She'll save us! She'll stop the noise!"

Butternugget rolled in the dust, howling. "No kings! No queens! No crowns!"

The circle shook, fractures racing outward like a spider's web catching fire. The Cognichonk's light pulsed with insane glee.

Choose.

CHOOSE.

ANCHOR. FRAGMENT.

I tried to hold myself together. My mind felt like glass dropped from a roof.

Bosco's voice roared. *Luis!*

Jake pressed in. *Mark them as yours! Before she does!*

Butternugget sobbed. *Don't choose!*

Shrimp whimpered. *Make it stop. Make it stop.*

My mouth opened. Words gathered. Orders that would chain them to me forever. I felt them boiling in my throat like confession and gasoline.

And I stopped.

The Cognichonk screamed. Visions collided. Overlapped. Wove themselves into a single nightmare of crowns and cages.

This is the game, it whispered in every voice I owned.

Anchor. Fragment.

Control. Chaos.

No middle ground. No mercy. It tried to push the choice into my mouth. Forced the words to my lips.

Say it.

Own them.

Break them.

Save them.

I bit down hard enough to taste blood. "NO!"

The Cognichonk's roar shook the alley as light flared hot enough to burn the chalk lines into vapor, filling our lungs with the stench of scorched symbols and charred intent while the concrete split wider beneath our trembling paws.

The counter-sigils Jessa had written in blood hissed, flared white, then black, then nothing.

The cats tumbled back in a riot of yowling bodies. Bosco crashed into the wall, gasping. Jake skidded in the dust, roaring in defiance. Butternugget spun and fell, shrieking with laughter and terror. Shrimp just lay on his side, panting, staring at nothing.

The Cognichonk shrank. Its glow collapsed in on itself. A final, furious pulse—then silence. Cold. Dead. No circle. No throne. Just ruin.

I felt them all in my head. Raw. Breathing. Alive.

Bosco rasped. *You didn't choose.*

Jake exhaled like an old gun cooling. *You rejected the alpha position.*

Butternugget sobbed quietly. *No kings.*

Shrimp whimpered. *Good. Good. No crowns.*

I didn't say anything. Couldn't. Just listened to the wind scrape through the ruined alley. And waited to see who would move first.

CHAPTER TWENTY-FIVE

My lungs burned in air thick with scorched prophecy and wet fur—the kind of atmosphere that hangs around after all the right decisions went wrong and all the wrong ones came due with interest. The chanting had stopped. The screaming too. All that remained was the ragged rasp of our collective breath, each inhale remembering what it had cost to say **no**.

The circle was gone. Lines reduced to smoldering powder. Cracks spidered outward in the concrete like a confession someone tried to burn before anyone else could read it. The Cognichonk lay at the center, a dull knot of yarn, blackened but not gone. Watching.

My body was leaden. Every borrowed muscle shrieked its protest. My paws were raw, claws splintered, crusted with blood. My mind was worse. Every thought was a raw edge, threads frayed and snarled.

I felt them all in my head, but the connection wasn't smooth anymore—just raw, unfiltered noise. Fear tangled with anger. Regret buried everything else. And underneath it all, hope that hadn't yet realized it was already dead.

Bosco moved first, of course. He rose with the slow deliberation of a pallbearer who'd been carrying the weight long before I added another ton to his shoulders. Old cats and old detectives—they don't rush toward bad news. They just nod at it like an old enemy across a crowded bar. When his eyes found mine, they pinned me there like evidence he'd finally collected enough of to close a case.

His voice growled in my skull, low and relentless. *You broke it.*

My tongue felt thick, stuck to the roof of my mouth like guilt. I forced the word out.

"Had to."

Bosco's tail lashed, stirring the dust like smoke from a gun that hadn't cooled. *You chose nothing. That's still a choice.*

I didn't answer. The words wouldn't come.

Jake lay sprawled in the ashes, one ear twitching in the silence. He didn't bother to look up. His voice rasped like an old revolver that hadn't been cleaned in years. *Pack scattered. Still free. Better hunting alone than leashed.*

He was right. That didn't make it feel better.

Butternugget was rocking in place, pupils wide as moons, his laughter a cracked teapot boiling dry. *No kings. No crowns. No me. No you. Hide. Hide now.*

He wrapped his tail around himself, pulled it tight like a promise he'd already broken.

Shrimp whimpered, his voice thin as a hairline crack in stained glass. *Too loud. Make it stop. Make it all stop. Please.*

He was shivering so hard I could feel it echo in my ribs. I

could feel all of them in my head, like a room full of suspects who wouldn't shut up long enough to hear the charge.

I sucked in air, let it scrape my throat raw before I dared speak.

"Listen."

Bosco didn't blink. Jake's ear twitched again, slower this time. Shrimp went quiet but didn't stop rocking. Butternugget's muttering slowed to a stutter.

"I didn't know this would happen," I said. My voice was smoke over embers. "Didn't know refusing would break it this badly."

Silence. Dense. Judging.

"But I *knew* I couldn't choose. Not for you. Not for anyone. I didn't have the right."

The wind hissed through the alley, cold against scorched stone. Nobody spoke. Even the Cognichonk seemed to hold its breath.

Bosco's stare didn't soften. *You didn't choose. You didn't save them.*

The words hit like brass knuckles.

My throat worked around the truth. I felt the network out there, twitching in the dark. Orange cats in alleys and attics, under cars and behind dumpsters. Crying. Screaming. Waiting for orders that never came.

I coughed. The taste was blood and failure.

"Yeah," I whispered. "I didn't save them. I don't know if I *can* save them."

I squeezed my eyes shut, but the ash found its way in anyway, stinging like tiny accusations. Like evidence I'd tried to ignore until it was too late. Same old story— detective sees the truth coming a mile away but still gets blindsided when it shows up with brass knuckles and a grudge. When I tried to speak again, my voice cracked down the middle.

"I don't even know how to fix this."

Nobody said anything.

Shrimp whimpered once, softer than before. Jake shifted, claws scraping concrete like he was testing the world for weakness. Butternugget's rocking slowed to a shudder.

I forced myself to keep going. My voice broke halfway through.

"But I won't—"

I swallowed, tasting iron.

"I won't abandon you."

The wind fell silent.

Bosco didn't answer. Jake's tail twitched once, deliberate as a threat that hadn't decided who it was for. Shrimp blinked slowly, his eyes wet and too wide. Butternugget stopped muttering, pressing his nose into the dirt like it might forgive him.

I felt them in my head. Broken. Bleeding. Mine. And for one heartbeat, that was enough.

The wind died down. For a moment there was only breathing. Ours. Shared. Fractured but alive.

Then I felt it. A vibration under my paws. Subtle. Wrong.

I opened my eyes. The Cognichonk twitched. Something dying that hadn't gotten the news. Something patient. Something that knew the house always wins.

Eventually. Blackened yarn unwound with a sound like teeth being dragged across stone. At its core, an ember flared—orange, sickly bright—before drowning itself in smoke.

It tried to purr. God help me, it *tried*—but what came out was guttural and broken, a cough that remembered being music once but couldn't quite recall the tune. It didn't soothe. It glitched. Purr-purr *SNAP*. Static. Sparks. The kind of sound that would make a baby cry and a priest change religions.

But it wasn't dead. It was *thinking*. Planning. Waiting for its next chance.

The pulse hit me in the chest. My vision went black. And then *orange*.

I was everywhere at once, my consciousness torn into scraps and scattered like bloody confetti.

I saw an alley miles away. A huddle of orange cats pressed together in fear, eyes round and luminous. One was chanting my name. LUIS. LUIS. LUIS. Another bit his ear bloody to make him stop.

I saw a rooftop. Cats in a circle. Glyphs scratched in pigeon shit and blood. A makeshift ritual. One cat, big and scarred, barking orders. He wore a child's plastic crown. It was cracked. He didn't care.

VEX. VEX. VEX.

I saw an apartment living room. A ginger tabby perched on a microwave, staring into the middle distance with glassy eyes. Crying. Whimpering. "Make it stop. Make it stop. Please."

I felt another cat under a car, howling at nothing, claws gouging pavement until they split.

Another in a basement, drawing spirals on the floor. One loop at a time. Over and over. Until his paw bled.

They weren't united. Weren't free. Just unanchored—driftwood in a flood where every piece thinks it's a boat. Freedom's just another word for nothing left to lose, but these cats? They'd lost everything and gained nothing. The worst kind of bargain. The kind I specialized in.

My refusal hadn't broken the network like I'd hoped. It had done something worse—*fractured* it into jagged pieces that were still trying to connect.

The vision flickered like bad reception. I clawed at my own consciousness, trying to pull away, but the Cognichonk dug in its hooks and dragged me deeper, forcing me to see more.

A circle in a warehouse. Cats pressed to the ground by force. Glyphs burning under them in gold and crimson. A voice commanding. Cold. Precise.

Vex. Her eyes gleamed with intent. No hesitation. No mercy.

"If he won't lead you, I will."

I felt them obey. Not willingly. But absolutely.

My heart lurched. I saw them all. They weren't just cats anymore. They were this city's dirty little secrets, spilled across alleys and rooftops like pockets turned inside out. Some praying. Some plotting. Some just waiting for the next lie that promised to hurt less than the truth. The city does that—turns even the innocent into either victims or accomplices. Sometimes both.

I ripped myself free with a snarl. My claws scored the concrete. The alley returned. Cold. Empty.

The Cognichonk twitched once. The ember at its heart blinked out. But I knew it was still listening.

I spat blood on the cracked ground.

"They're tearing themselves apart," I rasped.

Bosco's hackles rose. He didn't speak, but his eyes gleamed.

Jake's tail lashed once, slow and deliberate. *Your eyes track the same threat. Good hunter.*

Butternugget whimpered. Rocked. *No kings. No crowns. No gods. No gods. No gods.*

Shrimp just stared. His pupils huge, reflecting the ember that wasn't there anymore.

I wiped the blood from my mouth with the back of a paw.

"They're not free," I said. My voice was grave-dirt dry. "They're lost."

The Cognichonk didn't answer. It didn't have to. I could feel it in my bones. Waiting. Patient. Hungry.

And it would wait as long as it took for someone to put the crown back on.

The silence that followed wasn't just empty—it was ugly. Concrete dust settled on our fur with the finality of grave dirt while the Cognichonk pulsed once, like something dead that hadn't stopped dreaming.

I heard Shrimp breathing. Fast. Shallow. Like he was running in place in his own skull.

He wasn't looking at me. He wasn't looking at anything. His eyes were huge, bottomless, full of the kind of static that made radios hiss in abandoned houses.

"Shrimp," I rasped. "Talk to me."

He didn't blink. His mouth opened. And something else spoke.

The voice that came out of him didn't belong in any cat —or in anything that had ever wanted to be loved or fed or left alone in a sunny spot. It was older and hungrier, prophecy that had grown tired of waiting and bared its teeth.

"Twelve paws no longer bind."

Shrimp's head jerked sideways with a sickening crack. His voice wasn't his anymore—it belonged to something that had been waiting in the shadows long before any of us showed up with our petty little tragedies and second-rate redemptions. Prophecy doesn't ask permission. It just breaks in and rearranges your future like a crooked cop planting evidence

"The pantry god wakes."

His claws gouged the concrete. Blood welled up.

"The leash undone."

He arched, spine contorting like a wire being twisted.

"The yarn devours itself."

Then he collapsed.

For a moment, everything stopped—even the wind seemed to hold its breath. His body shuddered once, then again, before collapsing into a stillness more frightening than the convulsions.

Butternugget whimpered. Crawled backwards until his tail hit the wall. "No gods," he babbled. "No gods. No crowns. Hide. Hide."

Bosco's lip peeled back in a snarl. His voice in my head was the scraping of claws on a coffin lid. *It's starting.*

I blinked. Ash flaked off my whiskers. My mouth tasted like iron filings and old guilt.

"What's starting?"

Jake's head lifted. His eyes were flat, lethal. Certain. *Territory war.*

I didn't argue—couldn't argue—because the truth of his words had settled in my bones before he'd even finished speaking.

Shrimp's breathing hitched, caught, then finally evened out. He blinked, slow, confused. He looked at the blood on his claws and mewled once, small and broken.

Bosco's body moved before I could argue with myself. I stepped forward. Pressed my forehead to Shrimp's. Let him feel the connection. The promise. Even if it was one I didn't know how to keep.

The Cognichonk didn't glow, but I felt it anyway—the silent smile, the patient waiting, the calculation beneath. It had gotten exactly what it wanted all along.

We stayed like that for a moment.

Shrimp's breath rasped hot against my nose. His eyes fluttered, wet and dazed. But he was there. Alive. Lucid enough to tremble.

I pulled back slowly. My body—Bosco's body—creaked like old wood settling in a burned-out house.

The Cognichonk sat in the ruins of the circle, its yarn blackened and dull as old embers. But not gone—never gone. It no longer glowed, just pulsed once with slow deliberation, like a heart that refused to stop beating just because you'd put a knife through it.

I narrowed my eyes at it, feeling the certainty settle in my bones like an old bullet too deep to dig out. This wasn't over. Never is in this city. Power doesn't die—it just changes hands, puts on a fresh suit, and pretends it's working for you this time. Someday it would wake again to whisper in desperate ears hungry for salvation, promising crowns while forging chains.

And someone—*someone*—would listen.

Vex's face flashed behind my eyes. Cold. Beautiful. Merciless. A queen of sigils and cages.

If he won't lead you, I will.

I ground my teeth until my jaw ached with the pressure of everything still unsaid, then forced myself to turn to the others.

Butternugget was chewing on his own tail, muttering "No gods no gods no gods."

Shrimp was pressed against the wall, eyes huge, purring in relief or terror or both.

Jake hadn't moved, his body a question made of tense muscle and waiting, needing only a word to transform stillness into violence.

I gave it to them.

"All of you. Listen."

The wind cut through the alley, carrying the taste of blood and ashes, but I forced the words out anyway.

"That thing," I jerked my head at the Cognichonk, "isn't dead. Just waiting. It'll call again. It'll offer crowns. Collars. The whole damn kingdom if someone's desperate enough to take it."

No one argued.

I swallowed the taste of iron and failure. Let it coat my tongue so I wouldn't forget it.

"We'll stop her," I said. My voice low. Final. "We'll stop anyone. No more crowns. No more collars."

Bosco rumbled. A deep, broken growl of agreement. *Good.*

Jake lifted his head. Nodded once, grim and sure.

Butternugget's head snapped up. His eyes wild. "Bite everyone!" he shrieked.

Shrimp blinked slowly. Then purred. Low. Soft. Weirdly gentle.

I exhaled. My breath fogged in the cold. Just another ghost in a city full of them. And I let myself believe. Just for a heartbeat. That maybe refusing to be a king was the first real command I'd ever given worth obeying. That's the thing about lost causes—they're the only ones worth fighting for in this town.

The wind howled through the broken circle. And together, we turned to face it.

EPILOGUE

The world didn't end that night. But it cracked a little more. I felt it in the dark places—the kind only cats bother to haunt. The spaces between streetlights where shadows don't just gather, they take minutes and file them away for evidence later. And I felt them too: orange cats everywhere. My fractured jury. My broken mirror.

One perched on a windowsill with blood still wet on its claws, eyes narrowed at the dawn like it was a witness who'd seen too much and couldn't be trusted to keep quiet about it.

Another hunched in a subway tunnel with a candle guttering between his paws, his mouth forming sigils that would crack any sane tongue that tried to speak them.

A third under a rusted-out car, scratching spirals into the pavement until his claws split and bled—the kind of devotion that looks like madness until you realize madness is just devotion that picked the wrong god to follow.

Some lit candles to honor the dead. Others opened

throats to feed the living. The worst? They waited. Silent. Patient. Like bullets in a chamber waiting for fingers that haven't yet decided to pull the trigger.

And I felt it binding them all. That damned knot of memory and will—the Cognichonk. Like a crime boss who never shows his face at the scene but has his fingerprints on every trigger pulled in this town. It pulsed once in the dark with a rhythm that felt like hunger and amusement twisted together—the heartbeat of a city that feeds on its own citizens and calls it progress. It wasn't dead. Just waiting. Dreaming of thrones.

And I'm the fool who refused to wear the crown. The kind of mistake that comes with its own payment plan— daily installments of regret with compound interest. So now I have to break it. That's how these stories always end— with one last job that's really just the beginning of a longer fall.

Even if it kills me. Even if it kills us all. Some cases you solve. Others you survive. The worst kind? They survive you.

ABOUT THE AUTHOR

Kysa Steele is an IT professional by day, and by night an author, TTRPG GM, cat servant, and wife (though the order depends on which cat is asking). She grew up devouring books and plotting to write her own. While newly minted as an indie author, she's been telling elaborate, occasionally cursed stories at the TTRPG table for years. She spends her time building worlds and trying to unravel her cats' many conspiracies.

She lives in Texas with her husband and a cadre of furry overlords. Nori and Mochi are the latest recruits, while Nox, nicknamed the Demon Princess, claimed dominion during the writing of Curse Meow Not. Jake Speed and his sister Ripley occupy the middle ranks, and the eldest, Cid, remains her watchful shadow and self-appointed bodyguard.